PRAISE FOR *THE SHAPE OF THE RUINS*

FINALIST FOR THE
MAN BOOKER INTERNATIONAL PRIZE
2019

"This is the big, sweeping book of Colombia that Vásquez has been building up to—a novel that obsessively re-examines the fanaticism and deceptions at the heart of Colombia's past and present." —*Vanity Fair*

"Teeming with crackpots and idealists, doomed leaders and those who would avenge their deaths, this is a novel with a surplus of interesting characters. Its plot, meanwhile, is constantly churning. Readers who think they can foresee what's coming next will find that they're wrong."
—*San Francisco Chronicle*

"[A] sweeping and magisterial novel." —*The Washington Post*

"Juan Gabriel Vásquez is the most famous novelist to come out of Colombia since Gabriel García Márquez. . . . Deftly weaving fact into fiction, the novel asks if official history can ever add up to more than victors' propaganda that buries other versions of the past." —*The Economist*

"This compelling read is more than a standard mystery; it interrogates the way moments of violence in Colombia's past have retained their power long after they are over." —*Time*

"*The Shape of the Ruins* is far more than a tutorial; it's a gripping Deep State novel that richly illuminates how the powerful brutalize the powerless. Its implications should serve as a cautionary tale for other nations under authoritarian threats. Vásquez has written the epic of his people."
—Minneapolis *Star Tribune*

"Packed with history, alternate history, and a keen, mischievous sense of historical humor." —Lily Meyer, NPR Books

"Juan Gabriel Vásquez's *The Shape of the Ruins* is a highly sophisticated, fast-moving political thriller set in Colombia and an excellent read."
—Alan Furst

THE
SHAPE
OF THE
RUINS

THE
SHAPE
OF THE
RUINS

———

JUAN GABRIEL VÁSQUEZ

TRANSLATED FROM THE SPANISH BY ANNE McLEAN

Riverhead Books
New York

RIVERHEAD BOOKS
An imprint of Penguin Random House LLC
penguinrandomhouse.com

The Library of Congress has catalogued the Riverhead hardcover edition as follows:

Names: Vásquez, Juan Gabriel, author. | McLean, Anne, translator.
Title: The shape of the ruins / Juan Gabriel Vásquez ;
translated from the Spanish by Anne McLean.
Other titles: *Forma de las ruinas*. English.
Description: New York : Riverhead Books, 2018.
Identifiers: LCCN 2018008350 | ISBN 9780735211148 (hardback) | ISBN 9780735211162 (ebook)
Subjects: LCSH: Political fiction. | BISAC: FICTION / Literary. | FICTION / Political. |
FICTION / Historical.
Classification: LCC PQ8180.32.A797 F6713 2018 | DDC 863/.64—dc23
LC record available at https://lccn.loc.gov/2018008350
p.   cm.

First Riverhead hardcover edition: September 2018
First Riverhead trade paperback edition: September 2019
Riverhead trade paperback ISBN: 9780735211155

Printed in the United States of America
1   3   5   7   9   10   8   6   4   2

BOOK DESIGN BY LUCIA BERNARD

For Leonardo Garavito,
who put the ruins in my hands

For María Lynch and for Pilar Reyes,
who showed me how to shape them

Thou art the ruins of the noblest man . . .

<small>WILLIAM SHAKESPEARE</small>, *Julius Caesar* (act 3, scene 1)

CONTENTS

I

The Man Who Spoke of Inauspicious Dates

1

II

Relics of the Illustrious Dead

53

III

A Wounded Animal

111

IV

Why Swell'st Thou Then?

169

V

The Major Wound

217

VI

The Investigation

273

VII

Who Are They?

325

VIII

The Trial

385

IX

The Shape of the Ruins

441

AUTHOR'S NOTE

511

ACKNOWLEDGMENTS

513

I

THE MAN WHO SPOKE OF INAUSPICIOUS DATES

The last time I saw him, Carlos Carballo was climbing with difficulty into a police van, his hands cuffed behind his back and his head hunched down between his shoulders, while a news ticker running along the bottom of the screen reported the reason for his arrest: the attempted theft of the serge suit of an assassinated politician. It was a fleeting image, spotted by chance on one of the late-night newscasts, after the loudmouthed assault of the commercials and shortly before the sports update, and I remember having thought that thousands of television viewers would be sharing that moment with me, but only I could say without lying that I wasn't surprised. He was arrested in front of the former home of Liberal leader Jorge Eliécer Gaitán, now a museum, where armies of visitors arrive every year to come into brief and vicarious contact with the most famous political crime in Colombian history. The serge suit was the one Gaitán was wearing on April 9, 1948, the day Juan Roa Sierra, a young man with vague Nazi sympathies, who had flirted with Rosicrucian sects and often conversed with the Virgin Mary, awaited him as he left his office and shot him four times at close range in the middle of a busy street in the broad daylight of a Bogotá lunchtime. The bullets left holes in the jacket and the waistcoat, and people who know that visit the museum just to see those dark empty circles. Carlos Carballo, it might have been thought, was one of those visitors.

That happened on the second Wednesday of April in the year 2014. It seems Carballo had arrived at the museum around eleven in the morning, and for several hours had been wandering through the house like a worshipper in a trance, or standing with his head tilted in front of the books on criminal law, or watching a documentary with stills of burning tramcars and irate people with raised machetes shown repeatedly over the course of the day. He waited for the last group of uniformed schoolchildren to leave before going up to the second floor, where a glass case protected the suit Gaitán was wearing on the day of his assassination, and then he began to shatter the thick glass with a knuckle-duster. He managed to put his hand on the shoulder of the midnight-blue jacket, but he didn't have time for anything else: the second-floor guard, alerted by the crash, was pointing his pistol at him. Carballo noticed then that he'd cut himself on the broken glass of the case, and began to lick his fingers like a stray dog. But he didn't seem too worried. On television a young girl in a white blouse and tartan skirt summed it up:

"It was as if he'd been caught painting on a wall."

All the newspapers the next day referred to the frustrated robbery. All of them were surprised, hypocritically shocked, that the myth of Gaitán still awoke such passions sixty-six years after the events, and some made the comparison for the umpteenth time to the Kennedy assassination, the fiftieth anniversary of which had been marked the previous year without the slightest diminution of its power to fascinate. All of them remembered, in case anyone had forgotten, the unforeseen consequences of the assassination: the city set on fire by the populist protests, the snipers stationed on the rooftops firing indiscriminately, and the country at war in the years that followed. The same information was repeated everywhere, with more or less subtlety and more or less melodrama, sometimes accompanied by images, including those of the furious crowd, which had just lynched the murderer, dragging his half-naked corpse along the cobblestones of Carrera Séptima, in the direction of the Presidential Palace; but on no media outlet could you find a speculation, as gratuitous as it might be, about the reasons a man who wasn't mad might have for deciding to break into a glass case in a guarded house and make off with the bullet-ridden clothing of a famous dead man. Nobody posed that question, and our media memory gradually began to forget Carlos Carballo. Swamped by everyday violence, which doesn't give anyone time to even feel discouraged, Colombians allowed that inoffensive man to fade away like a shadow at twilight. Nobody thought of him again.

It's his story, in part, that I want to tell. I can't say that I knew him, but I had a level of intimacy with him that only those who have tried to deceive each other achieve. However, to begin this story I must first speak of the man who introduced us, for what happened to me afterward has meaning only if I first tell of the circumstances in which Francisco Benavides came into my life. Yesterday, walking around the places in central Bogotá where some of the events that I'm going to explore in this report happened, trying to make sure once more that nothing has escaped me in its painstaking reconstruction, I found myself wondering aloud how I've come to know these things I might be better off not knowing: how I had come to spend so much time thinking about these dead people, living with them, talking to them, listening to their regrets and regretting, in turn, not being able to do anything to alleviate their suffering. And I was astonished that it had all started with a few casual words, casually spoken by Dr. Benavides inviting me to his house. At that moment, I thought I was accepting in order not to deny someone my time who had been generous with his own at a difficult moment, so the visit would simply be one more commitment out of the many insignificant things that use up our lives. I couldn't know how mistaken I'd been, for what happened that night put in motion a frightful mechanism that would only end with this book: this book written in atonement for crimes that, although I did not commit them, I have ended up inheriting.

FRANCISCO BENAVIDES WAS one of the most reputable surgeons in the country, a drinker of fine single-malt whiskey and a voracious reader, though he made a point of emphasizing that he was more interested in history than in invented stories, and if he had read a novel of mine, with less pleasure than stoicism, it was only due to the sentimentalism his patients stirred in him. I was not, in the strictest sense, a patient of his, but it was a matter of health that had put us in touch the first time. One night in 1996, a few weeks after moving to Paris, I was trying to decipher an essay by Georges Perec when I noticed a strange presence beneath my jaw on the left side, like a marble under the skin. The marble grew over the next few days, but my concentration on the change in my life, puzzling out the rules of the new city and trying to find my place in it, prevented me from noticing the changes. In a matter of days, I had a growth so swollen that it deformed my face; in the street, people looked at me with pity, and a classmate stopped greeting me out of fear of some unknown contagious disease. I underwent many examinations; a whole legion of Parisian doctors were unable to reach a correct diagnosis; one of them, whose name I do not wish to recall, dared to suggest the possibility of lymphatic cancer. That was when my family back in Colombia turned to Benavides to ask if that were possible. Benavides was not an oncologist, but in recent years he had devoted himself to accompanying terminal patients: a sort of private labor he carried out on his own and for no payment whatsoever. So, although it would have been irresponsible to diagnose someone who was on the other side of the ocean, and more so in those days before telephones sent photos and cameras were integrated into computers, Benavides was generous with his time, his knowledge, and his intuition, and his transatlantic support was almost as useful to me as a definitive diagnosis would have been. "If you had what they're looking for," he told me once by telephone, "they would have found it by now." The complex logic of the sentence was like a life buoy thrown to a drowning man: you grab on to it without wondering if it might have a hole in it.

After a few weeks (which I spent in a timeless time, coexisting with the very concrete possibility that my life was ending at the age of twenty-three, but so numbed by the blow that I couldn't even feel true fear or true sadness), a general practitioner I met by chance in Belgium, a member of Médecins Sans Frontières recently returned from the horrors of Afghanistan, needed just one look to diagnose me with a form of lymphotuberculosis that had disappeared from Europe and could be found (it was explained to me without the quotation marks I will now use) only in the "third world." I was admitted to a hospital in Liège, shut away in a dark room, examined in a way that made my blood burn, then anesthetized, and an incision was made on the right-hand side of my face, below my jawline, so they could extract a lymph node and do a biopsy; a week later, the lab confirmed what the recent arrival had said without needing so many expensive tests. For nine months I followed a triple course of antibiotics that dyed my urine a lurid shade of orange; the inflamed node gradually shrank; one morning I felt dampness on the pillow, and realized something had burst. After that, the contours of my face went back to normal (except for two scars, one discreet and the other, the result of the surgery, more flagrant) and I was finally able to put the whole business behind me, although in all these years I haven't managed to forget it entirely, for the scars are there to remind me. The feeling of being in debt to Dr. Benavides has never left me. And the only thing that occurred to me when we saw each other in person for the first time, nine years later, was that I had never thanked him properly. Maybe that was why I accepted his entry into my life so easily.

We met by chance in the cafeteria of the Santa Fe clinic. My wife had been admitted fifteen days earlier, and we were trying the best we could to cope with the emergency that had forced us to extend our stay in Bogotá. We had landed at the beginning of August, the day after the Independence Day celebrations, intending to spend the European summer holidays with our families and return to Barcelona in time for her due date. The pregnancy had reached its twenty-fourth week in complete normality, for which we gave thanks every day: we knew from the start that any pregnancy with twins goes by definition in the column labeled high-risk. But the normality was shattered one Sunday, when, after a night of discomfort and strange pains, we visited Dr. Ricardo Rueda, the specialist in complicated pregnancies we'd been consulting since the beginning. After a careful ultrasound, Dr. Rueda gave us the news.

"Go home and get some clothes," he told me. "Your wife is staying here until further notice."

He explained what was happening with the manners and tone of someone announcing a fire in a cinema: the gravity of the situation must be made clear, but not so forcefully that people kill each other in a stampede for the exit. He described in detail what cervical insufficiency meant, asked M if she'd had any contractions, and finished by communicating the necessity of an urgent operation, to delay the irreversible process we'd begun without knowing. Then he said—finding a fire, trying to prevent a stampede—that premature delivery was an inevitable reality; now we had to try to see how much time we could gain in such an adverse situation, and on the length of this time my daughters' survival depended. In other words: We had begun a race against the calendar, and knew that the risks, if we lost, were the kinds that destroy lives. From then on, the objective of every decision was to delay the delivery. By the time September began, M had been hidden away in a room on the first floor of the clinic for two weeks, lying down, not allowed to move, and undergoing daily examinations that had put our endurance, our courage, and our nerves to the test.

The days' routine was built around cortisone injections to develop my unborn daughters' lungs, such frequent blood tests that very soon my wife had no unpunctured spots on her forearms, infernal ultrasounds that could last up to two hours and during which the health of their brains, spinal columns, and two hearts with their accelerated rhythms that never beat in unison were determined. The nightly routine was no less busy. The nurses came in at any moment to check some detail or ask a question, and the constant lack of sleep, as well as the state of tension we were living in, made us irritable. M had begun to have contractions she didn't feel; to reduce them (I never knew whether their intensity or frequency) she was given a drug called Adalat, responsible, as they explained to us, for her having violent hot flashes that forced me to open the windows wide and try to sleep under the inclement cold of the small hours in Bogotá. Sometimes, when sleep was already frightened off by the cold or the nurses' visits, I would go for a walk around the deserted clinic; I'd sit on the leather sofas in the waiting rooms, if I found a place with the lights on, I'd read a few pages of *Lolita* in an edition from the cover of which Jeremy Irons observed me; or I'd wander down the dim corridors, in those hours when the clinic shut off half the neon panels, walking from the room to the neonatal unit and from there to the waiting room for out-patient surgery. On those nocturnal strolls through white corridors I would try to remember the latest explanations received from the doc-tors, and to figure the risks the twins would run if they were born in that instant. Then I'd make mental calculations of how much weight the girls had gained in the last few days and the time it would take them to get up to the minimum required for survival, and it unnerved me that my well-being depended on that obstinate counting of grams. I tried not to get too far away from the room, and in any case to have my phone in my hand rather than in some pocket, so I'd be sure to hear it ring. I looked at it frequently: to confirm that I had coverage, that the signal was good, that my daughters would not be born in my absence due to the lack of four black lines on the small gray firmament of a liquid screen.

It was during one of these nocturnal excursions that I recognized Dr. Benavides, or rather he made himself recognized by me. I was te-diously stirring milk into my second coffee, sitting at one of the back tables of the cafeteria that never closed, far from a group of students who were taking a break in the middle of the night shift (which in my city is always busy, full of small and big violences); in my book, Lolita and Humbert Humbert were beginning to cross the United States, from Functional Motel to Functional Motel, filling parking lots with tears and illicit love, putting geography into motion. A man ap-proached me, introduced himself without any fuss, and asked me two things: first, if I remembered him; then, how had that whole story with my lymph nodes turned out. Before I could answer, he had sat down with his own cup of coffee clutched tightly between both hands, as if someone might suddenly take it away. It wasn't one of those refugee-camp plastic cups that the rest of us were given, but a solid ceramic mug painted dark blue, the logo of some university peeking out from between half-open fingers.

"And what are you doing here at this hour?" he asked.

I gave him the abridged version: the threats of premature birth, the number of weeks and the various prognoses. But I discovered I didn't feel too keen to discuss the matter, so I headed off any comments. "And you?" I asked.

"Visiting a patient," he told me.

"And what does your patient have?"

"A lot of pain," was his brutal summary. "I came to see what I could do to help." Then he changed the subject, but it didn't seem like he was trying to avoid answering: Benavides was not the kind of person who shies away from talking about pain. "I read your novel, the one about the Germans," he said. "Who would have imagined: my patient turned out to be a writer."

"Who could have imagined."

"And besides, he writes things for old people."

"Old people?"

"Things about the forties. Things about the Second World War. April 9 and all that."

He was referring to a book I'd published the previous year. Its origin went back to 1999, when I met Ruth de Frank, a German Jewish woman who, after escaping the European debacle and arriving in Colombia in 1938, witnessed how the government, in alliance with the Allies, broke diplomatic relations with the Axis countries and began to imprison citizens of enemy nations—propagandists for or sympathizers with European fascism—in luxury hotels in the countryside converted into internment camps. Over the course of three days of questioning, I had the pleasure and privilege of having this woman tell me almost her whole life story, which she remembered astonishingly well, and I took notes on the excessively small pages of a squared notebook, which was the only thing I could find in the hotel in the tropical lowlands where we met. In the thrilling confusion of Ruth de Frank's life, which spanned two continents and more than seven decades, one anecdote stood out in particular: the moment in which her Jewish family, in one of those cruel ironies of history, had ended up being persecuted in Colombia, *for being German*. This misunderstanding (but *misunderstanding* is an unfortunate and inadequate word) turned out to be the first heartbeat of a novel I called *The Informers*; and the life and memories of Ruth de Frank became, distorted as fiction always distorts, one of the fundamental characters of the novel, a sort of moral compass of its fictitious world: Sara Guterman.

But the novel was about many other things. Given that its center was in the 1940s, it was inevitable that at some moment the story or its characters would come across the events of April 9, 1948. The characters of *The Informers* talked about that nefarious day; the narrator's father, a professor of oratory, could not recall without admiration Gaitán's supernatural speeches; in a couple of brief pages, the narrator goes to central Bogotá and visits the scene of the crime, as I have done many times, and Sara Guterman, who goes with him that day, crouches down and touches the rails of the tram that still ran on Carrera Séptima in the 1940s. In the white silence of the nocturnal cafeteria, each of us in front of his cup of coffee, the doctor confessed that it had been that scene— an older woman reaching down to the surface of the street in front of the place where Gaitán was shot and touching the rails of the extinct tram the way one might take the pulse of an injured animal—that led him to look me up. "I've done the same thing," he said.

"You've done what?"

"Gone into town. Stopped in front of the plaques. Even crouched down to touch the rails." He paused. Then: "How did you get the bug?"

"I don't know," I said. "I've always had it, my whole life. One of my first short stories was about April 9. It was never published, luckily. All I remember is the snow falling at the end."

"In Bogotá?"

"Yes, in Bogotá. On Gaitán's body. On the rails."

"I see," he said. "No wonder I don't like reading made-up things."

That's how we started talking about April 9. I noticed that Benavides did not refer to it as the *Bogotazo*, the grandiloquent nickname that we Colombians gave to that legendary day a long time ago. No: Benavides always used the date, and sometimes the complete date with the year, as if it were someone's first and last name and deserved respect, or as if using the nickname was a gesture of intolerable familiarity: after all, one cannot allow oneself to take little liberties with the venerable events of our past. He began to tell me anecdotes, and I tried to hold my own. He told me about the detectives from Scotland Yard the government hired in 1948 to supervise the investigations, and about the brief correspondence he maintained with one of them many years later: a very polite man who remembered with fresh indignation the long ago days of his visit to Colombia, when the government asked the detectives for daily results and at the same time seemed to put all the obstacles in the world in front of them. For my part, I told him about my conversation with Leticia González, my wife's aunt, whose husband, Juan Roa Cervantes, was chased by a small band of machete-wielding Liberals who confused him with the assassin who shared his name; when I met him, he himself told me about those anguished days, but what he best remembered (making a visible effort to contain his tears) was the punishment the confused Gaitanistas inflicted on him: setting his library on fire.

"What a name to have on that day," said Benavides.

Then he told me the tale he'd heard from Hernando de la Espriella, a patient from the coast who'd found himself in Bogotá when the chaos broke out, and spent the first night facedown on top of a pile of corpses to keep from being killed as well; and I told him about my visit to Gaitán's house, which had been turned into a museum, where his midnight-blue suit was displayed on a headless mannequin in a glass case, with the bullet holes in the cloth (two or three, I don't remember anymore), for all the world to see . . . For fifteen or twenty minutes we stayed there, in the cafeteria after the night-shift students had left, exchanging anecdotes the way boys exchange stickers for football albums. But Dr. Benavides got the feeling at a certain point of having outstayed his welcome or interrupting my silent time. That's the impression he gave me: Benavides, like all doctors who have lived close to the pain or worries of other people, knew that patients and their relatives need moments of solitude, of not speaking to anyone and not having anyone speak to them. And so he said good-bye.

"I live nearby, Vásquez," he said as he shook my hand. "When you want to talk about April 9, come by my house, have a whiskey, and I'll tell you things. I never tire of the subject."

I sat for a moment thinking that there are people like that in Colombia: those for whom talking about April 9 is the same as playing chess or bridge for other people, or doing crossword puzzles, or knitting, or stamp-collecting. There aren't many left, truth be told: they've been dying out without replacing themselves or leaving heirs or founding a school, defeated by the implacable amnesia that has always stifled this poor country. But they still exist, and it's normal, for the assassination of

Gaitán—the lawyer of humble origins who had reached the heights of politics and was called to save Colombia from its own heartless elites, the brilliant orator able to blend in his speeches the irreconcilable influences of Marx and Mussolini—is part of our national mythology, the way the assassination of Kennedy might be for an American. Like all Colombians, I grew up hearing that Gaitán had been killed by the Conservatives, that he'd been killed by the Liberals, that he'd been killed by the Communists, that he'd been killed by foreign spies, that he'd been killed by the working classes feeling themselves betrayed, that he'd been killed by the oligarchs feeling themselves under threat; and I accepted very early, as we've all come to accept over time, that the murderer Juan Roa Sierra was only the armed branch of a successfully silenced conspiracy. Perhaps that's the reason for my obsession with that day: I've never felt the unconditional devotion that others feel for the figure of Gaitán, who strikes me as more shadowy than is generally admitted; but I know this country would be a better place if he hadn't been killed, and most of all would be able to look itself in the mirror more easily if the assassination were not still unsolved so many years later.

April 9 is a void in Colombian history, yes, but it is other things besides: a solitary act that sent a whole nation into a bloody war; a collective neurosis that has taught us to distrust one another for more than half a century. In the time that has passed since the crime, we Colombians have tried, without success, to comprehend what happened that Friday in 1948, and many have turned it into a more or less serious entertainment, their time and energy consumed by it. There are also Americans—I know several—who spend their whole lives talking about the Kennedy assassination, its details and most recondite particulars, people who know what brand of shoes Jackie was wearing on the day of the crime, people who can recite whole sentences from the Warren Report. And yes: there are also Spaniards—I don't know too many, but I know one, and he's enough—who never stop talking about the failed coup on February 23, 1981, in the Chamber of Deputies in Madrid, and who could find the bullet holes in the domed ceiling with their eyes closed. People are the same all over the world, I imagine, people who react like that to their countries' conspiracies: turning them into tales that are told, like children's fables, and also into a place in the memory or the imagination, a place we go to as tourists, to revive nostalgia or try to find something we've lost. The doctor, it struck me then, was one of those people. Was I as well? Benavides had asked me *how I'd gotten the bug*, and I'd told him of a story I'd written in my university years. But I hadn't told what had provoked the story or when exactly I'd written it. I hadn't remembered all that in a long time, and it surprised me that it should be now, in the midst of a particularly relentless present moment, that these memories should decide to return.

IT WAS DURING the arduous days of 1991. Since April 1984, when the drug lord Pablo Escobar had the minister of justice Rodrigo Lara Bonilla assassinated, a war between the Medellín cartel and the Colombian state had taken my city by storm and turned it into its theater of operations. Bombs exploded in locations carefully chosen by the drug traffickers to kill anonymous citizens who had no part in the war (apart from the fact that we all had a part in the war, and it was naive and innocent to believe otherwise). The evening before Mother's Day, to give one example, two attacks on Bogotá shopping malls left twenty-one dead; a bomb in the Medellín bullring—to give another example—killed twenty-two. The explosions blotted the calendar. With the passing months we began to understand that we weren't free of risk, because any one of us could be caught by a bomb blast at any time and in any place. The locations of the attacks, through a sort of barely discovered atavism, began to be off-limits to pedestrians. Bits of the city were gradually lost to us or turned into a kind of memento mori of bricks and cement, and at the same time we began to glimpse this still-timid revelation: that a new type of chance (the fate that separated us from death, which is, along with the fate of love, the most considerable of all and also the most impertinent) had entered our lives in the invisible and especially unpredictable shape of a wave of explosions.

Meanwhile, I had started to study for a law degree at a university in central Bogotá, an old seventeenth-century cloister that had served as a prison for the Independence revolutionaries, some of whom descended its staircase to the scaffold, and its thick-walled classrooms had produced several presidents, not a few poets, and, in certain unfortunate cases, some president poets. In our classes we barely spoke about what was happening outside: we argued over whether a group of speleologists, trapped in a cave, have the right to eat one another; we argued whether Shylock, in *The Merchant of Venice*, had the right to cut a pound of flesh from Antonio's body, and whether it was legitimate for Portia to prevent him from doing so on a cheap technicality. In other classes (in most of the classes) I was bored with an almost physical boredom, a sort of disquiet in my chest, similar to a light anxiety attack. During the ineffable tedium of procedural or property law I started to sit in the back row of the lecture hall, and there, protected by the motley bodies of the other students, I'd take out a book by Borges or Vargas Llosa, or by Flaubert on Vargas Llosa's recommendation, or by Stevenson or Kafka on Borges's recommendation. I soon reached the conclusion that it was not worth attending classes to play out this elaborate ritual of academic imposture; I began to skip classes, to waste my time playing billiards and talking about literature, or listening to recordings of poetry by León de Greiff or Pablo Neruda in the room filled with leather sofas in the Casa Silva, or walking around the neighborhood of my university, without a routine or method or destination, going from the shoe-shine stands in the square to the café beside the Chorro de Quevedo fountain, from the noisy benches in the Parque Santander to the tucked-away and quiet ones in the Palomar del Príncipe, or from the Centro Cultural del Libro, with its one-square-meter stalls and their crowded-together booksellers who could get their hands on every single novel of the Latin American boom, to the Templo de la Idea, a three-story house where they bound books for private libraries and where one could sit on the stairs and read other people's books while inhaling the fumes of the binder's glue and hearing the noisy machines. I wrote abstract stories with the poetic excesses of *One Hundred Years of Solitude*, and others in which I imitated Cortázar's saxophonist punctuation from "Bestiary," for example, or "Circe." At the end of my second year I understood something I'd been incubating for several months: that my law studies were of no interest or use to me whatsoever, for my only obsession was reading fiction and, finally, learning how to write it.

One of those days, something happened.

In a History of Political Ideas class, we were talking about Hobbes or Locke or Montesquieu when two detonations were heard outside. Our classroom was on the eighth floor of a building that overlooked Carrera Séptima and from our window we had a privileged view of the street and the western sidewalk. I was sitting in the last row, with my back against the wall, and I was the first to stand up and look out the window: and there, on the sidewalk, in front of the windows of the Panamericana stationery shop, the body that had just been shot was lying and bleeding in plain sight. I looked for the shooter, without success: nobody seemed to have a pistol in hand, nobody seemed to be running to vanish behind a complicit corner, and in any case there were no heads turned in the direction of someone fleeing, or curious gazes or pointing fingers, because the people of Bogotá had learned not to get mixed up in other people's business. The wounded man wore a business suit but no tie; the jacket had opened when he fell and revealed the white shirt stained with blood. He wasn't moving. I thought: He's dead. Then two passersby lifted the body up; someone else stopped the driver of a white flatbed truck. They put the body in the back of the truck, and one of those who had carried him got in beside him. I wondered if he knew him or if he'd just recognized him at that moment, if he'd been walking with him when he was shot (if he was his partner, for example, in who knows what dodgy business) or if he was simply moved by solidarity or contagious pity. Without waiting for the light on Avenida Jiménez to change to green, the white truck pulled out of the traffic, turned abruptly left (I imagined they were taking the wounded man to the San José hospital), and disappeared from view.

When the class ended, I walked down the eight flights of stairs to the university entrance hall and then out into the Plazoleta del Rosario, where there was a statue of the city's founder, Don Gonzalo Jiménez de Quesada, whose armor and sword appear in my memory eternally coated with pigeon shit. I walked down the narrow alley of Fourteenth Street, which was always cold because the sun reaches it only in the early morning and never after nine, and crossed Carrera Séptima at Panamericana. The bloodstain was the size of an open hand. I got close enough to see it between my feet, as if to protect it from the footsteps of the others, and then I did exactly that: I stepped in it.

I did so with care, with barely the tip of my shoe, like a child dipping his toes in the water to check the temperature. The clean and well-defined outline of the blood was damaged. Then I must have felt a sudden shame, because I looked up to see if anyone was watching me and silently condemning my behavior (which was somehow disrespectful or profane), and I walked away from the stain trying not to draw attention to myself. A few steps from there were the marble plaques that commemorated the assassination of Jorge Eliécer Gaitán. I stopped to read them or pretend to read them; then I crossed Carrera Séptima along Jiménez, walked around the block, went into Café Pasaje, ordered a black coffee, and used a paper napkin to clean the tip of my shoe. I could have left the napkin there, on the café table, under the porcelain saucer, but I preferred to take it with me, taking care all the time not to touch with my bare hand the man's dried blood. I threw the napkin away in the first bin I saw. I didn't speak to anybody about it, not that day and not in the days that followed.

However, the next morning, I returned to the sidewalk. Barely a trace of the stain remained on the gray concrete. I wondered what had happened to the wounded man: if he'd survived, if he would now be recovering in the company of his wife or children, or if he'd died and at this very moment his wake was being held in some part of the furious city. Just like the previous day, I took a couple of steps toward Jiménez and stopped in front of the marble plaques, but this time I read them in their entirety, every line of each of the plaques, and I realized I'd never done so before. Gaitán, the man who had formed part of the conversations in my family as far back as I could remember, was still virtually unknown to me, a silhouette passing through the vague idea I had of Colombian history. That afternoon I waited for Professor Francisco Herrera at the end of his oratory class and asked him if I could buy him a beer so he could tell me about April 9.

"Better make it a coffee," he said. "I can't go home with beer on my breath."

Francisco Herrera—Pacho, to his friends—was a thin man, with large black-rimmed glasses and a reputation as an eccentric, whose baritone voice didn't prevent him from perfecting imitations of almost any of our politicians. His main subject was the philosophy of law, but his knowledge of rhetoric and most of all his talent as an impersonator had enabled him to organize an evening class in which we listened to and deconstructed the great speeches of political oratory, from Antony in *Julius Caesar* to Martin Luther King. Not infrequently, the class ended up serving as a prelude to some of his students accompanying him to a nearby café and exchanging his best impressions for a brandy-laced coffee, to the curiosity, amusement, and sometimes sarcasm of the neighboring tables. He was especially good at imitating Gaitán, since his aquiline nose and his black slicked-back hair gave the illusion of resemblance, but also because his exhaustive knowledge of Gaitán's life and work, which had enabled him to publish a brief biography with a university press, filled each of the phrases he pronounced with a precision that made him seem more like a medium in a spiritualism session: Gaitán coming back to life through his voice. Once, I told him that: it seemed like Gaitán possessed him when he pronounced his speeches. I saw him smile the way a person might smile when he's devoted his life to an extravagance and just realized, to his own slight surprise, that it hasn't been a waste of time.

At the door to the Café Pasaje—we were on our way in as a boot-black was on his way out with his wooden crate under his arm, and we stopped to let him pass—Pacho asked me what I wanted to talk about.

"I want to know exactly how it happened," I said. "What Gaitán's assassination was like."

"Oh, well then, we won't even sit down," he said. "Come and we'll walk around the block."

That's what we did, and we did so without exchanging a word, both of us walking in silence, descending in silence the steps on the Jiménez side of the Plazoleta, waiting in silence for a break in the heavy traffic to cross Séptima. Pacho seemed to be in a hurry and I strained to keep up with him. He was acting like an older brother who had left home and was showing his younger sibling, who'd come to visit him, his new city. We passed in front of the marble plaques, and I was a bit surprised that Pacho didn't stop to look at them, that he didn't even show an awareness of their existence with a nod of his head or a wave of his hand. We arrived at the space where in the year 1948 the Agustín Nieto building stood (I realized that we were a few steps away from the spot where the bloodstain had been the day before and today only its ghost and its memory remained) and Pacho steered me to the glass door of a shop. "Touch it," he told me.

I took a second to understand what he was saying. "You want me to touch the door?"

"Yes, touch the door," Pacho insisted, and I obeyed. "Here, through this door, Gaitán emerged on April 9," he continued. "Of course, it wasn't this same door, because it wasn't this same building either: it's been a while since they demolished the Agustín Nieto to build this monstrosity. But at this moment, here, for us, this door is the door Gaitán came out of, and you're touching it. It was one o'clock, more or less, and Gaitán was going for lunch with a couple of friends. He was in a good mood. Do you know why he was in a good mood?"

"No, Pacho," I said. A couple came out of the building and stopped to look at us for a second. "Tell me why."

"Because the night before he'd won a case. That's why, that's why he was happy."

His defense of Lieutenant Cortés, accused of having shot dead the journalist Eudoro Galarza Ossa, had been less of a judicial success than a full-blown miracle. Gaitán had given an astonishing speech, one of the best in his life, alleging that the lieutenant had killed the journalist, it was true, but he'd done so in legitimate defense of his honor. The crime had occurred ten years earlier. The journalist, director of a newspaper in Manizales, had allowed the publication of an article that denounced the abusive way the lieutenant treated his troops; Cortés arrived at the newspaper office one fine day and complained about the article; when Galarza defended his reporter, saying he'd done nothing but print the truth, the lieutenant drew his pistol and shot him twice. And that's what happened. But Gaitán used his best rhetorical weapons to speak of human passions, military honor, the sense of duty, the defense of the values of the fatherland, of proportionality between aggression and defense, of how certain circumstances dishonor a military officer but not a civilian, of how an officer who defends his honor is also defending at one and the same time the entire society. It didn't surprise me that Pacho should know by heart the closing lines of the defense. I saw him transform himself slightly, as I'd seen him do so many times before, and I heard his changed voice, the voice that was no longer the deep and dense voice of Francisco Herrera, but the sharper voice of Gaitán, with his deep metronome breathing and his marked consonants and his exalted rhythms:

"Lieutenant Cortés: I do not know what the jury's verdict will be, but the multitude awaits it and feels it! Lieutenant Cortés: you are not my defendant. Your noble life, your pained life can offer me your hand, which I clench in mine knowing I shake the hand of a man of integrity, honor, and goodness!"

"Honor and goodness," I said.

"What a marvel, no?" said Pacho. "What vulgar manipulation, but what a marvel. Or rather: what a marvel *precisely* for being such a vulgar manipulation."

"Vulgar but successful," I said.

"Exactly."

"Gaitán was a magician at that."

"A magician, yes," said Pacho. "He was a defender of freedoms, but had just gotten a journalist's murderer out of prison. And nobody thought that might be contradictory. Moral: You must never believe a great orator."

The crowd exploded in applause and men carried Gaitán out on their shoulders, like a bullfighter. It was ten past one in the morning. Gaitán, tired but triumphant, ended up accepting the obligatory celebrations, drinking toasts with friends and strangers and arriving home at four a.m. But five hours later he was already back at his office, impeccably combed and dressed in a three-piece suit: a dark blue, almost black suit with very fine white pinstripes. He received a client or two; took calls from journalists. Toward one some friends had gathered in Gaitán's office just to congratulate him: Pedro Eliseo Cruz, Alejandro Vallejo, Jorge Padilla were there. One of them, Plinio Mendoza Neira, invited everyone out to lunch, for the events of the previous night had to be celebrated.

"Agreed," laughed Gaitán. "But I'm warning you, Plinio, I'm expensive."

"They came down in an elevator that would have been about there, more or less," Pacho told me, pointing at the entrance to the building. "The elevator didn't always work, because there wasn't always power in the Agustín Nieto. That day there was. That's where they came down, look." I looked. "And they came outside. Plinio Mendoza took Gaitán by the arm, like this." Pacho took me by the arm and made me walk ahead, away from the door of the building toward the edge of Carrera Séptima. Unprotected by the building's wall, Pacho had to speak up and lean closer to me to overcome the noise of the vehicular and pedestrian traffic. "There, on the other side of the street, was a poster for the Faenza cinema. They were showing *Rome, Open City*, the Rossellini film. Gaitán had studied in Rome, and it's not impossible that the poster might have caught his attention. But that we'll never know: we can't know what goes on in a man's head just before he dies, what buried memories might surface, what associations of ideas. Whatever the case, thinking of Rome or not, thinking of Rossellini or not, Plinio Mendoza took a couple of steps to distance them from their other friends. As if he had something confidential to discuss with Gaitán. And, you know what? Maybe he did."

"What I wanted to tell you is something really stupid," said Mendoza.

Then he saw Gaitán stop short, begin to back up toward the door and hold his hands to his face, as if to protect himself. Three quick shots rang out; a fraction of a second later, there was a fourth. Gaitán collapsed on his back.

"What's the matter, Jorge?" said Mendoza.

"What a stupid question," said Pacho. "But who could think of anything more original at a moment like that."

"Nobody," I said.

"Mendoza managed to see the assassin," said Pacho, "and grabbed him. But the assassin pointed his pistol at him and Mendoza had to back off. He thought he was going to be shot too and tried to get back to the building, to the door of the building, to hide or take cover."

Pacho took me by the arm again. We returned to the vanished door of the Agustín Nieto. We turned around, looking toward the traffic on Séptima, and Pacho raised his right hand to point out the place on the sidewalk where Gaitán had fallen. "From his head a trickle of blood spilled down onto the pavement. Juan Roa Sierra, the assassin, was over there. It seems he had been waiting for Gaitán beside the door of the Agustín Nieto building. This is not certain, of course. After the crime, witnesses thought they'd remembered him because they'd seen him enter the building and go up and down in the elevator more times than normal. They'd noticed that, rather. But it's not possible that they were sure: after such a serious event, a person starts to think he saw something, that something struck him as suspicious . . . Some said later that Roa was wearing an old, worn-out, gray striped suit. Others, that the suit was striped, but brown. Others said nothing about any stripes. You have to imagine the confusion, everyone shouting, people running. How was anybody going to notice anything? Anyway: Mendoza saw the assassin from here, where we are now. He saw him lower the revolver and point it at Gaitán again, as if to finish him off. According to Mendoza, Roa didn't fire. Another witness says that yes he did fire, that the bullet had ricocheted off the pavement, like this, and that it almost killed Mendoza. Roa began to look around everywhere, to look for a way to escape. There, on the corner," said Pacho, moving his hand in the air toward Avenida Jiménez, "was a policeman. Mendoza saw him hesitate for a second, a very brief second, and then draw his pistol to shoot Roa Sierra. Roa began to run toward the north, up there, see."

"I'm looking."

"Then he turned around, as if to threaten those who accompanied Gaitán, I don't know if you understand, as if to cover his getaway. And that was when the people in the street pounced on him. Some say that the policeman also pounced on him, the one who was going to shoot him or maybe another one. Others say that the policeman came up behind him and stuck his gun in his back, and that was when Roa put his hands up and the rest of the people pounced on him. Other people say that he tried to cross Séptima, over to the east side. They grabbed him there, at that point on the sidewalk, before he made it across. When Gaitán's friends saw that they'd grabbed the assassin, they went back to Gaitán, to see if they could help him. His hat had fallen off and was a step away from the body. The body was like this," said Pacho, drawing horizontal lines in the air. "He was parallel to the road. But the confusion was such that each one of his friends later gave a different version. Some said that Gaitán's head was pointing south and his feet north, others the exact opposite. They agreed on one thing: that his eyes were open and horribly still. Someone, maybe Vallejo, noticed he was bleeding from his mouth. Someone else shouted to bring water. On the main floor of the building was El Gato Negro, and a waitress came out with a glass of water. 'They killed Gaitancito,' it seems they were shouting. People approached Gaitán, bent down to touch him the way people touch a saint: his clothes, his hair. Then Pedro Eliseo Cruz arrived, who was a doctor, and crouched down beside him and tried to find a pulse."

"Is he alive?" asked Alejandro Vallejo.

"Just call a taxi," said Cruz.

"But the taxi, a black taxi, had approached without anyone having to call," said Pacho. "People fought over the right to lift Gaitán up and put him in the car. Before they lifted him, Cruz caught sight of the wound on the back of his head. He tried to examine the wound, but when he moved Gaitán's head he made him vomit blood. Someone asked Cruz how he saw the situation."

"He's lost," said Cruz.

"Gaitán emitted a series of moans," said Pacho. "Sounds that were like moans."

"So he was alive," I said.

"Still alive, yes," said Pacho. "Another waitress from one of the other cafés around here, El Molino or El Inca, later swore that she'd heard him say: 'Don't let me die.' But I don't believe it. I believe more in what Cruz says: that Gaitán was already beyond all help. At that moment a guy with a camera showed up and started taking photos."

"What, Pacho?" I said. "There are photos of Gaitán here, after the shots?"

"So they say. I've never seen them, but it seems there are. Or rather:

someone took some, that is known. Whether or not they have survived is another matter. One can't imagine that something so important might have been misplaced, but they might have been lost in a move, or something like that. But it's quite likely that's what happened. Otherwise, why haven't they reached us? Of course, it's also possible that someone destroyed them. Since there are so many mysteries about that day . . . Anyway: it seems that's what happened. The photographer pushed his way through the crowd and began to take pictures of Gaitán."

One of the witnesses present got indignant. "The dead man doesn't matter," he told the photographer. "Take a picture of the assassin."

"But the photographer didn't," said Pacho. "People were already lifting Gaitán to put him in the taxi. Cruz got in with him, and the rest of Gaitán's friends got into another one that had pulled up behind it. And they all drove off south to the Central Clinic. They say at that moment several people crouched down in the place where the body had been, took out their handkerchiefs, and soaked them in Gaitán's blood. Then somebody came with a Colombian flag to do the same."

"And Roa Sierra?" I asked.

"A policeman grabbed Roa Sierra, remember?"

"Yes. There, beside the building."

"Almost at the corner. Roa Sierra was backing away toward Jiménez when a policeman came up behind him and stuck his pistol in his ribs."

"Don't kill me, Corporal, sir," said Roa.

It turned out to be a private just coming on duty. He disarmed Roa (took a nickel-plated pistol from him and put it in the pocket of his trousers) and seized him by the arm.

"Jiménez he was called," said Pacho. "Private Jiménez walking the Avenida Jiménez beat: sometimes I think history is lacking a little imagination. Well, anyway, the private was taking Roa Sierra prisoner when a guy on the street jumped on him and punched him, I don't know if it was with a fist or a crate, and Roa Sierra was smashed up against the shop window and he stayed right here." Pacho pointed at the door next to the Agustín Nieto building. "This building was called Faux, I think, and there was a display window here that shattered, a Kodak shop, I seem to recall, though I'm not sure. We don't know whether from the blow he received or from crashing through the glass, but Roa Sierra began to bleed from his nose."

Seeing that people had begun to surround them, Private Jiménez sought refuge. He walked south, passing in front of the facade of the building. "That's him," the mob shouted, "that's the one who killed Dr. Gaitán." The private, leading Roa Sierra by the arm, began to move toward the door of the Granada Drugstore, but in that short distance he couldn't prevent the bootblacks from landing blows with their heavy wooden crates.

"Roa was scared to death," Pacho told me. "The people who'd seen him fire, Vallejo and Mendoza, said later they'd seen a terrible expression of hatred on his face: that they'd seen a fanatic's hatred. Everyone also said that at the moment of firing, Roa had behaved with total self-control. But later, when he was already surrounded by enraged bootblacks, when he was being beaten and thinking, I imagine, these people want to lynch me . . . then no longer, then there was no fanaticism or self-control. Pure fear. The change was so shocking that many thought they were two different guys, the fanatic and the fearful one."

Gaitán's assassin was pale. He had olive-colored skin and an angular face; his straight hair was too long and his mediocre shave had left dirty shadowy patches on his face. His general appearance was that of a stray dog. Some witnesses testified that he looked like a mechanic or a manual laborer, and one even said he had an oil stain on his sleeve. "Let's lynch the assassin!" someone shouted. With his nose broken from one of the blows, Roa let himself be shoved inside the Granada

Drugstore. Pascal del Vecchio, a friend of Gaitán's, asked the pharmacist to protect the assassin so he wouldn't be lynched. They got Roa inside; he seemed resigned to his fate and didn't put up any resistance, and they saw him crouch down in a corner of the drugstore that wasn't visible from the street. Someone lowered the metal shutters. One of the pharmacist's employees went over to him then:

"Why did you kill Dr. Gaitán?" he asked him.

"Oh, señor," said Roa, "powerful things that I can't tell you."

"People began to try to break through the metal shutters," said Pacho. "The owner was frightened or didn't want his place damaged, and ended up opening them himself."

"The people are going to lynch you," said the employee. "Tell me who sent you."

"I can't," said Roa.

"Roa tried to hide behind the counter, but they grabbed him before he could get to the other side," said Pacho. "The bootblacks pounced on him and dragged him out. But before getting him outside, someone found a dolly, you know those little iron carts for moving stacks of boxes. Well, someone grabbed that dolly and dropped it on top of Roa. I've always thought that was when Roa lost consciousness. People dragged him out onto the cobblestones. They kept hitting him: fists, kicks, smashing their crates on him. They say someone showed up and stabbed him with a pen several times. They started dragging him south, toward the Presidential Palace. There's a photo, a famous photo that someone took from an upper story of some building farther up, when the mob was almost at Plaza de Bolívar. You can see the people dragging Roa and you can see Roa, or his dead body. Along the way he has lost his clothing and he's almost naked. It's one of the most horrible photos that came out of that horrible day. Roa is already dead by then, and that means he died at some point between there and the

Granada Drugstore. Sometimes I think that Roa died at the same moment as Gaitán. Do you know exactly what time Gaitán died? At five minutes to two. One fifty-five p.m. It's not impossible that he might have died in the same instant as his assassin, is it? I don't know why it's important, or rather, I don't know that it is important, but sometimes I think about that. From here they took Roa Sierra. This is where the Granada Drugstore was and they took him from here. Maybe when he passed this point where you and I are standing now he was already dead. Maybe he died later. We don't know and we'll never know."

Pacho fell silent. He opened one hand and looked up at the sky.

"For crying out loud, it's drizzling," he said. "Did you need to know anything else?"

We were no more than five steps away from the place an anonymous man had fallen a few hours before. I thought of asking Pacho if he knew, but then it struck me as a superfluous piece of information leading nowhere, and even disrespectful to the man who had made me a gift of his knowledge. I thought they were two very different deaths, Gaitán's and that of the anonymous man, and they were separated by many years besides, but the two puddles of blood, the one where people had dipped their handkerchiefs in 1948 and the one that had dirtied the tip of my shoe in this year of 1991, were not so different really. Nothing linked them aside from my fascination or my morbid curiosity, but that was enough, for the morbid curiosity or fascination was just as strong as the visceral rejection of the city I was beginning to feel in those years, the murderous city, the cemetery city, the city where every corner had its corpse. That's what I was discovering in myself with something like dread, the dark fascination with the dead who swarmed the city: the dead of the present and of the past as well. There I was, in the furious city, going to look at the locations of certain crimes just because they horrified me, chasing the ghosts of the dead who died violent deaths, precisely out of fear of one day being one of them. But that was not easy to explain, not even to a guy like Pacho Herrera.

"Nothing else," I said. "Thanks for everything."

I watched him disappear into the crowd.

That night I arrived home and wrote in one go the seven pages of a story that repeated or tried to repeat what Pacho Herrera had told me, standing on Carrera Séptima, on the very sidewalk where my country's history had been overturned. I don't think I managed to understand how Pacho's tale had captured my imagination, nor do I think I realized how thousands of Colombians over the past forty-three years accompanied me in that. The story wasn't good, but it was mine: it wasn't written in a voice borrowed from García Márquez or Cortázar or Borges, like so many other attempts I made and would make around that time, but rather held, in its tone and its outlook, something that for the first time seemed all mine. I showed it to Pacho—a young man seeking approval from his elders—and at that moment began a new relationship with him, a different relationship, more complicit than before, based more on camaraderie than authority. A few days later, he asked me if I'd like to go to Gaitán's house with him.

"Gaitán has a house?"

"The house where he was living when he was killed," said Pacho. "It's a museum now, of course."

And there we arrived on a sunny afternoon, a big two-story house I haven't returned to since, surrounded by green (I remember a small lawn and a tree) and entirely occupied by the ghost of Gaitán. There was an old television downstairs that showed a documentary on his life in a continuous loop, farther on some speakers that spat out recordings of his speeches, and upstairs, at the top of the broad staircase, we encountered the square glass case in which the midnight-blue suit stood up straight. I walked around the case, looked for the bullet holes in the cloth, and found them with a shiver. Later I went to look at the grave in the garden and stood facing it for a while, remembering what Pacho had told me, lifting my face, watching the leaves of the tree rustle in the wind and feeling the afternoon Bogotá sun on my head. Then Pacho left, without giving me time to say good-bye, and got into a taxi he hailed on the street. I saw him close the door, saw his mouth move to give an address, and saw him take his glasses off, the way we do to get a speck of dust out of our eye, or an eyelash that's bothering us, or a tear that's clouding our vision.

THE VISIT TO DR. BENAVIDES took place a few days after our conversation. On the Saturday, I'd spent a couple of hours in the food court of a nearby shopping center, for a break from the routine cafeteria food, and then I'd spent another while in the Librería Nacional, where I found a book by José Avellanos that I thought might be useful for a novel I was trying to write in stolen moments. It was a picaresque and capricious story about a possible visit Joseph Conrad had made to Panama, and with every sentence I realized that writing it had only one purpose: to distract or distance me from my medical anxieties. When I got back to the room, M was in the middle of one of the examinations that measured the intensity of her clandestine contractions: her belly was covered in electrodes; a robot stationed close to the bed emitted an electronic murmur and we could hear, above the murmur, the delicate sweeping of a little pen tracing lines of ink on a roll of graph paper. With each contraction the lines altered, shook, like an animal whose sleep has been disturbed. "You just had one," said a nurse. "Did you feel it?" And M had to confess that she hadn't, that she hadn't felt it this time, either, and she revealed her annoyance as she did so, as if her own insensitivity absurdly bothered her. For me, on the other hand, the line on that paper was one of the first traces of my daughters in the world, and I even thought of asking the nurses if I could keep the printouts or if they could make me a copy. But then I said to myself: And what if it all goes wrong? If the delivery goes wrong and the babies don't survive or they do but in difficult circumstances and there's nothing in the future to commemorate, much less celebrate? That possibility had not yet lost validity; neither the doctors nor the tests had ruled it out. So the nurses left without my asking them for anything.

"How'd the examination go?" I asked.

"The same," said M with half a smile. "These two are ready to come out, seems like they've got a date." And then: "Someone dropped something off for you. Over there, on the table."

It was a postcard that I immediately recognized, or rather a photograph the size of a postcard and with a message written on the back.

Sady González not only had been one of the great photographers of the twentieth century but was now acknowledged as the preeminent witness of the *Bogotazo*. This was one of his best-known images. González had taken it in the Central Clinic, where they took Gaitán to try to save his life. By the time of the photo, the doctors' efforts have turned out to be in vain and the injured man has been pronounced dead, spruced up a little and strangers have been allowed in, so Gaitán appears covered in a white sheet—impeccably, disturbingly white—and surrounded by people. Some of those around him are doctors: one of them has his left hand, which wears a rough-hewn ring, on top of Gaitán's body, as if to keep him from falling; another, who might be Pedro Eliseo Cruz, is looking back, maybe at the policeman who is leaning in to appear in the photo (having sensed the importance of the moment). On the left of the frame is Dr. Antonio Arias, in profile, looking nowhere with an especially discouraged expression, or that looks especially so to me because Dr. Arias is the only one who seems

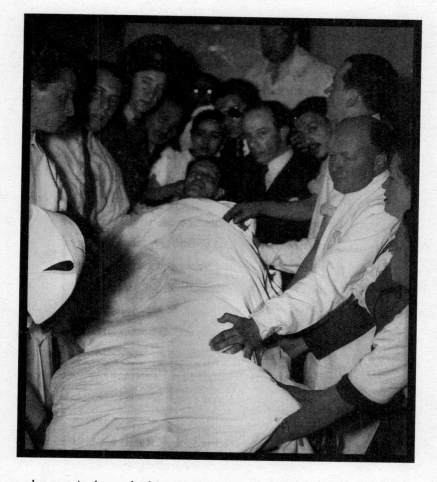

to be genuinely not looking toward the photographer, and whose un-affected sadness seems to be preventing him from noticing what's going on in the room. Between them all is Gaitán, whose head someone is raising a little—the position is not natural—so his face is very visible in the photo, for the photo was taken for this reason, as a testimony to the death of the caudillo, though for me its achievement is much greater, for what you can see on the face of Gaitán was, as a line of verse I like puts it, *the flat anonymity of pain.*

I don't know how many times I've seen that image before, but there, in the room in the clinic, beside my wife confined to her hospital bed, I seemed to see for the first time the girl who is behind Gaitán, the one who seems in charge of holding up the dead man's head. I showed the photo to M and she said no, it was the man wearing glasses who was holding it up, because the girl's hand was closed and at an angle that would make it impossible to support anything. I would have liked to believe she was right, but I could not: I saw the girl's hand, I saw it supporting Gaitán's head, which seemed to float above the white sheet, and that troubled me.

On the back of the postcard, with a ballpoint pen (so it wouldn't smudge on the laminated surface), Dr. Benavides had written:

Esteemed Patient,

Tomorrow, Sunday, I'm having a dinner party. A very *petit comité*, I'll invite you in French to pretend to be cultured. I hope to see you at 8 to talk about things that no longer interest anybody else. I know you're busy with more important things, but I promise I'll try to make it worth your while. Even if only for the whiskey.

Fond regards,
FB

That's how the next day, September 11, I found myself heading to the north of Bogotá, where the fraying city starts to turn into a haphazard alternation of gated clusters of buildings and malls and then, with no warning, a huge wasteland, broken here and there by constructions of dubious legality.

On the radio they were talking about the 2001 attacks in New York, and the newsreaders and commentators were doing what would soon become customary on each anniversary: remembering where they were at that moment. Where was I four years earlier? In Barcelona, finishing lunch. I didn't have a television at the time, so I didn't know anything about it until Enrique de Hériz phoned me: "Come over to my place right now," he said. "The world is ending." And now I was driving north up Carrera Novena and the station was broadcasting recordings from that day: the newscasters describing the events as they were happening, declarations full of astonishment and rage after the collapse of the first building, the reactions of politicians unable to show true indignation even in a case like this. One of the commentators said they'd deserved it. "Who?" asked another, as surprised as I was. "The United States," said the first. "For decades of imperialism and humiliation. Finally, somebody answered back." At that moment, as I was arriving at the address, I no longer had in mind the directions Benavides had given me to get to his house, but rather my visit to New York eight months after the attacks, my interviews with people who had lost someone and my experience of the pain of a city reacting to the attacks with solidarity and integrity. The commentator kept talking. In my head, disorderly replies were forming themselves, and I only managed to say, out loud, but to no one: "What a jerk."

The doctor was waiting for me, filling the entire doorframe. Although he was barely half a head taller than me, I sensed that he was one of those men who walk with their heads bent so they don't knock themselves on low beams. He wore glasses with metal frames and tinted lenses, perhaps the kind that change color according to the intensity of the light, and there, on the threshold, beneath the swift clouds passing over our heads, he seemed like a spy out of a novel, a sort of slightly chubbier, and most of all, more melancholy George Smiley. Just fifty years old, and barely protected from the cold of the Bogotá evening in an old, unbuttoned sweater, Benavides gave me the impression of a weary man. Other people's pain can wear us down in more or less subtle ways; Benavides had spent many years of his life fighting it, sharing patients' suffering and their fear, and that compassion had sapped his energy. Outside their workplaces, people age suddenly, and sometimes we attribute their aging to the first thing that comes to mind: what we know of their lives, a misfortune we've followed from afar, an illness someone told us about. Or, as in Benavides's case, the particular features of his work, which I knew enough about to admire him, or rather admire his dedication to others and regret the fact of not being like him.

"You're early," the doctor said. He led me into the interior patio, where there was still a bit of slanted evening light; in a few minutes of excited conversation he spoke to me again of my novel, asked how my wife was doing and about possible names for my daughters, and told me that he, for his part, had two children in their twenties, a boy and a girl; he then told me that the bench I was sitting on was a railway tie that he'd put legs on himself. The chair he was sitting in, he went on to tell me, had come from a hotel in Popayán that collapsed during the earthquake of 1983, and the only ornament on the table was part of a propeller from a merchant ship. "I still don't know how I put up with all these things, but I do," he said. I've since thought that the doctor was testing me at that moment: trying to find out if I shared that irrational interest in objects from the past, those silent phantoms.

"Well, let's go inside, the dew's catching up with us," his now invisible or blurred features said through the growing darkness. "It seems people are finally starting to arrive."

It turned out the *comité* was not as *petit* as Benavides had suggested. The small house was full of guests, most of them my host's age: they were, I thought without any proof, his colleagues. People clustered around the dining room table, each with a plate in hand, maintaining a precarious balance as they served themselves more cold meats, or attacked the potato salad, or tried to tame some unmanageable asparagus that fell from forks. Invisible speakers whispered the voice of Billie Holiday or Aretha Franklin.

Benavides introduced me to his wife: Estela was a small woman with a pronounced bone structure and an Arabian nose, whose generous smile compensated to some extent for her permanently ironic gaze. Then we made the rounds of the room (through its air now rarefied by smoke), for Benavides wanted to introduce me to some of my fellow guests. He began with a man wearing thick glasses who looked a lot like the one M thought was holding Gaitán's head in the photo, and another, short, bald man with a mustache, who had to make an effort to let go of the hand of a woman with dyed hair in order to shake mine. "A patient of mine," said Benavides to introduce me, and I thought it amused him to deliver this unimportant lie.

Meanwhile, I had begun to feel uncomfortable and uneasy and it wasn't hard to figure out why: some part of my consciousness had begun to wonder how my still-future family was, those girls growing precariously in my wife's womb. There, wandering around Benavides's house, I began to feel a new anxiety; I wondered if this—this sudden sensation of solitude, this conviction that the worst things happen in our absence—was what fatherhood amounted to; and I regretted having come to talk about banalities in society instead of staying with M to keep her company and help in whatever way I could. Someone, behind me, was reciting some lines of verse:

> *This rose was witness*
> *To this, which if not love,*
> *No other love could be.*
> *This rose was witness*
> *When you gave yourself to me!*

It was León de Greiff's worst poem, or in any case the one that had always struck me as the least worthy of his fantastic oeuvre, but the one all Colombians invariably know and which never takes long to crop up at certain types of gatherings. It seemed the gathering in Benavides's house was one of those. And again I regretted having come. Beneath a hanging fern, beside a sliding door that led to a small garden, now black in the night, there were two cupboards with glass doors that immediately caught my attention, for their contents were arranged like pieces in an exhibit. I stopped in front of the doors, looking without seeing, with the initial intention of escaping the social obligations occurring behind me. But little by little the contents of the cupboards began to arouse my curiosity. What was all this?

"That's a copper kaleidoscope," said Benavides. He had arrived stealthily at my side and seemed to have heard my thoughts, maybe from being used to first-time visitors stopping in front of this cabinet and starting to ask questions. "That's a real stinger of an Amazon scorpion. That is an 1856 LeMat revolver. That is the skeleton of a rattlesnake. Small, yes, but you know size doesn't matter."

"Your private museum," I said.

He looked at me with evident satisfaction. "More or less," he said. "They are things I've accumulated over the years."

"No, I meant the whole house. The whole house is your museum."

Here Benavides smiled a wide smile and pointed to the wall above the piece of furniture: two frames adorned it (though I don't know if I should say *adorned* in this case, since the intention of these objects was not aesthetic). "That's the cover of a Sidney Bechet album," said Benavides. Bechet had signed and dated it on May 2, 1959. "And that," he said, pointing to a small piece almost hidden beside the cupboard, "that's a set of scales someone once brought me from China."

"Is it original?" I asked stupidly.

"Down to the last piece," Benavides told me. It was a beautiful instrument: it had a carved wooden frame, and from the crossbar hung an inverted T with two bowls. "See that lacquered box? That's where I keep the lead weights, the prettiest thing there is. Here, I want to introduce you to someone."

Only at that moment did I realize there was someone with him. Behind my host, hidden as if out of shyness or prudence, a pale-skinned man with a glass of fizzy water in his left hand was waiting. He had large bags under his eyes, although he didn't look, in other respects, much older than Benavides, and in his strange getup—brown corduroy jacket, high-collared starched shirt—what most attracted one's gaze was a red cravat, red like the red of a bullfighter's cape. The man in the red cravat held out a soft, damp hand and introduced himself in a low voice, perhaps insecure, perhaps effeminate, the kind of voice that forces other people to lean closer to understand.

"Carlos Carballo," said the character alliteratively. "At your service."

"Carlos is a friend of the family," said Benavides. "Old, very old. I don't even remember when he wasn't here."

"I was a friend of his father's first, you see," said the man.

"First a student, then a friend," said Benavides. "And then my friend. An inheritance, rather, like a pair of shoes."

"Student?" I asked. "Student of what?"

"My father was a professor at the National," said Benavides. "He taught forensic science to law students. One day I'll tell you about it, Vásquez. He had more than a few anecdotes."

"More than a few," said, or corroborated, Carballo. "He was the best professor in the world, if only you could have seen him. I think he changed the lives of several of us." His face grew solemn and he even seemed to stand taller as he said: "A first-rate mind."

"When did he die?" I asked.

"In '87," said Benavides.

"Almost twenty years," said Carballo. "How time flies."

It unsettled me that someone who would wear that cravat—that affront of fine silk—should also speak in clichés and set phrases. But Carballo was, evidently, an unpredictable guy; perhaps for that reason he interested me more than the rest of the guests, and I didn't flee from his company or invent an excuse to escape that corner. I took my phone out of my pocket, checked the intensity of the small black bars and the absence of missed calls, and put it away again. Someone caught Benavides's attention then. I looked in the direction he was looking and saw Estela, who was waving her arms at the opposite end of the room (and the sleeves of her loose blouse bunched up and her arms looked as pale as a frog's belly). "I'll be right back," said Benavides. "It's one of two things: either my wife is drowning or we've run out of ice." Carballo was now talking about how much he missed his *maestro*— that's what he called him now, *maestro*, and perhaps in his head the word was capitalized—especially in those moments when one needs someone to teach one how to read the truth of things. The phrase was a gem found in the mud: at last, something that matched the cravat.

"Read the truth of things?" I asked. "What are you referring to?"

"Oh, it happens to me all the time," said Carballo. "Doesn't it to you?"

"What?"

"Not knowing what to think. Needing some guidance. Like today, for example. I was listening to the car radio on my way here, you know, the evening programs. And they were talking about September 11."

"I was listening to that too," I said.

"And I was thinking: how much we miss Maestro Benavides. To help us see the truth hidden behind the political manipulation, behind the criminal complicity of the media. He would not have swallowed that fairy tale. He would have known how to uncover the deceit."

"The deceit?"

"All this is a deceit, don't tell me you hadn't noticed. Al Qaeda. Bin Laden. Pure bullshit, pardon my French. These things don't happen like that. Does anyone believe that buildings like the Twin Towers can collapse just like that, because they get nailed by an airplane? No, no: this was an inside job, a controlled demolition. Maestro Benavides would have realized at once."

"Wait a second, let's see," I said, halfway between interested and morbidly curious. "Tell me about this demolition."

"It's quite simple. Buildings like those, with perfectly straight lines, only collapse the way those collapsed if someone sets off an explosion from below. You have to take their legs out, not shoot them in the head. The laws of physics are the laws of physics: Or have you seen a tree fall when you cut the top branches?"

"But a building is not a tree. The planes crashed into them, the fire spread and weakened the structures, and the towers came down. Wasn't that what happened?"

"Well," said Carballo. "If you want to believe it." He took a sip of his drink. "But a building like that doesn't fall in its entirety, doesn't fall so perfectly. The collapse of the towers was like a commercial, don't tell me it wasn't."

"That doesn't mean anything."

"No, of course not," sighed Carballo. "It doesn't mean anything if one doesn't want to see it. There is definitely no worse blindness than not wanting to see."

"Don't talk to me in silly proverbs," I said. I don't know where this unusual discourtesy came from. I dislike willful irrationality and I can't stand people hiding behind language, especially if it involves the thousand and one formulas language has invented to protect our human tendency to believe without proof. Even so, I try to control my worst impulses, and that's what I then did. "I'll allow myself to be convinced if you convince me, but up to now you haven't convinced me of anything."

"So it doesn't all strike you as strange?"

"What's strange? The way the towers fell? I'm not sure. I'm not an engineer, I wouldn't know . . ."

"Not just that. What about the air force not being in a state of readiness on that very morning? Or the air space defense system being turned off on that very morning. That the attacks led directly to such a necessary war, or a war so necessary at that moment to maintain the status quo."

"But they're two different things, Carlos, don't tell me I have to explain that," I said. "It's one thing that Bush used the attack as a pretext for a war he'd been wanting to wage for a while. His allowing the deaths of three thousand civilians is quite another."

"That's exactly how it seems. They seem to be two separate things. That's the great triumph of such people: to make us believe we should separate things that are actually right together. Nowadays, only a dupe believes that Princess Diana died in an accident."

"Princess Diana? But what does she have to do . . . ?"

"Only a dupe believes that there are no points in common with her death and that of Marilyn. But there are some of us who see clearly."

"Oh, don't talk nonsense," I spat out. "That's not clairvoyance, that's pointless speculation."

Benavides approached us at that moment, and heard the last sentence. I felt embarrassed, but found no words to make apologies. My irritation was exaggerated, of course, and I didn't quite know what mechanism had produced it: no matter how impatient I might be with those who read the whole world as a code of conspiracies, that didn't justify my rudeness. I remembered a novel by Ricardo Piglia where he says that even paranoid people have enemies. Contact sustained with other people's paranoias, which are multifarious and lie hidden behind the most tranquil personalities, work on us without our noticing, and if you don't watch out, you can end up investing your energy in silly arguments with people who devote their lives to irresponsible conjectures. Or perhaps I was being unfair to Carballo: perhaps Carballo was only a skillful reiterater of information obtained in the sewers of the internet, or even one of those men who has an involuntary addiction to more or less subtle provocation, to the scandal of easily shocked people. Or maybe it was all even simpler: Carballo was a damaged man, and his beliefs were defense mechanisms against the unpredictability of life—the life that at some unfathomable moment had done him harm.

Benavides had noticed the bad atmosphere; and also recognized that the bad atmosphere could transform into something else, after my rude reaction. He held out a glass of whiskey, apologizing as he handed it to me, "It took me so long to get from one side of the house to the other that the napkin is damp." I took the glass without a word and felt its solid weight in my hand, its hard crystal edges. Carballo didn't say anything, either: he was looking at the floor. After a long uncomfortable silence, Benavides said, "Carlos, guess who Vásquez is a nephew of."

Carballo grumpily answered the riddle. "Who?"

"José María Villarreal," said Benavides.

Carballo's eyes moved, or at least that was my impression. I can't say that they widened, according to the conventional expression of surprise or admiration we've come to accept, but there was something in them that interested me: not for what they showed, I also need to make that clear, but for the obvious attempt not to show too much.

"José María Villarreal was your uncle?" said Carballo.

He was alert again, just as when he'd been talking about the Twin Towers, while I was wondering how Benavides knew about that kinship. It wasn't too surprising given that my great-uncle José María had been an important member of the Conservative Party, and in Colombian politics everyone always knows everyone. In any case, that relationship was the sort of thing that might have come up in our first conversation, in the hospital cafeteria. Why hadn't Benavides mentioned it then? Why was Carballo interested in it? I couldn't know then. It was obvious that Benavides, mentioning my uncle, was trying to defuse the hostility he'd found. It was also obvious that he'd immediately achieved it.

"And did you know each other?" asked Carballo. "You and your uncle, I mean. Did you know him well?"

"Less well than I would have liked," I said. "I was twenty-three when he died."

"What did he die of?"

"I don't know. Old age." I looked at Benavides. "And how is it that you two know of him?"

"How wouldn't we know of him," said Carballo. He was no longer hunched over; his voice had recovered its previous vivacity; our clash had never taken place. "Francisco, bring the book and we'll show him."

"Not now, *hombre*. We're in the midst of a dinner party."

"Bring the book. Please. Do it for me."

"What book?" I asked.

"Bring it and we'll show him," said Carballo.

Benavides made a comical grimace, like a child who has to run an errand, which is really a whim of his parents. He disappeared into the next room and returned in a flash: it hadn't taken him long to find the book in question; perhaps it was the one he was currently reading, perhaps he had his bookshelves rigorously ordered so he could find a title without looking through all the rest, without passing uncertain fingers over the impatient spines. I recognized the red slipcase long before the doctor handed the book to Carballo: it was *Living to Tell the Tale*, the memoir Gabriel García Márquez had published three years earlier, copies of which had then flooded all Colombian bookshops and a good part of those elsewhere. Carballo took the book and began to flip through, looking for the page he was interested in, and before he found it, my memory (and instinct) had already suggested what he would show me. I should have known: we were going to talk about April 9, 1948.

"Yes, here it is," said Carballo.

He handed me the book and pointed out the passage: it was on page 352 of that edition, the same one I had at home in Barcelona. In the chapter in question, García Márquez was remembering the Gaitán assassination, which had caught him in Bogotá, studying law with no vocation for it and living from hand to mouth in a *pensión* on Carrera Octava downtown, less than two hundred steps from the place where Roa Sierra fired those four fateful shots. Speaking of the riots, the fires, and the violent and generalized chaos that the assassination provoked (as well as the efforts the Conservative government took to maintain control), García Márquez wrote: "In the neighboring department of Boyacá, famous for its historic Liberalism and its harsh Conservatism, the governor José María Villarreal—a hard-nosed Goth—not only had repressed local disturbances at the start but was dispatching better-armed troops to subdue the capital." *A hard-nosed Goth*: García Márquez's words about my uncle were even gentle, since they were about the man who, on the orders of President Ospina, had authorized a police corps whose members were chosen by the single criterion of their Conservative Party affiliation. Shortly before April 9 that overly politicized police force had already gotten out of hand, and it would soon turn into a repressive organization with pernicious consequences.

"Did you know about this, Vásquez?" Benavides asked me. "Did you know your uncle was mentioned in here?"

"I knew, yes," I said.

"'A hard-nosed Goth,'" said Carballo.

"We never talked about politics," I said.

"No? You never talked about April 9?"

"Not that I recall. There were stories."

"Oh, that's interesting," said Carballo. "Isn't it, Francisco? We're interested in this, aren't we?"

"Yes, we are," said Benavides.

"Tell us, let's hear," said Carballo.

"Well, I don't know. There are several. There was that time when a Liberal friend visited at dinnertime. 'My dear Chepe,' he told him, 'I need you to go find somewhere else to sleep.' 'Why?' asked my uncle. And the Liberal friend told him: 'Because tonight we're going to kill you.' He told me things like that, about the attempts on his life."

"And about April 9?" asked Carballo. "Didn't he ever talk to you about April 9?"

"No," I said. "He gave a few interviews, I think, nothing else. I didn't talk to him about it."

"But he must have known tons of things, no?"

"What kinds of things?"

"Well, he was governor of Boyacá that day. Everybody knows that. He received information and that's why he sent the police to Bogotá. One imagines that he would have continued finding out what was going on. He would have asked questions, he would have talked to the government, isn't that true? And over the course of his long life he would have talked to many people, one imagines, he would have known a lot about things that happen, how to put it, out of the public eye."

"I don't know. He never told me."

"I see," said Carballo. "Look, and did your uncle never talk to you about the elegant man?"

He wasn't looking at me when he asked me this question. I remember well because I, for my part, looked toward Benavides, and found his gaze absent or maybe evasive: I found him making an effort to appear distracted, as if the conversation had suddenly stopped interesting him. I later realized that it interested him more than ever in that second, but I had no reason to suspect hidden intentions in that apparently casual dialogue.

"What elegant man?" I asked.

Carballo's fingers started leafing back through the pages of *Living to Tell the Tale* again. They soon found what they were looking for.

"Read this," Carballo told me, putting the tip of his index finger on top of a word. "From here."

After killing Gaitán, García Márquez wrote, Juan Roa Sierra was chased by a furious mob, and had no choice but to hide in the Granada Drugstore to avoid being lynched. Some policemen and the owner of the drugstore were in there with him, so Roa Sierra must have thought himself safe. Then the unexpected began to happen. A tall man *wearing an irreproachable gray suit as if he were going to a wedding* incited the crowd, and his words were so effective, and his presence was so authoritative, that the owner of the pharmacy raised the iron shutters and let the bootblacks force their way in, hitting out with their wooden crates, and dragged away the terrified assassin. Right there, in the middle of Carrera Séptima, under the eyes of the police and at the urgings of the elegant, well-dressed man, they beat him to death. The elegant man—in his irreproachable gray suit—began to shout: "To the Palacio!" García Márquez wrote:

"Fifty years later, my memory is still fixed on the image of the man who seemed to incite the crowd outside the pharmacy, and I have not found him in any of the countless testimonies I have read about that day. I had seen him up close, with his expensive suit, his alabaster skin, and a millimetric control of his actions. He attracted my attention so much that I kept an eye on him until he was picked up by too new a car as soon as the assassin's corpse was dragged away, and from then on he seemed to be erased from historical memory. Even mine, until many years later, in my days as a reporter, when it occurred to me that the man had managed to have a false assassin killed in order to protect the identity of the real one."

"To protect the identity of the real one," repeated Carballo at the same time as I did, so that we sounded like a bad choir in the middle of the racket of the party. "How strange, don't you think?"

"Strange, yes," I said.

"It's García Márquez talking, not any old idiot. And he says it in his memoir. Don't tell me it's not strange. Don't tell me there's not something to this guy. To the fact that he's been swallowed up by oblivion."

"Of course there's something to it," I said. "A still unresolved murder. A murder surrounded by conspiracy theories. It doesn't surprise me that this interests you, Carlos: I've already seen that this is your world. But I don't know if you should latch on to a novelist's isolated paragraph as if it were the revealed truth. Even if he is García Márquez."

Carballo, more than disappointed, was annoyed. He took a step back (there are disagreements so strong that we feel assaulted, and little keeps us from raising our fists like boxers), closed the book, and, without yet putting it down or back in its red slipcase, crossed his hands behind his back. "I see," he said in a sarcastic tone. "And what do you think, Francisco? How can I get out of this world of mine where we're all crazy?"

"Now, Carlos, don't get offended. What he meant was . . ."

"I know very well what he meant to say. He already said it: that I'm an idle speculator."

"No, no, forgive me for that," I said. "That's not what . . ."

"But there are those who think the opposite, right, Francisco? There are those who can see where others are blind. Not in your world, Vásquez. In your world there are only coincidences. It's a coincidence that the towers collapsed when they shouldn't have. It's a coincidence that a man was in front of the Granada Drugstore able to get it opened without having to ask. It's a coincidence that your uncle's name appears fourteen pages after that incident."

"Okay, now I really don't understand," I said. "What does my uncle have to do with that guy?"

"I don't know," said Carballo. "And neither do you, because you never asked him anything. Because you never talked to your uncle about April 9. Because you don't know whether your uncle might have known the man who made them open the Granada Drugstore. Wouldn't you like to know, Vásquez? Wouldn't you like to know who that guy was who had Juan Roa Sierra killed in front of everyone, and then hopped into a fancy car and disappeared forever? We're talking about the most serious thing to ever happen to your country and you seem not to care. A relative of yours participated in that historic moment and might have known who the guy was, everyone knew everyone back then. And you seem not to give a shit. You're all the same, brother: you go live somewhere else and forget about the country. Or maybe not, now that I think about it. Maybe you're just protecting your uncle. Maybe you don't forget anything, but know very well what happened. You know very well that your uncle organized the Boyacá police. You know very well that the police force later turned into an assassination squad. What do you feel when you think of that? Do you worry about being well informed? Have you worried? Or don't you give a shit, do you think that it has nothing to do with you, that it all happened a quarter of a century before you were born? Yes, that's probably what you think, that this thing is for others to worry about, other people's problems, not yours. Well, you know what? I'm glad destiny has forced your children to be born here, has forced your wife to give birth here: I'm glad of that. So your country can teach you a lesson, teach you not to be so selfish. So maybe your daughters can end up giving you a lesson on what it means to be Colombian. That is, if they're born properly, right? If they don't die right there, like sickly kittens. That would be a lesson too, now that I think of it."

What happened next I remember through a mist. I do remember that in the next second I no longer had the glass of whiskey in my hand; in the next I realize I'd thrown it at Carballo's face, and I remember very well the crash of the glass as it shattered against the floor and I also remember Carballo on his knees covering his face with his hands, bleeding through his broken nose and the blood staining his cravat, red on red, dark red (black blood, the Greeks called it) on the brilliant red of a matador's spear, and also running down the edge of his left hand, dirtying the cuff of his shirt and his watch strap, which I remember being of white fabric and therefore more vulnerable to bloodstains than a leather one. I remember Carballo's shouts of pain, or maybe fear: there are people who are afraid of the sight of blood. I also remember Benavides taking me by the arm with a firm grip, full of authority and decisiveness (almost a decade has passed, but I can still recall the pressure of that hand on my arm, still feel it), and guiding me through the living room, the occupants of which parted to allow us to pass between incredulous or openly censorious stares, and out of the corner of my eye I caught a glimpse of Estela, my hostess, running toward the injured man with a bag of ice in her hand, and another woman, maybe the housekeeper, carrying a broom and dustpan with an irritated or impatient expression on her face. I had time to think that Benavides was throwing me out of his house. I had time to regret it, yes, to regret the end of a relationship that wasn't a friendship but might have become one, and in a flash of guilt I imagined the open door and the shove out of the house. I felt tired and maybe I'd had one drink too many, though I don't think so, but through my hazy understanding I was prepared to take responsibility for my actions, so in my head I began to rapidly sketch out excuses or justifications, and I think I'd begun speaking them when I realized Benavides was not leading me to the front door, but rather to the staircase. "Go upstairs, open the first door on the left, lock the door behind you, and wait for me there," he said, placing a key ring in my hand. "Don't open it for anyone else. I'll be up as soon as I can. I think we have a lot to discuss."

II

RELICS OF THE ILLUSTRIOUS DEAD

I don't know how long I waited in that jumbled, airless room. It was a study with no windows, obviously designed as Benavides's territory. There was an armchair for reading under the beam of light from a large lamp, which looked more like an old-fashioned hair dryer than anything else. And there I sat after walking several times around the room without finding a place that seemed destined for visitors: the doctor's study was not a space made for receiving anybody. Beside the chair, on top of a small table, was a pile of a dozen books that I amused myself by looking at without deciding to leaf through any of them for fear of breaking some hidden order. I saw a biography of Jean Jaurès and Plutarch's *Parallel Lives*, and I saw Arturo Alape's book on the *Bogotazo* and another leather-bound volume, this one more slender than the previous, the author's name unreadable and a title that struck me as too much like a pamphlet: *How Colombian Political Liberalism*

Is Not a Sin. The center of the longest wall was occupied by a desk, the surface of which was a rectangle of green leather, with two meticulous piles of paper, one of sealed envelopes and another of unfolded bills (a rare concession to practical life in this place devoted, it would appear, to various forms of contemplation), kept in place by the weight of a handcrafted pencil holder. Two pieces of equipment dominated the surface: a scanner and the screen of a computer, a huge white monster of the latest generation that occupied its place like an idol. No, I thought immediately: not like an idol, but like a great eye, like an all-seeing, all-knowing eye. Ridiculously I checked to make sure the computer was turned off, or at least that its camera was, in case anyone was spying on me.

What had happened down there? I still wasn't completely clear about it. I was surprised at my violent reaction, in spite of the fact that I, like most people of my generation, have a suppressed undercurrent of violence as a consequence of having grown up in a time when the city, my city, had turned into a minefield, and the great violence of bombs and shoot-outs recurred among us with their insidious mechanisms: anyone will remember the alacrity with which we'd get out of our cars ready to smash somebody's face in for a banal traffic incident, and I'm sure I'm not the only one who has seen the black hole of a pistol pointing in his face more than once. I won't be alone, either, in my fascination with scenes of violence, those football matches converted into pitched battles, those hidden cameras that register lost fistfights in the Madrid metro or a Buenos Aires gas station, scenes I look up on the internet to watch and feel the inevitable adrenaline surge. But none of that could justify what happened downstairs; however, the state of my nerves, due to lack of sleep and extreme tension, might help to explain it a little. That's what I clung to: yes, that wasn't me, and Dr. Benavides and his wife had to understand that: thirty blocks away, my unborn daughters were running life-or-death risks daily, and each day my well-being and that of my wife were facing the chance of a highly perilous birth. Was it not understandable that a comment like Carballo's would make me lose my sanity for a moment?

On the other hand, how much did Carballo know about my relationship with José María Villarreal? It was obvious he didn't have concrete particulars, but also that he and Benavides had been talking about me in some detail. Since when? Had Benavides invited me to his house for the secret purpose of introducing me to Carballo, or so that Carballo could meet me? Why? Because I was the nephew of someone who lived through April 9 firsthand and had a key role in what happened after Gaitán's assassination. Yes: that, at least, was true. It was a public event and formed part of official history: the governor loyal to the regime who sends a thousand men to control the riots. And of course, I had read García Márquez's memoir as everyone had, and I had felt uncomfortable, as everyone had, and even alarmed at the clarity with which the country's best novelist, as well as our most influential intellectual, suggested without foundation or euphemism the existence of a hidden truth. For that page was doing nothing else: by talking about the elegant man and suggesting his participation in the murder of the murderer, García Márquez put down in black and white his profound conviction that Juan Roa Sierra was not the sole assassin of Jorge Eliécer Gaitán, but that there was an elaborate political conspiracy behind the crime. *The man had managed to have a false assassin killed in order to protect the identity of the real one:* the words now acquired a new luminosity. But what had not occurred to me, of course, was that my uncle might have known who the elegant man was. The idea was outlandish, even if everyone back then knew everyone within the political elites. Was it outlandish? It was. But was it? Each of Carballo's words seemed to indicate a profound conviction: my uncle

José María could have been in the position to know something that would illuminate, although in a tenuous way, the identity of the man who had had *a false assassin killed in order to protect the identity of the real one.*

I was deep in these ruminations when someone knocked on the door.

When I opened it, I found a haggard and stooped version of Dr. Benavides, as if recent events had worn him down even further. In his hands he carried a tray with two cups and a fuchsia-colored thermos like the kind runners use, except that Dr. Benavides's thermos didn't contain water or an energy drink, but strong black coffee. "Not for me, thank you," I said. "Yes, for you. Thank you." And he poured me a cup. "Oh, Vásquez," he continued. "What a mess you got me into today."

"I know," I said. "I'm very sorry, Francisco. I don't know what got into me."

"You don't know? I do. It would probably have happened to anyone in your situation. Carballo got out of hand, I know that too. But that doesn't mean it's not a mess for me." He walked over to a corner of the room and pressed a button on a sort of robotic vent: the temperature in the room went down several degrees and I had the impression that the air was no longer humid. "You ruined my get-together, dear friend," said Benavides. "You ruined my party and my wife's."

"I can go downstairs," I offered. "I can apologize to everyone."

"Don't worry. They all left."

"Carballo too."

"Carballo too," said Benavides. "He went to the clinic. See if they can fix that septum."

Then he walked over to his desk, sat down, and turned on the computer. "Carballo is a very peculiar guy," he said, "and he might seem mad. I don't say he doesn't. But he's actually a worthwhile guy, so passionate that he sometimes goes too far. But I like passionate people. It's a weakness, what can I do. I like people who believe what they believe with real passion. And God knows that's how it is with Carballo." While he was talking, Benavides was moving the mouse over the green leather of his desk, and the elements on-screen changed, windows opened one on top of the other, and behind them I managed to see the image Benavides had chosen as his desktop background. I wasn't surprised to recognize another of Sady González's photos: the one of a burning streetcar during the April 9 disturbances. It was an image charged with violence, and must say something about the person who chose to see it every time he turns on his computer, but I didn't feel like thinking about that too much: it was also possible to stop seeing in that image a denunciation of the danger and destruction of that ill-fated day, and see only a spur to memory, a historical testimony. "Have you drunk your coffee?" Benavides asked.

I showed him my empty cup, its bottom adorned only with brown rings that some (not I) know how to read and interpret. "All of it," I said.

"Very good. Do you feel wide awake, or shall I pour you another?"

"I'm awake, Doctor. What happened downstairs was something else. It was . . ."

"Don't call me Doctor, Vásquez, I beg you. First of all because the word is so devalued in this country. Everyone, everyone gets called doctor. Second, I'm not your physician. Third, you and I are friends. Aren't we friends?"

"Yes, Doctor. Francisco. Yes, Francisco."

"And friends don't use formulas like that with each other. Do they?"

"No, Francisco."

"I could call you doctor too, Vásquez. You decided to devote yourself to writing, but first you graduated from law school. And lawyers also get called doctor in this country, don't they?"

"They do."

"And do you know why I don't call you doctor?"

"Because we're friends."

"Exactly. Because we're friends. And because we're friends, I trust you. And you trust me, I imagine."

"Yes, Francisco. I trust you."

"Exactly. And because we trust each other, I'm about to do something I only do with people I trust. I'm doing it with you because I trust you and I feel I owe you an explanation. You owe me a whiskey glass and a dinner party with my friends, but I owe you an explanation. And even if I didn't, I would give it to you. I think you can understand what I'm going to show you. Understand it and appreciate it. There are not many people who can. I think you can. I hope I'm not mistaken. Come here," he said, pointing an authoritative finger to the space beside his chair, in front of the desk with his papers. "Stand here."

Obeying him, I found the computer screen transformed. Occupying it entirely, apart from the colorful icons that run along the bottom, was an image I immediately recognized as an X-ray of a thorax; in the middle of the X-ray, embraced by the shadows of the ribs, resting on the spinal column, a black stain in the shape of a bean. I asked, "What's that bean?" and Benavides told me it wasn't a bean but a bullet deformed by its impact with the vertebrae: one of the four bullets that had killed Jorge Eliécer Gaitán on April 9, 1948.

GAITÁN's BONES. The bullet that had killed Gaitán. I was seeing them: there they were. I felt the privilege, the rare privilege of being there. I thought of Gaitán, of the famous photo of his lifeless face and of my visit to his house in my student days, when I began to be interested in his life story and his death and what that death and that life

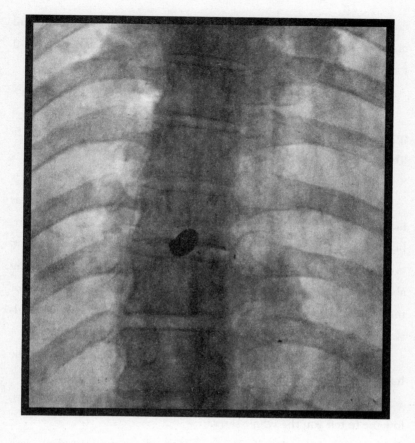

said about us Colombians. I remembered the glass case and the three-piece suit Gaitán was wearing when he was killed: I remembered the perforations in the dark cloth caused by the assassin Juan Roa Sierra's bullets. Now I was seeing one of those bullets inside the body, the now lifeless body. Benavides made comments and notations like a good professor, counted vertebrae and pointed out invisible organs and recited, as if they were poems, entire phrases someone had written on Gaitán's autopsy. One of them, "the heart intact without malicious signs of any cardiac arrest," struck me as worthy of a better destiny (it would have been those *malicious signs, señales aviesas,* that struck me as fantastic), but this was not a moment for making literature. I could only ask inwardly how it was possible that this was in his hands. Until I stopped wondering inwardly and asked out loud:

"How is it possible? How is it possible that you have this?"

"The original is in a locked drawer," said Benavides, answering a question no one had asked. "Only normal, no? Although nobody knows it's here."

"But why is it here?"

Benavides allowed something approaching a smile to appear on his face. "My father brought it," he said. He didn't say *"papá,"* as we Colombians tend to say even when we're adults and talking to another adult, even to strangers. In other Spanish-speaking countries, an adult talking about one's *papá* to another adult is an inevitable sign of affectedness or infantilism. Not so in Colombia. And nevertheless, Dr. Benavides always referred to his as his father. For some reason, I liked that.

"He brought it?" I asked. "Where did he bring it from? Why did he have it?"

"I'm glad you asked," said Benavides. "Now have patience, and allow me to tell you the whole story."

He dragged the chair he'd been sitting in—a modern black desk chair on wheels, with a sort of elastic webbing as a back and umpteen levers and switches for unknown functions—and moved it over beside the armchair. Benavides made a sign to me: *You sit here.* He sat in the armchair, crossed his hands over the buttons of his sweater, and began to tell me his father's story.

Don Luis Ángel Benavides had studied bacteriology at the National University. His scant vocation for the science did not prevent him from getting the best marks in his discipline, and during the final year of his studies he received a visit that changed his life: on the recommendation of his professor, the legendary Guillermo Uribe Cualla, the university authorities invited him to found the forensic laboratory. He never opened another bacteriology book. He traveled to the United States to specialize in ballistics and forensic sciences, and returned to Colombia ready to become the campus celebrity and great professor of his day. "He taught classes at the Institute of Penal Sciences in the Faculty of Law," Benavides told me. "A lot of capital letters for a couple of rooms, don't you think? In any case, there are twenty years' worth of Colombian judges whose only knowledge of forensic science comes from what my father taught them." Over the course of his long career, the first Dr. Benavides collected objects—objects he used for his classes, but also rare or odd things that his innumerable disciples or colleagues gave him: firearms, old swords, a lunar rock, a *Homo habilis* skull—and one day he arrived at his dominion in the university and looked around melancholically. "Damn it," he said. "This is like living in a museum." And at that moment he decided: as if it were the most natural thing in the world, he founded and began running, within the facilities of the National University, the Luis Ángel Benavides Carrasco Museum of Forensic Sciences.

"During the 1970s, when students at the National went on strike once a month, my father brought the most valuable pieces from the museum home," Dr. Benavides told me. "To protect them, you understand. Because one could never know what was going to happen in one of those strikes: stone-throwing, destructive impulses, confrontations with the police. Still, nothing ever happened to the museum. The students threw stones as if they were deranged, but they never touched a brick of the museum. They took care of it, they loved it. I saw it, Vásquez, I remember. Well anyway, this is one of the things my father brought home every once in a while. At that time he had a lab at the back of the house, behind the kitchen, and in that lab another museum of things that interested him gradually began to accumulate. Well, that's where he kept the things he brought home from the university while the strikes were going on. For example, this X-ray, which was very important to him. More than once I saw him looking at it against the light in the courtyard, trying to find who knows what, and I felt what you feel when you watch a musician reading a score. It's one of the clearest memories I have of his life: my father standing at the brightest hour of the day beside a window, trying to see through the image to a hidden truth."

Luis Ángel Benavides had died in 1987. "And one fine day," Dr. Benavides told me, "one of my brothers shows up and tells me there's an insurance policy. He tells me we have to collect on it, that we can't let it go to waste, that we have to move quickly, that we might lose it . . . To collect on the policy, I can't remember why, we had to take an inventory of the museum. And by then, my father's museum had a large number of pieces: fifteen hundred, two thousand. Who could deal with all that? It was a Herculean task, but also a mere administrative formality, and neither my brothers nor I had time to spend on it. So we got in touch with a lifelong student of my father's, a woman who worked at the Department of Administrative Security. She agreed to help us and began to compile the inventory, and was working on it when the bomb exploded."

The bomb at the DAS building. I was sixteen years old (in my last year of high school) when the drug traffickers Pablo Escobar and Gonzalo Rodríguez Gacha conspired to park a bus loaded with five hundred kilos of dynamite beside the building where the Department of Administrative Security operated. Their objective was not, in a strict sense, the state intelligence organization, but the general who directed it and symbolized, at that precise moment, the enemy the Medellín cartel had declared war on. It was December 6, 1989; it was 7:30 a.m. when the explosion shook the neighborhood of Paloquemao.

I was already sitting in my classroom, on the other side of the city, and I remember well the fear on the face of the teacher who told us the news, and I remember well classes being canceled, going home, and that feeling of surprise and displacement, of incomprehension and anxiety that I would learn to associate with those days when terrorism disrupted our routines, even those who'd had the good fortune to be somewhere else. The DAS bomb killed almost eighty people and wounded more than six hundred. Among the dead were civil servants, security agents, unsuspecting passersby on whom blocks of concrete rained down. One of those killed, then, was Dr. Luis Ángel Benavides's student. "Was she one of those killed?" I asked. "Precisely," answered the doctor, "she was one of those killed.

"The inventory was never finished," Benavides told me. "And one day I went to the museum, thinking of looking over the objects there to see if I could carry on with the inventory myself, and I found it closed. This was at the beginning of 1990, but classes hadn't begun yet. Inside there were just two guys, both dressed in suits and ties. They weren't professors: I could see that just from looking at them. One had a repugnant little mustache, like Rudolph Valentino's, do you remember who Valentino was? Well, that's what his mustache was like, the kind of mustache that has always made me unsympathetic to a man who would choose to have one like that. The guy was walking back and forth, walking like this, with his hands behind his back, and saying to his colleague that this was useless, that they were going to have to close the museum. And then I got scared, because in a second I imagined all that was in there, all the beautiful things that had been so important to my father, and I imagined them stuck in boxes and rotting away in some dank and dusty basement somewhere, more or less like piling up in the cupboard under the stairs of this country of indolent people. So it cost me no effort, nor did I feel any guilt: I grabbed a bag and stuffed three things into it, the first ones I found. And I walked slowly out of there, so I wouldn't alarm anyone or arouse suspicion. I think I did the right thing, because later they closed the museum, as they'd suggested. They really closed it: with a brick wall. Yes, they bricked it up, and with everything inside. Imagine, Vásquez, imagine the treasures that were there."

"The X-ray was one of them," I said.

"One of the ones I rescued, yes."

"But not the only one."

Benavides stood up and turned to the wall on his left. He took in both hands the only frame that adorned it: it was a poster in homage to Julio Garavito, that ancestor of his who more than a hundred years ago had calculated the latitude of Bogotá and invented a method for measuring the lunar orbit: there was the man, with his thick mustache, beside an illustration of the moon on which you could see the Sea of Tranquility. Benavides unhooked the picture; on the back, stuck with a piece of masking tape on each of its four corners, was an airmail envelope, an old-fashioned envelope, with its red and blue lines along the edges. Benavides slipped two fingers carefully inside and extracted a shiny object. It was a key.

"No, it's not the only one," said Benavides. "It's not even the most important. The importance of these things cannot be measured, of course. But I'm sure you'll agree with me. Let's see what you think of this."

He used the key to open a cabinet in his desk, and a drawer, freed from its latch, slid forward as if springing to life. Benavides reached in and handed me a heavy glass jar with a pressure seal. It was meant to look utterly banal: it could have contained apricots in brandy, sundried tomatoes, or eggplant slices roasted with basil. Inside the jar, an object impossible to identify—not eggplants, tomatoes, or apricots, obviously— seemed to float in the translucent liquid. Once I'd accepted that it was the fragment of a spinal column, I understood that the shaggy bits covering it were flesh, human flesh. When an impression is so strong, only silence seems advisable: any question, one suspects, will be redundant or even an offense. (We mustn't offend the objects of the past.) Benavides didn't even wait for me to put into words what was rushing through my head. In the center of Gaitán's vertebra, a black hole looked at me like the eye of a galaxy.

"My father believed there'd been a second shooter," said Benavides. "At least for a time."

He was referring to one of many conspiracy theories surrounding Gaitán's assassination. According to this one, Juan Roa Sierra did not act alone on April 9: he was accompanied by another man, responsible for other shots and one of the lethal bullets. During the 1950s, the theory of the second shooter was gaining ground, in large part due to an incontrovertible fact: one of the bullets that killed Gaitán had not appeared in the course of the autopsy. "And of course, people's imagination does what it does," said Benavides. "More and more witnesses became convinced they'd seen a second assassin. Some even described him. Some even said that the missing bullet was the only truly lethal one; they decided that the missing bullet had been fired by a different gun and that therefore Roa Sierra was not even the assassin." Since these witnesses were serious and respectable people, and since the phantoms of April 9 were still wreaking havoc among us, in 1960 an examining criminal magistrate was assigned the job of confronting the theory of the second shooter, whether to confirm it or rule it out definitively: to silence the paranoid. The judge was called Teobaldo Avendaño, and had the rare distinction of not being hated by the Liberals or the Conservatives. In this country, that was the greatest of virtues. "And the first thing the magistrate ordered," said Benavides, "was the exhumation of the corpse."

"To look for the bullet?" I asked.

"The thing is, the initial autopsy had been very frugal. Imagine, Vásquez, what the doctors who performed it in 1948 might have felt. Imagine what it would be like to be in front of the dead body of the great Liberal caudillo Jorge Eliécer Gaitán, hero of the people and future president of the Republic of Colombia. How could they not feel intimidated? Once the causes of death were declared, they decided not to destroy the body any further, even though they hadn't found the other bullet. They didn't open up his back, for example, in spite of knowing that one of the bullets had entered through it. But this happened in the early evening, just past six, and at that moment the truth was only one: a guy called Juan Roa Sierra had killed Gaitán and then the furious mob had killed him. And that was all: What did it matter how many bullets the assassin had fired? That became important only later, with the versions that arose, with the contradictions, the unanswered questions, the problems: with all the speculations that clutch at whatever they can. Conspiracy theories are like creepers, Vásquez, they grab on to whatever they can to climb up and keep growing until someone takes away what sustains them. For that they had to dig up Gaitán and open up his back and look for the missing bullet. And who did Avendaño ask to do that? Do you know who that task fell to? Well, yes: my father. Dr. Luis Ángel Benavides Carrasco."

"To the expert," I said, "in Ballistics and Forensic Sciences."

"Exactly. They kept the date and time of the proceedings secret. Gaitán was buried beside his house, in Santa Teresita. Have you been to that neighborhood, to Gaitán's house? Well, that's where he's buried. They disinterred the coffin and put it in the courtyard of the house. I don't know where, but I imagine in that small courtyard at the back of the main floor. There was my father. How many times he told me that story, Vásquez: thirty, forty, fifty times in my life, since I was a boy. 'Papá, tell me about when they exhumed Gaitán,' I used to say, and off he'd go with the story. Anyway, my father waited for the casket and asked that it be opened in his presence, and he was surprised at how well preserved Gaitán's body was. Some bodies last longer, some not so long. Twelve years after his death, Gaitán looked as though they'd embalmed him . . . But as soon as the air touched him, he began to decompose. The house filled with the smell of death. My father said the entire neighborhood filled with the smell of death. Apparently it was unbearable. Those present began to leave one by one. Pale, queasy, hiding their faces in their coat sleeves. And after a while they'd come back as if nothing had happened, fresh and healthy-looking. My father found out later that Felipe González Toledo, the only journalist present, took them to a nearby bar and had them rub *aguardiente* in their nostrils, so they could stand it. González Toledo knew all the tricks. That's why he was the best chronicler the crime pages of this country ever had."

"And did he write about that day?"

"Of course. The chronicle's out there for you to look up and read, with my father's name in black and white. The chronicle describes the moment that my father and the coroner removed the bullet. But he doesn't tell any details, and I know them, I know they found the vertebra where the bullet was lodged, I know they extracted the vertebra and reburied Gaitán. They didn't want some madman to decide to steal the body."

"And the vertebra?"

"They took it to the institute."

"To the Legal Medicine Institute," I said.

"And there they confirmed, or my father, who was the one who knew about these things, confirmed that the bullet had come from the same pistol."

"Juan Roa Sierra's pistol?"

"Yes," said Benavides. "The same pistol as the rest of the bullets. You must know how it works, because these things are on television every night, so I'm not going to explain what the barrel bore is, or how rifling of any gun leaves a virtually unmistakable trace on a bullet. You just need to know that my father did the analyses, took the images, and concluded that they'd come out of the same gun. So there was no second shooter. At least according to that. And then, obviously, the vertebra with the bullet was not returned to Gaitán's body. They stored it securely away. Or my father did, who used it for years during his classes at the university. This is the other image I have of my father, on the trolley bus route. He never liked driving, and to go from home to the university and the university home, he took the trolley. Did you know the Bogotá trolley buses, Vásquez? Well, imagine the scene, a regular guy, because my father was the most regular guy on earth, getting onto the trolley with his briefcase in his hand. Looking at him, nobody would ever have imagined that inside his briefcase were the bones of Jorge Eliécer Gaitán. Sometimes I went with him, a boy hand in hand with his father, and my father would then have a living boy in one hand and a briefcase of dead bones in the other. Bones, furthermore, for which anyone would have killed right there. And he took them out and brought them home on the trolley bus, safe and sound in his leather briefcase."

"And that's how the vertebra ended up in this house."

"From the university to the museum, from the museum home, and from there to your hands, courtesy of yours truly."

"And the liquid?"

"Formaldehyde in a solution of five percent."

"No, no, I'm asking if it's the same."

"I change it every once in a while. So it doesn't get cloudy, you know? So it can be seen clearly."

There are some of us who see clearly, I remembered. I held the jar up to the light and looked at it. Flesh, bone, formaldehyde in a solution of five percent: human remains, yes, but most of all objects from the past. I have always been sensitive to them, sensitive or even vulnerable, and I accept that in my relationship with such things there is an aspect of fascination or fetishism, and also something (impossible to deny) of an ancient superstition: I know that some part of me sees them and has always seen them as relics, and that's why the cult in which believers profess to a splinter of wood from the cross of their Lord or a certain famous shroud where the image of a man has been imprinted by magic has never seemed incomprehensible or, much less, exotic to me. I can understand very well the devotion with which the first Christians, persecuted and murdered, began to conserve and venerate the mortal remains of their martyrs: the chains that bound them, the swords that fatally wounded them, the instruments of torture that inflicted pain on them for long hours of captivity. Those early Christians who watched their fellows die in the arena, who from a distance watched the condemned bleed to death after the attacks of beasts or lances, threw themselves on top of bodies at grave risk to their own lives to soak their rags in the still-fresh blood. That night, in Dr. Benavides's study and with Gaitán's vertebra before my eyes, I could not help remembering the Bogotá witnesses to the April 9 crime doing the same thing: falling to their knees on the paving stones of Carrera Séptima, in front of the Agustín Nieto building, a few steps from the streetcar tracks and therefore risking their own lives, to collect the black blood of the dead leader, the spreading pool of blood spilled by Juan Roa Sierra's four shots. An atavistic instinct urges us to these desperate acts, I thought with Gaitán's vertebra in my hand.

Yes, that's what the vertebra was: a relic. That energy I felt through the glass and the formaldehyde: what perhaps the early Christians felt, let's say Saint Augustine, holding in his hands the remains of a martyred body: let's say Saint Stephen. Augustine even speaks—though I no longer remember where I read this—of one of the stones that killed Stephen; this stone had also been preserved in his day, that murderous stone was also a relic. And where was the bullet that had killed Gaitán? Where was the bullet I'd just seen in the X-ray, the bullet blunted after exploding against the bones? Where was the bullet that had penetrated Gaitán's body through his back, and that had been extracted and analyzed by Dr. Luis Ángel Benavides after it had been deformed by the impact? Where was the bullet that, again according to Dr. Benavides, was no longer lodged in that vertebra? Benavides watched me looking through the jar and the formaldehyde. The lights of the room played with the dense liquid; in the glass of the jar danced brief sparkles of colors that weren't in the vertebra, colors that came from the light broken by the prism: phantom colors. And I thought of the stone that killed Saint Stephen and the bullet that killed Gaitán. "Where is the bullet?" I finally asked.

"Oh, yes, the bullet," said Benavides. "Well, there's no way of knowing."

"They didn't keep it?"

"Maybe they did, maybe someone thought of keeping it. Maybe it's put away somewhere, gathering dust. But I don't think my father kept it."

"But it would have been useful to him," I said. "For his classes, at least."

"Yes, that's true. For his classes. What can I tell you, Vásquez, I've thought the same thing. And yes, it is entirely logical that my father would have wanted to keep it. But I never saw it. Maybe he did keep it and even used it in his classes before I was aware of any of this. But he never brought it home as far as I know." There was a silent pause. "Although one could fill whole books with all that I don't know."

"Who else has seen these things?"

"Since I've had them, you're the first. Outside of my family, of course. My wife and children know that these things exist and they know they're here, in my safe. For my children it's as if they didn't exist. For my wife, they're a crazy pastime."

"And Carballo?"

"Carballo knows they exist. More than that: he knew long before I did. My father talked to him about these things. He talked to him about the 1960 autopsy. It's possible, though I don't know, that Carballo had seen them in his classes. But he doesn't know I have them."

"What?"

"He doesn't know they're here."

"And why haven't you told him? I saw Carballo's face when we started talking about Gaitán. When you mentioned my uncle. His face lit up, his eyes widened, it was as if he were a child who'd been given a present. It's obvious that he has as much interest as you do, or even more intense, if possible. Why don't you share this with him?"

"I don't know," said Benavides. "Because I have to keep something just for myself."

"I don't understand."

"For my father, Carballo was not just any student," said Benavides. "He was his favorite student. His heir, his disciple. All professors are vulnerable to admiration, Vásquez. More than that: many teach just to feel that admiration. What Carballo felt for my father went much further: it was adulation, idolatry, something almost fanatical. Or that's how I saw it. He was also a brilliant student, this Carballo. When I met him, when my father started bringing him home for lunch, he was at the top of his class, but my father said that the class was nothing: he was the best student he'd had in his whole career. 'What a shame he was studying to become a lawyer,' my father said. 'Carlitos should have been a forensic doctor.' He had a real weakness for him. So much so that I was sometimes jealous."

"Jealous of Carballo, Francisco?" I laughed. The doctor laughed, too: a crooked laugh, a grimace of both complicity and embarrassment. "Jealous of that character, begging your pardon? This is something I wouldn't have expected of you."

"Why not? First of all, let me tell you that he's much less of a weak character than you think. A brilliant guy, that's what he is, even with his ridiculous scarves, Carballo has one of the liveliest minds I've ever come across. It's a shame he never practiced his profession, because he would have been a brilliant lawyer. But I think he didn't like the law. He liked my father's class and he was at the top of his year, but the rest of the courses he didn't like, it was as if he were obliged to study law. In any case, this is all beside the point. Or is it that one is supposed to stop feeling things like this as an adult? None of that, Vásquez. Jealousy and envy make the world go round. Half of all decisions are taken out of such basic emotions as envy and jealousy. Feelings of humiliation, resentment, sexual dissatisfaction, inferiority complexes: there you have the engines of history, my dear patient. Right now someone is making a decision that affects you and me, and they're making it for reasons like these: to harm an enemy, to get revenge for an affront, to impress a woman and sleep with her. That's how the world works."

"Well, yes. But none of that is comparable to this business of yours. Why were you jealous? Because your father paid more attention to Carballo than to you? But you weren't even a student in the same class."

"I wasn't even a student on the same *course*," Benavides said. "As a matter of fact, I wasn't even a student in the same university: I went to Javeriana, because I never wanted to take advantage of my father's prestige to get into the National. And besides, Carballo was several years older than me—seven or eight years, depending on who you talk to. None of that mattered: I'd come home for lunch and there he'd be: sitting in my place and talking to my father."

"Hang on a second, Francisco," I interrupted. "What do you mean?"

"Well, sometimes I'd come home for lunch and there was Carballo, sitting at the dining room table, and the table would be covered in open books, notebooks, diagrams, sketches, rolls of paper."

"No, no. Explain to me the age difference."

"What?"

"You just said that Carballo was seven or eight years older than

73

you," I said. "Depending on who you talk to, you just said. I don't understand."

Benavides smiled. "Yes, it's true. I'm so used to the matter that I forget how strange it is. But it's quite simple: if you ask Carballo when he was born, he'll tell you 1948. If you ask the civil register, you'll discover that's a lie: that he was born in 1947. Guess the reason for the difference. I'll give you one chance. Guess why Carballo says he was born in 1948."

"To coincide with April 9."

"Spot on, Vásquez. Carballo no longer has any secrets from you." He smiled again, and then I couldn't figure out what was behind that smile: pure sarcasm, a bit of affection, a certain blend of sarcasm and comprehension and tolerance, the tolerance one has for children or madmen? I, meanwhile, remembered that García Márquez had done something similar: for many years he maintained that he was born in 1928, when he was actually born a year earlier. The reason? He wanted his birth to coincide with the famous massacre at the banana plantation, which became one of his obsessions, and which he described or reinvented in the best chapter of *One Hundred Years of Solitude*. I didn't mention this to Benavides, in order not to interrupt his tale too much.

"Tell me more about the dining room," I said.

"Yes. I would arrive and there would be Carballo, chatting with my father, with the table covered in papers about the latest case. And the whole family had to wait until my father finished explaining what he was explaining to his student. To his disciple. Envy, Vásquez, is nothing more than the conviction that someone else has the place that belongs to you. And that's what I felt about Carballo: that he supplanted me, replaced me, robbed me of my place at the dining table. It was fine for my father to stay at the university to give all his theories about the world to his favorite student. It was fine that he told him things he would never have told me. But coming to my house and carrying on with the same things, that bothered me. My father talking to him and not to me: that bothered me. If something happened to him at the university, he told him and not me. And yes, Vásquez, yes: that bothered me. It poisoned my life. I was a grown man, as they used to say, but that poisoned my life and there was nothing to be done about it. Anyway, I was still very young then. I got married when I was twenty-four, graduated as a surgeon, and got over it. I had other things to think about . . . All this to say that no, Carballo does not know that this is here. And I'd prefer it to stay that way. I'd prefer him not to find out. I don't know if you understand why."

"I understand more than you think," I said. "Can I ask you something?"

"Maybe."

"Did your father's relationship with Carballo remain the same?"

"The same as ever," said Benavides. "Master and disciple, mentor and protégé. It was as if my father had found his heir apparent. Or as if Carballo had found his father, that could also be a way to put it."

"Who is Carballo's father?"

"I don't know," said Benavides. "I think he was killed in the *Violencia*, back when so many Liberals and Conservatives were killing each other. Carballo comes from a humble family, Vásquez, he's the first ever to go to university. Anyway, I don't know anything about his father. Carballo has never liked talking about that."

"No, of course not. Understandable, then. Understandable that he stuck to Dr. Benavides and didn't let go. A sort of substitute father."

"I don't like that expression, but I suppose so. That explains it in part. They saw each other often, spoke on the phone . . . They lent each other books, or rather, my father lent him books. They carried on repairing the country by night, identifying the exact moment Colombia had screwed up. And that's how the last five years of my father's life went by. Five or six, let's say. That's how they went."

"Which theories?"

"What?"

"You said your father gave all his theories to Carballo. What theories were they?"

Benavides poured himself another cup of coffee, took a sip, and stepped over to his desk. He opened a deep drawer full of purple folders with typed labels, but I was too far away to read them. He took out one of the files, returned to the armchair, placed it on his lap, and began to pass his hand over it, stroking it as if it were a cat. "My father didn't have a lot of hobbies," he said then. "He was one of those fortunate men who do what they most enjoy for a living and are only happy when they're doing it. His work was his distraction. But if there was something similar to a hobby or a pastime in his life, it was this: reconstructing famous crimes from the point of view of forensic science. One of my grandfathers was famous in the family for assembling jigsaw puzzles of two or three thousand pieces. That was his hobby: gigantic puzzles. He did them on the dining room table in his house, and while he was doing one, the family couldn't eat at the table. Well, these forensic analyses of murders were my father's puzzles. He got up early on Saturdays and Sundays, very early, and started studying them as if they were his most recent cases. The murder of Jean Jaurès. Archduke Franz Ferdinand. For a while he was even working on Julius Caesar, imagine. He analyzed it for months and wrote a detailed report based, among other sources, on Shakespeare's play. There was a time when he started turning deaths that weren't crimes into murders: I remember, for example, the months he spent trying to prove that Bolívar hadn't been killed by his tuberculosis, but had been poisoned by his Colombian enemies . . . This is to explain that it was all a game. A serious game, like puzzles for those who do them, but a game after all. Oh, you should have seen the way that grandfather of mine would get if someone moved a piece: there would be hell to pay.

"And that file is one of his puzzles?" I asked.

"Yes," said Benavides. "The puzzle of John Fitzgerald Kennedy. I don't know when he got into it, but this was one of his toys, if you allow me the frivolity, that accompanied him for his whole life. Every five or six years, he'd get out the file again, put the puzzle together again, or try to. Look at these papers, for example: they're clippings from Colombian newspapers that refer to the Kennedy assassination. Look at the dates: February 4, 1975. This other one, from *El Espacio*, is from 1983. The date can be seen on one corner, but besides, it was published on the anniversary: 'Twenty Years Since the Kennedy Assassination,' you can clearly read. Imagine my father reading a rag like *El Espacio*! But everything he saw about Kennedy ended up in this file. Here are, I don't know, twenty or thirty pieces, some more important, others less so. But all part of my father's hobby. That's why I keep them, that's why they're valuable to me. I don't think they'd have any value for anyone else."

"Can I see them?"

"That's why I got them out. I want you to see them." He stood up and arched his back: the movement of those who have back trouble. "Have a look at these while I go see what's going on in the rest of the house. Would you like anything from the kitchen?"

"No thanks," I said. "Can I ask you a question, Francisco?"

"Maybe."

"Why this folder and not another? You've got a drawer full of file folders. Is there any reason for choosing this one to show me instead of any other one?"

"Of course there's a reason, Vásquez. This one has a lot to do with Carballo. And we're here talking about Carballo, we've been talking about Carballo the whole time, even if you haven't realized. To put it a better way: have a look at that. I'll be right back to tell you more things."

And after saying that, he closed the door and left me alone.

I OPENED THE FILE still sitting in the revolving desk chair. But the papers slipped out, some fell on the floor or forced me to catch others with my left hand while trying to flip through the rest with my right, so I ended up sitting right on the floor, on the carpet the color of untreated wool, to spread them out there, one beside the other. "L. H. Oswald Did Not Kill J. F. Kennedy," the oldest of the cuttings shouted at me from the carpet. Dr. Luis Ángel Benavides had noted its date, but not its source; I thought I recognized, however, the typography of *El Tiempo*. The news item spoke of a film that had just been shown in Chicago that reached an irrefutable conclusion: President Kennedy had been shot at by "as many as four, possibly five persons." The film, the newspaper article informed us, was the work of Robert Groden, "a New York photographer and optical expert"; a political activist named Dick Gregory declared that the film "will change the destiny and fate of the world." They were both new names to me, but the rest of the article allowed me to deduce that the film in question was that of Abraham Zapruder: the famous eight-millimeter film clip shot by an amateur the day of the assassination, those twenty-seven seconds that are still the most direct witness we've ever had of what happened and the source of all the conspiracy theories that have been born since. Zapruder's film clip is now part of the twentieth century's popular consciousness (its frames live on our retinas and we identify them immediately), but at the date of the news item, it wasn't yet: it was still more or less secret, or it was known by just a few, and that's why the reporter didn't even give the name by which we now know it. The way the article is written, it was even possible that the writer attributed the authorship of the film to Mr. Groden, when the truth was that Groden—photographer, optical expert—had only been responsible for enlarging it, examining it, and denouncing in strong words what he saw in it: that is, the one responsible for arriving at the hair-raising conclusions that were going to change the destiny and fate of the world.

"The film," I read, "shows the moment in which the bullet reaches President Kennedy's head. According to Groden, the force of the projectile threw Kennedy back and to the left, which indicates it was shot from in front of and not behind the president, as had been thought up till now." It was fascinating: in the world of the article, the world of February 4, 1975, those revelations were still revelations. Now they are a

Febru 4/75

L. H. Oswald no matò a J. F. Kennedy

J. F. KENNEDY   L. H. OSWALD

CHICAGO, 3 (UPI). Lee Harvey Oswald "no tuvo nada qué ver con el asesinato" del Presidente John F. Kennedy, según prueba una película hecha por un fotógrafo y experto óptico de Nueva York, que fue exhibida en Chicago en rueda de prensa.

Según Robert Groden, "4 ó tal vez 5 personas", dispararon contra Kennedy, y se hicieron 6 disparos y no 3, como estableció la Comisión Warren, que investigó el asesinato del Presidente, ocurrido en Dallas, el 22 de noviembre de 1963.

Oswald fue arrestado y, a su vez, fue asesinado en el cuartel general de la Policía de Dallas por Jack Ruby, dueño de un bar nudista.

Dick Gregory, un activista político, dijo que la película "cambiará el destino y la suerte del mundo". Agregó que ella "salvará la vida del senador Edward Kennedy".

La semana pasada, Gregory y un profesor adjunto de filosofía, Ralph Schoenman, dijeron que tenían pruebas de que la Agencia Central de Inteligencia (CIA) había intervenido en el asesinato de Kennedy.

Groden exhibió el filme en una conferencia de prensa realizada en Chicago y dijo que se trataba de una ampliación de la película original sobre el asesinato. El filme original es de propiedad de la empresa periodista "Time Inc.".

La película, ampliada a gran tamaño y utilizando la cámara lenta, muestra el momento en que el Presidente Kennedy es alcanzado por una bala en la cabeza. Según Groden, la fuerza del proyectil lanzó a Kennedy hacia atrás y a la izquierda, lo que indica que fue disparada de frente y no de espaldas al Presidente, como se ha pensado hasta ahora.

En la película también se ven dos hombres que, según Groden, estaban disparando a Kennedy. Uno desde detrás de un pedestal, en un prado, frente a la comitiva. El otro está semioculto bajo un arbusto y también de frente a la comitiva, empuñando un fusil, según Groden.

Gregory dijo que él, Groden y Schoenman viajarán el sábado a Washington para mostrar el filme ante la comisión que investiga las actividades de la CIA, que preside el vicepresidente Nelson Rockefeller.

commonplace: we all know that the movements of Kennedy's head flagrantly contradict the official version, and are the principal stone in the shoe of those who still maintain that Oswald acted alone. The article continued: "Two men are also seen in the film, according to Groden, who are firing at Kennedy. One from behind a pedestal, on a grassy knoll, in front of the motorcade. The other is half hidden under a low tree and also in front of the motorcade, pointing a rifle, according to Groden." The repetition of those three words, *according to Groden*, was like a window through which you could see the attitude of the journalist: cautious, fearful, careful to underline (in the name of the newspaper, perhaps) that those subversive revelations belonged exclusively to the protagonist of the news. How much that word, *according*, had changed in the thirty years since: how it had filled with new meanings, how it had cast aside vacillations and assumed certainty. It's always difficult, I thought, the exercise of reading a document from another time with the eyes of those who read it in the moment of its appearance. There are those who never manage it, I thought; and that's why they'll never communicate with the past: they will remain forever deaf to the whispers, the secrets it tells us, to the comprehension of its mysterious mechanisms.

Another of the cuttings had six stills from the Zapruder film. The newspaper had laid out the illustration like a strip of film, and Dr. Luis Ángel Benavides had numbered the blank spaces, although I wasn't sure what the numeration corresponded to. The doctor hadn't bothered to identify the cutting, so it wasn't possible to know where it came from or when it had been published, but I imagined it was quite a bit later than the item about Robert Groden, for several years had to have passed since that exhibition of Zapruder's film in Chicago before any media outlet in the world would have the right to reproduce its content. Those photograms. That film. There, sitting on the floor of Benavides's study, I thought: I would never get accustomed to them. I thought: They'll never stop being extraordinary. What heap of coincidences were necessary for a man with a good camera to find himself in the perfect spot and manage to film from there one of the defining events of our time? In our day of tablets and smartphones everybody now has a camera in their hand all the time, and there is no scandal or public event, as innocuous as can be, able to escape those public witnesses who see all, those ubiquitous digital gossips who film everything and make everything immediately available on the Web, solicitous but unscrupulous, indignant but indiscreet. However, in November 1963 it still seemed strange, or fortuitous, that an unexpected moment of life should be filmed by anonymous men with private equipment. And that's what Zapruder was: an anonymous man, a man in the crowd, by nature but

also by his own volition. A man who had no reason to be where he was at midday on November 22, with a movie camera in his hand.

Zapruder could very easily not have been there. If his Ukrainian family had not emigrated in 1920, expelled by the violence of the civil war, if he'd died in the Russian Revolution or chosen a different country in which to seek exile, Zapruder would not have been there. If he hadn't learned to cut patterns for clothing in Manhattan shops, Zapruder would not have been hired by Nardis, a Dallas sportswear factory, and he wouldn't have been there. If he hadn't liked cameras and hadn't bought the latest model Bell & Howell the previous year, he wouldn't have filmed what he filmed. We now know that the film very nearly did not exist. We know that Mr. Zapruder had planned to film the presidential motorcade from the beginning, but when he saw that it was raining that morning, he left his camera at home and went to work without it; we know that it was his assistant who pointed out the cleared sky and suggested he go home for his camera, to not miss that important event. And it was an important event—it was— but Mr. Zapruder could very easily have refused, or not bothered, or not had time, or not wanted to leave his workplace, or had other errands to run . . . Why did he do it? Why did he rush home from work to pick up his Bell & Howell?

I imagine Zapruder as a shy, bald man in his fifties, with large black-framed glasses and a slight Russian accent, who just wanted to work quietly in his sportswear shop and feel like an American. One might think that in those days, after the installation of the missiles in Cuba and the confrontation with Khrushchev, neither his origins nor his accent would be feeling too comfortable. Was his admiration for President Kennedy a way of being in the middle of what surrounded him, a display of loyalty to the United States in those days of the Cold War? When he followed his assistant's advice and returned home for

his camera, was he demonstrating that Kennedy's visit was also important to him, that he too felt committedly democratic, that he too was
participating in the patriotic celebration of the presidential visit? How
big a part did his deep, old immigrant's insecurities play—even if he'd
been in the United States for four decades—in the fact that he decided
to go down to Dealey Plaza, bring out his Model 414 PD Bell & Howell, and start filming? Ah, but that could also have happened another
way: for we know that Mr. Zapruder initially thought to film from the
window of his office, and it was only at the last minute when he decided to look for a better angle and went down to Elm Street; once
there, thinking of the route the motorcade would cover, he realized
the ideal vantage point would be from the top of a concrete abutment
at the north end of the street, near the viaduct, above a small hill covered in well-kept grass. He went there, climbed up on the abutment
with the help of his secretary, Marilyn Sitzman, and asked her to keep
hold of his raincoat to neutralize the vertigo he'd suffered since he was
young. When the presidential motorcade appeared from Houston
Street, Zapruder forgot his vertigo, forgot the hand clutching the back
of his coat, forgot everything except his Bell & Howell camera, and
began to film the 27 seconds, the 486 frames that registered forever, for
the only time in the history of humanity, the moment when several
bullets destroyed the head of a leader of a nation. "Like a firecracker,"
he would later say. "His head exploded like a firecracker."

What followed was a world at war. Screams of hysteria, men throwing themselves to the ground to protect their children with their bodies, uncontrolled crying, fainting. In the midst of the commotion,
Zapruder, not yet entirely understanding what had just happened, was
returning to his office with his secretary when a reporter from *The Dallas Morning News* approached him. His name was Harry McCormick;
he'd seen him filming and offered to take him to a Secret Service agent,

Forrest Sorrels, who would undoubtedly know how to deal with the extraordinary document he had in his hands. Zapruder agreed to hand over the film to Agent Sorrels, but he put one condition on it: that it should be used only to investigate the assassination. After reaching an agreement, the men went to the WFAA television station to develop the film, but without success: the technicians did not have the necessary equipment at the studio. So Zapruder ended up taking the film to the Kodak processing plant, waiting until 6:30 in the evening, then going immediately to the Jamieson Film Company to have two copies made, and arriving home after the most exhausting day he would ever live. That night he dreamed he returned to Manhattan, where he'd lived for his first twenty years in the United States, and when he arrived at Times Square he saw a booth advertising: "See the President's head explode!"

I have seen it explode. Millions of people have seen it explode (like a firecracker), and we've also seen what comes next, the improbable seconds when Jackie lunges to recover the fragments of her husband's recently shattered head; and there, among Dr. Luis Ángel Benavides's cuttings, the frames showing the elegant and well-groomed woman on top of the back of the Lincoln limousine (midnight blue, the same color as Gaitán's suit), reaching for pieces of cranium or brain matter. What was Jackie looking for? What instinct told her to recover fragments of a body she had loved and that had now stopped living? We can speculate: we can think, for example, of an instinct that, for lack of a better word, I call *completist*: the urge not to allow something that was together to disintegrate. Whole, the body of John Fitzgerald Kennedy lived and worked, it was the body of a father and a husband (and also of a president, a friend, a promiscuous lover); fragmented by the impact of the bullets, broken into pieces that now slid across the midnight blue of the limousine, that living body had stopped existing. Maybe that's what Jackie desired, even if she was unaware of it: to repair the ruined body to return it to its original state, the state it had been in seconds before, with the illusory impression that in doing so, returning the lost fragments to the destroyed body, that body would come back to life. Would the professor of forensic sciences have thought the same thing when he looked at this page of a newspaper and when he cut out the frames from Zapruder's film? Maybe Luis Ángel Benavides read the images in a different way; maybe he had good reasons to believe that Jackie, acting the way she did, was thinking in forensic terms: collecting evidence to help the eventual investigators, the discovery of the guilty party and his efficient punishment. It's possible that he'd had that opinion at the moment of cutting out the page and adding it to his dossier, his puzzle; it's possible, I say, because we all see the images Zapruder's camera captured coldly and with distance and it's legitimate to imagine Benavides the elder seeing them like that when he cut out these pages; but believing such considerations could have passed through the consciousness of Jackie Kennedy on November 22, 1963, believing those methodical reasons inspired her in the moment of losing all her composure and climbing on top of the trunk of the Lincoln, with her husband's blood still fresh on her tailored suit, seeping into its fabric and staining it irremediably, is to ignore the power our atavisms have over us. If a religion had formed around JFK (the idea is not preposterous), each of its threads would have become a relic as well. And we would adore it, yes, we would worship it, and we would construct altars or museums, and conserve it over time like a treasure.

I WAS ABSORBED in those thoughts when Dr. Benavides returned. "Everybody's asleep now," he said, and dropped with fatigue into his reading chair. It was as if he made me notice—with his movements, with the weight of the sigh he let out—that I was tired too: my head ached a little, my eyes were beginning to sting, and the claustrophobia I'd suffered since childhood (yes, like Mr. Zapruder's vertigo) perked up: I wanted open spaces, to go out into the cold air of the Bogotá night, to get out of that windowless room that smelled of papers from the past and leftover coffee, to get back to the clinic and see M and hear about my daughters, who were still living in a distant world incomprehensible to me. I took out my phone: there were no calls and all the bars that indicated a good signal were still there, at the corner of the screen, firm and parallel, standing up in order of stature like a children's choir. Benavides pointed to the carpet covered in clippings and added: "Well, I see you've been making progress."

"How dedicated your father was," I said. "Admirable."

"Yes, that's what he was. But he was already old when he got feverishly determined. That was in '83, the twentieth anniversary: at that moment his dedication turned into something more. One day he said to me: I'm not going to die without resolving the Kennedy case. He died, of course, without resolving it, but his papers are still here. Why isn't . . . ?" He bent down, moved his hand through the papers and grabbed one. "Yes, here it is. This is from that time, look: an analysis of the hypotheses of the crime, in his own handwriting. Read it, please."

"You want me to read it?"

"Please."

I cleared my throat. "'Hypothesis one,'" I read. "'Two shooters, page ninety-five.' Page ninety-five of what?"

"I don't know. Some book he was consulting. Go on."

"'Two shooters,'" I obeyed, "'one in the window of the sixth floor, another on the second floor. Note: At 12:20 a film shows two silhouettes in the sixth-floor window.' In parentheses: 'At 12:31 the president

is shot. The superintendent of the building, Roy S. Truly, going upstairs with a policeman immediately after the shots were fired, meets
Oswald drinking a Coca-Cola in the second-floor hallway.' I think
that's what it says, your father's handwriting isn't that easy to decipher."

"As if I didn't know. Go on."

"'Hypothesis two. Page ninety-seven. Oswald fired from the second-
floor window and the other shooter, who was a more expert sniper,
fired Oswald's rifle from the sixth floor. Hypothesis three . . .'"

"No, not that one. That one's useless."

"It says that maybe Oswald wanted to kill the governor."

"Yes, exactly. It's useless. The important thing is in the others, those
contain my father's convictions."

"His conclusions?"

"No, not his conclusions, because he never had a definitive one. But
he did arrive at the conviction, as definitive as it could be, that Oswald
didn't act alone. That the lone-wolf theory, as the Gringos call it, is
completely false. Lone wolf, isn't that what they say? Even the name is
absurd. Nobody could have done that alone, it seems obvious. You'd
have to be blind not to see it. Or rather: you have to not want to see it
not to see it."

"You're talking like Carballo," I said.

Benavides laughed. "Maybe, maybe." Then: "You've seen the Zapruder film, I imagine?"

"Several times, yes."

"Then you remember."

"What?"

"The head, Vásquez. What else?"

Perhaps it was because I didn't answer immediately, or due to the
tiniest instant of silence that opened up after his words, but Benavides
leaped to his desk, and there, standing in front of the enormous screen

Hipótesis ①

2 Tiradores ?: pág 95

uno en la ventana del
6° piso

otro en el 2° piso

Nota: a las 12,20 una
película muestra dos
siluetas de personas
en la ventana del
6° piso (A las 12,31 dio
pasaron entre el Presidente
el Jefe de las oficinas
Roy STruly al salir en
en Policía inmediata-
mente de todos pa...

of his computer (I had his chair and he didn't ask for it back), bending over with difficulty as if taking a bow, he moved the mouse and began to type. In seconds a YouTube page opened: *The Zapruder Film*, I read. And there was the shiny Lincoln, advancing at that frighteningly slow pace, accompanied by white-helmeted motorcyclists, and there was Kennedy. There was the president: sitting so close to the door that he could rest his right arm on it, waving to one side and the other with the same relaxed hand, swallowing up the world with his propaganda smile and his hairstyle so perfect it didn't even get ruffled in the open air, sure of his life and his deeds or at least pretending a seamless

encontrarme Oswald
tomándose una bre...
en el pasillo del 2º
piso.
Hipótesis ② pág 97 - 106
Oswald disparó desde la
ventana del 2º piso y
el otro tirador...
...disparó en
la cabeza de Oswald
desde la ... ventana del
6º piso
Hipótesis ③ pág 72-7
Oswald quería matar era al
Gobernador de quien era
enemigo?

self-confidence. The motorcade is partially hidden behind some object that might be a placard or a street sign, and when it comes out again, comes back into view, something happens that no one seems to understand: Kennedy makes a strange motion with his arms, a gesture that would not have seemed normal in anyone, much less in a president with the eyes of the world on him at that moment. He brings his fists together at his throat—in front of the knot of his tie, shall we say— and raises his elbows symmetrically like a marionette. The first shot has wounded him. The bullet came from behind and went right through, and it's possible that Kennedy had lost consciousness in this

instant, because then he closes his eyes, as if he were sleeping, and begins to lean toward Jackie. It's horribly slow, the calmness with which
death settles on the Lincoln limousine: in full view of everyone, without hiding, without arriving surreptitiously as it usually does, but intruding in broad daylight. The president's wife doesn't yet know what
has happened; she knows something strange is happening, because she
sees her husband leaning toward her, as if he suddenly felt ill, and then
she tilts her head toward him (her impeccable pillbox hat, her haircut
that marked a generation) and speaks to him or appears to speak to
him. We can imagine her words, her apprehensive words still ignorant
that he is no longer able to hear them: "Are you okay?" Jackie Kennedy
might have said. Or perhaps: "What's the matter? Do you feel all
right?" And then her husband's head explodes: yes, like a firecracker.
It's the second bullet, which shatters the occiput and scatters his bone
fragments, his relics. The video lasts a few seconds more and then the
screen goes black. It took me a moment to emerge from its spell. Benavides had returned to his armchair and gestured to me (with an almost
imperceptible motion of his open hand) to also return to my place.

"You see it, right?" he said then. "The first shot comes from behind
and goes through Kennedy. My father believes that he was killed at
that moment. The second shot comes from the front. Look at his head:
it goes back and to the left, because the bullet comes from the front
and to the right. Agreed?"

"Agreed."

"Okay. Then tell me: How is it possible that Oswald was behind the
president at the moment of the first shot and in front of the president
one second later? If the second bullet was fired by the same assassin as
the first, the head would have been driven forward by the impact. And
Jackie would not have flung herself on the back of the car to pick up
pieces of his skull, because the pieces would have flown forward toward

where the governor was sitting, or toward the driver's seat. No, Vásquez, it's not possible that both shots came from the same direction. It's not me who says so and it's not the conspiracy theory: it's the laws of physics. That's what my father said: 'It's a matter of physics.' And we've known this for some time, although official history refuses to accept it. My father knew it too. He knew there were at least two, two shooters."

"In the book depository. One on the sixth floor and one on the second."

"Exactly. But that doesn't explain the provenance of the shot that makes Kennedy's head explode. My father believed that shot hadn't come from the book depository, but from somewhere in front of the motorcade."

"That's what the 1975 article says. This Groden fellow's theory."

"Yes. One or two snipers fired from the front. Groden says there was one behind a pedestal and another behind a shrub. And that the one behind the shrub had a rifle. Now then: Do you know what Zapruder said after the assassination? A special agent took his statement, and Zapruder was sure the assassin was behind him. Later, in front of the Warren Commission, he retracted: he said there were too many echoes in Dealey Plaza, and that he couldn't be sure. But in his first version, the version he gave on the very day of the assassination, he was as sure as he could be. He didn't doubt, he didn't say 'I believe that,' he didn't say 'It might have been like that.' No: he was sure. And my father was also sure."

"But in the notes he doesn't mention that."

"These notes I showed you are just a part of his studies. There are whole pages, much longer than these, but they're not here. Do you know who has them?"

"Don't tell me: Carballo."

"Well, yes, I will tell you. Carballo has them. Why? Because he had them when my father died, as simple as that. Carballo kept many pa-pers, and it was because my father lent them to him. Or rather: he gave them to him and never wanted them back. And although it's hard for me to admit, I can understand why: no one was as close to him as Carballo in his final years. Carballo visited him, devoted time to him, listened to him discuss his theories, and that company, for an old man like my father, becomes the most important thing in the world. I made a mistake, Vásquez, I was mistaken and I'll never forgive myself. I was the one who neglected my father in the last years of his life. I was very involved in my own stuff, understand. I was devoted to my career and my family, fascinated by this new stage of adult life. And with my first child, who was born the year after our wedding. When Kennedy had been dead for twenty years, my second child had just been born. My daughter. So in 1983 I had to be a father of two children, a husband, a surgeon trying to make his way in the world, and on top of that I had to take care of my father. And of course, it was very, very handy for me to have Carballo there."

"To keep your father distracted," I said.

"I'm not the only one, either, am I?" said Benavides. "All sons of widowed fathers are grateful to have someone keep them company. Carballo fulfilled this role for me: he was the perfect companion for my father, he made him feel alive and awake, and best of all he did it without thinking he was doing anyone a favor. Just the opposite, feel-ing privileged: feeling that my father was making him a gift of his time and his ideas. Which is pretty close to the truth, besides. 'How I envy you,' Carballo would say to me. 'How I would have liked to be the son of a man like the doctor,' he'd say. It was a perfect arrange-ment. I didn't even pay him, I paid him in kind. In writings in my fa-ther's hand. In books and documents. In a whole bunch of things that had value to me, although I only realized too late."

"And among those things are papers that should be in this file," I said.

"Exactly. But for Carballo they're more than that: they're clues."

"Clues to the Kennedy case," I said, as if stating the obvious.

"No," said Benavides. "Clues to the Gaitán case. Let's see, let's see if you can understand: the only thing that interests Carballo is Gaitán. April 9 is his only obsession, and there's nothing else. The Kennedy case interests him as far as it illuminates Gaitán's. Carballo says that in the Kennedy case there are clues about Gaitán, about figuring out who murdered him and how they covered up the conspiracy. What happened to Kennedy points to what happened to Gaitán."

"But Kennedy was much later," I said.

"And you don't think I've told him that? A thousand times and in every tone of voice. But he thinks everything contains clues. He finds clues in everything. And when he sees them, he jumps on them."

Benavides had bent down to pick up the purple file, and from his armchair, stretching his long arms so much that his cufflinks strained against his skin, he began to pick up the cuttings. He did so carefully, lifting each rectangle of paper with his thumb and index finger held in the shape of tweezers. "How yellow they're getting, poor things," he said with an affectionate tone, as if he was talking about a litter of newborn puppies. I also bent down and began collecting cuttings, and the whole scene was strangely intimate. Benavides separated one of the papers out and set it on his reading table; when the rest were sorted back in the folder, he picked it up again and asked me if I'd seen it.

"Of course," I said. "Jack Ruby killing Oswald. Everybody in the world has seen that photo, Francisco. Just like the Zapruder film."

"I wasn't asking if you'd seen the image," said Benavides. "I was asking if you saw *this* image, this reproduction that *El Tiempo* published in 1983 and which is underlined by my father." Benavides pointed to the underlined sentence, the second beneath the photo, and

El 25 de noviembre de 1963, Jack Ruby dispara mortalmente sobre Lee Harvey Oswald, quien había sido detenido acusado de ser el asesino del Presidente John F. Kennedy tres días antes. En ese momento comenzaron las dudas sobre la verdadera autoría del magnicidio de Dallas que conmocionó al mundo. (Foto archivo de EL TIEMPO).

recited it without needing to read it: *"At this moment doubts began,"* he said, *"about the true authorship of the Dallas assassination."*

"I saw the underlined sentence," I said. "What about it?"

"I remember, Vásquez, I remember as if it were yesterday," said Benavides. "I remember the day Carballo arrived at my office with the memoirs of García Márquez in his hand. This was two years ago, a little more. In January of 2003, I remember because New Year's Eve had just passed. The first working day of the year, I arrived at my office and there, in the waiting room, sitting there like a patient, was Carballo. He jumped up when he saw me come in, accosted me. 'Have you read it?' he asked. 'Have you read this? Your dad was right!' During the following days, no, the weeks and months that followed, he became increasingly obsessed with the things he saw by looking at the two crimes together, one beside the other. He made me a list. He went to my office or to my house and listed them. First: the assassin. What did Juan Roa Sierra and Lee Harvey Oswald have in common? They were both accused of acting alone, of being lone wolves. Second: they both represented the enemy in their historic moment. Juan Roa Sierra was later accused of having Nazi sympathies. I don't know if you remember that Roa worked at the German embassy and brought Nazi pamphlets home. Everybody soon found out about that. Oswald, of course, was a Communist. 'That's why they were chosen,' Carballo told me, 'because they were people who wouldn't awaken solidarity of any kind. They were the public enemy of the moment: they represented it, they incarnated it. If it were now, they would have been Al Qaeda. That makes it much easier for people to swallow the story.' Third: both assassins were in turn murdered almost immediately. 'So they wouldn't talk,' Carballo told me, 'isn't it obvious?'

"And then he took out García Márquez's memoirs and read the part where the elegantly dressed man manages *to have a false assassin killed in order to protect the identity of the real one.* He savored the phrase, Vásquez, he repeated it over and over, it was a spectacle to see him: an increasingly worrying spectacle, but a spectacle. In time he began to refer to that phrase at the same time as the one in the caption of the Jack Ruby photo. *At this moment doubts began . . .* Later he began to play with them, to interchange them, for example. 'Wasn't it true that Jack Ruby killed *a false assassin in order to protect the identity of the real one?* Wasn't that true, Francisco? Wasn't it true that the elegant man urging on the crowd in the Granada Drugstore was the *moment when the doubts about the true authorship of that assassination began?* The doctor knew it,' he repeated. 'Why else did he underline that sentence? Why was he obsessed with the second shooter in the Kennedy case, he who had looked for bullets from a second shooter in the body of Gaitán? Was he not getting close to something even if he didn't know it? There are too many similarities, this cannot be a coincidence.' I made fun of him: 'What are you saying, Carlos? That Kennedy was killed by the same people who killed Gaitán?' And he would say, no, of course not, that he wasn't crazy . . . but there were still too many similarities. 'There's a method here. The people who killed Kennedy maybe learned from the ones who killed Gaitán. Weren't there Gringos in Bogotá on April 9? Were there not CIA agents here? And the people who killed Gaitán had to have learned from someone else, didn't they? Such a perfect conspiracy is not set up by an amateur.' I told him to stop spouting nonsense, that these were nothing but coincidences. And he would say: 'There's no such thing as coincidences.' He'd open his eyes wide when he said this: that coincidences didn't exist. I never saw anyone open their eyes wider or raise their eyebrows higher."

"But there was no second shooter in the case of Gaitán," I said. "Your father was the one who carried out the autopsy."

"I said that to him too. I reminded him that my father had done ballistic tests. That he'd confirmed what had been said from the beginning, since the investigation of 1948: all the bullets that killed Gaitán came from Roa Sierra's pistol. But Carballo looked away or made one of his incredulous expressions. Of course, for him everything the '48 investigation said was a lie. 'What happened is that on April 9 we didn't have a Zapruder,' he'd say. 'If we'd had a Zapruder, another cock would have crowed in this country.' Yes, it's difficult to talk to him. I imagine you noticed that this evening. In any case, what happened this evening corresponds to that obsession. Carballo desperately wants to know who the elegant man at the Granada Drugstore was. He wants to know who made the crowd kill Roa Sierra. Why? Because then he can compare him to Jack Ruby, I suppose, and then see if they had things in common. What he really wants is to know what happened on April 9, to reach the depths of the matter. And if you think about it, Vásquez, isn't that what we all want?"

"Well, yes," I said. "But within reasonable limits, I would say."

"People like Carballo we can call crazy, paranoid, unhinged, whatever you want. But these people devote their whole lives to discovering the truth about something important. They might use the wrong means. Their passion might lead them to commit excesses and convince themselves of stupid nonsense. But they're doing something that neither you nor I could do. Yes, they might be inconvenient, might ruin get-togethers with their outbursts or their politically incorrect opinions. They might be socially clumsy, put their foot in it more than occasionally, be impertinent or even insulting. But they are doing us a service, it seems to me, because they remain vigilant, because they don't swallow everything, even if what they imagine is preposterous. And the problem with this theory, the problem with thinking that Kennedy's and Gaitán's assassinations have a lot in common, is precisely that: that none of this, if you look closely, is really preposterous."

"Nothing seems preposterous, because everything is," I said. "It's like talking to the Mad Hatter."

"Well, that's what you think. Each person can think what they like."

"But you can't take this seriously, Francisco."

"As serious as it seems to me is the least of it. Don't kid yourself, Vásquez. Dig deep. Learn to see beyond the obvious. For Carballo this is his life's mission. It's not just time and energy, but money too. He's spent more money than he's ever had on this, because he believes in his vision. Other times he's told me: my mission is my vision. Or the other way around, I can't remember. It doesn't matter. For him, if there is a truth in these assassinations, it's this: we haven't been told the truth about them. And can we say he's wrong? No, Vásquez, everyone knows we haven't been told the truth. Only an innocent or someone who knows nothing of history believes that Juan Roa Sierra did it without anyone's help or instigation. At this point, only an innocent thinks that Lee Harvey Oswald fired all the expert sniper's shots that killed Kennedy. So, what can we do with this coincidence? Leave it alone or do something about it? Yes, I realize that for you Carballo is nothing but a nutcase, an irresponsible nutcase. But ask yourself, Vásquez, look yourself in the mirror and wonder if Carballo disgusts you because he's absurd or because he's dangerous. Does he irritate you or does he frighten you? Ask yourself, look at yourself. Maybe I should never have introduced the two of you, I now realize, maybe I was mistaken. If that's the case, forgive me. I have to confess something to you, Vásquez: he asked me to, as a favor. He wanted to meet you, and he asked me to introduce the two of you. He's convinced you can tell him something, I imagine. He's like that with April 9: if he finds a clue he hasn't explored, he lunges after it like a bloodhound. And you, with your uncle being who he was . . . that's what you are, a clue. Maybe what happened this evening was also my fault, for not gauging things properly. In any case, don't worry: I don't think you'll see him again. Today you met for the first time. I don't think there'll be a second. What happened happened, and it was a rather unfortunate accident, it was. But you can relax, Vásquez. You two don't lead the sorts of lives whose paths are likely to cross."

I hope he's right, I thought as I left his house. I hope I never see that man ever again.

I THOUGHT about our conversation that night and I still thought about it the following day, although for different and unpredictable reasons: because nothing could have presaged the contradictory mixture of repugnance and fascination, of seduction and rejection, that I was going to feel when I remembered what I'd seen and heard in Benavides's house: remembering Carlos Carballo and Jorge Eliécer Gaitán and Lee Harvey Oswald and Juan Roa Sierra and John Fitzgerald Kennedy. There was not a single hour that went by after I left Benavides's house in which I did not think of those men and their sad fate, and nor did I do a single thing to banish those images and that information from my memory but rather I flirted with them, enriching them with my own imagination, constructing stories in my mind to give them a verbal beginning. Tuesday morning I went out early to the neighborhood of Candelaria, in central Bogotá, for no other reason than to stand in the place where Gaitán fell and remember the tale that Pacho Herrera had told me one afternoon in 1991. I then repeated the walks I'd taken when I was a law student, from Quevedo's fountain to the Palomar del Príncipe, from the benches in Parque Santander to the steps of the Primada Cathedral; in those days the walks had been disorderly and haphazard, willfully given over to chance and the whim of each day (which are never the same), but after a certain point they began to impose some sort of order on themselves, and that order, which I've gradually refined over successive visits to Colombia, was now a fixed routine. Drawn over the map of the neighborhood, my route was a parallelogram, the vertices of which, like in "Death and the Compass," were points of violent events, except that in the Borges story they're conscious artifices plotted out by a literary bandit, and mine answer more to the pitiless contingencies of history.

I tend to begin at the Café Pasaje, by drinking a coffee with a dash of brandy, and then I cross the Plaza del Rosario and walk east along Fourteenth Street, passing along the high sidewalks in front of the house where the poet José Asunción Silva shot himself in the heart in 1896; then I continue south and down Tenth Street, taking careful steps on the cobblestones that cover that street like dead turtles, and walking slowly beside the window Simón Bolívar jumped out of on that nefarious night in 1828 when a band of conspirators burst into that house brandishing swords and tried to kill him in his own bedroom; I come out onto Carrera Séptima at the Capitol, and twenty steps away from there, in 1914, in front of two marble plaques that, with a certain awkward redundancy, regret the General Rafael Uribe Uribe crime; then I walk four more blocks north, until I arrive at the site of the disappeared Agustín Nieto building, or rather the spot on the sidewalk where the slain Jorge Eliécer Gaitán fell. Sometimes (but not always) I finish a few meters farther on, where in 1931 there was a bar where the cartoonist Ricardo Rendón, whose drawings I'd admired without understanding them since I was a boy, made a sketch of a head with a bullet entering it, drank a last beer, and then shot himself in the temple for reasons no one has ever been able to confirm.

I repeated all this on that Tuesday, September 13, but this time I didn't do it thinking of these deaths we've inherited, who fell in such a small area over so many years and make up part of our landscape whether we know it or not, and it shocks me that people should pass by the plaques without ever stopping to glance at them and in all probability without devoting the briefest of thoughts to them. We living are cruel.

I did this very early, as I used to when I was wrestling with my legal studies and had seven a.m. classes every morning. But this time I returned to a place I hadn't been—hadn't even thought of—for the last twelve years. One day near the beginning of 1993, I had gone out to walk around downtown, as I frequently did, to escape the mortal boredom of my law classes. That morning I was in search of the two-volume *Último Round* by Julio Cortázar, in the Siglo XXI edition that had become so hard to find; after stopping in at the Librería Lerner I decided to take a stroll around the Centro Cultural del Libro, an unusual building that seemed like an industrial storehouse: three stories of brick walls with narrow cubicles where you could find almost any secondhand book you might want. But before getting lost in its labyrinths, I remembered a bookshop embedded in a school supply shop on the other side of the street on the same block, and I thought I'd try my luck there first. I didn't remember that the new school year had just begun that day and I was annoyed to find myself, when I got to the shop window, among a crowd of unruly children shouting their heads off among the skirts of their innumerable mothers. No: there'd be time some other day to come here. I carried on walking, turned the corner heading east, and was approaching the next corner, where I'd have to turn south to find the first entrance to the bookshop storehouse, when a huge noise I'd never heard before but recognized immediately, shook the walls. I was amazed the building hadn't collapsed, for the explosion was so loud that many of us wondered if the bomb had gone off right there. I ran toward Avenida Jiménez with one single thought in my head: to make my way through the people running in contradictory directions, get to the university, make sure my sister was all right, and get away from the area as fast as possible. It was only later when, watching the evening news, I found out the explosion had left dozens dead and injured (as well as a huge crater in the pavement), and that several of the victims were mothers and children who'd been buying school supplies at a local stationery shop.

And now, arriving at the spot where the bomb exploded according to my fallible memory, looking for the stationery shop I'd almost gone into (and finding that it was gone, like so many things in my inconstant city), I remembered that day, the pain in my eardrums, and the revelation, which I accepted without blowing it out of proportion or romanticizing, that I could easily have been one of the dead. And I relived those difficult early months of 1993: the bomb on Séptima and Seventy-second, the one at 100th and Thirty-third, the other two that exploded downtown, one on Trece at Fifteenth and the other at

Twenty-fifth and Novena, and the one that exploded at the mall in the north, on Ninety-third Street.

Now no trace remains, of course, of that bomb, or of its twenty-three dead. I was thinking not of ruins or physical traces of destruction, but of some plaque like the ones that reminded us of the famous or important individuals, public figures whose deaths had repercussions in other people's lives. No, this had undoubtedly been one of terrorism's successes in my country: group deaths (what a dreadful expression), collective deaths (no, that's no better), were never remembered, didn't seem to merit the tiniest homage on the walls of buildings, maybe because the plaque would inevitably be large (to fit twenty-three names, imagine, or triple that in the case of the DAS bomb), maybe because marble plaques are reserved by some implicit or silent tradition for those who drag others to their deaths, those whose unexpected fall can take down a whole society and often does, and that's why we protect them—and that's why we fear their deaths. In ancient times no one would have hesitated to give their life for their prince or their king or their queen, for all knew that their downfalls, whether due to madness or conspiracy or suicide, could well push the whole kingdom into the abyss.

That happened with Jorge Eliécer Gaitán, I thought, whose death we could maybe have averted, and I don't think there is a single Colombian who hasn't wondered what would have happened if we had averted it: we Colombians don't agree on many things, but we do all think that Gaitán's murder was the direct cause of the *Bogotazo*, with its three thousand casualties, as well as the opening shot of the political violence that would end eight years and three hundred thousand deaths later. If Gaitán had not been killed, how many anonymous deaths might we have been spared? What sort of country would we have today? Since memory behaves unpredictably, always doing what it wants, a phrase appeared in mine that is attributed to Napoleon: "To understand a man, you have to understand the world he lived in at age twenty." The world at twenty, for me who was born in 1973, was this one: the one of bombs from January to April, the death of Pablo Escobar, who fell under a hail of bullets on a Medellín rooftop. But I didn't know what that could mean about my own life.

I turned the corner and went inside the brick building, but I'd barely started looking through the stalls when my cell phone rang (there at last was the call I'd been fearing for days). With a firm voice, undoubtedly trying to transmit to me the tranquility she obviously wasn't feeling, M told me that her water had broken. The doctors had explained that an emergency cesarean would begin in an hour. I asked if I'd be able to see her before.

"I think so," she said. "But hurry, please."

WHEN I ARRIVED I found the clinic in a state of shock. There were lines at all the entrances: lines of cars to get into the parking lot, lines of people to get through the glass doors of the building. An armed guard was looking through women's purses and men's briefcases and anything that looked like a bag. After I passed through that control another guard stopped me, asked me to lift my arms and started to frisk me. "What's going on?" I asked. "Security measures," he told me. "President Turbay just died." But the security measures had held me up for several minutes, and walking quickly down the corridors of the clinic, avoiding unhurried people (obviously free of the rush that was overwhelming me), I thought I was going to be late, that I wouldn't manage to see my wife before she went into surgery, that I wouldn't be able to make her feel my company or my vigilance, and then—a head under pressure functions in strange ways, and the tension flows in the most unexpected directions—I despised Turbay with a puerile and violent resentment of which I'm now ashamed, a private and brief tantrum that soon disappeared, leaving just an uncomfortable sensation of degradation that wasn't even justified. For despite the lines, despite the searches and frisking, I ended up arriving in time. M, lying on a cot that blocked a dimly lit corridor, answering the anesthetist's questions while waiting for someone to arrive to take her into the operating room, was pale and her palms were sweating, but on her face was an expression of someone in control of the situation, and I could do nothing but admire her.

The girls were born at 12:00 noon and 12:04. At that moment the doctors wouldn't let me see them: the stretcher that took them from the operating room left with such urgency that for an instant I sensed a gust of impending disaster. All I could see was a mess of white cloth; from that inert bundle arose the oval and translucent air pumps, which the nurses squeezed to help my daughters take their first breaths with their cortisone-matured lungs. M was still anesthetized and would take a few minutes to come around, but I asked permission to be with her when she did, and in those minutes I thought of the disappointment that would now accompany her forever: that of not having seen her daughters as soon as they were born. She would wake up and I would tell her that everything had gone well, that the girls were in their incubators and starting to recover; but none of that would change the fact that she hadn't seen them. That made me sad; I thought, however, that my sadness was not comparable to what she would feel. In any case, what mattered now was the obligation, after the emergency of the premature birth, to confront another task: the uncertain survival of thirty-week creatures whose bodies weren't ready for life.

Hours went by before I was allowed to see them for the first time. I was alone when that happened: after being immobilized for twenty-seven days, M had suffered a slight atrophy of her leg muscles, and couldn't even stand up; so as soon as I received authorization to visit my daughters, I found the camera we'd brought for this moment (although we'd imagined this moment would be very different) and I headed for the neonatal unit. There, between six or seven other newborns that were never more than blots on the landscape to me, were the two girls, each identified with a white card, and each card affixed to the incubator with insulating tape. They were bathed in a beam of bright light; otherwise they were well wrapped up, with little fleece hats on their heads, white blindfolds over their eyes so the light wouldn't hurt them, and oxygen masks covering their mouths. Not one of their features was visible for me to meet, learn, and begin to memorize as we do with new faces that enter our lives. One thousand four hundred and one thousand two hundred sixty grams were their exact weights, according to the card: what the pasta weighs that you cook for a dinner party. Seeing them (seeing the arms as thick as one of my fingers, the skin with its purple tones and still covered in lanugo, the electrodes that barely fit on the narrow surfaces of their chests), I had this terrifying revelation: that the survival of my daughters was not in my hands and there was nothing I could do to protect them from the troubles that lay in wait for them, because those troubles came from within. They were in immature bodies like time bombs that might or might not go off, and I knew it even though I hadn't yet received the complete inventory of the risks. I would receive it later: as the hours and days went by, the doctors would tell me about ductus arteriosus, a duct of the heart that would require surgery if it remained open for an imprecise time period, and also what exactly cyanosis meant, the indications of oxygen saturation, the fragile retinas and risk of blindness that still threatened. I took a series of photos of terrible quality (the plastic of the incubators reflected the flashes and partially hid what was on the other side) and took them back to M.

"There are your daughters," I said, forcing a smile.

"There they are," she said.

And then, for the first time since all this began, she burst into tears.

Occupied as I was with the care of my daughters, I didn't tell M what I'd seen in Benavides's house. Something else had to happen before I did. It happened shortly before she was finally discharged; by that point she was able to walk around the clinic a bit, and together we'd begun to visit the girls as often as the neonatology department rules permitted. They were brief visits, twenty minutes maximum, during which we could take them out of the incubators, hold them for a little while, feel them and let them feel us. In those moments the nurses took off the electrodes and the unpleasant noise of the machines—that memorandum of mortality—was shut off. It wasn't possible, however, to take out the oxygen tube that had replaced the CPAP mask of the first days: the girls had them taped to their faces (a piece of surgical tape on each side of their tiny nostrils), and we, the visitors, had to sit very close to the incubators so the tube wouldn't tauten or run the risk of coming loose. And so, connected to the oxygen tanks, leaning back in uncomfortable positions, with those tiny bodies sleeping on our chests, we spent minutes that were at once times of timid happiness and buried concern, because never was their vulnerability so clearly evident. I held one of my daughters' hands between my thumb and forefinger and realized perfectly how easily I could break it into pieces if I wanted; I kept an eye on the main door to the room, because I'd convinced myself that a breeze could cause havoc to their lungs; I disinfected my hands more than necessary with a transparent gel with an alcoholic smell that burned the eyes, for the immune systems of premature babies are not able to defend themselves from the most innocuous bacteria. And little by little I began to notice, with more anxiety than interest, that the whole world had turned into a threat. The presence of foreign objects and the nearness of other people made me nervous and even aggressive, even if they were acquaintances and even if those acquaintances were doctors and worked in that very clinic. I blamed these anxieties for my reaction on the day I went in to see my daughters while M packed up her things to be discharged, and I found Dr. Benavides leaning over one of their incubators and manipulating the oxygen tube with his bare hands. Without even saying hello, I asked what he was doing.

"The little tube had slipped out," he said, smiling but without looking at me. "I just reattached it."

"Take your hands out, please."

Benavides finished smoothing down the surgical tape with the tip of his little finger, took his hands out of the incubator, and turned toward me. "Don't worry, it's quite simple," he said. "The little tube—"

"I prefer," I cut him off, "that people don't put their hands into my daughters' incubators when I'm not here. That they don't touch them, I don't know if you understand."

"I was putting the tube back in."

"I don't care what you were doing, Francisco. I don't want you touching them. Even if you are a doctor."

The doctor was genuinely shocked. He walked over to the door and pressed the disinfectant lever once and then again. "I came to say hello," he said, "and to see how your daughters were doing. To put myself at your disposal, rather."

"Well, thanks, but we're fine. This isn't your specialty, Doctor."

"Excuse me, Daddy," said a nurse who arrived at my side.

"What's the matter?"

"You know you can't be in here without a gown on, rules are rules."

I was given a pale blue bundle that still had the warm scent of freshly ironed clothes. By the time I had put on the sterile gown and cap, Benavides had gone. I treated him badly, I thought, offended him; and then I thought: Screw him. He didn't cross paths with M, who came to sit beside me a few minutes later, well wrapped up in her gown and cap, ready to receive the other baby. She must have seen something in my face because she asked me if I was all right. And I was about to tell her the whole story at that moment—tell her about Benavides, his father, Carballo, Gaitán's vertebra—but I couldn't. "Nothing, nothing's wrong," I said. "I don't believe you," she said, having always had infallible instincts, "something's up with you." And I told her yes, something had happened, but I'd tell her later, when we left: because it was uncomfortable for me to talk with one of our girls lying on my chest, and because my voice and my breath might even bother her and disturb her sleep, the most peaceful and silent sleep I'd ever seen. None of that was true, of course, but I was unable to pinpoint the reasons why I didn't want to tell her there. The few bits of self-knowledge we manage to collect never arrive in time; I, for the moment, had to wait several days to realize that M was completely right when she said, after hearing my detailed and slightly contrite tale of my clash with Dr. Benavides, these simple words about our daughters: "What it is, is that you don't want dirty people near them."

I was going to answer that the adjective did not apply to Dr. Benavides, who from the start had struck me as one of the most honest and most transparent—yes: cleanest—people I'd ever met, but then I realized she meant something else: not Francisco Benavides's moral condition, but what Benavides brought with him like a snail's shell: the legacy of his father. In other words, the too-present probability that the hand that had smoothed the surgical tape on my daughter's left cheek had held, in some moment of its past, the vertebra of a man who'd been shot dead, and not just any man, but one whose crime was still living among us Colombians, and fed in obscure ways the multiple wars in which we keep killing each other fifty-seven years later. I wondered if it wasn't possible that a door might open in my life and the monsters of violence enter through it, able to invent strategies and ruses to get into our lives, into our houses and our rooms and our children's beds. Nobody is ever safe, I remember having suspected, and then I remember having promised, with the secret anxiety of unwitnessed promises, that my daughters would be. I told myself that every day, whether visiting the girls, taking them out of their incubators, letting them take turns sleeping on my chest, whether it was at my in-laws' house—a chilly studio with a terrace overlooking an army of eucalyptus trees—while I added a page or two to the file of my novel about Joseph Conrad in Panama. (That one, for example, in which the narrator's baby girl is born after six and a half months of pregnancy, and he says she's so small his two hands could cover her completely, so scrawny her legs still showed the curve of her bones, and her muscles so weak that she was unable to feed from her mother's breasts.) And one night, while M was trying to stimulate the girls' sucking reflex by putting the knuckle of her little finger of her right hand in their mouths, I realized I was thinking not about my daughters but about Francisco Benavides, not about the mother's milk we had to leave for them to get through the night but about the X-ray of a torso with a bullet inside, not about the jabs in a minuscule heel or about blood tests, but about the luminous tones of a vertebra preserved in formaldehyde. "It's turning into an obsession," M reproached me one night. "I can see it in your face."

"What do you see?"

"I don't know. But I wish it wouldn't happen to you now. All this is exhausting, I'm exhausted, you're exhausted. And I'd rather not have to do this alone. The girls, I mean. I don't know what's going on with you, but I'd rather you were here, with me, and that we do this together."

"We are doing it together."

"But something's going on with you."

"Nothing's going on with me," I said. "Absolutely nothing."

III

A WOUNDED ANIMAL

Carballo reappeared in my life at the end of November. My daughters had emerged from their incubators and were now spending the nights with us, in M's family home (where we always stayed when we visited), in the room that had been M's before she left for Europe: we'd prepared a crib with adjustable railings big enough for both of them, one on each side, each connected to her own medicinal oxygen tank, which watched over her through the rails like a silent relative, and each with her own little plastic tube covering her upper lip. On the twenty-first, around six o'clock, in the middle of a diaper change, I received a call from a friend who gave me a piece of news: Rafael Humberto Moreno-Durán, one of the most notable novelists of his generation and my friend for the last several years, had died that morning. "He died already," she said, putting all the weight of her voice on the resigned adverb, and then she told me the time of the funeral, the name of the church, and its exact address. And there I was the next morning, sharing with the family and friends of R.H. (as we all called him) sadness but also relief, for the illness had been difficult, more intense than long, but in any case very painful, although he'd borne it with humor and something I can only call courage.

We'd met when I was a law student whose only intention was to learn how to write novels, just as he'd been three decades earlier, and we started to become friends without my really knowing how; he visited me in Barcelona, the city where he had arrived in the early seventies and where he had spent twelve happy years, and I visited him in Bogotá whenever I had the chance, sometimes for lunch at his house, sometimes to accompany him on his daily walk to pick up his mail from his post office box. It was a sacred routine for him: arrive on foot at the Avianca building, enter the tunnels lined with locked boxes, and come out with letters and magazines. It was on one of those walks that he told me of his illness. He told me that one afternoon, climbing the stairs of his building, he'd lost his breath all of a sudden, his vision had clouded over—the world turned into a black space—and he was on the brink of fainting right there, on the hard brick steps. The doctors didn't take long to diagnose anemia and find its cause, a cancer that had been living clandestinely for a long time in his esophagus and which, at the time of that encounter, had obliged him to undergo various treatments and had disrupted his appetite. His alien, he called it. "I have an alien," he told people who asked about his sudden weight loss. And when he was gloomy or irritable, he'd apologize: "It's just that my alien isn't behaving today." Now, not much more than a year after the diagnosis, he'd lost the battle against that fucking disease that respects neither dignity nor truces.

And there we were, his acquaintances and friends, filing into the spacious nave of the church, looking for a free spot on the wooden pews, moving within the four walls while we greeted people in that half voice we use on sad occasions. But most of all we were freezing to death, for around the church rose up a conspiracy of office towers and dense eucalyptus trees that wouldn't let a single heartbroken ray of sunshine through. We were all there: I mean, those who loved R.H., those who respected him, those who neither loved nor respected him but admitted to admiring his books, those who admired his books but didn't admit it out of envy, those who had once been the target of his derision or his direct attacks and now came to rejoice, in their corner of silent bitterness, that R.H. was no longer here to throw their mediocrity in their faces. In few places is there such a high concentration of hypocrisy as at a writer's funeral: there, in the church, surrounding the coffin where R.H.'s body rested, there was in those moments at least one person devoting himself to the old art of pretense, of pretending sadness or desolation or depression, when deep down they were thinking that neither R.H. nor his books would be around anymore to cast a shadow.

While I made myself comfortable in my place, a seat next to the aisle of a pew in the middle (not so close to the coffin to feel like an intruder, not so far away as to feel like a mere onlooker), I was trying to remember the last time I attended a religious farewell to someone who didn't believe in religion. Would R.H. have drawn nearer to God in his last days, as happened to so many agnostics? Those metamorphoses of souls occur in places one's friends don't even see, so I couldn't even speculate, but someone should study the number of conversions due to cancer (of course the thing does not work the other way: I don't know of any illness that leads to apostasy). When the priest began to speak, a man who was sitting on one of the front benches, on the edge of the central aisle, caught my attention as his silhouette nodded at the end of every phrase that came out of the speakers, like a campaign director approving his candidate's oratory. But then there was a movement in the church nave, murmurs and heads turning, because Mónica Sarmiento, R.H.'s wife, had stood up after a slight nod from the priest, and was advancing toward the pulpit. She adjusted the microphone, took off her dark glasses and passed her hand over her tired eyes, and announced, with integrity and strength drawn from the unfathomable depths of her sadness, that she was going to read a letter that R.H. had left for Alejandro.

"Who's Alejandro?" someone beside me asked.

"I don't know," said someone else. "A son, I imagine."

"Dear Alejandro," said Mónica. A silence fell over us. "It's very likely that now, about to turn eleven years old as you are, you won't yet understand the reasons I'm writing you this letter. But I'm doing it to be on the safe side. I'll explain: sooner or later every son comes down with the Kafka syndrome, that is, he feels the need to write a letter to his father, give him a piece of his mind, reproach him for how arbitrary and egotistical he is or has been, for his lack of compassion and tolerance. Because the son, at a certain age, believes himself to be the king of creation and asks only for devotion and attention and if his father does not offer them he opts for retaliation, personal ill will, disobedience, antagonism, or, as in Kafka's case, terrible, vindictive writing. So, to be on the safe side, this letter is a possible preventative measure. Many years ago I read something that now regains all its meaning. I'll never forget the first line of one of the essays by Francis Bacon, Lord Chancellor of England—a moralist so wise that he did the exact opposite of all that he preached—which says: 'He that hath wife and children hath given hostages to fortune.' And I think, my dear Alejandro, that today I am a hostage to fortune, to fate, to the chance that involves us one with the other; that my will is not what it was in my times of wandering the world, when nothing and nobody limited my liberty and when everything was for me a wide map of open roads. I believed myself to be eternally young and indomitable and I was convinced—I swear—that life began at eighteen and all who don't reach that age belong to the order of protozoa. Children were for me the eleventh plague of Egypt, to the point of my initials' almost turning into an infanticidal slogan: R.H. didn't stand for Rafael Humberto, but for that famous king, *Rey* Herod. Until the day that you were born and that was when I discovered that Francis Bacon's phrase hid unexpected surprises: when you were born I became a hostage to your fortune."

People smiled in the church, and I thought: Typical of R.H. Typical of him to convert a sad, lamentable occasion into an opportunity for humor, for wordplay, for the ingenuity that spoils solemnity. I also thought of my daughters: Had I become a hostage to their fortune? Through Mónica's mouth, R.H. was now speaking of the birth of his son, or rather was speaking to his son of his birth, and was accepting the inevitable sentimentality of every father who speaks of his children, and was telling amusing anecdotes as fathers tend to do about their sons, well aware that the anecdotes might be completely lacking in charm for anyone else. One of these anecdotes recalled the day that a Mexican friend gave Alejandro a stuffed Pegasus. R.H.'s son asked why that horse had wings, and R.H. explained that Pegasus had been born from the blood of Medusa when Perseus cut her head off, and that instead of hair she had snakes with which she paralyzed her victims. "Don't make me laugh, Dad," said Alejandro. "As consolation for the fool of myself I'd just made," said R.H. in Mónica's voice, "I knew from that moment that you'd been born with an immunity to magical realism."

In the nave various guffaws rang out.

"Against what?" someone else near me asked.

"Let me listen," was the answer.

"Why am I bringing up these anecdotes?" Mónica continued. "Because in some way the father, in his maturity, believes himself and wishes to be the son's memory, for whom, at his tender age, all is ephemeral and insignificant, as if he sensed that all he has lived so far is worth very little and the only important events are those he has yet to be involved in. Childhood doesn't exist for children; however, for adults childhood is that former country we lost one day and which we futilely seek to recover by inhabiting it with diffuse or nonexistent memories, which in general are nothing but shadows of other dreams. That's why we seek to become notaries of our child's memory: of something that he will forget very swiftly but that for the father is proof that he has engendered his own posterity. How to forget that repertoire of childish philosophies with which the son, unintentionally, seeks to underline with his own concepts a world that is beginning to be his own? One night, while waiting for the news to begin, you and I were watching television. They were showing a live broadcast of the final—and most torrid—hours of the Carnival in Rio de Janeiro. Comfortably settled on the sofa you avidly observed the ample profusion of tanned skin and flesh on display in the Sambadrome. You were five years old and I couldn't contain myself, so I commented to you, as if we were a pair of dirty old men: 'Alejandro, women are absolutely spectacular.' And you, without even turning your head and as if you were an expert on the subject, answered: 'They are, Papá. And they give milk too.'"

This time the laughter filled the whole church. People laughed, but were still uncomfortable: Was this allowed? they all seemed to be wondering. R.H., from the past or from his absence, didn't seem to care, or rather it must have caused him true pleasure to be provoking such inoffensive discord.

"Dear Alejandro: If there's one thing I regret, it's not having told my father how much I admired and loved him. My only gesture of affection was a quick kiss on the forehead two days before he died. The kiss tasted like sugar and I felt like a thief who furtively stole something that no longer belonged to anybody. Why do we hide our feelings? Out of cowardice? Out of egotism? With a mother it's different: we cover her with flowers, gifts, and sweet phrases. What is it that prevents us from affectionately confronting our father and telling him, face-to-face, how much we love or admire him? On the other hand, why do we curse him under our breath when he puts us in our place? Why do we react with wickedness and not affection when the occasion presents itself? Why are we brave with taunts and cowards with affection? Why did I never tell my father these things but I tell them to you, who are probably too young to understand them yet? One night I wanted to speak to my father in his room but found him asleep. As I quietly began to leave the room, I heard my sleeping father, in a desperate voice, say: 'No, Papá, no!' What strange, agitated dream was my father experiencing with his father? And if one thing caught my attention, beyond the enigma of the dream, it was that my father was seventy-eight years old at that time and my grandfather had been dead for at least a quarter of a century. Does a man have to die to speak to his father?"

Then a light rain began to fall. No, not a light rain, but a sparse one: a rain of thick, heavy drops but few of them. From outside its delicate rattle on the metal roofs and parked cars reached us, and from then on it was harder to understand the words Mónica was reading. My attention drifted as it tends to do; for the second time I wondered if I, too, now that my daughters had been born, was a hostage to fortune, and I didn't know the answer or where to begin to look for one. How would they behave toward me in the future? What was a father's relationship with his daughters like? It was undoubtedly different from that between two men, a father and son, and especially two men from different generations. But if I had had sons, I thought, male children, I would be facing similar difficulties, wouldn't I? Would my sons hide their feelings from me? Would they react with wickedness and not affection? And why not think that my daughters might have a tense and difficult relationship with me too? All my life I've gotten along better with women than men, maybe because masculine camaraderie and complicity have always struck me as ridiculous: How would it be with my daughters? Then I saw Mónica pronouncing words that were obviously the final ones and folding up the pages and stepping down to men and women who received her with open arms. She did not do so amid applause, but amid the repression of that applause. R.H.'s letter to his son had broken the conventions of a funeral Mass, and the audience had felt disoriented, beautifully disoriented, and in their faces you could see they were pleased at not knowing very well how to act, of having come to say good-bye to someone by way of a ritual that everyone knows and having ended up on uncertain ground, laughing and feeling like laughing, not applauding but feeling like applauding, and maybe all thinking of their sons and daughters as I was thinking about mine.

I don't know what else happened during that Mass. I don't remember the communion I didn't take or the peace that, out of distraction, I didn't wish anyone. The coffin containing R.H.'s body passed before me and I waited for it to pass, and I allowed myself to be devoured by the river of mourners, by the noisy silence in which they advanced. I couldn't take my eyes off the coffin; the coffin, for its part, moved stubbornly toward the rectangle of light of the main door, rising and falling according to the movements of the pallbearers. From behind I saw it exit into the midday air and go down the steps toward the hearse, its hatch open like a mouth. I waited, watching in silence from the first step, until the driver closed the hatch, and then I saw, written in golden letters on a sash with a purple background, the name I'd seen so often on book covers and spines, in interview headlines, at the bottom of reviews in the newspapers. When had Rafael Humberto decided to be R.H.? The first edition of his first novel, *Juego de Damas*, had appeared in 1977 with his complete name on its cover and spine, and in the dedication he wrote in my copy twenty years later, while we had pasta with too much sauce for lunch in La Romana restaurant, are all four of his names. When had his name decided to become its initials, as if preparing to fit onto a purple sash on a hearse? The church was slowly emptying, people were going down into the parking lot and getting into their cars and the cars began to emerge in single file; and we, those who remained on the top step, were watching the convoy leave with its terrifying discipline. Very few people were still there—in my memory, there were six or seven people—when the rain began to get worse. I was getting ready to go down the steps and across the adjacent park to hail a taxi on Carrera 11 before the downpour broke, but at that instant I felt a heavy hand on my shoulder, and turning around I found myself face-to-face with Carballo.

It was him. It was the man who had caught my attention before the reading of R.H.'s letter to his son. Why hadn't I recognized him then? What had changed in his appearance? I wasn't able to pinpoint it, but at the same time I had the invincible conviction that he had recognized me immediately. More than that: I knew or thought I knew that Carballo had been aware of my presence during the entire funeral and had been keeping an eye on me from a distance, following me like a spy and standing beside me, intruding on my casual conversations, waiting for the opportune moment to enact an unexpected encounter. And his infallible instinct, his predatory instinct, had told him this was the best moment to attack his prey. *He's like a bloodhound,* Benavides had told me.

And also: *You're a clue.*

And now I was thinking: *I'm his clue. He's a bloodhound. I'm his prey.*

"FANCY MEETING YOU HERE," said Carballo. "I certainly didn't expect this."

I had absolutely no doubt he was lying. But what for? Impossible to know and I couldn't think of any question that might reveal it. In fact, just then, I couldn't think of a better option than lying too. (There is almost never a better option: the lie has a thousand uses, it's as malleable and submissive as a child: it does what we ask of it, it's always prepared to serve us, it's neither pretentious nor egotistical and it never asks for anything in return. Without it, we could not survive for a second in the jungle of social life.) "You were here, at the funeral?" I asked. "I didn't see you. Where were you hidden?"

"I arrived early." He waved his arm in the air. "I was up front, on that side."

"I didn't know you and R.H. knew each other."

"We were very close," Carballo told me.

"You don't say."

"Yes I do. It was one of those brief but fruitful friendships, you see. Look, why don't we sit inside? It's really starting to come down."

It was true. The day had darkened and the rain intensified against the church; the thick drops lashed the paving stones and began to form the first puddles, and immediately splashed in the puddles and spattered our shoes, socks, and the bottoms of our trousers. If we remained standing there, I thought, we'd end up drenched from head to toe. And so we decided to cross the threshold of the church and sit down in the last pew, the two of us alone in the nave empty of mourners, so far from the altar that we couldn't make out the features on the crucifix. The moment had for me the curious familiarity of a scene from a movie: a clandestine meeting between Italian mafiosi, for example. Carballo took a seat toward the middle of the long wooden pew; I stayed as close to the center aisle as possible. Our voices sounded distorted by the echoes, but also by the racket of the rain falling outside, and after a while we noticed that we'd imperceptibly been moving closer, to be able to hear each other without shouting. I noticed the plaster on his nose. I counted the days since the incident at Benavides's house, and it seemed to me that no septum in the world takes more than two months to heal. "How's the nose?" I asked.

He raised a hand to his face, but didn't touch it. "I don't bear you a grudge," he said.

"But you still need to wear that bandage?"

"That's why I said hello," he carried on as if he hadn't heard me. "To prove it with irrefutable, as they say, actions. That I bear you no grudge, I mean. I won't even tell you how much I've spent on painkillers. And the days off work."

"Oh. Well, send me the bills, I'll . . ."

"No, no," he cut me off. "Don't insult me, please."

"Sorry. I thought . . ."

"No, no, sir. I came here to say good-bye to a friend, not to charge you for a couple of painkillers."

I'd offended him: his feeling of offense seemed genuine. Who was this guy? With every word he inspired more aversion but also more intrigue. I thought, not without some involuntary cynicism, that the plaster on his nose was part of an elaborate disguise, or rather a sophisticatedly simple disguise: I thought it must help him obtain things. What things? I couldn't imagine. Carballo had begun to talk about

R.H. His death was very sad, although he couldn't say it had taken him by surprise, because this disease was hell, and it was hellish precisely because of that: because it gave notice. No matter how short it was, how sudden, it always spent several months with the person, giving notice. That's why it was cruel. It had treated R.H. brutally, it had to be said: it was always brutal to the best people. No, we were definitely nothing, and when you win the lottery, well, it's your turn and there's nothing to be done . . . There it was, I thought: there was the same indiscriminate mixture of clichés and unusual perceptions I'd witnessed during our first encounter.

"The death of R.H. is a loss for national literature," he said. And he added: "It's not like a Moreno-Durán is born every day."

"Well, that is certainly true," I said.

"Isn't it, though? These things have to be said. *The Chancellor's Felines*, what a novel! *Mambrú*, what a novel! You reviewed it, didn't you?"

"What?"

"For the *Banco de la República* magazine," said Carballo. "A really good review. I mean, very positive. Although for my taste, it didn't go far enough."

My review of *Mambrú* had appeared in 1997. In that stage of my youth, book reviews for *Boletín Cultural y Bibliográfico del Banco de la República*—a quarterly publication that allowed me to review up to four books per issue—had become my main source of income. In the *Boletín* you could praise anything to the skies, not that it was a publication with massive distribution: it was read in academic circles, among library users and fanatical bookworms. Had Carballo been researching me? How much did he know about me, and why? Was it just, as Benavides had said, out of the interest awoken by my being related to José María Villarreal, important witness to the events of

April 9? Although it was also possible that he was what he appeared to be: an intelligent guy with too much time on his hands, an irrational obsession . . . and similar literary tastes to mine: for the two novels he'd mentioned out of R. H. Moreno-Durán's prolific oeuvre were just the ones I would have chosen. Now Carballo had begun indiscriminate praise of R.H. "And what can you say about his opening sentences? Oh, those first sentences! 'Bride's perspiration is the Arabic name for talcum powder.' That's from *The Gentleman of the Undefeated*. 'When you and I made love, death won a chess match against the Knight of the Seventh Seal.' That's from *Diana's Touch*. 'Like a salmon leaping in the night, that's dawn in Manhattan . . .' Oh, those first phrases, Vásquez, always those openings! A person picks up a book like that and doesn't put it down again! At least I don't, I who read to be told a well-told story well. I'm what they call a *hedonic* reader." And he went on like that, alternating stock phrases with perceptiveness that seemed to belong to someone else, when he said something that gleamed in the middle of his chatter like a fire on a mountainside at night.

"Wait a second," I interrupted him. "Say that again."

"He was a writer capable of slipping us clues about the life of the nation. He was capable of speaking between the lines of the most difficult things. He was a master of allusion."

"No, not that," I said. "You just said something about what remained to be written."

"Oh, yes," said Carballo. "I know something about that and I think you do too, although you know less than I do. And in any case, what I do know I owe to you. Render unto Caesar the things that are Caesar's. If it weren't for that conversation, R.H. would never have enriched my life like he did. Although now there's nothing left of that."

"What conversation?"

"You really don't know?" he said, exaggerating his surprise. (I thought: He's an actor, a histrionic. I thought: Don't believe a single word he says.) "I'm going to have to spoon-feed it all to you. The conversation in the new magazine, Vásquez. 'The Contemporary Novel and Other Illnesses,' wasn't that what it was called?"

Yes, that's exactly what it was called. Carballo was full of surprises. In August of the previous year, Moisés Melo, publisher of the recently founded magazine *Piedepágina*, had invited us to his house to talk about what was happening to R.H. since his cancer diagnosis: his illness and his pain seen through literature. It was a two-hour conversation that could be distinguished from our normal conversations only by the lack of whiskey, the presence of a running tape recorder, and an editorial process that organized our words to give them a coherence and purpose they don't always have. The magazine came out in December; between Christmas and New Year, Carballo, who was consulting certain documents in the Luis Ángel Arango Library, came across it by accident on a table in the cafeteria. "I almost fell off my chair," he said. "In that interview I found everything I was looking for."

"And what was it you were looking for," I asked.

"A guy with an open mind," Carballo told me. "A guy willing to listen. Ready not to allow himself to be guided by prejudice, ready to break out of the straitjacket or the official version."

"I don't remember our having discussed straitjackets," I said.

"No? What a shame. But I imagine you remember talking about Orson Welles."

I did remember, but vaguely. However, now, as I write these memories down a decade later, I have in front of me the first issue of *Piedepágina*, and I can look up my conversation with Moreno-Durán, nate mediático representado y destruido en *Ciudadano Kane...*

RH: Sospecho que Welles vino, en el fondo, huyéndole a Rita Hayworth, que era bastante "intensa". En realidad, vino a hacer el documental y permaneció en el Brasil, ininterrumpidamente, por siete meses. Luego fue a Buenos Aires, habló con Borges, para el estreno de *El Ciudadano*, que así se llamó su película en Argentina. De ahí surgió la bellísima nota que Borges escribió en *Sur*. Luego fue a Chile, y ya de despedida llegó a Lima, y el 12 de agosto las agencias de prensa le hicieron la última entrevista y le preguntaron: *¿Y qué va a hacer a partir de ahora, viaja a Los Ángeles?* Dijo: *No, mañana viajo a Bogotá, Colombia.* Le preguntaron por qué, y contestó: *Tengo grandes amigos en Colombia, me encantan los toros, Colombia es un país de toros y soltó todo un rosario de tópicos sobre nuestro país.* Al día siguiente, agosto 13, en la primera página de *El Tiempo* se lee: ORSON WELLES LLEGA A BOGOTÁ, y los mismos titulares reproducen *El Espectador* y *El Siglo*. Pero Orson Welles no llegó nunca a Bogotá. Ese capítulo forma parte de una novela que se llama *El hombre que soñaba películas en blanco y negro*, que cuenta lo que le ocurrió a Welles en Bogotá los días 13, 14 y 15 de agosto, ocho días exactos después que Eduardo Santos entregara el poder y lo asumiera por segunda vez Alfonso López Pumarejo. Esto tiene una importancia política que nadie recuerda, y es que Laureano Gómez, en una entrevista que tuvo con el embajador norteamericano, le dijo que si Alfonso López se posesionaba, él daría un golpe de estado con la ayuda de sus amigos del Eje. La cuestión es que Orson Welles llega a Bogotá, una ciudad convertida en un nido de espías, corresponsales de guerra, y con el agravante de que en ese momento el país estaba completamente conmovido, dolido y rencoroso por el hundimiento de varias fragatas colombianas en el Caribe. En ese ambiente Orson Welles sufre una serie de peripecias impresionantes. Es una novela larga, de unas cuatrocientas y pico de páginas, donde reconstruyo un determinado momento histórico colombiano. De alguna forma constituye un díptico con *Los felinos del Canciller*.

confirm its exact words, and carefully transcribe them here in this narration that's gradually coming to resemble an evidence brief. R.H., in a black suit and a purple shirt, was talking about the novel he'd just finished. The plot had come from a short story, "First Person Singular," that told of Orson Welles's trip to Colombia in August of 1942: a special trip, because it never actually happened. After the success of *Citizen Kane*, explains R.H. in our conversation, "Welles became an internationally famous figure. The United States, the Department of State, and RKO Pictures decided to send him to Latin America to make a documentary, and thus use his presence as a way of uniting Latin America's interest to that of the United States against the Axis." Then the interview carries on in this way:

J.G.: They probably also wanted to get him off their backs for a while, pressured by William Randolph Hearst, the media magnate portrayed in *Citizen Kane*.

R.H.: I suspect that, deep down, Welles came here to get away from Rita Hayworth, who was pretty intense. Actually, he came to make a documentary and stayed in Brazil, uninterruptedly, for seven months. Then he went to Buenos Aires for the Argentine premiere of *El Ciudadano*, as it was called there. He spoke to Borges. That's where the beautiful review Borges wrote for *Sur* came from. Then he went to Chile, and as a farewell he passed through Lima, and on August 12 the press agencies interviewed him one last time. They asked him: And where are you going next, Los Angeles? He said: No, tomorrow I'm traveling to Bogotá, Colombia. They asked him why and he answered: I have some great friends in Colombia, I love bullfights and Colombia is a bullfighting country. And then he came out with a whole lot of clichés about our country. The next day, August 13, on the front page of *El Tiempo*, the headline reads: "Orson Welles Arrives in Bogotá," and *El Espectador* and *El Siglo* followed suit. But Orson Welles never arrived in Bogotá.

In the published conversation the question I asked him does not appear: "Why, R.H.? Why didn't Orson Welles come to Colombia?" Nor does the crafty expression appear, the brief second when his face goes from being that of a man who's dying of cancer to that of a boy:

"I'm not going to tell you," he said. "You're going to have to read the whole novel." The magazine did, however, record his following words:

R.H.: The novel is called *The Man Who Dreamed Movies in Black-and-White*, and tells the story of what happened to Orson Welles in Bogotá on August 13, 14, and 15, exactly eight days after Eduardo Santos handed over power and Alfonso López Pumarejo assumed it for the second time. This has a political importance that no one remembers, which is that in a conversation with the U.S. ambassador, Laureano Gómez told him that if Alfonso López did take power, he would stage a coup d'état with his friends in the Axis. The thing is that Orson Welles arrives in Bogotá, a city converted into a nest of spies and war correspondents, and with the aggravating factor that at this moment the country was completely shaken, hurt and resentful over the sinking of several Colombian frigates in the Caribbean. In that atmosphere, Orson Welles suffers a series of impressive adventures.

J.G.: It's another turn of the screw in the relationship between history and the novel. The novel is becoming the great instrument of historical speculation.

R.H.: I don't think that the novel is trying to colonize new spaces, but that all spaces belong in the novel's territory. There is a very curious fact: during the Rio Carnival in 1942, Orson Welles met Stefan Zweig, who told him what a wondrous country this was where he was going to live because a friend had invited him. In my novel, when Orson Welles gets to Colombia, he is invited to a gathering to be introduced to some important people, and at that gathering there is one very silent man, six and a half feet tall, whom everyone calls Viator, who speaks with a Brazilian mountain accent and with whom Welles has an immediate rapport. Viator turns out to be no more and no less than João Guimarães Rosa, who lived in Bogotá at that time. He was a secretary at the embassy and had just been consul in Hamburg, where the Nazis had put him in a concentration camp. Once liberated, upon his return he was assigned to Bogotá. The Guimarães facts are reliably true. I take advantage of all these marvels though I suspect some critic will say: This guy got carried away . . . and it turns out it's all true. Welles and Guimarães Rosa ended up becoming friends here, in Bogotá.

All this R.H. said in the conversation we had, and that's what Carlos Carballo had read. But in the church, sitting in the last wooden pew, I didn't remember these details: I didn't remember that R.H. had talked about the Liberal presidents Santos and López, or about Laureano Gómez, the Conservative leader who admired Franco and prayed for an Axis victory, or about the Colombian frigates sunk by Nazi submarines in the Caribbean, which served as a pretext for the government to break off diplomatic relations with the Third Reich. I didn't remember our having spoken about Stefan Zweig, whose time in Brazil has been sadly encoded in the macabre photograph of his suicide by barbiturate overdose (accompanied by his wife, Lotte, who died dressed in a kimono and nothing else), or the mention of Guimarães Rosa, who died of a heart attack in 1967 (eleven years after having described his own death, his own heart attack, in a famous novel).

The details of the conversation had dissolved in my memory; not so, apparently, in that of Carballo, who was paraphrasing away. Outside, the downpour rattled on the roofs of empty cars and a strong wind had begun to jostle the tops of the nearby eucalyptus trees. Something moved in the depths of the church, beside the pulpit; I saw a shadow or a silhouette that was hiding; I thought someone was watching us (keeping an eye on us) from afar. Then a child dressed in black peeked out, looked at us, and disappeared again. The sound of the door banging shut reached us late, like thunder.

"I read that conversation, and do you know what happened?" Carballo was asking me now. "Do you know what I did when I read it? It was as if the ground had shifted. *Literally.* I couldn't keep working."

He had spent the morning in the Luis Ángel Arango Library, looking unsuccessfully for information about an author unknown to me: a certain Marco Tulio Anzola. When he found the copy of *Piedepágina*, he'd gone out to get some air; he had every intention of going back in to look through microfilm, but the discovery prevented him: how could he carry on scouring old newspapers, old photographs of a city that no longer existed? No, it wouldn't have been possible: because there, in the pages of a literary magazine, something had arisen for which Carballo had been searching for a long time. "It was like an electrical charge," he told me, "and how could I sit still at a library desk when my body wanted to shout, run around downtown, and keep shouting?"

He immediately knew what he had to do. He began his investigations that afternoon and before the day was over he already knew that R. H. Moreno-Durán (b. Tunja, 1946), author of the trilogy *Femina Suite*, would soon be giving a lecture to present his latest work, the nonfiction *Women of Babel*. The event would be taking place at the Central University at six-thirty. Entrance was free. "It was my opportunity," said Carballo. "I didn't think twice." Two days later, he grabbed his briefcase, put a few papers and the copy of the magazine in it, went to the university auditorium, bought the book at the stall by the entrance, and went to drink a fruit tea in the café next door until the lecture ended. Then he watched the people line up by a desk with a tablecloth, all with their books in hand; instead of joining the line, Carballo waited until everyone had left, saw Moreno-Durán say goodbye to the organizers, and leave on foot heading for Carrera Séptima. Only then did he approach him.

"Maestro," he said without any ado, "I've got the book of your dreams."

R.H. could have looked at him the way you look at a lunatic, but he didn't. Then he noticed his own book, the copy of *Women of Babel* Carballo was carelessly carrying, and said:

"Well, not quite the book of my dreams, but here let me sign it for you."

"No, no," said Carballo. "I didn't mean . . ."

Carballo didn't know how to explain the misunderstanding; he mumbled a couple of incoherent phrases, his jumbled hands moving through the air, but Moreno-Durán already had the book open to the title page. "Who is it for?"

Carballo had to snatch it out of his grip: "No, *maestro,* you don't understand. I've come to give you a subject, the subject of the best book you're going to write in your life. It's a book that nobody has done yet in Colombia. Because to make this book you need two things: information and daring. And that's why I've come to propose it to you, *maestro.* Because only you can write this book. You and I, to be precise: I'll supply the information and you'll supply the daring."

"Ah," sighed R.H. And then: "Well, no. Many thanks, but I'm not interested."

"Why not?"

"Because I'm not," R.H. cut him off. "But thanks."

He started to walk toward Carrera Séptima. Carballo walked along with him. He noticed that his briefcase was similar to R.H.'s, both of black leather, both with metallic clasps. In this detail he saw a confirmation or at least an incentive: coincidences, in Carballo's experience, did not exist. While he made way between the pedestrians, keeping an eye on the cracks in the sidewalk and trying to keep Moreno-Durán from escaping, Carballo kept asking him to listen to his story, please, even if only to banish doubt, even if only to keep himself from wondering for the rest of his life what that marvelous book he'd been offered might have been, even if only not to die suspecting he'd let the train pass without boarding.

"I didn't know what the cancer might have done to him," he told me. "I'd never seen R.H. before in my life and had nothing to compare him to. I couldn't think: Oh, how thin he's become. I couldn't think: Oh, he must be very ill."

But after his last words, he noticed that R.H. was looking at him differently. What was it in his look? Intrigue, contempt, the uncomfortable feeling that the most private thing in the world—a terminal illness—had just been violated? R.H. kept walking. He turned north up Séptima and Carballo turned with him. But he was no longer talking. Out of weariness or resignation, he carried on walking in silence, avoiding people, trying not to step on the blankets of the street vendors. He'll never know if it was to fill the silence, but then R.H. asked: "And why me?" It was a simple question, but it was enough to switch on a sort of momentary lucidity in Carballo. "For the same reason I'm not writing it myself," he said. "I could fill three hundred pages, sure I could. But that would be a failure, that would be throwing all I've achieved into a garbage can. No, this book cannot be written by just anyone. It has to be written by the same person who wrote *The Man Who Dreamed Movies in Black-and-White*."

It was as if a hand on his chest had stopped R.H.

Carballo thought: *This is my chance.*

"Orson Welles in Bogotá," he said. "Who would have dared tell that story? Official history doesn't include that visit, *maestro*, the official version denies it ever happened. But you dared to tell it, you gathered it up. And now, thanks to you, Orson Welles will forever be among Bogotá's visitors. He was in Brazil with Stefan Zweig. He was in Argentina with Borges. And now he was in Bogotá with Guimarães Rosa. Your novel rescues some events that would otherwise have been lost forever. If not for you, those hidden truths would never have come to light. And I have another of those hidden truths, *maestro*, and I want to tell it to you. It's taken me more than ten years, no, more than twenty, thinking about how to reveal this to the world. But now I've discovered it: it's with you that I have to do it. With a book of yours. The story I want to entrust to you, the silenced truth that I want to entrust to you to turn into a book, is going to turn the world upside down."

"Is it, now?" R.H.'s lips curled into a sneer of brutal skepticism, and Carballo felt the weight of his authority. "And what truth might that be?"

"Give me two hours, *maestro*, I won't ask any more of you," said Carballo. "No, I don't even need two. One will be more than enough. In one hour I'll explain it all and show you the documents, and then you can decide if it's worth the trouble or not."

They'd arrived at Twenty-sixth Street, where Carrera Séptima turns into a viaduct and pedestrians can lean over the edge to believe, magically, that the cars disappear under the soles of their shoes. A fit of vertigo shook Carballo as R.H. said: "Look, my friend, I'm in a hurry. And you haven't convinced me of a single thing. Either explain what you're talking about now or we'll leave it here." A bus sped past, so close to the curb that the sidewalk trembled and the gust of wind in its wake almost ripped out of his hand the sealed envelope Carballo had just taken from his briefcase.

"And what's this?" asked R.H.

"It's a letter. Addressed to you. I wrote it to leave for you in case we weren't able to talk today. No, it's not a letter, it's a report. Just five pages, but it's all explained here, all that I know, all that I've discovered in my studies of the last forty years. As soon as you read it you're going to realize. What we have in our hands, what we can do with this information, the turn this country will take when this becomes known. Everything will change when we bring this truth to light. It's going to change this country's past, of course it will, but most of all it's going to change its future. It's going to change the way we relate to each other. Listen to what I'm telling you, *maestro*: after you've written this book of ours, life in this country will never be the same."

"AND HE AGREED?" I asked.

"I couldn't believe it either at first," Carballo told me. "But R.H. was a believer, you know? He *believed*. Great writers are like that: they have intuition, they have the faith that goes with that intuition. They know how to recognize the truth when you put it in front of them. And they fight, they fight to the death to make the truth known. No, R.H. didn't disappoint me." He paused and said: "But death took him before he had a chance to finish the work."

Could what he was saying be true? Everything, everything about Carballo made me distrust him. Each of his words sounded fraudulent; however, I didn't manage to do what I should have done: stand up and denounce his lie out loud. But was it a lie? Apart from the mystical rhetoric about *believers*, about *the truth*, about death *taking* a person before he'd *finished the work*, was Carballo lying to me? What for? Again this thought passed through my head: If all this was a lie, then Carballo was the best liar in the world. If all this was a performance, this man was the best actor. *He's a histrionic,* I thought again, *he's his own character,* and then it occurred to me for the first time that this man was ill. A page of *The Emigrants* came to mind in which Sebald talks about Korsakov's syndrome, that disease of the memory that consists of inventing memories to replace true ones that have been lost, and I wondered if it weren't possible that Carballo suffered from something similar. Wasn't that more likely than the crazy story of stalking and accosting a well-known writer, giving him a letter in the middle of the street, and the clandestine agreement about a crazy book? Wasn't it more plausible than imagining R.H., a serious and dedicated novelist, as the voluntary ghostwriter of a conspiracy theory enthusiast?

"Oh, so he died before finishing the book," I said. "But he did start it?"

"Of course he started it," said Carballo. "He thanked me every time we saw each other. 'This is going to be my swan song,' he told me. 'And to think I was about to tell you to go to hell, Carlitos.' Yes, that's what he called me, Carlitos. He was working on the book up until the end. I only wish I'd known more about his illness. To appreciate his effort as much as he deserved."

"Where did you meet?"

"Sometimes at La Romana. A restaurant on Jiménez, I don't know if you know it."

"Yes, I know it. Where else?"

"Sometimes he asked me to walk with him to pick up his mail. He had a post box."

"Yes, yes, I know. And where else?"

"What's the matter, Vásquez? Are you testing me?"

"Where else did you see him?"

"Once he invited me to his house, to have lunch with his friends."

"Oh, yeah? And who was there?"

He looked at me sadly. "You don't believe me," he said. "I see that now. You think I'm making it up."

It was like shaking a venetian blind: I managed to see, for the briefest instant, an expression of vulnerability that I'd never seen before and in any case was not an impostor's vulnerability. I had a sort of revelation: to get rid of him once and for all, I had only to say yes. *Yes, Carlos, I think you're making the whole thing up. I think you're lying, I think you're deceiving me, I think you're talking nonsense or you're ill.* But I didn't. I was dissuaded by La Romana restaurant, by the walks to pick up the mail, details Carballo could not have known without direct and close contact with R.H.; but I was also dissuaded more than anything by curiosity, the terrible curiosity that has gotten me into so many scrapes without my ever having been able to learn my lesson, the curiosity I've always felt for other people's lives in general and in particular for those of tormented people, for all that works in the secret of their solitude, everything that happens, to put it another way, behind the blinds. We all live hidden lives, but sometimes the blind is shaken and we glimpse an action or a gesture and we suspect that there's something behind there, and we don't ever know if what's hidden interests us because we can't manage to see it or because of the immense effort someone's made to prevent us from seeing it. It doesn't matter what secret it is (it doesn't matter if it's banal or if it's defined a whole life), keeping a secret is always a difficult task, full of tactics and strategies, which demand memory and narrative arts, conviction and even a degree of good luck. And that's why lies make people interesting: because no lie is perfect and monolithic; because if we just watch for a sustained period of time or with a stubborn and constant attention, the blinds will move and what the other person doesn't want us to see will be briefly visible. That happened there, in the church pew, when Carlos Carballo realized I didn't believe him. And that's how I knew, with the same instinct wild animals have, that a word of mine at that moment would be enough to destroy him (or destroy our relationship) and get rid of him forever. And I decided not to do it. It wasn't out of compassion, but simple curiosity. Or rather: curiosity converts the best emotions—compassion, solidarity, altruism—into instruments to achieve its twisted aims.

"No, Carlos, I don't think you're making anything up," I said. "But please understand. I've known R.H. for almost ten years. Or I knew him, rather. And the writer I knew does not fit at all with the guy you're telling me about."

"Don't be naive, Vásquez. Do you really think you knew R.H. entirely? Do you really believe you can know anyone entirely?"

"You can know someone *reasonably*."

"As if people had only one face," said Carballo. "As if everyone weren't more complicated than one might think."

"Maybe so," I said, "but not to such an extent. Not so far as to take on board someone else's idea for a book in the middle of Carrera Séptima. Not so far as to devote the last months of his life to a delirious idea."

"What if it wasn't delirious? And if the one who proposed it wasn't a stranger?"

"I don't understand," I said. "You didn't know R.H. when you proposed the book. Isn't that what you just told me?"

"I'm not talking about R.H. anymore," said Carballo. He stared at the floor and then at the stained-glass windows. "R.H. is no longer here. But the material is still here, my discoveries are still here, the truth is still waiting. The truth is patient. The book is still here, alive and kicking, and someone has to write it."

I don't know how I didn't see it coming. Now, as I recall that long-ago scene in order to write, I feel the same surprise I felt then and I ask myself the same question: How did I not guess? How did I fail to read the signs? I remember I looked toward the door and noticed the rain was stopping, and as I did so, as if my body realized what was awaiting it, I felt less cold. Of course, I thought: of course this encounter is not a coincidence, of course Carlos Carballo knew he'd find me there, attending a friend's funeral Mass. Or rather, even if he hadn't been certain of finding me, he knew the probabilities were high and had decided to try his luck: and luck had been on his side.

"Oh, I see," I said. "You want me to write it now."

"Look, Vásquez, you're not R.H., no offense," he said. "I read your stories, the ones that happen in Belgium. Tell me, why waste your time with that bullshit? Who cares about those characters who go hunting in the woods and separate from their wives? With a civil war here at home, with more than twenty thousand dead every year, with an experience of terrorism that no other Latin American country has witnessed, with a history marked from the start by assassinations of our great men, and you're writing about little divorces in the Ardennes. I don't understand you. And your novel, that novel about the Germans, well, that's better, of course. I can tell you there is something worthwhile there. But I also have to be honest: the general result is a failure. A worthy failure, especially for someone of your age, but a failure. The novel has too many words and not enough humility. But that's not the serious thing. The most serious thing, what spoils the novel, is its cowardice."

"Its cowardice."

"Just what you heard. The novel passes over the great themes as if stepping on eggs. It mentions drug trafficking and even the murder of that football player, but does it go into them? It mentions Gaitán, but does it go into what happened to Gaitán? It mentions your uncle José María, but does it go any further? No, Vásquez, you lack commitment, brother, commitment to this country's difficult issues."

"Maybe I chose other difficulties," I said.

"Foreigners' things," he said. "Not ours."

"Well," I said, laughing, or pretending to laugh. "That's the stupidest thing I've ever heard."

"R.H. left you a note," Carballo interrupted me. "I'm carrying out his wishes by giving it to you."

He handed me a sheet of white paper. A professional obsession told me it was a letter-sized 80-gram sheet, the same that Moreno-Durán used to write his heterogeneous first drafts. (Only in his later years did he make the transition to a computer, and that's why I needed only a glance to know it was a recent document.) Six sentences filled the space.

Dear Juan Gabriel,

A short time ago an extraordinary possibility fell into my hands. Or rather, I received it as a gift from an extraordinary man, who is presenting you with this letter. Life has not given me time to transform this gift into a book, but I think, given the circumstances, I have honored the obligation. Now it's up to you to inherit this wonderful material and bring it into port. You have in hand something great and I have no doubt you're a worthy recipient of these secrets.

As ever I send you an embrace and my friendship.

I read and reread the note with the profound emotion the words of the dead cause in us: we imagine their hands and their skin passing over the paper we're now touching, and every line and every curve and every period is a trace of their passage through the world. There was my name and some words written with affection, and then I thought that I could no longer reply to this note as I would have done before and that's how the dead begin to drift away: with everything we can no longer do with them.

I asked Carballo when he had received this letter.

"Three days ago," he said. "When R.H. went into the clinic. He had me summoned, gave me back all the papers, and put this note on top of them. "Juan Gabriel is the person," he told me.

"To write the book."

"I don't agree either. But R.H. must have his reasons. To trust you, I mean, to bequeath this to you. He must have seen something in you that escapes me." He looked ahead, toward the crucifix, and said: "What do you say, Vásquez? Are you ready to take on the book you were born to write?"

I read the note again, looked again at the signature. "I need to think about it," I told him.

"Oh, how ridiculous!" he exclaimed with a snort. "This bullshit way of thinking and thinking. You people think too much."

"It's not that easy, Carlos. Yes, you found three or four banal coincidences between two assassinations. I don't know how strange that is, when they were in plain sight. Two assassinations of important people resemble each other. Very good. But from there to thinking they've really got something to do with each other is a big stretch, don't you think? Or how many different ways are there to kill a politician?"

Carballo started. "Who told you that?"

"Dr. Benavides, who else. What's the matter, isn't it true? That's your theory, isn't it? That the Gaitán and Kennedy assassinations have too much in common?"

"Of course not," he said with a misunderstood-artist's pout. "That is a gross simplification of something much more complicated. Obviously my dear friend has understood nothing, has inherited nothing from his father. What a disappointment. What else did our little doctor tell you?"

"We talked about the second shooter," I said. "In the Kennedy case, but also in the Gaitán case. We talked about your teacher, Carlos: Dr. Luis Ángel Benavides. The great Luis Ángel Benavides, yes, the ballistics expert who discovered the presence in Dallas of more than one shooter. And without anyone's help. But who also exhumed Gaitán in 1960 and confirmed beyond the shadow of a doubt that the missing bullet came from the same pistol. That Gaitán, unlike Kennedy, had been killed by a single person."

"But that wasn't confirmed."

"Of course it was confirmed."

"It was not confirmed."

"What do you mean it wasn't? Didn't he do the autopsy? There's the evidence, Carlos, no matter how much you want to deny it."

"The evidence disappeared," said Carballo, lowering his voice. "Yes, Vásquez, just as you heard. The doctor did the autopsy, extracted the vertebra that had been struck by the missing bullet, and found the bullet. But neither the vertebra nor the bullet exists anymore. They've disappeared. Who knows where they are, or whether they've been destroyed. You have to wonder why those pieces of evidence disappeared, don't you think? You have to wonder in whose interest it might be that they could no longer be consulted after a certain time. You have to wonder who realized that science was advancing and the evidence to a past crime was beginning to reveal more things. The fact is they succeeded, Vásquez, like they always do, and now we'll never again have that evidence to examine by the light of new scientific discoveries, and who knows what it would have told us, what revelations it might still hold. Ballistics has really come a long way. Forensic sciences have made major advances. But it's no use to us, because those with power have made the evidence disappear. And so they're winning, Vásquez, they're hiding the truth from us, they—"

"Oh, Carlos, shut up for a moment," I blurted out.

"What, certainly not," he protested. "That's no way to—"

"Gaitán's vertebra is at Benavides's house," I said.

"What?"

"Nobody has made it disappear, there's no conspiracy. Francisco took it home when they were going to close the museum, and that's all there is to it. He took it so it wouldn't be lost, not to hide it from anybody. I'm sorry to spoil your theories, but someone had to tell you one day that Santa Claus was your parents."

This time the cruelty I spoke with was deliberate, and I was very aware I was talking to someone whose father had disappeared. Was there some relationship between his father's disappearance and Carballo's tendency to believe in ghosts? I considered it briefly, but then I was distracted by the expression on his face: I had never seen anything like it. I saw him crumble in a second and then manage, who knows with what interior efforts, to recover his composure.

He's wounded, I thought, *he's a wounded animal.*

Watching it was painful and at the same time captivating, but most of all eloquent: for something in that fleeting struggle with himself, something in that attempt to hide his disappointment or disillusion, showed me I'd been mistaken in making that revelation. By telling Carballo about the vertebra—the clandestine vertebra, I thought—I'd betrayed Benavides's trust, and there was no use alleging the doctor had not expressly forbidden me from telling him, since during our conversation in his study, as much by his tone as by his words, his intention to hide from Carballo the existence or survival of the vertebra and the X-ray had been obvious. Now I had betrayed that secret. I had done so on an impulse, carried away by a moment's instinct, but these excuses didn't even seem reasonable to me. What was going through Carballo's head, what disappointments, what memories of conversations when Benavides had lied to him about the vertebra, to a man who'd always considered himself his brother and the spiritual heir of Dr. Luis Ángel Benavides? Would Carballo be nursing his own feelings of betrayal, different from mine but perhaps even more valid? The sky began to clear and daylight to enter the church more strongly; a strange optical illusion made it look like Carballo had gone pale. He had his gaze fixed on the crucifix behind the altar. It didn't seem like he was going to speak again. I folded the piece of paper he'd given me in thirds, the way you fold a letter, and put it in my breast pocket. "I'll think about it," I said, and stood up.

"Yes," said Carballo, without looking at me. I could suddenly hear, in the midst of his precise and convinced voice, an uncontrolled note, the imbalance of someone who gets shoved in the street. "Think it over, Vásquez. But don't think lightly of it. I'll tell you the same thing I told R.H.: Don't let this opportunity slip away."

"What opportunity?" I asked. "To make history?"

The question sounded sarcastic, but that wasn't my intention. I asked him because I really wanted to know: to know whether that was what was within reach.

Carballo, staring at the crucifix behind the altar, didn't answer.

IN THE MIDDLE of December, three weeks after the funeral, I called Mónica and asked if I could visit her. During this time, Carballo wrote me two e-mail messages (I'll never know how he managed to get my address), but I didn't answer either of them. Then he wrote a third message: *Cordial greetings Juan Gabriel, the more I think about it the more convinced I am that this book is meant for you, don't squander the chance, regards, CC.* This one also went unanswered.

When I arrived at what had been R.H.'s apartment, I found that someone else had also had the idea of visiting Mónica. Hugo Chaparro was a guy with a brown mustache and freckles spattered across his pale skin; he'd seen all the films in the world and written about most of them, and his relationship with R.H. during the last months of his life had been very close: Hugo had accompanied him to chemotherapy, had helped him organize his papers, had gone with him to collect his mail at the Avianca building, had showed up at his house anytime R.H. needed help related to his work. The apartment was a spacious place in the northern sector of Bogotá with fine large windows through which all the sounds of the noisy city rushed in. We had lunch there, talking about R.H.'s books and what should be done with them, but also about his illness—which he'd always discussed freely, with a mixture of bravery and disdain, without portraying himself as a victim but wanting to be heard—and the same conversation continued without interruption in the small open study R.H. used for reading, in front of the dark wooden bookcase where he kept the first editions of his books, all bound, due to an old superstition, in real leather. Hugo was looking at books: he went shelf by shelf, reading spines, taking some down and putting them back, as if it were the first time he'd visited that library. Mónica was sitting in a wicker rocking chair, but without rocking, the heels of her shoes securely planted on the carpet; behind her head there was a narrow, vertical window that looked out onto an interior patio, and a cold, tired sun, which would soon be disappearing, a reticent sun of a city in the Andes shone through that window.

"Well, now," said Mónica in her firm voice. "What was it you wanted to tell me?"

"Yes," I said. "It's silly, but just to make sure, do you know a guy called Carlos Carballo?"

A brief silence. "No. Who is he?"

"A guy," I said, "an acquaintance of R.H. Well, I don't know if he was an acquaintance. At least, a guy who said he knew him. I was wondering if you'd heard of him."

"Doesn't ring a bell," said Mónica.

"Are you sure?" I said. "He told me they knew each other well. He wanted R.H. to write a book."

As soon as I said the last sentence, Hugo straightened up and turned toward us. "Oh, I know who he is," he said. "That book guy, yeah, I know. A pain in the neck, an impertinent beast."

"Carlos Carballo," I said to be sure.

"Yeah, yeah, that guy," said Hugo. "He followed us all the time, he was unbearable. We'd arrive for chemotherapy and there he'd be, as if he were R.H.'s long-lost brother. You know him too?"

I didn't give them all the details, but enough so they'd understand. "He approached me after the funeral Mass," I told them. "He told me he'd read my conversation in *Piedepágina*, and that conversation led him to R.H. Or rather, that he'd read what R.H. said about his Orson Welles novel and had thought that this was the guy he needed."

"What for?" asked Mónica.

This time Hugo answered. "He says he knows things that nobody else knows. He says he has some research about Gaitán, apparently, about April 9. Isn't that it? Something like that. And he followed us even into the chemotherapy ward, sat there, beside R.H., calling him *maestro*, saying: 'You have to write it, no one else can write it, you have to write it.' Toward the end it was almost scary, I swear. R.H. said he'd turned into a Hollywood producer."

"Why?"

"Because now he had an alien and a stalker."

Mónica laughed. It was a sad laugh.

"But R.H. didn't agree to do it?" I asked.

"Of course not," said Hugo. "He was close to calling the police, the guy was really troubling."

"Well, he told me he'd agreed. That he'd even started writing the book."

"But I don't understand," said Mónica. "Why did it have to be R.H.? Why did it have to be him?"

"I don't know if I can explain it," I said. "This guy, this Carballo, read my conversation with R.H. In the conversation R.H. talks about his Welles novel and tells me that Welles was never in Bogotá. That the newspapers of the time announced his trip, but the trip never took place. And nevertheless, R.H. tells it, he describes that trip, the three days Welles spent in Bogotá, and he tells them in minute detail. The novel describes what happened to Welles when he spent those three days in Bogotá, the people he met, the political strife of the moment, et cetera. At least, that's what R.H. told me in that conversation. I don't know whether it's true, because I haven't read the manuscript. Have either of you read it?"

"No," said Hugo.

"I have," said Mónica. "But go on."

"Well, Carballo was convinced of that: the man who wrote a novel about something that official history denies was the only person authorized to write his book. Why? Because his book tells something that official history denies."

"But what is it?" said Mónica. "What does his book reveal?"

"That's what I don't know. He didn't tell me. But it's something to do with Gaitán and April 9. I met Carballo in September, at a friend's house, and talked to him for quite a while, so I can imagine where things are heading. It's simply a conspiracy theory, one more of the thousands already out there."

"A conspiracy theory," said Mónica. "How interesting."

"And how original," said Hugo. "As if every madman in this country didn't have one."

"No, no," said Mónica. "I meant it. You haven't read the novel."

She stood up and we watched her disappear down the darkened corridor that led to the bedrooms and R.H.'s office. On Hugo's face a mocking smirk had now appeared, or was it the same mocking smirk his face usually displayed: his short eyebrows raised above his nose, as if outlining a roof, and on his mouth, beneath the sparse mustache, an amused and mischievous smile, sly and melancholy at once. In moments like that, for Hugo the whole world seemed to transform into a Charlie Chaplin film: *The Gold Rush*, say, or *City Lights*.

When she came back, Mónica was carrying a red notebook. No, it wasn't a notebook: when she sat down and set it on her lap I realized it was a manuscript bound at a stationer's, with black rings and red cardboard covers. "It's the Orson Welles novel," she told us. She started leafing through the manuscript, looking for something precise, the whereabouts of which she remembered imprecisely, and from my chair I could see the printed pages, numbered by hand in black ink and with corrections in red ink, sometimes a phrase crossed out or something written in the margin, sometimes encircling whole paragraphs and murdering them with two strokes in a merciless cross incapable of pity. One page caught my attention and I asked Mónica if I could read it. There, R.H. had eliminated some lines that made me feel sorry for them: sorry for their condemnation to the hell of words that will never be read. I asked permission to take a photo with my phone.

"You writers are crazy," she said, but didn't object.

The lines were these:

If our times have taught us anything—said Welles all of a sudden—it's to be aware of all the beings we have inside of us. We are multitudes within our individuality, as many men as opinions we display or moods we experience.

Rusia. Hitler se oponía a la ruptura de Japón y los Estados Unidos".

-Si algo nos ha enseñado nuestro tiempo -dijo de pronto Welles- ha sido tomar conciencia de los muchos seres que llevamos dentro. Somos multitud dentro de nuestra individualidad, tantos hombres como opiniones manifestemos o estados de ánimo vivamos.

-Welles dejó de hablar y fijó su mirada en algunas manchas de tinta fresca que descubrió en la parte inferior del periódico que hojeaba su amigo. Husmeó dentro del portafolios y comprobó que su estilográfica tenía una pátina de tinta azul justo a la altura del anillo donde la tapa protege a la pluma.

-Supongo que son cosas de la despresurización -dijo sin que Crews advirtiera su maniobra.

Tras comprobar que el depósito de la tinta no había sufrido ningún desperfecto secó la pluma con un trozo de papel y enroscó la tapa con gran pericia. A continuación devolvió la estilográfica al portafolios y se miró los dedos, felizmente libres de manchas.

-Somos como las visiones de un calidoscopio -prosiguió Welles su discurso, como si nada lo hubiera interrumpido-. Quien me vea o escuche tiene que ordenar las diferentes partes de un todo. Ni yo mismo sé quién soy.

-¿Quiere eso decir que no somos más que lo que la visión de los otros dice que somos?

-Sospecho que sí -dijo Welles, mientras paseaba el índice de la derecha por la primera página del periódico-. Fíjate, si no, en Stalingrado. Aquí arriba aparece la noticia general sobre la situación de los nazis ante la estrategia del ejército rojo. Es la noticia desnuda sobre los hechos. A la derecha, un mapa nos ilustra sobre el orden de la batalla. Abajo, a la izquierda, dos o tres opiniones de autores especializados comentan lo que puede

147

Meanwhile, Mónica found what she was looking for and gave it to me to read. In the scene they're discussing the sinking of the schooner *Resolute*, a famous incident during the Second World War in Colombia. I knew it quite well, having come across repeated mentions of it while researching my novel *The Informers*, and I remembered that it had been this attack, always attributed to a Nazi submarine, which led the Colombian government to break off diplomatic relations with Germany, confine Germans in camps, confiscate their property, and close their bank accounts. All their riches—and Germans in Colombia were generally people with money—had passed into the state's coffers, which almost always meant into the hands of the powerful corrupt and the corrupt powerful. In the novel, one character asked another: "Do you mean that the sinking of the ships in the Caribbean was nothing more than a setup so that our country would join the Allies and, along the way, to enrich a few patriots at the expense of the Germans?"

"You see?" said Mónica.

"What?" I said.

"What?" said Hugo.

"Wait," said Mónica.

Her ringless hands turned more pages, but this time they took less time to find what they were looking for. Again she passed me the manuscript; again she asked me to read it. "What do you think about the death of Gardel?" said the narrator of the novel (but I didn't know who that narrator was). "Many say it was no accident, but an attack, you know what I mean, someone put a bomb on board and adios, Zorzal." A character called Salcedito replied: "That's a perfect idea for a thriller. Besides, nobody would think it strange for such a thing to happen in our country, which is the country of death." In this case the references were also familiar, and the epithet, as will be seen, is not gratuitous. In June 1935, while on a tour of three Colombian cities,

Carlos Gardel, the most important tango singer in history, had died in a plane crash at the Olaya Herrera Airport in Medellín. His airplane, an F-31 whose nickname, "The Tin Goose," must have worried some people, was ready to depart two minutes before three in the afternoon, but then the pilot received the news that they were going to have to carry several film canisters in the plane. There was no room in the cargo compartment, so the crew ended up stowing the reels of film under the seats. Later it would be said that this excessive weight caused the accident. In any case, the pilot (Ernesto Samper, he was called, just like a president six decades later) saw the squared flag and began to taxi. But the F-31 didn't manage to pick up speed. "This plane is like a Lacroze tram," it seems Gardel joked. That was when the plane started veering to the right, off the runway, and would have crashed into an office building full of people if the pilot hadn't managed a last-second maneuver. The F-31 swerved brusquely, avoided the office building, and crashed into another plane that was waiting its turn to take off for Manizales. The two planes burst into flames immediately: fifteen men died; Gardel was one of them. The official investigation concluded that excess weight, a strong south wind, and most of all the terrible topographic situation of the airfield had caused the accident. Among the experts who signed the official report was an engineer, Epifanio Montoya, whose granddaughter would tell me in 1994 that her grandfather had been present at Gardel's accident, and five years later would marry me.

But I didn't mention that frivolous coincidence to Mónica and Hugo, because they had no reason to share my interest in the oddest cameos of history, and besides, it didn't seem pertinent. What was pertinent was remembering that in the case of Gardel's death several conspiracy theories also circulated at the time: some spoke of a rivalry between the two big Colombian airlines; others, of a rivalry between the pilots themselves; others, finally, of a flare gun, mysteriously missing a cartridge.

"Now you see, don't you?" asked Mónica.

"I think so," said Hugo.

"Look, I don't know who this Carballo is," said Mónica. "But if he needed someone to listen to him talk about conspiracies, he'd come to the right place. R.H. was sensitive to these things. He liked to think that everything had its dark side. The sinking of the schooner in the Caribbean? A conspiracy to take Germans' property away from them. The accident that killed Gardel? A conspiracy of one airline to take business away from the competition. What can I say? He liked this sort of thing."

"That doesn't mean anything," I said.

"Of course not. But the novel is full of things like that. We have to accept that the guy knew what kind of tree he was barking up."

"But the guy couldn't have read the novel," said Hugo.

"It doesn't matter," said Mónica. "What I mean is that R.H. was receptive to that kind of craziness. Or understanding, or curious, however you want to put it. And it doesn't strike me as odd that he would have sat in a café listening to crazy stories, and maybe even feigning a bit of interest, to see if he could get something useful out of him to use in a novel. Now I suppose you two are going to tell me that you novelists aren't like that: always stealing people's stories, always taking advantage of other people's oddness. Anyway, as I said before: I don't know who this guy is."

"He told me he and R.H. were very close friends."

"Well, that I can refute. R.H. barely left the house in the last months. Any close friend I would have seen around here. And a new one would have caught my attention, it seems to me."

"Me too," I said.

"There you go."

"But this is really strange," Hugo said. "The guy said that R.H. agreed to write the book?"

"Not just that he agreed," I said. "That he was happy. That it was going to be his great novel, his swan song. And that he would have finished it if the illness hadn't beaten him. That's why he left it to me."

"Wait a second. What does that mean?" said Mónica.

I was pleased to have foreseen this moment. I reached into the inside pocket of my jacket, where I keep a pencil and a pen, and took out the letter that Carballo had given me after the funeral. I unfolded it and handed it to Mónica; I watched her read it—saw her small eyes, which had always seemed to me to watch the world with a certain suspicion, moving like flies over the paper—and then pass it to Hugo, who read it in turn, in silence, without comment.

"He gave you this note," said Mónica. It wasn't a question anymore in her voice, but an affirmation. "This Carballo."

"Yes. He told me that R.H. had left it for me. That R.H. wanted me to write the book, now that he wasn't going to be able to."

"Well, it's impressive," said Mónica.

"What is?"

"It's fake, this letter. But it's very well done. That's what's impressive: that it's so well done."

"And how do you know it's fake?" asked Hugo.

"R.H. had one signature for life and one for literature," said Mónica. "One to sign checks or contracts, for example, and another for signing books. The signature he used for letters was the same one he used for books." She held the paper close to her face. "And this is his signature for going through life. It is perfect, though."

"But where could he have seen it?" I said. "That's what I can't figure out."

"I can," said Hugo. "R.H. had to sign papers at every chemotherapy session. It's not impossible . . ."

"Impossible no, but very strange."

"Whoever copied it is an artist, in any case," said Mónica. "But the fact is, R.H. would never have used this signature for a letter, and much less a letter about literature to a friend."

"What you're saying is that the letter is false," I said.

"That's what I'm saying."

"Are you sure?"

"Completely sure. You tell me: Have you ever seen this signature on anything R.H. has ever signed for you?"

It was true: I'd never seen it. I felt relief, but also a vague frustration, and added to the frustration a shameful admiration I was very careful not to mention. I imagined him devoting several hours to studying

---

Bogotá, 17 de noviembre de 2005

Querido Juan Gabriel:

Hace poco tiempo me cayó en las manos una posibilidad extraordinaria. Mejor dicho, me la regaló un hombre extraordinario, que es quien te entrega esta carta. A mí la vida no me ha dado tiempo para transformar este don en libro, pero creo que dadas mis circunstancias he cumplido a cabalidad. Ahora te toca a ti heredar tan maravilloso material y llevarlo a buen puerto. Tienes en tus manos algo grande y no dudo al decir que eres digno depositario de estos secretos.

Recibe como siempre mi abrazo y mi amistad,

---

documents and then devotedly copying the signature, navigating with difficulty its curves and corners, learning them bit by bit, inhabiting them, it occurred to me then, as Pacho Herrera allowed himself to be inhabited by the spirit of Gaitán. Yes, I admired the intensity of the lie, or rather the intensity of the desire that had justified or created the lie, and I also admired the details of the lie, the investigation that sustained and informed it (and I wondered where he'd gotten certain details, such as La Romana restaurant and the visits to the post office box; I couldn't come up with satisfactory answers, and I admired him more). I thought that we should invent a new word for a lie so elaborate that

it transcended and exceeded mere verbal deceit, that demands a complex and articulated staging, that requires certain props and the talent to manufacture them. What was Carballo? He was not a simple forger, though he was also that. What was he? He was someone capable of forging a letter from a dead man to achieve his aims, to fulfill his obsessions in the world. "He's someone with passion," Benavides had told me in those or other words,

MUJERES DE BABEL

–La experiencia leída–

*Para
Juan Gabriel,
magister in Joyce,
con el
ánima complacida
y la pluma
complaciente.
Un abrazo de
tu amigo de
siempre,
R.H. Moreno Durán*

taurus

Bogotá / septiembre 2004

but I saw, more than a passion, an unhealthy obsession, a demon tormenting a human being, because only by following a demon could someone go to the extremes Carballo had gone to. And I couldn't not respect that.

"He's talented, even so," I said to Hugo as we were leaving.

"Very," said Hugo. "One could only wish for such talents."

That night, when I got to the apartment, I immediately noticed that something wasn't right. The girls were sleeping in our room and the baby carriage was under the stairs as if M had just come in. She didn't have to tell me what had happened: as soon as I saw her annoyed or maybe disappointed expression, I remembered we'd had an appointment at the clinic and was ashamed of myself for not having showed up. The reason for the appointment was an oximetry that would determine whether our daughters could finally begin to breathe on their own, without the help of supplementary oxygen; in the last little while we'd had similar tests every three or four days, and the results so far had always been disappointing, so the leaving behind of the rented tanks and the need to take them everywhere had acquired a symbolic value for us: the cannulas that encircled my daughters' faces had turned into our last obstacle to normality. This time we hadn't got the hoped-for result either. The disappointment was palpable in the atmosphere, on my wife's face and in her body, but I didn't know if it was just disappointment at the results or also at my blameworthy absence. She handed me the headed paper with the results of one of the two tests:

- With cannula 1/8: HR 142. SpO2 95%
- Awake without oxygen: HR 146. SpO2 86%
- Asleep without oxygen: HR 149. SpO2 84%

"And the other one?" I asked.

"The same," she said. "They are actually twins."

"So, no then?"

"So, no," said M. "And I would have liked to find that out together. It would have been nice if you'd been there when they gave us the news." And then: "Where were you?"

"At R.H.'s house," I said. "Talking to Mónica. We were deciding . . . We were seeing if what Carballo said was true."

"Carballo? The friend of Benavides?"

"That's the one," I said. "Sorry. I lost track of time."

"No, you didn't lose track of time, you forgot about the test," said M. "It slipped your mind." And then: "You're not here. You're not in this."

"What do you mean?" I said. Although I knew perfectly well what she meant.

"That your head is somewhere else and I don't know where. What's happening to us is important. You have to pay attention. We still haven't come out the other side, there are still lots of things that could go wrong, and the girls depend on us. I need you to be with me, concentrated on this, and you seem more interested in what a paranoid madman says. And it's true, it's not the first time you've been interested in a guy like that, but this time it's different. These girls were born in a country where people kill each other all the time. That's the way it is. But the worst thing is that those dead people are more interesting to you than they are. Maybe I'm exaggerating, maybe I'm being unfair, I don't know anymore. I don't want to be unfair. But now the girls are here, I don't know if you understand me. Don't bring those things home. You just spent all day talking about that crazy man and thinking about horrible things. Don't bring all that to the girls, all those things in your head and hands. Don't stop thinking about them in order to think about that. Later there'll be time, but don't do that now, now there are more important things." She began to walk toward the swinging door to the kitchen. "But if you can't, if you don't want to put all your attention on this, you better go back to Barcelona," she said before disappearing. "I'll do it on my own."

I stayed in the living room, then went up to our room and found my daughters awake, four gray eyes wide open, trying to focus on some point in space with an expression halfway between alarmed and curious. Ninety days had passed since their birth, and only now were resemblances starting to emerge in their features, only now could I detect genetic forces doing what they do in bones and muscles, and it was a sort of miracle to see my mouth in their mouths and M's eyebrows in their thin brows, traces of us repeated in the two symmetrical faces that couldn't look at me yet but soon would: they would focus their lost gazes, and their eyes would no longer be gray but will have taken on the color of mine to look at me. Some Paul Éluard lines that I'd once put in a book and whose meaning had never been clear to me came to mind, though it was clear they didn't refer to a newborn baby:

> *She has the shape of my hands*
> *She has the color of my eyes*
> *She is swallowed up by my shadow*
> *Like a stone against the sky*

I stupidly wondered whether they'd noticed my absence, if they'd reproached me for it; I wondered if I'd failed them for the first time. I thought: *He that hath wife and children hath given hostages to fortune.* I seemed now to truly understand the meaning of the words, as if days ago, when I heard them during the Mass, they'd been abstract, unconnected to me, too far removed from my awareness or experience. *I am a hostage to fortune,* I thought. And then I went back downstairs, sat at the desk that wasn't mine, turned on my computer, and wrote a few sure words to Carballo.

> Look, Carlos, I have thought it over carefully and arrived at a decision. This is not for me. Not only because I realize that you don't want a writer (you want a patron for your raving, someone who will give your paranoia the false prestige of the printed word), but because I don't think you're telling me the truth. I don't believe that R.H. left me anything with you. I think you're a liar and a charlatan, forgive my frankness. I am not interested in what you're proposing, do not wish to remain in contact with you, and all I ask of you is that you respect my decision and not try to insist.

I received his reply in a matter of minutes:

> go to hell

Three little words, no punctuation: that was it. I imagined Carballo with an expression blending disappointment and disdain, an intense disdain, a disdain that was almost an insult and even a threat.

I didn't answer.

And he didn't write again.

IN JANUARY 2006, our stay in Bogotá reached its end. I landed in Barcelona—the city that had been my home for the previous seven years—prepared to forget my excessively close contact with the old violence of my country, and to concentrate on the life I had in front of me, not on what I'd left behind. I must have achieved it almost without noticing, for the encounter with Benavides and Carballo soon began to recede in my memory, and after a moment I can't pinpoint, ceased to exist, ceased to contaminate my present with images of famous murders (a head that explodes like a firecracker and a fleshy vertebra that once contained a bullet) and with preposterous stories of conspiracies that only feed our paranoia, our general sensation that the whole world is our enemy. I devoted myself to the classes that earned me my living while trying not to disappoint my daughters, for I knew that my errors would soon be in the past for me, but would mark each of them from the first moment and forever. Everyone says that the power to mold at whim the lives of our children is terrifying, but I thought the impunity I'd enjoy if I were mistaken in doing so was even more terrifying, if I wounded or deformed them or hurt them or taught them, unintentionally, to hurt others. I found it satisfying to be able to devote myself to them, without distractions, without contaminations from the past. It was a willful and conscious effort, and the results, fruit of my forgetful stubbornness. It had been a mistake to grant my time and ear to Carballo's obsessions, and also, why not admit it, to those of Benavides. This mistake could be corrected.

But can one really forget at will? In *De Oratore*, Cicero tells the story of Themistocles, an Athenian whose wisdom had no equal in his time. It was said that Themistocles had received a visit from a cultured and successful man who, after a flattering introduction, offered to teach him the science of mnemonics. Themistocles, curious, asked what could be achieved by this new science, which was only just beginning to be spoken of, and the visitor assured him with pride that mnemonics would allow him to remember everything. Disappointed, Themistocles answered the visitor that the real favor wouldn't be in teaching him how to remember everything, but in how to forget what he wanted to forget. I can think of events of my life (seen, heard, decided in some cases) without which I would be better off, because they are not useful but instead uncomfortable, shameful, or painful, but I know that willfully forgetting them is not possible, that they'll remain hidden in my memory. It's possible they'll leave me in peace for some length of time, like hibernating animals, but one random day I'll see something or hear something or make some decision that makes them return to my head; guilty or simply disturbing memories return to our recollection at the most unexpected moments. And there is then a sort of muscular reaction—a reflex action in our body—that always accompanies those returns; there are those who duck their heads between their shoulders as we do when someone throws something at us, others bang their fists on their desks or dashboards as if this brusque gesture will frighten away the undesirable memories, and others make a revealing expression, closing their eyes, tightening their jaws and lips, showing their teeth, and if we were spying on them we could even recognize those moments. There it is, we'd think: he's just remembered something uncomfortable, or disturbing, or guilty. No, we cannot control our forgetting, we haven't learned how to do so in spite of the fact that our minds would work better if we could: if we could somehow manage to master the way in which the past meddles in the present.

I was successful, in any case. During the six years that followed, I didn't think again of those crimes. It was as if I'd never visited the house of Francisco Benavides: the forgetting was a solid triumph. I wrote and taught and took what I considered necessary trips, translated sentences by Hemingway or books of conversations with Al Pacino, taught literature classes to North Americans in their twenties and tried, sometimes successfully, to interest them in Rulfo and Onetti, read *Under the Volcano* and *The Great Gatsby* feeling that they wanted to teach me valuable lessons and that I was too dim to understand them; and meanwhile I let time pass over me. Cities, like the face of a child, give us back what we show them: the Barcelona of those years welcomed and embraced me, but that was only a reflection of my private satisfaction, the strange equilibrium that family life had supplied to my days. I began to live without being aware of it, which must be one of the metaphors of happiness. My daughters learned to walk in the long corridor of our apartment on Plaza Tetuán, whose living room windows overlooked some palm trees agitated all year round by parakeets, and later, when we moved to a ground-floor apartment on Córcega Street, they already spoke with a hybrid accent that would turn them into little foreigners in either of their two homelands, and in the process their language turned into a rare mirror that reflected my feeling of strangeness or foreignness. I wondered, more seriously than ever, if I wouldn't return to live in my city, if the years gone by since my departure (which were now getting to be quite a few) would be taking me further and further away irremediably, until they made a return impossible. A good friend summed it up with a linguistic twist that contained a profound truth:

"It's not that we Colombians leave Colombia," he said. "We're just always leaving."

But where was the limit to all this? How long was it possible to spend as an inquiline before losing the sacred right to go home? In English dictionaries the word *inquiline* is defined as an animal that exploits the nest or den of another species; the definition helped me begin to explain my situation without recourse to the grandiloquences that harass us, for I was not an "exile," being an "ex-pat" bored me with its simple-mindedness, and not even by force would I have agreed to belong to a "diaspora." But for a while I lost sleep wondering whether the condition of inquiline could be inherited, if my daughters, no matter how settled in their Barcelona lives, were inevitably condemned to be from elsewhere, to continue to belong to another species.

No, maybe this wasn't their den as it wasn't mine, as comfortable as I felt in it, as fond as I was of its people and its bends and curves. Never had I felt so at ease as during the years of my life in Barcelona, watching my children and my friends' children grow and reading books I'd never read and wondering how I'd gone through life without reading them. I took long nocturnal walks, sometimes after having a drink with friends or coming home with M from the Méliès cinema after seeing a Hitchcock or Welles or Howard Hawks movie. I'd return home to give my daughters a kiss on the forehead, for a moment watch them sleep under the blue glow from their night-light, check that the windows and doors were locked, and go to bed as well. There was in all that the impression of having left behind the shadow line that Conrad spoke of, that age when we become adults once and for all, we take our place in the world and begin to unearth our secrets. By thirty-three, it had been at least five years since I'd crossed that imaginary frontier, and I felt capable of confronting whatever came. And all this seemed to me mysteriously inseparable from the luck, the immense good fortune, of having been able to escape.

Yes, that was it. It was as if I'd escaped, yes, it seemed right to me to put it in those terms, because that's what all Colombians do: our lives get used up in trying to escape or wondering why we don't, in arriving on good terms with life elsewhere or struggling with the decision not to pursue that life. And so it happens that some of us inhabit Barcelona or Madrid, as we've done New York, the city with the third-largest Colombian population in the world, some of us end up in Miami or Paris or Lima or Mexico City, filling requirements as water fills the spaces it is let into. During that time I began to translate *The Tunnel*, an extraordinary novel by William Gass, whose epigraph didn't impress me then as much as it should have and most of all as much as it does now:

Anaxagoras said to a man who was grieving because he lay dying in a foreign land, "The descent to hell is the same from every place."

No, Colombian violence is not escapable, and I should have known that. Nobody escapes, but much less the people of my generation, who were born with the drug trade and reached adulthood as the country was shipwrecked in the blood of the war Pablo Escobar declared on it. One can leave the country as I left in 1996 and believe it left behind, but that would be deceit, we'd all be deceiving ourselves. The teacher that life chose to show me this lesson, when it could have chosen so many other ways, would never cease to amaze me: a hunted hippopotamus.

It was a beast weighing a ton and a half that had spent two years on the loose after escaping from the Hacienda Nápoles, the property that had been Pablo Escobar's headquarters and also a zoo open to the public. It was summer when I saw the photo, the dense and hot summer of 2009. One of the many guests we had during that time had forgotten a copy of *Semana* magazine, but several days had to go by—the magazine tumbling around like a lost soul—before I opened it mechanically in an idle moment, having taken a cold beer out of the fridge. The effect, however, was immediate. The image of the soldiers who had shot the hippopotamus, dark men in uniform who stood around the body with their weapons pointing at the sky and a rude smile of victory on their faces, caused me an impression I couldn't have foreseen, a sort of unease that had nothing to do with the present moment, the inexplicable sensation that something was wrong. What was going on? It took me a long while of staring at the photo, of reading and rereading the account of the escape and hunt in the magazine, to comprehend it: the image of the hippopotamus surrounded by his hunters had capriciously superimposed itself over that of Pablo Escobar, pursued and shot dead on the rooftops of Medellín, his body surrounded by his own hunters, all uniformed men pointing their own weapons at the sky, all with their own victorious smiles, and one of them lifting the corpse by his shirt, as if to show the cameras and onlookers the bearded face of the man who had flooded the country with blood for a decade.

Suddenly I recalled the visit I made, in the company of a friend from school and his parents, to the Hacienda Nápoles zoo, a fabled place that held, as well as hippopotami, pink Amazonian dolphins, several pairs of giraffes, gray rhinoceroses and African elephants, zebras that gathered together to create in the observer the mirage of a herd, an army of flamingos that colonized several different lakes as their numbers swelled (drawing a long pink line beneath the gigantic palm trees), a kangaroo that knew how to kick a football, and a parrot that recited the starting eleven of the national team. The year was 1985; it must have been July, because school holidays had just begun; so I would have been twelve years old when I went through the gate into the hacienda, passing beneath the small white plane that Pablo Escobar had mounted there, above the entrance, to commemorate his first *coronation*, as they called a successful delivery of a shipment of drugs into the United States; a pawn crossing the lines of defense and turning into an opulent queen, upon arrival. Later I would learn that plane—HK-617 was its registration number: one of those fragments of perfectly useless information that persist in my capricious memory—was a replica of the original, which had been lost at sea with a shipment of drugs. But at that moment, passing beneath the wings with my friend and his parents, I felt a twinge of childish guilt, for I knew very well that my own parents would not have been amused by my visit to the property of the man who was by then the most notorious drug trafficker in the country: the man who, since April of the previous year, was known to be responsible, as yet unpunished, for the assassination of the minister of justice.

All these memories arrived in my head with meridian clarity. The impulse was irresistible: I reached for my notebook and began to record memories: about life in those years, about the zoo, about what my parents would have thought if they'd known I'd been there. No, it would not have amused them; and I, at twelve years of age, already had the necessary principles to understand why not: the assassination of Minister Rodrigo Lara Bonilla had destroyed in a single blow their idea of the country they lived in. "Things like this hadn't happened since Gaitán," my father said during those days, or at least he says it in my memory. They—the generation of those in their forties at that time—had grown up in a country where *that didn't happen anymore.* A few months before the assassination, during a weekend get-together at the house of one of our neighbors, some grown-up stated his opinion that the minister better be more careful, because if he kept annoying them, the drug barons were going to kill him. The whole party—four couples of parents who were playing cards and drinking *aguardiente* wrapped in ponchos from Nobsa—burst out laughing, because it was unimaginable to all of them that it could happen, and those who remembered the *Bogotazo* (in their own memories or inherited memories) held on to the illusion that it would never happen again. But the illusion broke apart on April 30. Rodrigo Lara left his office that evening, and it was dark by the time the hit men caught up with him. The one with the machine gun shot in the shape of a cross, as he'd been taught at the *sicario* school an Israeli mercenary had set up in Sabaneta, south of Medellín. When he was killed, Lara had with him a hardback book called *Dictionary of Colombian History.*

The next day there was a special silence in the streets, the silence that settles on a house where someone is dying. Later, when I asked my elders about it, they all repeated the same idea: yes, it was a different city, the city had woken up unhinged. The country was also different, of course: something had broken in it, something had changed, but it was not yet possible to know that it had changed *forever*, we couldn't yet know that a dark decade had begun that night, nine years, seven months, and a number of days whose effects we would try to elucidate for the rest of our lives. A dark decade, yes, a zone of shadows, the stinking pit of our history. The Colombian government had to react in some way, and it did so by hitting the drug cartels where it hurt them most, by announcing, with great media hype, that it would immediately start extraditing drug traffickers. The extradition treaty between Colombia and the United States, signed in 1979 by Jimmy Carter and Julio César Turbay, came back out onto the streets like a zombie, frightening the narcos. For there was one thing they knew very well: a Colombian judge could be bought or killed—*plata o plomo*, money or lead, was their famous slogan—but that was more difficult to do abroad, far from their stashes of dollars and hungry *sicarios*. That was when the first bomb exploded, or at least the first that I remember. It happened in front of the American embassy and killed one person. Two months later, the United States received the flights with the first extradited prisoners. Escobar and his associates, determined that the same thing would not happen to them, formed a group with its own name, the Extraditables, and their own war cry: *Give us a grave in Colombia rather than a jail cell in the USA.* And they proceeded, with admirable perseverance, to dig graves for their fellow citizens.

A long time later I was able to hear a recording of Escobar's voice issuing what is almost a manifesto and leaves no room for doubt:

"We have to create real fucking chaos so they'll beg us for peace," he says. "If we take it to the politicians, burn down their houses and make a real bloody civil war, then they'll have to call us to peace talks and our problems will be fixed."

But it wasn't just politicians, it was all of us who saw our houses burned down, who saw ourselves involved in that civil war, which wasn't a civil war, of course, but a cowardly and merciless and devious massacre of vulnerable and innocent people.

TWENTY-FOUR YEARS after my visit to the zoo, there I was, remembering from Barcelona all that I'd seen in those years, spending long hours on the internet to collect all the information possible (videos of the blood-covered upholstery of Lara's car or Galán collapsing on the wooden platform), talking on the telephone with friends or family members to ask them what they remembered and also remembering other victims, as if I'd be committing an injustice by not doing so, as if someone might be watching over my shoulder ready to reproach me for not remembering their dead, and also remembering that city discombobulated by bombs, that city that woke up after every attack converted into a chicken with its head chopped off still running around in circles. And I wondered what had happened to us: to all Bogotanos, of course, but in particular to those of us who were children when it all started and who learned how to live in that difficult decade. We pretended that it was normal to crisscross our windows with masking tape, so pieces of glass, if a bomb went off, wouldn't turn into lethal shards. We pretended it was normal to sleep in other people's houses each time that, after a bomb exploded or a politician was murdered, a curfew was declared before we'd managed to get home.

A year and a half. For a year and a half I filled page after page with memories like those, with notes and facts, in a desperate attempt to transfigure them by way of the imagination, that illuminates everything, and through storytelling, which sees further than we do, and thus finally understand what happened during that decade: understand the public and visible events, of course, the legions of images and tales that were stored up in chronicles and histories and the memory-laden labyrinths of the internet, but also to understand the private and invisible events, which are not contained anywhere because not even the best historian, or the best journalist, can tell what goes on in someone else's soul. A year and a half, yes. It was a year and a half I spent ceaselessly remembering those days, a year and a half remembering the dead, living with them, talking to them, listening to their laments and lamenting in turn not being able to do anything to alleviate their suffering. But most of all thinking of us, the living, who continue to try to understand what happened, who so many years later continue telling stories to explain it to one another. That's what I did: I tried to explain it, I told a story, I wrote a book. And I swear that I thought, after finishing *The Sound of Things Falling*, that I had settled my debts with the violence it had fallen to me to live through. Now it seems incredible that I hadn't understood that our violences are not only the ones we had to experience, but also the others, those that came before, because they are all linked even if the threads that connect them are not visible, because past time is contained within present time, or because the past is our inheritance without the benefit of an inventory and in the end we eventually receive it all: the sense and the excesses, the rights and the wrongs, the innocence and the crimes.

IV

WHY SWELL'ST THOU THEN?

In July 2012, after living for sixteen years in three different European countries, I moved back to Bogotá. One of the first things I did was to call Dr. Benavides to ask when we could see each other. Our last encounter had ended in a less than satisfactory way, and I wanted to rectify that discomfort: smooth things over, and apologize, because the error, the misjudgment, and also the poor behavior, had been mine. A sad-sounding voice told me that the doctor wasn't feeling well and couldn't take my call. The job of beginning a new life in a new country is no easier when it's your own; concentrated as I was on the enigmas of arrival, on interpreting the thousand and one ways in which the mentality and temperament of my city had transformed in the years of my absence, I didn't call Benavides back, and I didn't even think about his health. A year and a half went by. I wrote another novel; I took what I considered to be necessary trips; slowly, habit by habit, I gradually arrived in Colombia. In that year and a half, which now stretches out in my memory, I didn't hear anything more about Benavides. I barely thought about him. The man had opened the door of his study to me, had involved me in things he considered secret, had confided in me. What had I done to repay that confidence? One fine day it dawned on me that eight years had passed since our last uncomfortable and troubled conversation, and I thought it wasn't the first time someone had disappeared from my life due to my own fault: due to my tendency to solitude and silence, due to my sometimes unjustifiable reserve, due to my inability to keep relationships alive (even those I have with people I love or who genuinely interest me). This has always been one of my great defects, and it has caused me more than one disappointment and has disappointed others more than once. There's nothing I can do about it, however, because nobody changes their nature by the mere force of will.

But at the beginning of 2014, something happened.

ON JANUARY 1, I found myself at a nineteenth-century hacienda in the coffee-growing region, a house with wattle-and-daub walls and floors of varnished wood the name of which, Alsacia, made me think of Prussian War veterans leaving a piece of their nostalgia in the Colombian Andes. I had arrived there with the ostensible aim of seeing in the New Year in good company, but I ended up spending more time than planned worrying about the last news of the previous one: on December 24, while returning to her house in Belgrade from Sarajevo, the Serbian writer Senka Marniković, author of a book of short stories that was for me clearly a masterpiece, lost control of her car on an icy, slippery road, broke through a guardrail, skidded across a high embankment, and ended up crashing head-on into the wall of a mechanic's workshop. The death on the other side of the world of the author of a single book, whose photo I'd never seen and whose voice I'd never heard, provoked an unexpected and surprising melancholy in me, especially as a few short years ago I had no idea of her existence.

I came across her name in the spring of 2010, during a seventy-two-hour visit to Belgrade where I went to speak about literature to an audience of scholars of the Spanish language. My hostess, a professor of Latin American literature who was translating the poetry of César Vallejo in her spare time, took me to see the apartment of the novelist Ivo Andrić after my talk. Over the course of the following day she arranged to show me a park from which you could see the Danube as well as a dive where curious foreigners could buy devalued money from the era of the Bosnian War. It was there, in that bar, where she asked me if I'd read *Fantasmas de Sarajevo*. When I said not only did I not know the book but I'd never heard of the author, the professor said, in a perfect Madrid accent, "*Coño*, that can't be," and the next morning I discovered that she'd left for me at reception a copy of Marnikovic's book in the only Western language into which it had so far been translated. I began to read *Fântomes de Sarajevo* in the Belgrade airport, and by the time I arrived home in Barcelona, after a stopover in Zurich and a delay for bad weather, I'd finished it and was rereading some of the stories, cursing the fact that I'd never found this formidable book before and feeling I hadn't made such a marvelous discovery since the day in 1999 when I opened the strange book of a certain W. G. Sebald. And now Marnikovic was dead, dead at seventy-two, thirty-nine years after publishing her marvelous book, and the melancholy that I felt at that news now transformed into an almost physical need to reread it, to immerse myself in her voice that knew more things than I did, to pay attention to the world through eyes that were more attentive than mine. I took the book off my shelf and put it in my black bag, and there it was that January 1, accompanying me in the nineteenth-century hacienda, silent even in the neutral tones of its cream-colored covers, tactful as if we both had lost a common friend.

It was a holiday, of course, but it was also a Wednesday: the day of the week that I had devoted during the preceding seven years to writing my column for *El Espectador*. I'd grown used to writing it in the morning when my head was less fuddled, but this time the New Year's Day leisureliness (the unconscious conviction that the world has started over again and there's no hurry for anything) had broken my discipline. So after a late lunch, when the old house with its wooden floors fell into an invincible drowsiness and nothing broke the silence except the agitation of the cicadas and parakeets, I poured myself a beer, made myself comfortable at a card table whose green cloth had been burned by cigarettes during the previous night's revelries, and got down to work like a hunter who goes out to try his luck with no certainty he's going to find anything. I opened Marniković's book at random, reread the openings of a few stories, and ended up reading all of "The Long Life of Gavrilo Princip," the best in the book and the most pertinent to this year that was just waking up. With those characters in mind I wrote the first sentences of my column; in a matter of minutes, Marniković's tale had associated with other subjects and other characters that had touched me more closely, so the column came together around a relatively simple idea: the possible correspondences between two well-known crimes, one of universal importance and the other of more restricted consequences, that took place within a few months of each other. I gave the text the title "Memories of the Year to Come." I wrote fairly quickly:

This will be a year of commemorations, but not the good kind. Of course, the Panamanians will celebrate the SS *Ancon*'s passage through its recently inaugurated canal; of course, Julio Cortázar's readers will remember his birth in Brussels. But I'm very much afraid that most of the following months will be spent talking about certain assassinations and their consequences. The year 1914, runs the cliché, is the true port of entry into the afflicted twentieth century, and that is not exactly because an Argentine writer was born in Belgium or a route opened between two oceans. The assassinations that took place that year were midwives to a good deal of the history that followed, and it sets one's teeth on edge to observe, with the falsely reassuring perspective of the years, how little we imagined the debacle awaiting us around the corner. In "The Long Life of Gavrilo Princip," one of the best pieces of fiction that has ever been written about the legacy of that year, the Serbian writer Senka Marniković invents a world in which the First World War has not happened. Gavrilo Princip, a young Serbian nationalist, arrives in Sarajevo to kill Archduke Franz Ferdinand, but his pistol jams and the archduke carries on living. Princip dies a year later, of tuberculosis, and the world is otherwise.

But it wasn't like that, of course. Gavrilo Princip did kill Archduke Franz Ferdinand of Austria. He was about to turn twenty; he had tried to join the Black Hand guerrilla group, but was rejected because of his short stature; after learning to throw bombs and shoot pistols, he joined a group of six conspirators whose objective was to assassinate the heir to the throne of the Austro-Hungarian Empire and thus force the separation of the Slavic provinces from the Empire and the creation of the great Serb nation. The conspirators joined the crowd that flanked the route the archduke would pass in a car whose roof had been removed so the public could see their nobles. The idea was that all the conspirators, from the first to the last, would attempt the assassination. The first failed from fear. Princip, in spite of Marniković's wonderful speculation, did not fail.

In October of the same year, but on the other side of the world, a man who was not an archduke, but a general and a senator of the Republic of Colombia, was assassinated, not by bullets but by hatchet blows, by two poor young men like Princip. Rafael Uribe Uribe, veteran of several civil wars, uncontested leader of the Liberal Party (in those days when being a liberal meant something), and the model for the character of García Márquez's Aureliano Buendía, was attacked at midday on the 15th by Leovigildo Galarza and Jesús Carvajal, unemployed carpenters. He died early the following morning in his house on Ninth Street, in Bogotá; beside the sidewalk where he received the murderous blows there is a plaque that nobody looks at, because it is at knee height. And nevertheless, Colombians will remember him this year. They'll write about him, they'll celebrate his life although they don't know anything about it, and they'll mourn his death even though they don't know why he was killed. And so the time will go by; thinking of Princip and Franz Ferdinand, of Galarza and Carvajal and of Uribe Uribe; thinking of those crimes; thinking of their causes and consequences. The year is just beginning.

The column was published on January 3. The following Monday, Epiphany, I woke up a little before first light; trying not to let the squeak of a floorboard under my feet or the creak of any hinge in the old house give me away, I got out my computer and started reading the newspapers. Many years ago I'd dropped the habit of reading the online comments my column inspired, not only from lack of interest and time, but out of the profound conviction that they displayed the worst vices of our new digital societies: intellectual irresponsibility, proud mediocrity, implausible denigration with impunity, but most of all verbal terrorism, the schoolyard bullying that the participants got involved in with incomprehensible enthusiasm, the cowardice of all those aggressors who used pseudonyms to vilify but would never repeat their insults out loud. The forum of opinion columns has turned into our modern and digital version of the Two Minutes Hate: that ritual in Orwell's *1984* in which an image of the enemy is projected and the citizens ecstatically give themselves over to physical aggression (they throw things at the screen) and verbal aggression (they insult, shriek, accuse, defame), and then go back to the real world feeling free, unburdened, and self-satisfied. Yes, I haven't read those comments for many years; however, that morning I did: I went over the insults with their spelling mistakes, the invariably badly punctuated libel, all those symptoms that something was rotten in the state of Colombia. Toward the end of the page, one commentary caught my attention. The signature (so to speak) was FreeSpirit. This was the text of his commentary:

> *What a stupid column, who cares what happened over there!! What happened here?? We Colombians KNOW why they killed Uribe Uribe no matter how hard they try to DECEIVE us, that the truth hasn't come to light is another matter. Gentlemen of El Espectador with columnists like this you're losing prestige day by day. Mr. so-called columnist you'd be better off dedicating yourself to your failed novels. One day the truth will come to LIGHT!!!*

In the days that followed, I couldn't shake the ridiculous certainty that I had found Carlos Carballo again. Then I thought it wasn't like that: I hadn't found him, but rather he had put himself deliberately in my path. Then I thought it was neither one nor the other, but the truth was simpler and even more annoying: Carlos Carballo had never gone away. In these eight long years that had passed since our encounter in the church, Carballo had not lost sight of me for an instant: it was not impossible that he would have read my books, I thought, and he had surely followed my columns, leaving after many of them his anonymous smears. Then I thought that FreeSpirit might, incredibly, not be Carlos Carballo, but any other of the millions of individuals who populate the republics of paranoia in a country with a convulsive history like ours. What I should do, I thought, was to call Francisco Benavides, inquire about his health and whether he'd been in touch with Carballo recently, whether Carballo had talked about me, if he'd told him what he'd proposed to me in the church and what my response had been. I called him; he didn't answer; I left a message with the secretary at his office. He didn't call me back.

My brief stay at the nineteenth-century hacienda came to an end. I returned with my family to Bogotá, ready to get back into my work routine, but I didn't try to contact Benavides. Two things distracted me: on the one hand, a novel that I'd been trying to write for five years, that seemed to have come unstuck now, after many false starts, and from which it had been very difficult to tear myself away to go on holiday; on the other hand, the search for information about Senka Marniković, whose death had turned her into someone interesting all of a sudden. But the internet, which knows everything, knew very little about Senka Marniković. As tends to happen to us when something preoccupies us or obsesses us, life seemed to suddenly be conspiring so that everything, directly or indirectly, referred to or reminded me of her. And so, a Spanish couple I'd just met, Asier and Ruth, turned out to have lived in the Balkans, and talked to me nostalgically of those days and offered to lend me books on the siege of Sarajevo, and a friendship started to grow. And so, the novelist Miguel Torres wrote to me saying he'd read my column and asking me who this Serbian writer was, if her books had been translated into Spanish, and where he could find them, for he was very interested in fictions that change or twist the real course of history. I didn't answer him: it was rude and an act of egotism, especially considering it concerned a colleague I appreciate (whose novels about April 9 are among the best that have ever come out of my country); but one of the mysteries of the life of a fiction reader is that possessiveness that sometimes takes us over with respect to the books or authors that have told us something important and new, something we'd never heard before. I didn't want to talk about Senka Marniković because Senka Marniković belonged only to me. It was a primitive emotion, but that's what I felt at the time.

At the beginning of February, I finally wrote to Dr. Benavides. I told him that I regretted the silence we'd fallen into for so many years; I told him I took responsibility for that silence and its consequences, but that I'd very much like to get back in touch. This time he replied immediately.

Esteemed patient:

I was very pleased to receive your message, why should I deny it. Every once in a while I think of those long-ago days and also regret that we'd lost touch. I've heard that you're now honoring us with your presence as a resident, are you not? Tell me when you want to get together and we'll catch up. Life has not been kind to me and I think I'd like to talk to somebody who understands my troubles (insert melodramatic music here). Anyway, for various reasons that I won't go into here, at this moment you are that someone. I'm working late shifts these days, I'm usually at the clinic until eight. Let me know one way or another before you come.

Warm regards,
Francisco

I went to see him the following Friday. Since the days of my daughters' birth, when I spent long nocturnal hours of uncertainty and anguish, arriving at a medical building at night makes me feel immediately uncomfortable. We had made an appointment, furthermore, in a place that reminded me of those days as if I were reliving them: the cafeteria in the basement, that windowless space that filled, at mealtimes, with two types of people: either relatives of patients with their permanent masks of uneasiness, or the usual and occasionally idle doctors and nurses. When Benavides arrived, two minutes after the hour, I saw on his face the ravages of time, and then, like an epiphany, I remembered the reasons I'd appreciated him with an appreciation that approached admiration. For it was not just the passing of years etched on Benavides's tired face, but also the wear produced by other people's suffering, that kind of reciprocal labor he'd taken on years before and that consisted basically of keeping the dying company. He came wrapped in his white coat and carrying a green book in his hand; before arriving at the table where I was waiting for him he had to greet four different people who stood up as he came through the glass doors, and he received all of them with the same kindness of a tired man, shaking hands with pleasure but with a sort of invisible weight on his shoulders. Now he wore frameless glasses, two lenses that would have seemed to be floating in front of his eyes if it hadn't been for the bright red of the arms and the bridge over his nose.

"I brought you this," he said as he sat down.

It was a university publication with a frightening title: *Looking Death in the Eye: Eight Perspectives.*

"What is it?" I asked.

"Variations on a theme," he said. "There are philosophers, theologians, literary writers, people you might be interested in. The doctor's me." After a modest silence he added: "For when you don't have anything else to read."

"Well, thank you," I said, and I said it sincerely (which isn't always the case when one receives a book). "Look, Francisco, the last time we saw each other . . ."

"Eight years ago? Are we going to talk about what happened eight years ago? No, Vásquez, that's a waste of time. Let's talk about important things. For example, tell me how your daughters are doing."

I did so. While we stood in line to be served dinner, while we walked back to the table and began to eat, I talked to him without too much detail of the experience of paternity, which seemed more difficult every day, and how I sometimes felt nostalgia for the first days, when the only obstacles were medical ones. Now I had to confront the world, this fucked-up world so skilled at harming everyone, and already at my daughters' age you could see so many of their friends damaged forever. I told him about the last two years in Barcelona and the decision to return to Colombia. I told him about my impressions of returning to live in my city after sixteen years: that sensation of partial foreignness, of not being completely from here like I used to be, in Barcelona, not totally from there; I told him how it was this strange foreignness that had allowed me to come back, for I had always fed off it. On the other hand, the city had turned angry, hostile, and intolerant on me, and in an unpredictable way: contrary to what was happening when I left, the violence was not coming from well-defined actors at war with the citizens, but was in the citizens themselves, who all seemed to have embarked on their own crusades, all seemed to walk around with their accusing fingers outstretched and ready to point and condemn. When did this happen? I asked Benavides. When did we get like this? Several times a day I arrived at the irritating conviction that the people of Bogotá, if they had the opportunity, would not hesitate to press the button that would forever erase the detestable others: atheists, workers, the rich, homosexuals, blacks, communists, businesspeople, supporters of the president, supporters of the ex-president, Millonarios fans, Santa Fe fans. The city was poisoned with the venom of small fundamentalisms, and the venom ran beneath us, like dirty water in the sewers; and yes, life seemed to go on normally and Bogotanos went on seeking refuge in the embraces of their friends and sex with lovers, and went on being parents and sons and brothers and husbands and wives without letting the venom affect them at all, or maybe believing that the venom didn't exist. But there were marvelous people like Francisco Benavides, who invested whole hours of all his days to give a hand to the terminally ill and speak to them of the best possible death, without ever avoiding affection, without rationing empathy or sparing his feelings, leaping headfirst and without closing his eyes into a relationship the only outcome of which could be sadness.

I spoke to him about Carballo. People came into the cafeteria and people left, there was a background noise of cutlery clashing against plates and heels clashing against tiles and voices clashing against tense voices, and I spoke to Benavides about Carballo. I told him about the encounter at R. H. Moreno-Durán's funeral Mass, told him what Carballo had told me, told him about the Orson Welles novel and listened to him mock that novel in particular and novelists in general, who couldn't leave history alone or respect things that really happened, as if they weren't interesting enough. He told me that was why novelists had lost the truly important fight a long time ago, which was not to get people to stop thinking about their disagreeable or gray or incomplete reality, but rather to get them to grab reality by the lapels and look it in the eye and insult it unceremoniously and then slap it across the face. I told him anyway it had been more than eight years since R.H. had died and the novel still hadn't been published, so he was surely right: people had enough and more than enough with knowing how things actually happened, and no longer had any interest in knowing how they might have happened. And neverthe-less, that was the only thing that interested me as a reader of novels: the exploration of that other reality, not the reality of what really happened, not the novelized reproduction of true and provable events, but the realm of possibility, of speculations, or the meddling the novelist can do in places forbidden to the journalist or historian. I told all this to Benavides and Benavides, feigning patience or interest, listened to me.

Soon I told him about the forged letter and the offer to write a book. "Are you sure it was fake?" Benavides asked. "Completely sure," I told him. And then I looked at an elderly couple who had sat down at the back, in the section with the soft chairs. I didn't stare at them because they'd caught my attention in any way, but as a way to avoid looking Benavides in the eye when I told him I had to confess something. Im-mediately, without giving him time to ask what it was about, I ex-plained how I had revealed to Carballo the survival—and location—of Gaitán's vertebra.

"It was unintentional," I said stupidly. "It just slipped out."

Then I saw on his face something I'd never seen before, a new shape emerging out of his profound depths. A stretch of time passed that to me felt very long: four, five seconds, perhaps six. Then Benavides emerged from his silence, and he did so with one of the shortest mono-syllables in existence.

"Ah," he said.

"I'm sorry," I said.

"I see."

"I know you didn't want that."

"I see," Benavides repeated. And then: "I had my suspicions." And then: "You've confirmed it, but I did suspect." Then he looked at my plate, I saw him staring at the position of my cutlery. "Have you finished?" he asked. "Would you like dessert, a coffee?"

"No, nothing, thanks."

"No. Me neither."

I saw him stand up and lift the tray with a slight bend of the knee, not the torso. He started to walk over to the place where used or dirty trays are left. I stood up and followed him.

"Sorry, Francisco, forgive my carelessness," I said. "I know you wanted to keep that secret. But I was arguing with Carballo, it got heated and I ended up letting that out, almost spitting it out at him. You have to understand, it was the only way to get him to stop annoying me. Yes, it was clumsy on my part. A stupid thing to do. But surely it's not the end of the world."

He smoothed his white coat and looked at me.

"I don't know about the end of the world," he said. "But it is the beginning of the night. To put it another way, our night just got longer, Vásquez, I hope you haven't told them you'll be home early. Come on, come with me on some rounds and I'll tell you what happened to me. See what you think."

And he started to tell me.

"A few years ago I organized a party at my house," said Benavides. "For my wife's birthday, the best-worn fifty years I've ever seen. Some friends of hers came, some friends of mine, some friends of both. One of the guests, as is probably obvious, was Carballo, who arrived first and was the last to leave. Carballo is like a piece of furniture in my house, Vásquez. We've grown used to him; he's like the unmarried uncle who always shows up, who is as much part of the family as any of us and wanders around the house as if it were his. That day he made my wife a photograph album, a beautiful thing. He got hold of the paper, paper manufactured in the early 1960s, when Estela was born. He got this thread to sew the pages together. He got the photos. I never found out how: I didn't worry about finding out how Carballo had gotten photos of my children when they were three and five and seven years old, photos of walks I'd taken with my wife when we were dating, photos of my father. A very special gift, in truth, made by hand, made with time and dedication. For my part, it came out well: Estela isn't usually a fan of mariachis, but I risked it that day, and she liked the mariachis. After the serenade, people started leaving gradually, until we were left sitting on the railway sleeper on the patio, watching night fall slowly. My family and I: that's who was there. That patio is the same one you saw, Vásquez, except for one little detail: the heater. An electrical appliance that heats like a bonfire and allows us to stay outside even after dark when it's starting to get cold. That was my children's gift, because Estela would never stay outside chatting on the patio at night, she feels the cold too much. My children gave her this heater, we tried it out for the first time that evening and it worked like a charm. Anyway, there we were, sipping *aguardiente*, because my children thought that was the best way to celebrate, talking nineteen to the dozen, laughing ourselves silly, when I chose that moment to give my family a piece of news. 'It's about the things my father left me,' I told them, 'the ones I have upstairs. I'm going to return them.'

"I can still see their shocked faces. 'What do you mean, return them?' they asked. I said yes. That I wanted to start making decisions about certain things. I'm getting close to sixty, I told them, and at this age one starts to think and sometimes one gets strange ideas. These things, the things I took from the museum, have been with me a long time. And I've never deceived myself, I never believed they were mine. I know I was justified in taking them from there. I know it was correct and necessary, but I also know they don't belong to me. These things have been with me for decades, moving around with me, being part of my life . . . And the proof that I did the right thing is that nobody's missed them. The rest of the things that were there, the ones I didn't take, have been lost. But these haven't. These were saved and nobody has asked about them. And I won't deny it, Vásquez, as I didn't deny it to them that evening or night: the happiness they give me is immense. Coming home at night and pouring myself a drink and touching these things, and reading about them and their moments, all that is for me what stamps are for a collector. Or butterflies. Or coins. Over these last years, these things have given me moments of great satisfaction. I told them all this. I looked at Estela, at my son, at my daughter, and I told them to relax, that I wasn't going to philosophize about it, not to worry: but that that was just the way it was. And then I explained the heart of the matter: that in spite of that happiness, in spite of those moments of mad obsession I've spent in the company of my old things, never, never have I forgotten they don't belong to me. They're not mine, they've never been mine. They're not my family's, either, although I sometimes like to think they are, that I had a right to inherit them and my children could inherit them as well. But it's not true: I have no right. They're not mine, they're not my family's: they belong to the country. Or the state, yes, patrimony of the state. That's what I told them, that's the long-winded speech I inflicted on them, and then I asked: 'You all agree with me so far?'

"It was my son who answered: 'Yes, Papá, all right,' he said. 'But you saved those things. Nobody cares about them, only the one who saved them. They belong to the man who saved them, it seems to me.'

"I told him no. That they didn't belong to me, and that was the end of it. They belonged to a public institution and now they were in private hands. 'I mean,' I told them, 'that no one knows I have them. Someone could say I stole them. And what could I say to refute that? I couldn't, no, I have no arguments to refute it. Well, this is what I wanted to talk to you about, to my family. I don't want to leave this problem for you when I die. I know there's a whole lifetime to go before that happens, but we have to think the matter through carefully so as not to make a mistake. Well, I've thought about it now.' I told them I knew they weren't interested in the things. Not my wife, who had tolerated them rather than accompanied me in my interest. Not my children, who had more relevant things on their minds. I'm telling you what I told them, Vásquez: Can you imagine the terrible predicament I'd be leaving them in if I died? 'In short,' I told them, 'I've been thinking, I've been thinking for a long time, and I've arrived at the conclusion that now is the time, that the hour has come. That's it. The time has come to give them back.'

"Estela asked me the obvious question: 'But to whom? You know very well that place no longer exists. Who are you going to give these things back to after so many years? And besides, what might happen afterward? I don't know what the law says about situations like this, but I can assure you you're going to get yourself in trouble. Colombia is a place where no good action goes unpunished. Who knows what might befall us. And I don't know if it's worth the risk to change the location of some things from other times that nobody has been missing, that nobody's going to look after the way you have. No, it seems stupid to me. The things from your father's museum are your treasures. They've survived thanks to you. If you hadn't kept them years ago, they would have been lost. And mark my words: they'll be lost if you return them. Apart from the fact that I don't know who you would return them to.'

"I told her to the National Museum, for example. They have uniforms from the civil wars there, swords, the pen of some founding father. Would it not be natural for my father's things to be displayed there, so people can go and see them? 'And what if nobody goes?' said my daughter. 'What if they're not interested in displaying them?' 'They will be interested,' I said. 'They will display them. And if they're not interested and don't display them, it doesn't matter. This is the right thing to do, the decent thing, even if no one knows what those things mean to the world anymore.' 'And if they take them from you and bring charges against you? Or levy a fine against you, the kind that bankrupts people? Have you thought of that? Or do you think they're going to be grateful for the care you've taken in secret of the country's historical treasures? Do you think things like this happen in Colombia, Papá? Tell me the truth: Do you think they're going to give you a medal for having spent twenty years playing with a few bones?'

"I never imagined they'd react like that. 'What matters to me now is knowing that these things are going to be left in good hands when I die,' I explained. 'And that they're not going to cause trouble for anyone. And that people won't think badly of me. I understand that you don't agree,' I said, 'and I understand your objections. That's why I need to do this properly, aboveboard. I've thought a lot about it and I've made the decision. But I agree that it must be done properly, to avoid disagreeable situations. So then: How do we do it? Help me to think it through. It occurs to me that I should speak to someone about it first, someone from some museum, someone from the Ministry of Culture. That would be essential.'

"There was a silence of the kind you only get at family gatherings. Family silences are different, Vásquez, don't you think? When you're with friends uncomfortable silences get filled any way they can, everybody feels the need or the advisability to fill silences before it's too late. But families are places you can be silent and nothing happens. When those silences are good, when they are the silences of trust and comfort, it's the best thing there is. But when they're the other kind it's different. Among families the silences of disagreement or conflict are painful, or at least I've always thought so. The first to break it was my wife: 'Why don't you do something with the media first? A radio interview, for example. All this would be easier and you'd run fewer risks if there were an intermediary, a messenger, if people found out first through an interview. That would allow you to explain the situation, to say that you actually saved national artifacts and history and have been protecting and looking after them for twenty years, that the country is in your debt. It would allow you to control the message, as politicians say. And it would even put pressure on the museum or wherever to treat the objects with appropriate respect. So you won't be going asking for favors, because the one doing them a favor is you. You've saved from disappearing some things that in another country would each have its own museum. Imagine what they'd do in the United States if someone said they had one of Lincoln's bones. Imagine what they'd do in France if someone showed up saying they had, I don't know, one of Jean Jaurès's ribs. That they had protected and cared for it and maintained it all this time and now they want to make a donation to the Republic, a donation to the people. They'd erect a statue to him. I don't want a statue, they're never flattering. But I do think you've earned the right to a thank-you.'

"As usual, she was right. I've grown accustomed to Estela being right, however it always surprises me. She's like Occam's razor in the guise of a woman: an injection of common sense, a total incapacity for foolishness. So everyone immediately agreed that this was the most intelligent, most sensible and beneficial course of action. My children, each on their own, were going to speak to people they knew in the media. To sound out some contacts. Estela, as well. She knew someone who knew someone who worked at Caracol or RCN, I can't remember. And I thought of you, Vásquez. You came to mind right there, I didn't even have to think about it. The only person to have seen these things, not all of them, but some of the most important . . . Of course, that day, when you were at my house breaking my guests' noses, you didn't have a column in *El Espectador* yet. But now you do and my children read it, and Estela reads it. They almost always agree. I mean, they almost always agree with you. Less when you get aggressive, Estela detests that. She says you undermine your argument. That you might be right, but when you're right with sarcasm, mocking others between the lines with that arrogant tone that slips out sometimes, then you're not right anymore. And if she were here now, she'd tell you as she told me once. 'Your friend doesn't care about convincing anyone, he cares about going for the jugular. And that's no way to do it. No dialogue can be built on that. It's a shame.' Anyway, I'm going off on a tangent: the thing is that I thought of phoning you, asking you to help me with this matter. With your column, with an interview in your newspaper, in whatever way. I thought: Vásquez will help me, for sure. I thought, I won't contact him right now because it's the Friday night before a long weekend. The next morning, very early, we were going to Villa de Leyva, to stay at a friend's house. So I thought: On Tuesday I'll write to him. And I said, I think I said: 'Okay then, that's what we'll do. Everybody look where they can. I'll write to Vásquez first thing on Tuesday.'

"All four of us stood up and went into the kitchen to tidy up the house a little, wash the dishes, and take out the garbage. We were all in there, each busy with some task, with the tap running, with the noise of the plates and cutlery and garbage bags being pulled out of the bin and fresh ones shaken open to replace them. And in the midst of all that bustle, we heard the bells on the front door. On the door of my house we have a set of those bells that let you know when it opens or closes, I imagine you know the sort of thing. Anyway, we heard them ring, and Estela said to my son: 'Go see who's here.' He took off the rubber gloves, left the kitchen, and came back a minute later saying the door hadn't opened but had closed. Nobody said another word about the door and I suspect nobody gave it another thought. At least for my part I'd forgotten it the next second. And we only thought of the door again when Estela and I returned from the long weekend, the night of the following Monday, and found that we'd had a break-in.

"They'd broken one of the windows by the door, those small, rectangular windows on the right as you enter the house. Remember? They reached a hand in and opened the door from the inside. Has anything like that ever happened to you, Vásquez? Do you know what it's like coming home for the first time after thieves have been in your house? It's a feeling of desolation, of total frustration, impotence, and injustice. Stupid feelings, because who's going to be so ridiculous as to talk about justice when someone's just broken into your house, right? It's like saying that was impolite to someone who's just shot you three times. But that's what you feel. I told Estela to go back to the car and I would take a look. One doesn't say *look and see if they're still here*, one just says *take a look*. 'Oh, spare me the heroics,' she said, and went in first. We looked through room by room, but you know in these cases that nobody's there, that they left hours ago. And of course, there was nobody there. And they hadn't wrecked the place either. They took small things: jewelry, a laptop, loose change that had been on my

bedside table. From the downstairs cabinet they'd taken the kaleidoscope and the old pistols. They hadn't taken my big computer, because
of its size, but they did break the lock on my desk drawer and took
everything that was in there, including what I inherited from my father: all that we were going to return as soon as we could.

"Yes, that's right: what you saw that night in my house, they took
that. Other things that you didn't see, all that too. Everything, Vásquez.
They took it all, those things all ended up in the same bag as the valu-
ables. I imagined them emptying the drawers and later asking themselves what all that shit was, excuse me, a piece of bone in a yellowish
liquid, and I imagined them pouring the liquid into a toilet I imagined
to be green, I don't know why, and throwing the bone and jar away
separately. I never cried over lost things, not even as a child, but that
night I cried. I wept because my father was not there to weep for
me. Or rather, I wept because my father was not there, and he would
have wept for his things. I wept to replace my father's absent weeping.
That's why I didn't get in touch with you, Vásquez, I suppose I don't
need to explain it. Because there was no longer any need for any column or interview. Because now there was nothing to return.

"I've been full of regrets for two years now. Regretting that I hadn't
decided to return my father's inheritance earlier. Regretting not having kept them in a safe, as Estela had sometimes advised me. I'd say
what for, since I'm the only one the things matter to, and besides, no
one knows they're here. But Estela said that things that matter only to
you should be cared for more than other things, because usually they
cannot be replaced, and *that's why they matter only to you*. But I didn't
take her advice, of course, and what happened happened. And during
all this time I've tried to mourn them, as if someone had died. And I
have to tell you that I had achieved it or I was achieving it, Vásquez.
When I wrote you that e-mail, what I had in mind was to tell you what

I've just told you: explain that what happened to thousands of people in Bogotá had happened to me. Tell you: 'Now I'm one more, Vásquez, now I'm part of the statistics. The incredible thing is getting to this age without it having happened to me before.' Or tell you: 'Imagine, Vásquez, what bad luck. They grabbed a handful of things, a bit by chance. They took everything from the drawers of my filing cabinet and there went my father's things. And what can you say? What bad luck: that's all you can say. That's what they call a rotten break. They don't know what they took, Vásquez. The bastards don't know what they took or the hurt they caused.' I was going to tell you all that. That's probably all I would have told you if you hadn't gotten ahead of me. Because now, with what you just told me, with that little detail that would be superficial or dull in other circumstances, everything's changed."

"I don't understand," I said finally. "What is *everything*? Why has *everything* changed?"

"How long ago did we leave the cafeteria, Vásquez? How long have we been talking about this matter? Fifteen, twenty minutes? Let's say twenty. If you could see what was going through my head, what has gone through my head in these twenty minutes, you'd die of fright. A whole life has turned upside down in these twenty minutes. Do you know why, Vásquez? Because while we were walking side by side down corridors, while we were going up and down in elevators, I have done nothing but remember what Estela used to say. You already know: if I thought my things were safe, if I thought nothing would ever happen to them, it was *because nobody knew they were here and because they didn't matter to anyone else*. But now you tell me what you told me and all those certainties begin to change. In these twenty minutes everything that's happened over the last few years has changed, and what I see now frightens me and would frighten you if you could see it, if you could enter my head and see the difference between what I thought I was experiencing and what I now think I experienced. Because you just made a confession that was unimportant to you, and the only thing I can think about those bones my father left to me before he died is this: that two years ago there was a person in the world who knew of their existence, that there was someone else in the world they mattered to. Or rather: another. There were two of us, you and I, and now there's another. Now there's Carballo. Now Carballo is with us. Two years ago, when I came home from a trip and found that my inheritance from my father had been stolen, Carballo already knew it was there. How did he know? Because you told him, Vásquez. Because you told him."

YES, IT WAS TWENTY MINUTES, twenty long minutes that Benavides spoke to me nonstop while guiding me through the labyrinths of the Santa Fe clinic, from the cafeteria to the door to the first floor, from the door to the corridor with the tall windows that leads to the buildings, and arriving through that narrow corridor (where one has the impression of pressing oneself against the wall to avoid running into a person coming the other way) to the elevators that go up to the doctor's offices. I accompanied him to his while he talked. I saw him pass between the secretaries' large desks, sad and deserted at this hour of the night, and open his office door and look for something in the filing cabinet, and then turn into the other room, where the blue examining table stood covered with a paper sheet, and tug a white lab coat exactly like the one he was wearing off a hanger, all this while he kept talking. He handed the white coat to me—"Hold this for me," he said—and kept talking. He did not stop talking. I accompanied him down in the elevator, back to the second floor of the towers and then back, through the corridor with the windows, to the main door, and he did not stop talking; and I accompanied him up that stairway of speckled steps and metal handrail that left a sour smell on one's palms, and he did not stop talking; I accompanied him to the fourth floor, and we walked together until we reached a glass door where a woman with an exhausted face and a large mole on her forehead, sitting behind a chipboard desk, greeted him: "Dr. Benavides, how wonderful to see you. Are you going to room 426?" A bell rang and Benavides pushed open the glass door. Only then did he stop talking about Carballo and the things stolen from his private drawer.

"Dr. Vásquez," he said, "are you going to put that coat on or not?" and then he spoke to the woman with a mocking smile. "Oh, Carmencita, doctors these days."

I was taken by surprise. And when one is taken by surprise in front of a third person, the instinct is always to play along or hold up the fiction the other has embarked us on: one feels like an actor who must maintain the illusion while in the scene, and only later ask for explanations. Carmencita looked at me with concerned eyes.

"Of course," I said. In order to put the coat on, first I put the book Benavides had given me between my knees. It was not an easy operation. "Sorry, I was a bit distracted," I said. But when the glass door had closed behind us I grabbed Benavides by the arm: "What is this, Francisco? What are you doing?"

"I want you to come with me."

"Where? Don't you think our conversation's been left half finished?"

"No, it's been left *interrupta*. Like the occasional coitus. We'll finish it later."

"But what you just told me is huge," I insisted. "Do you really think Carballo could have done that? Do you think he's capable of such a thing?"

"How ingenuous you are, Vásquez. Carlos is capable of that and much more. How is it possible you haven't realized by now? What happens is that something is one thing and something else is quite another. But what I'm telling you is we'll continue this later. This conversation, I mean: I swear we'll continue it later." He delicately removed my hand. "Right now I have other things to think about."

I followed him to the end of the corridor, the way a member of a cult follows his leader: the white coat I'd recently put on made me vulnerable to Dr. Benavides's magnetism. We went into a room on the right-hand side. The blinds were up and the window was an imperfectly black cloth. First I noticed a bald man reading the newspaper sitting at the far end of a green sofa, right up against the armrest as if the rest of the sofa were reserved for someone else. When he saw us come in he closed the newspaper (a dexterous flick of the wrists), folded it twice, and left it on the armrest to stand up and greet Benavides. It was a normal greeting—he shook his hand, smiled, said a couple of words—but something I couldn't figure out made me feel the power that the presence of Benavides had in this room, or rather the respect and even admiration he inspired in the man on the sofa. That was when I noticed the other presence: that of the woman lying in the bed, who seemed to be asleep or resting when we came in and who was now opening her eyes, big eyes that not even the gray rings under them could make ugly, eyes of a disproportionate size that nevertheless fit mysteriously into the proportions of that face and its tired, corroded, wasted beauty.

"This is Dr. Vásquez," Benavides introduced me. "I spoke to him about Andrea's case. He has my complete trust."

The bald man held his hand out to me. "Pleased to meet you," he said, "I'm Andrea's father." The woman in the bed smiled with a genuine but forced smile, as if the movement hurt. I got a better look at her: from the skin on her face and the color of her hair I thought she must be a little over thirty, even though her posture and attitude were those of a woman already worn out by life. Benavides was talking to me: he mentioned the words *immunological problem*, he said the patient had been bedridden for several years without any real possibility of improvement or cure, and I thought how astute he was. He spoke in simple terms so that I would understand, but it seemed as though he was doing so for his patient's benefit. He explained that the latest medical advice, after a diagnosis of ischemia, had established the necessity of amputating the left leg. Andrea received these words without flinching: her immense eyes stayed open, looking at the top of the wall, where a metal arm supported a television that was turned off. The father squeezed his eyes shut and opened them again, and it seemed obvious to me that the daughter had not inherited her formidable eyes from him. Benavides sat down beside him on the sofa; there was not room for me but I didn't care: the image of the three men seated as if in an audience for a show starring Andrea would have been a bit ridiculous. So I remained standing beside the sink, as I had sometimes seen doctors do in these situations: associates, assistants, nurses, or mere onlookers. I did not fit into any of those categories: I was an impostor and had been dragged into this imposture by Dr. Benavides. Why? What reasons could Benavides have for laying this ambush for me? He had planned it from the beginning, for he must undoubtedly have been thinking of this moment when he went back to his office for his spare lab coat. The coat smelled clean; in the breast pocket was a blue pen; I put my hands in the side pockets, but I didn't find anything in them. "Okay, I'm listening," Benavides said then.

"The thing is," said the father. Then he stopped. He turned to his daughter. "Do you want to tell him?"

"No, you tell him," said Andrea. She had a deep, mellow voice.

There was something about her that, in spite of her circumstances, I could only call charisma.

"Well," said her father. "We've been thinking, thinking very hard."

Andrea interrupted him. "No, I'd rather tell him myself," she said. "If you don't mind."

"I don't mind," said her father.

"We don't want," said Andrea. Now she was speaking to Benavides: her eyes had fixed on him like two beacons in the night. "Or rather, I'm the one who doesn't want it. Papá agrees."

"You don't want to go ahead with the amputation?" asked Benavides.

"It's not that," said Andrea. "It's that I don't want to go ahead."

Benavides said: "I understand." His voice at that moment was also one I hadn't heard before: affectionate but not paternalistic, capable of solidarity and sympathy but careful not to overstep. "I understand," he said again, "I do understand." He lowered his voice. "Well, we've talked about this a lot. You've kept in mind all that we've talked about, I imagine."

"Yes," said the father.

"I'm tired, Doctor," said Andrea.

"I know," said Benavides.

"I am very, very tired. I cannot go on. And anyway, what can happen if we do it? What can happen if they take my leg off? Is there any possibility I'll get better?"

Benavides looked her in the eyes. He placed his two hands on the file, as if referring to it without doing so. "No, there is not," he said.

"No, right?" said Andrea.

"No," said Benavides.

"That's why," said Andrea. "You tell me if I'm mistaken, Doctor, but the only thing we'll gain by this is more time. More time for me to live like this, without any changes, just waiting until they have to amputate the other one. Because that's how it is, isn't it? Within a few months we'll have to amputate my other leg, won't we? Tell me, Doctor, tell me if I'm wrong."

"No, you're not wrong," said Benavides. "As far as we can predict, that's exactly how it is."

The doctor hadn't taken his eyes off her for an instant. I admired the courage that must take, because not even I, who kept to the fringes of the conversation, could look at Andrea for long, and when Andrea's father looked at me I was unable to hold his gaze: I sought refuge in my telephone, where I pretended to take notes, or in the transparent bags of IV solution, or even in Andrea's profile: her tied-back hair, her pale neck where a thick artery was visible, or her athletic arms.

"In other words," said Andrea, "all care is palliative. There is nothing else to be done: all they can offer is time. Isn't that true?"

"That's true."

"Well, Papá and I," she said, "have been talking. And we've decided we don't want more time." The father hung his head and began to sob. "I'm just so tired," said Andrea. And then: "Forgive me, Papá." And she started to cry as well.

Benavides went over to the bed and held Andrea's left hand in both of his. Hers was pale, strong but small, and the doctor's seemed to devour it. "It's fine," said Benavides. "You have every right. You also have every right to ask for forgiveness, but you don't have to. You are living through this, nobody else. And you have been brave: you've been very brave, I have seldom seen people as brave as you two. I'm not going to try to convince you of anything. First, because I've given you all the necessary information. Second, because I would do the same thing in your position. Doctors should cure when possible. When it's not possible, we should alleviate. And if that's not possible, there's nothing more to do than accompany and support, so all this will happen under the best conditions. I am going to continue to accompany you as I have been doing, but only if you want me to, Andrea, only if you allow me to because it seems useful or necessary."

Andrea wept briefly: the disciplined weeping of someone who has already suffered a lot. She ran a hand over her eyes, softly, and then reached for a tissue on the bedside table and used it to clean the tip of her nose, as if out of vanity, as if wanting to dull the shine on her skin.

"And now what?"

"We have to do some paperwork," said Benavides. "Tomorrow we can check you out of the clinic. You can go home."

"Home," Andrea said with a smile.

"We're going home," said her father.

"Yes," said Andrea. "Yes. And then? What are you going to do, Doctor?"

"We'll do some palliative care," said Benavides.

"And then?"

"Then nothing."

"Then you'll do nothing," said her father. It seemed like a question, but it wasn't.

"Sometimes," said Benavides, "not doing anything is the correct thing to do."

"Thank you," said Andrea.

"Tomorrow you can leave," said Benavides.

"Yes," said Andrea. "Oh, yes, tomorrow I'm leaving. I'm leaving this place, going home, to my own bed."

"To your own bed," said her father.

"Now I need you, Mr. Giraldo," said Benavides. "To sign a few things for me." And to Andrea: "We won't be long."

They left. Andrea and I remained alone in the room. She was

looking at the ceiling and I was looking at her and painfully aware that all the empathy in the world wouldn't be enough for me to guess what was going through her head. She had just made the decision to die: Who does one think of when that happens? Where was her partner, if she was in a relationship? Where were her children? Maybe she was regretting errors she hadn't rectified, or maybe she was remembering some long-ago moment of happiness. Or maybe she would be frightened: frightened of what was to come. I saw her blink once, twice, squeezing her eyes the way we do to get a tear out, and then she looked at me. "And what's your opinion, Doctor?"

"Pardon?"

"You know my case. What do you think? Am I mistaken?"

"That's something only you can know," I told her. Then I thought that was cowardice, even more glaring in the face of the courage Andrea had shown: not just in making the decision, but in asking another doctor. Someone less gutsy would prefer not to seek out other opinions, in case they made her doubt something she'd decided at the cost of so much effort. "No," I said. "I don't think you're mistaken."

She kept looking at me.

"I'm scared," she said. "The problem is that I'm also tired. And I'm more tired than scared."

"Look, Andrea," I said. "I cannot know what you're feeling. Most doctors act like they do know, but it's not true. They don't know, they just read your medical history and try to guess. I can tell you one thing: Dr. Benavides is one of those who does know. And if he offers you his companionship and his support, you shouldn't be afraid: you're in the best hands in the world."

I truly believed this, of course, and I was sure Andrea would share that banal diagnosis. But had I foreseen her surprising question, I would have liked to tell her something else: that I admired her, that I envied her courage and her tenacity and her incredible maturity, that I was infinitely grateful (though I didn't know why) for the privilege of having been present at this moment. No, *maturity* wasn't the word I was looking for, maturity wasn't what I was seeing in the body and eyes of this woman. It was sovereignty, yes, that's what it was: sovereignty was what her body and her eyes were radiating. Death would take Andrea and her big eyes in a matter of months, but even at the moment of death, I thought, she would still be in perfect command of her body. And death would have no right to pride itself on anything. I thought: *Death, be not proud.* I translated the line into Spanish in my head and was about to say it aloud to Andrea, but then I thought Andrea might take me for a lunatic or insensitive, because who starts quoting old English poems at a moment like this (poetry is not a consolation or lifesaver for everyone, although it's taken me years to discover that). But I couldn't keep my mind from putting itself to the task of translating another of those lines: when death is called *Slave to fate, chance, kings, and desperate men*; when death is accused of dwelling *with poison, war, and sickness.* What this old poem was saying is that death depended on these instances, illness, war, poison, desperate men, kings, chance, and fate. Why, then, should death be proud, the poem said, and I thought, Yes, why? Andrea, however, had all the reasons in the world to be proud of herself, of her courage and her mettle, and also of the courage and mettle that had been very visible on her father's exhausted face. But I couldn't tell her. No, I couldn't tell Andrea that, I couldn't tell her that I barely knew her but was already proud of her, and death had nothing to pride itself on. Andrea picked up the electrical control of the bed and raised the back until she was almost sitting up, she leaned on her arms, made a straining effort, and her body, changing position, was no longer that of a dying woman.

I saw her cover her face with her hands, not to cry, but to take a deep breath; her shoulders raised. When she uncovered her face, her expression had transformed: it was as if the decision had lifted a weight, I thought, as if the accepted desire to abandon the struggle and die in peace had brought here, to this room on the fourth floor of the Santa Fe clinic, to the hospital bed she occupied in the middle of the room, a new serenity. It was a moment at once terrifying and beautiful, but I didn't know how to say where the beauty was. Of course, I could be misinterpreting the situation. That would not have been rare or unusual, either, for we spend most of our time doing that: misinterpreting others, reading them in the wrong key, trying to take a leap toward them and then falling into the abyss. There is no real way to know what goes on inside, though the illusion might be never so attractive: all the time vast spaces open between us and others, and the mirage of comprehension or empathy is just that, a mirage. We are all enclosed in our own incommunicable experience, and death is the least communicable experience of all, and after death, the most incommunicable experience is the desire to die. That's what was happening there: between Andrea and me an immense abyss was yawning, for there was no common ground between her, who had decided to die and in some way no longer belonged to the world of the living, and me, who was firmly installed in that world, who could make plans for myself and for my family. I remembered another line: *And soonest our best men with thee do go.* It wasn't true, of course (poetry can also lie to us, it is also capable of the occasional demagoguery), but maybe it was in this case.

"What book did you bring?" Andrea asked.

She'd noticed my gift from Benavides. I'd almost forgotten it: I had set it down on the edge of the sink, under the disinfectant dispenser, and seeing it again surprised me as an object found on the sidewalk at night might have done.

"Oh, this," I said. "Dr. Benavides just gave it to me. There's an article of his in it."

"An article by the doctor?"

"Yes."

"You don't say," she puffed. "So my doctor is also a writer." She leaned back a little more, or made herself comfortable. "And what is it on?"

There was no sense in pretending. "On death," I said.

"Oh, no," she said. For the third time I saw her smile. "I don't like silly coincidences." And then: "Unless it's not a coincidence."

"What do you mean?"

"Nothing, Doctor, don't pay any attention to me," said Andrea. "And what's the article called?"

"Dr. Benavides's article?"

"Of course. What do I care about the rest?"

I turned to the table of contents and scanned it for Dr. Benavides's article. I found it after "Explorations of Death, from Tolstoy to Juan Rulfo" and before "The Virtue of Suffering: Death as an Opportunity for Christian Charity." The title was a single word, "Orthothanasia," and its rounded shapes floated above its author's name like a badly made cornice. I pronounced it and felt something in my mouth. "Let's see, let me see," said Andrea. I handed her the book and saw her squint to see better; in a fraction of a second I decided she was farsighted and used reading glasses, but that she'd given them up or forgotten them somewhere and not bothered to go back for them because in any case she wasn't such a regular reader, or because her recent days had been filled with an intense depression and nobody reads a newspaper in the midst of a depression, or simply because what for anymore. I thought: Her life is a *what for anymore*. "Orthothanasia," Andrea was saying and repeating, as if measuring the word before deciding whether to buy it. "Orthothanasia."

"A correct death," I said.

"And what did you think of it?"

"I haven't read it."

"You haven't? But it's been underlined," she said. "You didn't underline it?"

"I haven't opened the book yet," I said. "Dr. Benavides just gave it to me."

"Who would have underlined it? Do people underline things they've written themselves?"

"I don't write," I said. "I wouldn't know."

But for an instant I considered adding: *It runs in the family. Benavides's father also underlined things he read: a newspaper article on the assassination of Kennedy, for example.* But I kept quiet.

"It says here the doctor is a physician and surgeon, specializing in bioethics, full professor, and I don't know what else. He has more titles than this contents page, our Dr. Benavides."

"Like I said: you're in the best hands."

"Oh, don't talk nonsense, Doctor," she scolded me. "I know I am, but it's not because of his diplomas." I immediately saw on her face an expression of embarrassment, as if she regretted being impolite, when all she'd done was denounce my frivolous or stupid comment. "Listen, listen to this," she said then. She half closed her eyes, held the book close to her face, and read: *"Physicians' feelings of guilt at the death of their patients emerge from the profound negation that contemporary medical science accords natural death.* That's underlined. *We can recall Alexander the Great, who is said to have exclaimed, 'I am dying from the treatment of too many physicians.'* That's also underlined. Here's a long section. Almost the whole paragraph is underlined." Andrea began to read: *"I received a phone call from an old friend,"* she said, but then she stopped. She carried on reading in silence; in the silence of the room I saw her eyes moving, but her mouth did not speak the words. "Ah," she said then.

"What's the matter?" I asked.

She closed the book and handed it back to me. "Nothing," she said. "What's taking them so long?"

"You're not going to keep reading to me?"

"They're taking too long," said Andrea, but I had the impression that she was no longer talking to me. "Paperwork, always red tape. Even to die in this country you have to do paperwork."

The miraculous buoyancy had vanished from her face, from her gestures. "Even to die," she repeated, and then started to cry. Something in Benavides's article had produced this metamorphosis; I realized, with some panic, that I didn't know what to do. "Andrea," I said, because in difficult situations we tend to use people's names as charms, imputing magical properties to them. But she didn't hear me: she was crying with her eyes open, at first soundlessly, then allowing herself a little girl's delicate sobs. I sat down on the edge of the bed, beside her, without knowing if this was something doctors did or if I was violating some rule, written or unwritten, of behavior or even ethics. Andrea hugged me and I let her hug me and soon was hugging her as well. I felt under my palm the hardness of her vertebrae and then I heard her speak. "I don't have any stories to tell," she said. "What do you mean, Andrea?" I asked. But she didn't want to explain anything. She pulled back. Then I heard footsteps in the hall and the latch of the door as it opened, and I jumped up, as if to avoid being caught out, as if Andrea and I had been doing something forbidden: flirting or inappropriate contact masking an illegitimate attraction. There, on the sheet, the imprint of my weight remained when Benavides and Andrea's father walked in. I thought that the man had just signed for the death of his daughter. Benavides was going to say something, but I beat him to it:

"I'll wait for you outside, Doctor," I said. "Take your time."

I left the room and returned the way we'd come. Carmencita

opened the glass door and said good-bye: "Have a nice evening, Doctor." But I didn't leave: there was no one in the waiting room, and I sat down there, in front of a muted television where three men in ties and a woman in a tailored suit argued over something so important it deserved their simultaneous gesticulations. I opened the book, looked for the article, found the sentence Andrea had read out loud and read what followed, the phrases underlined by Benavides with intentions that were perhaps less transparent than one might think. It was a brief paragraph-long tale, which told of a friend of Benavides with a hematologic problem by then incurable. "He was clear that the possibility of continuing with transfusions indefinitely no longer made sense," wrote Benavides, so he had decided to abandon all treatment and begin to die a natural death. "Sharing with him and his family his last days in his house, with gentle nursing care, in a serene and restful way, listening to his stories of times gone by, long before mine, I received one of his many teachings. I was able to see what was a good way to die." I looked up; on the screen, the woman was still gesturing and talking with a twisted sneer on her face. I thought: It's a sneer of hatred. I turned back to the book: "His universe was gradually reduced to the room, his close family, and his memories," wrote Benavides of his friend. "One afternoon, he closed his eyes like when we fall asleep after an arduous day's work, with the satisfaction of a duty fulfilled." The woman on the screen was showing her teeth, jutting out her jaw, running her dark tongue over her lips, hating her opponents or those who contradicted her, but I wasn't thinking of her, I was thinking of Andrea and what she'd tearfully told me: "I have no stories to tell."

Then I thought I understood. I understood (or believed I understood) that this brave woman had been undone by Benavides's tale: those affectionate words about his friend who was ill beyond recovery, the man who told him stories about the distant past, beside his close family, wrapped up in his memories. At thirty-odd years of age, Andrea was too young to have stories to tell or memories to protect her. "I have no stories to tell," she'd said, and the more I thought of it, the clearer it seemed that this moment of profound sadness had overcome her as a consequence of an underlined sentence in the article by Benavides. A sentence about a man who, like her, had stopped belonging to this world, who had taken, as she had, the free and sovereign decision to die a natural death, who had defeated death, as she had: had told it not to be proud; had reclaimed that pride for himself. Yes, the two of them were equals, that anonymous, dying friend and Andrea, the patient: the patient Andrea. Only one thing distinguished them, and that was the stories they could tell to those who wished to hear them, the memories they could surround themselves with in order to die in peace. That tiny difference, I understood or believed I understood, had provoked a sort of epiphany in Andrea the origins of which I was unable to track or even conjecture, but which left me in such a state of distraction I didn't notice the moment the glass door opened and Benavides arrived at my side.

"Which way are you going?" he said. "Would it be too much trouble to give me a lift? See if we can finish these incomplete conversations."

I was going to the opposite side of the city: I was going south and he lived in the north. And besides, it was almost eleven at night.

"No trouble at all," I said. "Conversations need to be finished."

WE WERE DRIVING north up the illuminated avenue, repeating together the route I had taken alone nine years earlier, and doing so in silence by imposition or order of Benavides. As we pulled out of the clinic parking lot, it had felt urgent to ask him about the extremely strange mise-en-scène we'd just shared; I asked him, in other words, why he had stuck me into that whole matter: why he had lent me the white coat, why he had forced me to participate in that imposture, why he had thought it necessary or beneficial or perhaps amusing for me to witness his conversation with a patient and the moment when that patient decides to set out for her own death. But Benavides, without taking his eyes off the windshield and the Carrera Novena stretching out in front of us, answered: "I don't want to talk about that."

"Let's see, Francisco," I said. "First you put me into such a situation. You oblige me to pass for someone else and see something that has nothing to do with me. And now you say you don't want to talk about it?"

"Exactly. I don't want to talk about it."

"But it's not that easy," I said. "I'm going to need . . ."

"Outside the hospital," said Benavides with a hint of impatience, "I do not speak of my terminal patients. It's a decision I made many years ago and it still seems the best decision I ever made. One has to keep one's lives separate, Vásquez, if not one can go crazy. This is exhausting, it sucks one's energy. And like any other person, I have limited energy."

It seemed like an excuse to me, of course. But it was such a sensible excuse, and the tiredness on the doctor's face was so plausible, that I could do nothing but accept it. I had also left Andrea Giraldo's room feeling that I'd left my strength inside it: tangled in the sheets I'd sat on, or maybe absorbed into the body of the woman who'd decided to die: those fragile bones that my embrace had briefly encircled in an attempt to offer a little clumsy consolation to someone who seemed to need it. After twenty blocks of perfect silence, I realized Benavides had closed his eyes. He seemed to be asleep, but his neck was straight: he wasn't nodding off, his chin wasn't dropping onto his chest. I didn't dare to pull him out of the refuge he'd improvised, for that's how I imagined it, a refuge, what he needed at that moment. For my part, I still had the same questions: What had Benavides sought by tricking me into a scene for which I was not prepared? What did he want me to see or hear, if that's what it was about? Did he know that Andrea would make her decision at that exact moment? And what had happened with the book? Had he planned that Andrea and I would somehow end up leafing through the pages of his article and reading the sentences he'd underlined? Had he given it to me with that intention? When he left the room and left us alone, had he foreseen what ended up happening? This idea had also passed through my head that long-ago night when I first met Carballo: that Benavides knew and controlled much more than he seemed to control and know.

Benavides came back to life only when we arrived at his gate. The doorman came over to the car to check my identity; I opened the window and a cold wind invaded the car like a cloud of flies. "I'm here with Dr. Benavides," I said in a loud voice. "Interior twenty-three." When I pointed to him so the doorman could see him, Benavides opened his eyes: not like someone who'd been sleeping, but as if a couple of seconds of reflection had gone by.

"Well, here we are," he said. "Thank you."

The house was dark. Even the entrance light was off, the one you always leave on to pretend somebody's home and deter thieves. In front of the door, Benavides put a hand on a small pane of glass and said: "This is the one they broke." I did as he had: put my hand on the new pane of glass, which had replaced the broken one, and meanwhile Benavides was telling me: "They didn't break the upper one, they didn't break the lower one. They broke this one: the one at the exact level of the door latch."

"All doors in the world have the latch at the same height," I said.

But he didn't hear me. "They walked in here," he said, "as if they owned the place." He turned to the right, toward the living room. "I thought at first that they'd seen my cabinet: the kaleidoscope, et cetera. And then they'd gone upstairs to see what else there was. But not anymore."

"You don't think so now."

"No."

"Now you think it was Carballo."

"Come here, Vásquez," said Benavides. "Come with me."

He went up the stairs and I went up behind him, with the feeling of going over a crime scene: not a broken-into house, but the place where someone had been killed. It was cold, as if uninhabited, and everything was dark, so Benavides had to turn on lights—making the world come to life in front of us—as we went along. "What I believe is that they came first of all here, to my study," said Benavides. "Because they already knew. They knew perfectly well what they were looking for and where to find it. And once they'd found it they had a look around, messing the place up a bit. They found some jewelry, a bit of cash, a couple of gadgets they could sell, a couple of things that looked like antiques. But that was after the main objective. That was when the main objective was already in the bag, in a manner of speaking, and it's very possible that it might have been just a cover-up. The problem is that it's difficult to imagine the details of the business. Imagining others is always difficult, but it's more difficult to imagine someone we thought we knew and now it turns out we don't know. I have tried to imagine Carballo since we left the cafeteria, but I can't complete the picture. First I think: No, it couldn't be him, it couldn't have been him. Carballo, my father's disciple. Carlos, my friend, Carlos Carballo, the friend with whom I've always shared an interest in things from the past . . . And then I think: The *only* friend with whom I share these interests. *The only one* who could have an interest in my inheritance from my father, in the bones of a politician assassinated sixty-six years ago. Thanks to you, *the only one* who could imagine where they were kept. You see, Vásquez: the only one, the only one, the only one."

"But what for?" I asked. "Why was he going to want to steal these things now?"

"Not now. Two years ago."

"Whatever. I told him you had these things in your possession nine years ago. If it's true that he stole them, why did he wait seven years?"

Benavides sat down in his black chair. "I haven't the slightest idea," he said. "But I don't have to find a thief's reasons. I only have to consider the facts and make a logical deduction. Who else, Vásquez? Who else would have wanted to take it?"

"Someone who didn't know what it was," I said.

"I don't think so."

"Someone who saw a locked drawer and took everything inside it. Probably thinking, also logically, that nobody locks a drawer unless it has something valuable in it. *This* is logical, Francisco. Not thinking that a lifelong friend is going to decide to break windows and sneak into other people's houses from one day to the next. Look, Carballo and I never hit it off. And it's true that he's a pathological liar and an impostor and even a forger. But from there to thinking he's a thief is a big leap."

"You don't know him the way I do," said Benavides. "You don't know what he's capable of. I do, because I've lived with him for many years now. With him and his obsessions. We all have obsessions, Vásquez, big or small. But I've never known anyone like Carballo, someone who organizes his entire life around a single idea. Carlos is divorced, did you know that?"

"No, he never told me. Nor was there ever any reason for him to tell me about his private life."

"Well, he is. He married a woman from Cali toward the end of the 1970s. Really nice, with one of those smiles that cheer up anyone's day. And she was also a woman with both feet on the ground. Carlos eventually left her. Do you know why? Because she didn't understand April 9."

"What part of it?"

"She didn't understand that Gaitán could have been killed by more than one person. That he could have been killed by someone other than Roa Sierra. She made fun of that. She said to Carballo: 'Tell me, my love, how many fingers fit on the trigger of a pistol?' Carballo couldn't stand it. He packed up his things one day and left. He spent a few weeks sleeping on my father's sofa."

"But that doesn't necessarily mean anything, Francisco."

"You don't think so?"

"I don't think so."

I crouched down beside the violated desk drawer. I saw its broken lock, the wood splintered along the edge of the drawer, and thought of the screwdriver and hammer that would have produced this effect. Dust had accumulated inside, as if it had been left open for too many days, and an earwig was walking around in one corner. "What is a fanatic, Vásquez?" said Benavides. "A fanatic is a person who's only good for one thing in this life, who discovers what that thing is and devotes all his time to it, down to the last second. That thing interests him for some special reason. Because he can do something with it, because it helps him to get money, or power, or a woman, or several women, or to feel better with himself, to feed his ego, to earn his path to heaven, to change the world. Of course, changing the world feeds an ego, brings money and power and women. People also do what they do for that, even the fanatic. Sometimes the fanatic does what he does for much more mysterious reasons, reasons that do not fall under any of the categories we've invented. With time these reasons get mixed up, confused, and converted into an obsession that borders on the irrational, a feeling or a personal and inevitable mission, of having been born for something. In any case, this person is distinguishable in many ways but one of them is extremely clear: he does what he has to do. He eliminates from his life all that does not serve the cause. If it's useful, he does it or gets it. No matter what it takes."

"And you think Carballo is a fanatic."

"Well, he acts like a fanatic, at least," said Benavides. "There are many kinds of fanatics, Vásquez. There are fanatics who kill and others who don't. There are a thousand ways to be a fanatic, a thousand different ways, stages going from a hunger strike to keep trees from being cut down to planting a bomb because the Quran says such and such a thing. I might be wrong, but I think in that progression of stages someone who breaks into a friend's house and steals certain things that will be useful to him fits the bill. Or someone who feels, due to some twisted mechanism, that these things belong to him, that they belong more to him than to his friend, that they should be his property and that they're not because of life's unfairness. Is it impossible that things happened that way? Carballo finds out by accident that Gaitán's vertebra is here in my house, the vertebra that belonged to my father since the autopsy of 1960. He flies into a rage: those things were his *maestro*'s, his mentor's, and they would be better in the hands of the beloved disciple than the prodigal son. What mistake, what grave mistake had his *maestro* committed in leaving these things in the hands of his son, who does not understand them or appreciate them as much as he, the disciple, does. For the son, they are a simple historical curiosity, a collector's pleasure, a pastime, or a fetish in the best of cases. For the disciple, on the other hand, they are a mission. Yes, that's it: they are part of a mission, they are things that serve a more elevated goal. And nobody else realizes. Everybody else is an amateur."

"God gives bread to the toothless."

"Exactly."

"And the mission is the book?"

"I can't think of another one," said Benavides. "Yes, Vásquez, the book. That book that he wanted you to write. Or rather: the information or the story that book was going to bring to light. His theory of the conspiracy that killed Gaitán. That obsession he's been turning over his whole life, like my father before him. With the difference that for my father it was a game. A serious game, but a game after all." The same words he'd used nine years earlier. I don't have a good memory, not for names or faces or messages, but I do remember words, their order and rhythm and secret music. And these were the same words Benavides had pronounced the night he showed me Gaitán's vertebra. "My imagination doesn't stretch far enough to know what's happened over these years. Carballo does not confide in me, but then he confides in no one. Nothing changes the fact that he is such a friend of the family, or the fact that he's such a regular visitor to my house. There is a whole part of his life still in the dark for me, a secret. Something must have happened over the years: a discovery, an idea. I don't know, I haven't been able to form a chronology, a logical sequence. But it does seem very coincidental that the robbery should occur just after I decided to return my father's legacies. Better yet: right after I spoke to my family about the matter. When we all went to bed that night, the decision was already irreversible: we were going to start making contacts to bring my inheritances out into the world and try to get them exhibited in a museum, which is where they should be. And right then thieves break into the house. Is it not too big a coincidence? I think so: I think Carballo found out what we were planning to do and prevented it. I don't know how, I don't have that much imagination. But it's the simplest explanation. And experience and my wife have taught me that when there is a simple explanation, it's better not to look for a complicated one."

"But yours is super-complicated," I said. "The simple one is the other, Francisco. Regular, everyday burglars."

Benavides didn't hear me, or pretended not to hear me.

"The question now is: What do we do? What do we do to recover these things? We accept, for the sake of argument, that Carballo has them in his possession. How can we confirm it? The guy hasn't stopped coming to my house, Vásquez. His relationship with me and my family hasn't changed since the robbery. I didn't tell him about the robbery, of course, because I didn't want to tell him about my inheritances. I didn't want to confess that I'd hidden them from him for so many years. But now that I'm suspicious of him, I start thinking of every time I've invited him to lunch or dinner in the last couple of years. The poker face, Vásquez, the perfect performance! Not a twitch that might have given him away, it's impressive. I don't know how many times he sat in the dining room and talked to me about Gaitán, about Kennedy, about the coincidences he saw between the two crimes, and all *exactly* as he used to before the robbery. And me feeling guilty because now, after the robbery, he was never going to have the vertebra in his hands. I never wanted to show it to him, of course, but after the robbery it wasn't that I didn't want to: it was that I couldn't. And I felt bad about that, as if I'd taken something away from him. Me from him! Life's ironies, eh? There I was, listening to him talk about Gaitán, feeling bad for depriving him of a great satisfaction unbeknownst to him, and him meanwhile knowing that when he went home he could have the vertebra in his hands, see it with his own eyes, use it for his own ends that I was unable to imagine. To contribute to the dossier of his paranoia, to the body of evidence for his conspiracy theory."

"If he has it."

"Yes, if he has it," said Benavides. Then he went silent for a moment. I saw him stand up and walk around the chair, and then grip the black chair-back with both hands, like a shipwrecked man clutching a tree trunk. "Look, Vásquez, pay attention, please," he said. "What I'm about to tell you might seem like an indiscretion, but it's not. I was thinking about it at the clinic at the same time as I was telling you other things. I was thinking about it in the car, on the way here. I've been thinking about it since we got home, while we've been talking. The thing is: my father's things are mine and nobody else's. But I also know they're my country's patrimony and I want them to go back to being so after all these years. And what I don't want, what I definitely do not want, is for them to serve a fanatic's speculation about a painful past. Now, then: you are the only person who can confirm whether or not Carballo has these things or not. Life put you in this strange situation, Vásquez, and there's nothing to be done. Carballo wanted you to write a book. I suggest you go and offer yourself. Yes, just what you heard. Track him down, offer to write his fucking book, get inside his house, and find out. Nobody else is in the position you're in. If your friend Moreno-Durán were still alive, we'd ask him. But he's not alive. The one who's alive is you. And Carballo would open the doors of his house to you, he'd show you his documents, his evidence, all the material he has to reveal to the world the truth about the assassination of Gaitán. Place yourself at his side, tell him all he wants to hear, lie and act as much as you need to. And find out. I know the idea seems outlandish, but it's not: it's perfectly sensible. So do me this favor, Vásquez: go home, think it over tonight, and call me in the morning. And do not forget for a single moment that I am asking for your help. I need your help and I am asking for it. I am in your hands, Vásquez. I am in your hands."

V

THE MAJOR WOUND

One Sunday night I wrote to Carlos Carballo—to an address that Benavides gave me, since the one I had saved on my computer was long out of date—and told him I needed to talk to him. He answered immediately, and he did so with his customary disdain for those features of more conventional mind-sets: grammar, punctuation. *Cordial regards Juan Gabriel,* I read. *And what do I owe the surprise to?* I told him that many things had happened since our last encounter; that I had changed and my circumstances had changed; in the last few years, I explained, some curiosities that didn't previously exist had manifested themselves (that's what I said: "manifested themselves"), and bit by bit I had reached the conclusion that the book he had once offered me was part of my destiny (that's what I said: "part of my destiny"). I thought this rhetoric would fulfill Carballo's expectations; I felt like an impostor, but I also felt that this pretense was part of the mission

Francisco Benavides had entrusted to me, and that the end, therefore, justified the means. Then, seeing that Carballo didn't reply, I began to think that I'd shown my hand, and that this expert cardsharp had guessed or glimpsed my true intentions. I went to bed with that idea, thinking already of a subsidiary plan to carry out my mission without giving myself away. But at half past six in the morning my telephone rang. It was him.

"How did you get this number?" I asked.

Carballo didn't answer me. "So glad to hear you," he said. "Are you busy on Friday night?"

"No," I said. It was true, but I would have canceled any engagement anyway. "We could have dinner, if you want."

"No, not dinner," he answered. "I'm inviting you to come on my program."

That's how I found out about this unpredictable man's new incarnation. Carballo had managed to get his own radio program, a four-hour broadcast every night that went on air at midnight on which he interviewed (although that word was too *professional* for what happened in that space) one and sometimes two guests. For the last five years, *Night Owls* had enjoyed the presence of politicians, football players, conceptual artists, retired military officers, singers, soap opera actors, novelists, poets, poets who were also novelists, politicians who thought of themselves as poets, and singers who thought they were actors. It took me only a brief internet search to come to realize that this program I'd never heard anyone mention was for its faithful audience a sort of radio institution, valued even more for its necessarily minority and, so to speak, clandestine character. Guests received two assignments: bring their own music—ten or so songs to personalize the broadcast—and their own drinks, which could be a thermos of coffee, a flask of *aguardiente* or rum, or a water bottle. Apart from that, all he asked them to bring was an open mind and an appetite for conversation, for their participation took up the first two hours of *Night Owls*. During this time, Carballo talked with his guest and took calls from his listeners; during the following two hours, now on his own in the studio, he went on taking calls, often to comment on the guests' contribution after their departure, and he played music and delivered monologues over the airwaves; and thus he had become in recent years company for insomniacs and solitary people, those who stayed up all night by vocation or for work and also those who got up extremely early. Now he was inviting me to be part of that; it didn't seem too high a price to pay to be accepted back into his life.

So the next Friday, at half past eleven on a cold night, I was parking my car in front of the Todelar studios, and asking a bored doorman under a yellow light where I could find Carlos Carballo. He hesitated, looked in a ring binder; this man was apparently not part of *Night Owls'* captive audience. I listened to his imprecise directions, walked up a dim stairway to the second floor and down a carpeted and deserted corridor, barely lit by the occasional neon tube and the brightness from the occupied studios. I had a small bottle of whiskey in my hand; in the pocket of my jacket, on a memory stick, were my ten favorite songs, and as I handed the small plastic cylinder to Carballo I realized that every one of them, from "Eleanor Rigby" to "Las Ciudades," from one by Paul Simon to one by Serrat, spoke of solitude.

"The guest has arrived!" Carballo exclaimed, to nobody. "Come in, come in, make yourself at home."

Carballo was wearing faded jeans and a shirt that his belt didn't quite manage to control, and around his neck a black-and-white-checked scarf, although it wasn't cold. He looked paler than before, and I immediately associated this pallor with his current job: he had become a man who lives by night and sleeps during the day, and therefore sees little sunlight. That was undoubtedly the reason for the olive-colored circles under his eyes, the blue veins very visible through the stubble on his cheeks. Carballo did not ask me the questions people usually ask each other—what's up, how's it going, how've you been—but had me follow him straight into the studio and asked me to make myself comfortable in front of a microphone adorned with a tiny Colombian flag, while he closed the padded door and bent over the sound technician to give him a series of inaudible explanations. When he came back and took his seat and put on his headphones, motioning me with his long fingers to do the same, I thought he was being evasive on purpose: perhaps he wanted us to be on air when our conversation began, so we wouldn't have to go through frivolities or false courtesies. I thought he'd grown impatient with the formulas of social life. I also thought he'd grown shy or reserved. But I never thought he was setting a trap for me.

"Today we have a very special guest," he said. There was the Carballo I remembered: mixed in with his eccentricities, clichés flourished like weeds among his words. He introduced me in a perfunctory manner, and then told his listeners that this was not the first time we'd spoken. "Do my listeners, my night owls, know how we met?" asked Carballo, lowering his voice, adopting with no effort an intimacy that was, visibly, one of his tricks. "He broke my nose with a glass tumbler. That's how we met. This is the first time I've brought someone who has sent me to the hospital on the show. And I hope it'll be the last, don't you?" He let out a complicit little laugh, but it wasn't directed at me: before my eyes, Carballo was inventing a private relationship with the thousands of anonymous people listening to us at this moment. It was fascinating. "That was nine years ago now, nine years less a few months. And here we are, dear listeners, night owls: here we are as casual as can be. Do you know why? Because everything happens for a reason. How are you, Juan Gabriel?"

"Fine, thanks, Carlos," I said. "I wanted . . ."

"You are the author of several books, but you're also a columnist for *El Espectador*. And as a columnist you surprised us at the beginning of the year revealing an interest we didn't know you had: the assassination of Rafael Uribe Uribe."

That caught me off guard. By that point, I had almost completely forgotten that improvised column, but in a flash I remembered the commentary of an unhappy reader behind whose pseudonym lurked, I speculated, Carlos Carballo. Now I thought I must have been right.

"Well, actually the column was not only about Uribe Uribe," I said. "It was, most of all, about a book I liked. *Ghosts of Sarajevo*, it's called, and I recommend it to everyone. Furthermore, the column was about two different anniversaries, two crimes that happened—"

"How did you come to be interested in Uribe Uribe?" the host of the program interrupted me.

"I don't know," I told him. "It's a recent interest."

"Oh, really? But you mention it at the beginning of one of your novels, *The Secret History of Costaguana*. You mention Uribe Uribe and Galarza and Carvajal, his murderers. That was seven years ago now, so your interest can't be that recent."

"That's true. I'd forgotten about that, but it's true. I don't know, Carlos, I'm interested in that crime the way all Colombians are. I . . ."

"Do you think so? I'm not so sure. I don't know how many of my listeners, my night owls, know about Rafael Uribe Uribe. How many know how he died. Do you know how he died? Do you know how that happened?"

I knew something. That's what I would have liked to tell him: that I knew something, but it wasn't much. Mere generalities, a more or less fixed scene that my memory stored without knowing how it had come to be formed there: that's how we know the past. I knew, of course, what I had written in my column: that on October 15, 1914, a hundred years less eight months before that radio conversation, General Rafael Uribe Uribe was walking along the eastern sidewalk of Carrera Séptima when he was fatally wounded with hatchet blows by two carpenters. Yes, this I knew, and I'd known it since I was a child. I must have been nine or ten when my father took me to the place where it had happened, showed me the sad marble plaque that commemorated the event and told me about the assassins. Galarza and Carvajal: the music of those two surnames had been with me since then, like the chorus of a popular song, though it must have been some years before their respective first names would accompany them, before my juvenile awareness would finally separate them and begin to imagine the owners of those names as two individuals, not as a mysterious insoluble unity, a two-headed monster. I don't know how I thought of them as a boy there, walking with my family across Plaza de Bolívar, nor can I remember how I imagined the cruel and brutal scene that Bogotanos must have seen in 1914. I realized that my ignorance, beyond these generalities, had decorated the scene with falsehoods and inexactitudes.

I could have explained all that to Carballo, but I didn't. I just talked about Galarza and Carvajal and the sidewalk on the east side of the Capitol building. My interviewer grimaced with displeasure (invisible to his listeners, luckily) and kept talking.

"That's what history tells us," he mocked. "But my listeners know that history can be, how shall we put it, a tiny bit of a liar. Isn't that true, my dear Juan Gabriel?" Now his tone was sickly-sweet or condescending, or both at once. "The truth might be different, right? Just like the truth about Gaitán's assassination, as a random example, is different from the one we've been sold in our school textbooks."

"Yes, I wondered how long it was going to take you to bring up

Gaitán," I said, trying to regain control of the conversation with a bit of humor. I thought: *Gaitán, whose vertebra you've stolen.* "You know, my dear Carlos, that I don't believe in conspiracy theories very much. I know they are popular, I know that people—"

"One moment," he interrupted me again. "We have a call." He took his eyes off me (I felt like I was freed from a weight) and said with his gaze focused on the void: "Yes, good evening, with whom do I have the pleasure?"

"Good evening, Carlitos," said a man's voice. "Ismael, at your service."

"Don Ismael, what do you want to tell us tonight?"

"I also read young Velásquez's column," said Ismael's voice, distorted by static. Carballo didn't correct him on my name; I wasn't going to interrupt him to do so. "And I want to tell him something: if he's so interested in the First World War, he shouldn't rule out what he calls 'conspiracy theories' with such disdain."

"But it's not disdain," I tried to intervene. "It's—"

"In the column, you spoke of Franz Ferdinand," said Ismael. "You spoke of Gavrilo Princip. You said that the First World War began with that. May I ask you a question?"

I tried to be affable. "As many as you wish, Ismael."

"Do you know how the United States entered the war?"

It was unbelievable. I looked at my watch: not half an hour of the program had gone by and already I was being forced to sit through a sort of telephonic Western history exam. Carballo's eyes were wide open and he wore an expression of absolute seriousness, as if the most important thing in the world at that moment was the reason I was going to give for the United States joining the First World War, which at that moment was not the first, since they were unaware of the possibility of a second, but the Great War. That's what they called it: the

Great War. They also called it, with populist optimism, the War to End All Wars. The name of that conflict has changed over the years, as perhaps has its nature or the explanation we've invented to talk about it. Our capacity to name things is limited, and those limits are that much more sensitive or cruel if the things we're trying to name have disappeared forever. That's what the past is: a tale, a tale constructed over another tale, an artifice of verbs and nouns where we might be able to capture human pain, fear of death and eagerness to live, homesickness while battling in the trenches, worry for the soldier who has gone to the fields of Flanders and who might already be dead when we remember him.

"Let's see," I said. "President Wilson, if I'm not mistaken, declared war against Germany after the sinking of the *Lusitania*. It was a passenger steamer sunk by a German submarine. More than a thousand people died in the attack. Wilson didn't declare war immediately, but soon afterward he did."

"Okay, and tell me something," asked Ismael. "When was the *Lusitania* sunk?"

"I don't remember the exact date," I defended myself. "It must have been—"

"May 7, 1915," said Ismael. "And when did the English decipher the German codes?"

"When what?"

"The German codes. The secret military codes. When did the British crack the code?"

"I don't know, Ismael."

"In December of 1914," said the voice. "Some five months *before* the *Lusitania* went down. So tell me, then: if Sir Winston Churchill, who was then the First Lord of the Admiralty, was able to know the location of all German submarines, how could one of those submarines get close enough to a passenger liner to torpedo it? The *Lusitania* was anchored in the channel, near the port, when it was hit by the German torpedo. Do you know why it was there, what it was waiting for? It was waiting for the boat that would escort it into the English port. That boat was the *Juno*. And it never arrived: it never arrived because Winston Churchill ordered it back to port. And there's the question I want to put to our guest: Why? Why did Winston Churchill give the order for the *Juno* to return to port before it reached the *Lusitania*? Why did Churchill, who knew of the presence of three German submarines in those waters, *voluntarily* leave the *Lusitania* exposed? Tell me. Why?"

I suddenly felt tired, very tired, and it was not because it was so late. As if a door opened a crack, I saw in the depths of the night a long series of monologues reproaching me, from anonymous places, for my unbelief or my ingenuousness. I looked at Carballo, thinking I'd see an amused grin: that of someone who has laid a trap and returns to find his prey has fallen in. But I didn't discover any such thing on his face, but rather a genuine interest in Ismael's information and in my next response. Maybe Carlos Carballo's audience was entirely composed of people like this Ismael, an army of night owls: it took me no effort to imagine those solitary people who carry out unsatisfying functions during the day and only really come back to life at night, when, in the solitude of their small apartments, surrounded by books that are not on shelves but in piles, turn on their computer or their radio and wait for midnight: then, the opposite of what happens to Cinderella, the magic begins. In Carballo's company, or that of his voice, these men and women will dedicate hours to examining the underside of the world, the truth of things that have been silenced by official history, and will find in the camaraderie of paranoia, in the pleasure of those shared indignations, the thing that can most unite two people, even if they don't know each other or have never seen each other—the feeling of sharing a persecutor. All this occurred to me in a fraction of a second, and only now, when I write it, does what happened next make sense. I understood something: I understood why Ismael had phoned in so quickly, as if he knew beforehand my opinion of conspiracy theories; I also understood why Carballo had invited me onto his program. Of course it wasn't out of any interest in my opinions, much less in my books. He had invited me to test me. To put it a better way: he hadn't invited me because of my past books, but to find out if I deserved, beyond all doubt, a certain future book. The clarity of the revelation dazzled me. I hastened to reply.

"Because he expected them to sink it," I said.

"What?" said Carballo.

"Of course," I said. "It was to get the United States to join the war, wasn't it? But the United States was not in the habit of getting involved in foreign conflicts, that was a sort of tradition since the Founding Fathers. I think even Washington made it clear as a kind of national philosophy." This was a vague memory from long ago and undoubtedly inexact readings. But I didn't think anyone was going to discredit me. Nobody did. "Nevertheless, it was in many people's interest for the United States to join the war because war generates profit. Everybody knows that the rich of the United States wanted their country to go to war, for the opportunities it would offer. But President Wilson stubbornly refused to get involved. An act of violence against U.S. citizens was needed, an act that would inflame public opinion and line it up behind the president, demanding retribution, demanding revenge."

Carballo had leaned back in his chair. He crossed his arms behind his head and observed.

"Have you heard of the papers of Colonel House?" asked Ismael.

I could not reveal the truth: that I didn't have the slightest idea what they were. But I knew that wouldn't be necessary, for Ismael wanted to talk, he was dying to talk. So I let him.

"Who hasn't heard of Colonel House's papers?" I said.

"Exactly: Who hasn't?" said Ismael. "Well then, in those documents, as you know, there is a very eloquent conversation."

"But let's explain to the listeners," I said, "let's explain to our night owls who Colonel House was."

"Yes, you're right," said Ismael. "Colonel House was President Wilson's most trusted adviser, his right-hand man. His papers record a conversation with Sir Edward Grey, Great Britain's Under-Secretary of State for Foreign Affairs. This occurred shortly before the *Lusitania* went down. Grey asked him what the United States would do if Germany sank a transatlantic liner full of Gringo passengers."

"We say North Americans here," said Carballo.

"Sorry, North American passengers. What the United States would do if the Germans sank a boat full of North Americans. And Colonel House answered that he thought the public indignation would be so great, that it would drive them into the war. That's more or less what he answered."

"And that's what happened," I said. "Without any more or less."

"Many people got rich from the United States joining the war. The Rockefellers earned more than two hundred million dollars. J. P. Morgan received more than a hundred million in loans from the Rothschilds. And you know, of course, what cargo the *Lusitania* was carrying."

"Of course," I said. "But tell them, Ismael, tell our night owls."

"Ammunition," said Ismael. "Six million bullets, property of J. P. Morgan himself. If you made these things up, nobody would believe it."

"But we don't have to make them up," I said.

"No. Because there they are."

"In the history nobody tells."

"Exactly."

"But you have to know how to see it."

"Know how to see it," Ismael repeated.

"You have to read," I said, "the truth of things."

Carballo—on his face the expression of a professor or a father or a leader of a sect—looked at me with approval.

FOR THE REST of my spell on *Night Owls*, I had time to argue how the French Revolution was actually a bourgeois plot, how the Illuminati secret society had declared war on all the world's religions, how the true origin of Nazi philosophy—someone used that expression, *Nazi philosophy*—could be traced back to 1919, the year that Adolf Hitler joined a secret society called Thule. Toward the end of the program I heard it said that evolution was one of the tools socialism used to penetrate our civilizations and that the United Nations was a front for those who wanted to impose a new world order. I also learned that the war on drugs, proclaimed by President Richard Nixon in the early 1970s, was the most successful imperialist strategy in the history of the United States, because it had enabled them to impose their laws on Latin America, at the same time as the black market money of the drug trade financed their economy. And then around two, while the program took a break and a Van Morrison song played and then one by Jacques Brel, I thanked Carballo and held out my hand to say goodbye. My hand hung in the air for an instant; it was a brief instant, but it gave me time to feel a change in Carballo's gaze, as if the approval I'd felt a while ago had disappeared. That wasn't so: it had just turned reflective and tenuous, like a candle flame.

"Well, I'm going to get going," I said. "But I'm ready to write the book, so give me a call when it suits you."

I began to walk away, but Carballo grabbed my arm.

"No, no," he said. "Wait for me. I'll finish the program and then you can drive me home."

"Carlos, I'm not a night owl," I said, trying not to offend him. "It's too late for me. We better see each other another day."

"None of that. You've heard the expression *worth the wait*? Well, that's what it is. Patience, my friend, patience. Believe me when I say you won't regret it."

Were his words the promise of a stolen vertebra? Nobody could ask me to keep the idea from crossing my mind. And that vertebra, after all, was my sole mission. Carballo was inviting me to his house: that would be after four in the morning, but still, how could I refuse?

"Well, okay," I said. "Where shall I wait for you?"

"Come on, I'll put you in a good spot," he said. "So you can hear the rest of the program."

He showed me to a darkened studio, on the other side of the corridor, with my now empty bottle of whiskey and a plastic cup full to the brim of coffee that tasted like burned leather. It was true: the sound of his studio, the music from *Night Owls*, was perfectly audible. When Carballo reached a hand out to switch on the neon lights, I said no, to leave them off, that I liked it as it was. The semidarkness and the silence of two in the morning in that half-deserted building, or just occupied by ghosts of the night world, calmed and suited me, because sitting there the tension that had accumulated over the last two hours fell upon me: during that time much nonsense had been spoken, but some pertinent things had also been said, other new things and still others that had remained with me and made me feel uncomfortable without being able to know why, the way an intuition makes us uncomfortable, after a conversation when we feel someone was trying to tell us something and—out of fear, timidity, excessive caution, to spare us displeasure or sadness—they haven't. For example, Carballo's interest in the assassination of Rafael Uribe Uribe was news to me; in my aforementioned column it had just served as a pretext, a way to complete a more or less attractive idea one day when my columnist's creativity was on vacation. During a break—while the voice of Maxime Le Forestier played—my host had reproached me briefly.

"That column is the reason you're here," he told me. "So don't spurn it."

And now someone was talking about Uribe Uribe again on the program. Having been distracted by my own meditations, I didn't know who it was: I caught up with the conversation when it already seemed to be quite far along. Or maybe they weren't talking about Uribe Uribe, but had just mentioned him in passing; the voices reached me clearly but at the same time from afar, perhaps through the illusion radio produces: although it was being transmitted ten meters from where I sat, the sound of *Night Owls* reached me as it would have if I were in Barranquilla, for example, or Barcelona, or Baltimore.

The listener who had called in had a rough smoker's voice, wasted and weak, mixed with the static (the bad quality of the phone line didn't help), so only his impeccable diction allowed me to understand his words. It was he who first mentioned my name, I think. We are programmed to become alert at the sound of those syllables: we distinguish them even in the midst of a crowd or confusion, and that's what happened to me. But my name didn't come up again. They were now talking about someone called Anzola.

"He did know," said Carballo. "You, my night owls, know as well as I do that Anzola was one of us: a courageous man, a bearer of truth, someone with the ability to see the other side of things. Don't you agree, Don Armando?" The man with the invalid's voice was called Armando. "Of course," said Armando. "And one has to ask, Carlos, what would have happened if Anzola's discoveries had survived. But they fell into oblivion, because this country has no memory, or only remembers what is in its interest." "For me it's not a question of amnesia," Carlos said now. "Anzola and his discoveries being forgotten is an interested forgetting. So, it's not forgetting, it's the suppression of an inconvenient truth. The perfect example of a successful conspiracy." And then Armando said: "That's what Vásquez doesn't know." And Carballo confirmed it: "Yes. That's what he doesn't know."

Just before four in the morning, Carballo left the last song in my list playing (the longest one; he always saved the longest for last) and said good night to the sound engineer with a half-dead embrace. He gestured to me from the hall, I stood up and followed him down dark corridors. He moved confidently as I felt my way along the walls, and in minutes we were pulling out of the side street heading north then up Eighty-fifth Street and then taking Carrera Séptima south. When we got to Avenida Chile, I decided to ask him: "Who is Anzola?"

Carballo didn't look at me. We were driving through a deserted and threatening city, because the early hours are always threatening in Bogotá: despite things going better than in the days before my departure, it is still a place where no one stops at a traffic light without a tinge of apprehension. Carballo had his eyes on the road, and the yellow light of the streetlamps and the red brake lights of the few vehicles played on his face. "Afterward," he said.

"After what? I heard you talking about me. And also talking about a certain Anzola who discovered I don't know what. Who is he?"

"Was," said Carballo.

"Who was he?"

"Afterward," said Carballo. "Later."

Carballo was giving me directions: he was one of those people who can't give a destination at the moment of getting into the car, but has to give instructions to the driver at every corner, as if mentioning his address at the beginning would be giving away a secret: giving too much information to the enemy. And so we passed behind the Hotel Tequendama and up to Carrera Quinta and took it south and got to Eighteenth Street. At a corner, in front of a closed parking lot, a few meters past a lean-to where a couple of bodies slept under dirty blankets, Carballo's hand moved in the darkness.

"Here it is." He pointed. "That's my window. Leave the car here."

"Here?"

"Nothing's going to happen, don't worry. We take care of each other on this street."

"But it's blocking the way."

"There's nobody around at this time. We'll move it later. That parking lot opens at six or six-thirty, when the students start to arrive."

Carballo lived in a first-floor apartment with two small rooms and windows with bars over them as if to prevent a prisoner from escaping. The floor was practically covered in little piles of books, and it wasn't easy to walk without tripping, but I did: I followed Carballo along the path his daily life had carved through the piles. Against one wall, in the middle of the living room, was the fridge; on top of the fridge, more books. "Do you want a drink?" he asked me, but before hearing my reply he was already pouring me a glass of Domecq brandy. As he did so I noticed the only cabinet, an unsteady structure where mugs, cups, and glasses fought for space with books, and on the top shelf books fought for space with empty bottles of Nectar *aguardiente*, lined up like collector's items. Among the bottles, a portrait of Borges watched us distractedly. I pointed to it with curiosity. "Oh, yes, I interviewed him," he said, as if it were the most normal thing in the world. "That was in sixty-something. A journalist friend told me the university radio station was looking for someone to interview Borges, because someone else had canceled, a professor, I think. I accepted, of course, even though I knew nothing about how to conduct an interview. But it was Borges, you understand. They said: 'They'll expect you tomorrow at eleven.' After a while I started to panic, realizing what I'd just done, and by the time I got home my stomach had begun to turn. I threw up, had diarrhea, my whole endocrine system went to shit. I wondered whether to prepare a list of questions or not. I prepared one, I tore it up, I prepared another. With the terror a famous Argentine can produce in a person, can you imagine? I arrived and Borges was already there, alone, because back then he wasn't with María Kodama yet. I interviewed him for two and a half hours, it was broadcast, and the next day, when I went to ask for a cassette to have a copy, they'd erased it. They'd recorded a football match over it." He handed me the glass and added:

"Wait for me a second. I have to get something."

Carballo the unpredictable. Decidedly, this was an unfathomable man: as soon as I thought I had understood him, that I now knew *what he was about*, Carballo revealed another of his facets and made my satisfaction look ridiculous. I imagined him leaving one of Dr. Benavides's classes to go and read *Ficciones* or *El Aleph*, or maybe the essays, yes, because the essays would have suggested more questions to an improvised interviewer than the stories, or at least questions less at risk of seeming silly or repetitious. Carballo, the pursuer of conspiracies, reading Borges's reflections on Whitman or Kafka: the image, I don't know why, struck me as irresistible. Then I remembered "The Modesty of History," an essay by Borges that I'd always liked and that there, in that man's apartment, seemed to acquire a mysterious pertinence, for in it

Borges sustains that the most important dates in history might not be the ones that appear in books, but other, hidden or private dates. What would Carballo have thought? What secret dates were more important than April 9, 1948, day of his unhealthy obsession? Or maybe my memory was distorting the essay? It was possible. But then I remembered "Theme of the Traitor and the Hero," a story about conspiracies that talks about Julius Caesar, and then I remembered a poem called "Los Conjurados" (The Conspirators), the title of which invites us to think of secret conversations and espionage and assassinations, when it only talks about Swiss people gathering to create Switzerland. In any case Borges stopped seeming exotic in Carballo's apartment: I wondered if he'd offered him his finds before offering them to R. H. Moreno-Durán. The idea didn't seem preposterous.

I was caught up in these reflections when Carballo came out. He was carrying a file folder in his hands.

"I have my routine at this hour," he said. "I get home, heat up some soup, and go to bed, because if not, the rest of my day is ruined. But today is a special day, and before going to bed I have to get you comfortably settled. But I hope we'll later drink a toast: we'll drink to our project. Are we in agreement so far?"

"Agreed," I said.

"I understand that if you're here, that's why. For our project. To write this book that so wants to be written. Do I understand, or am I mistaken?"

"You're not mistaken."

"Well then, we have to start as soon as possible," he said. He handed me the folder he was carrying and ordered: "We'll start here."

It was the same kind of folder I'd seen years ago in Francisco Benavides's house. It was labeled with three figures: *15.10.1914*. Nothing else was written on it, no words, no names, no tags of any sort, but I recognized the date.

"The Uribe Uribe crime," I said. "Why, Carlos? What does it have to do with this?"

"Start reading," he said. "Right now, because all the rest is withheld until you know certain things. I'm going to sleep, if you don't mind. If I don't get a few hours' sleep, how will I prepare tonight's program? And if I don't sleep at this hour, what sense will I make to my night owls, how will I lend them my ears and my attention, which is so important to them? These people depend on me, Vásquez, and I cannot let them down. I owe it to them, you understand."

"I understand, Carlos."

"I'm not so sure, but it doesn't matter. I'll repeat what I said earlier: make yourself at home. There's a pitcher of water in the fridge. You can make coffee if you want, because what's in the pot is no longer drinkable. I ask you one favor: Don't make noise. Don't wake me up. I can get very annoyed if I get woken."

"Don't worry," I said.

"When you have to go, leave the file there for me, on the table. Make sure the doors are closed, mine as well but especially the main door to the building. We don't want thieves getting in."

And he closed the door—the one on the right, at the back—and I didn't hear any more from him. I found myself alone in Carlos Carballo's living room, alone in the place of the mission a friend had entrusted to me. So I didn't start to read the contents of the folder with the date that was now echoing in my head, but rather to look for the vertebra in the jar of formaldehyde. I looked in the fridge, I looked among the books on the shelves and behind the empty *aguardiente* bottles, I looked in the drawers of a sort of bureau that someone

seemed to have abandoned in a corner, and I went so far as to scrutinize the spaces between the towers of books that grew like weeds beside all the walls. But I didn't find it anywhere. There were no locked
drawers or cupboards that could hide anything. Everything was within
sight in this place. I soon thought Carballo would not have left me
alone and at my leisure in the same room where he kept a stolen object;
and then I thought that maybe Carballo hadn't stolen it and that Francisco Benavides was completely mistaken and this whole business was
a cheap farce, grotesque as well as unfair. Carballo was a paranoid eccentric, but not a thief. Did he not have hundreds of people who adored
him, who listened to him every night with the devotion of worship-
pers? Was his program not a sort of nocturnal church, a clandestine
work of charity and empathy? While my hands took books off shelves
to check behind them, where all readers hide things, I thought of these
words and was soon ashamed of my thoughts. *Charity and empathy*:
the arrogance of thinking myself superior to those solitary insomniacs:
the insufferable paternalism of thinking they were living mistaken
lives, or that their lives revolved around fantasies or speculations, while
mine . . .

After a few minutes I gave up. My brief burglary had produced
nothing of interest: neither the missing objects nor clues or signs that
might lead to them. I returned to the folder and opened it unenthusi-
astically; I planned, I think I remember, to leaf through it enough to
be able to lie to Carballo later, and thus preserve my right to be here, in
his house, which was more like a fort. The folder contained a meticulous chronology: hour by hour, everything that happened on the day
Rafael Uribe Uribe died. I took off my shoes and lay back on the sofa
so the light would shine directly on the pages. I noticed that the curtains were drawn, so the dawn would not come through the windows,
or perhaps would enter timidly around the edges. It must have been

just after five when, armed with a fresh pot of coffee (and a mug where Mafalda had hung a sign warning her world: *Caution: Irresponsible people at work*), I began to read; it must have been six or almost six when I understood the contents of what I had in my hands, that opened like a secret to reveal to me the extent of my ignorance of that fateful day, the first of so many that marked the last century in my country. I began taking notes, and those notes are in front of me now, serving me as guides and memoranda to give those documents the form of a story and the illusion—but it's only an illusion—of an order and a meaning.

ON OCTOBER 15, 1914, at about half past one in the afternoon, General Rafael Uribe Uribe, indisputable leader of the Liberal Party, senator of the Republic of Colombia, and veteran of four civil wars, left his house at 111 Ninth Street and began to walk down the middle of the road, in the direction of the National Capitol. He was wearing a black suit and a bowler hat, his customary attire for days when the senate was in session, and clutched under one arm some papers that contained, according to those who knew him, a proposal for a law on work-related accidents. He knew the offices would be closed at this hour, but he always liked to arrive early: the general used the quiet times to prepare his fearsome speeches. He reached the corner of Carrera Séptima, crossed the street, and walked a few meters along the western sidewalk heading north, without noticing that two men wearing ponchos and straw hats were following him. Later their names would be known: Leovigildo Galarza, in the black poncho, was the taller one, with a lighter complexion and a copper-colored mustache; the one in the brown poncho—the shorter of the two, with a dark mustache and more slanted eyes, whose dark skin had the greenish tinge of illness—was called Jesús Carvajal. It would later be known, as well, that they were tradesmen, or, more precisely, carpenters by trade, and that they'd spent the morning preparing the hatchets they each carried beneath their ponchos: sharpening the blades, drilling holes in the wooden handles, threading a loop of rope through the hole to go around their wrists so the hatchets wouldn't slip at the crucial moment: they undoubtedly foresaw sweaty palms. And there, a few steps ahead of them, walking along his street as he had so many times before, was General Uribe Uribe, deaf to the prophecies that had been announcing an attempt on his life for months.

The threats had accompanied him for the last several years. The general had become used to them: since the war of 1899, when he had to sign a humiliating peace accord to keep the whole country from sinking into a bloodbath, he had lived with the feeling of being hated by his enemies, yes, but also by some of his friends. The Conservative press had blamed him for the hundred thousand dead of that war, perhaps because they didn't know that he blamed himself. But that's how it was. And the blame, or something like it, had transformed him: in the last decade, General Uribe, emblem of the most recalcitrant Liberalism, had suffered a metamorphosis that seemed scandalous to his supporters. It wasn't just that he had forever laid down his weapons or that he'd sworn never again to pronounce a word against one group of Colombians or in favor of another, but seeing him devoted to the defense of old enemies, exercising diplomatic labors in favor of Conservative presidents, and giving long speeches in which he repeated, over and over again, that he'd moved to more tranquil regions and that peace in Colombia was his only objective.

The army of his enemies, which in wartime had been very visible, in peace became as hazy as a ghost. It was impossible to know who endorsed it or what its intentions were, but Uribe began to hear hostile rumors, veiled threats, and friendly messages of alarm, which for some reason seemed different from those he'd always received. Friends told him to take care, that they'd heard strange things; his family asked him not to go out alone. For his staunchest supporters, he continued to be the symbol of progress, the defender of the workers and the last bastion of true Liberalism; for others, the perfect incarnation of moral decadence and the enemy of tradition and faith. For Conservatives, Uribe was a *propagator of corrupting doctrines* and was *condemned to Eternal Fire as a Liberal*; for half of the Liberals he was a *Conservative, a traitor to his party and their cause.* This last accusation, which must have seemed the strangest one to him, took on new life during the presidential elections of that year of 1914. Senator Uribe—the diplomat, the conciliator, the man of peace whose only obsession was to achieve the country's reconciliation—gave his support to the Conservative candidate. José Vicente Concha, as was predictable after such backing, came out victorious. General Uribe could not know it, but that would be the last election of his life.

The Liberals accused him of treason. On the walls of Bogotá posters defaming him began to appear. An artisan called Bernardino Tovar was heard to say that the Conservatives owed their triumph to Uribe. "The general's days are numbered," he said. Someone called Julio Machado was heard to say that the general had turned against his own. "The tradesmen are going to assassinate him," he said. After the new president took power, two anonymous messages arrived at Uribe's house. One of them spoke of Concha's election and of the "just indignation this has produced on the part of the workers of this city," and gave him this warning: "We believe it prudent to make you aware that we will release someone's hand to unburden you of your heart." The second anonymous message was less poetic and more peremptory:

> Rafael Uribe Uribe: We warn you that if you do not explain
> in a satisfactory manner your part in the naming of the
> Concha cabinet, that is, without deflecting the belief that
> you've miserably sacrificed the Liberal Party, your
> remaining days will be very few.

Underneath the threatening text, in a single line inclined to the right, came the signature in bombastic capital letters: *TRADESMEN*. Later the rumor spread that on that Thursday morning, just before leaving to walk to his session in Congress, the general had been arguing with his family about the advisability of taking a bodyguard with him. But he did not: he went out alone, looking at the ground, not noticing that two men were following him—two tradesmen—armed with hatchets and determined to bring about his death.

According to Jesús Carvajal's later confession, the decision had been made the night before. The assassins had met, by chance, drinking *chicha* in the Puerto Colombia, and from there they left together to go to Puente Arrubla, another bar they frequented. They played cards, drank, and smoked, and then, when a small band of *tiple* players and guitarists arrived, they danced (in the words of Carvajal) "men without women." It was after the dance that they were left alone. They walked down Thirteenth Street to La Alhambra *chicha* bar. They were talking about how difficult it was to find work these days, since the Ministry of Labor employed only members of the so-called Block, the faction of the Liberal Party that followed Uribe. The general, they decided, was directly responsible for the unemployment and hunger of the workers who weren't affiliated with his faction or who hadn't voted according to his suggestions in the last election. They accused him of caring about workers only in times of war and forgetting about them in peacetime: of treating people like cannon fodder. "Instead of starving to death in this land," said Carvajal or maybe Galarza, "we must punish the cause." And so, to determine the form and strategy of the punishment, they arranged to meet in Galarza's workshop, on Ninth Street, the next morning at eight.

Galarza's carpentry workshop was a small but well-located place, right in downtown Bogotá, a block and a half down from the Santa Clara Church. It had just two rooms, one for the tools and another to sleep in, and another carpenter, a wood carver, and two apprentices, one of whom was nine years old, worked there under Galarza's orders. Later a carbine with a broken butt was found there, along with two military berets, eleven cartridges for a revolver, and a knife and its sheath, and nobody could satisfactorily explain what five carpenters might need that small arsenal for. Galarza had learned his trade from his father, a violent man with a drinking problem. He was called Pío Galarza, and in 1881 had been sentenced to ten months in prison for the premeditated shooting death of Marcelino Leiva, another carpenter. Leovigildo was not even a year old yet and he was already the son of a murderer. At the age of nineteen he was recruited by the government troops to fight, with the Villamizar Battalion, in the War of a Thousand Days; he emerged victorious and also benefited from the war, as he got work as an army carpenter when it was over. It was at this time that he met Carvajal. He hired him in his workshop; ten years later, when he decided to become independent, he proposed that they should share the lease for the place on Ninth Street. The partnership did not last long (they separated over accounting discrepancies), and they didn't see each other again until running into each other on the evening of Wednesday, October 14, at the Puerto Colombia.

That Thursday dawned cloudy and cold. Carvajal arrived at the workshop at eight on the dot, but Galarza wasn't there. He went to look for him at his mistress's place. María Arrubla was a tired little woman who'd been washing his clothes and feeding him for more than two years. He found him drinking milk soup to get over his hangover, greeted him with an affectionate insult—How's it going, knucklehead?—and then, when he saw María, suggested they go to the shop next door for a quick *aguardiente*. On the way back to the carpentry shop, they reaffirmed their plan to punish the man they held responsible for their misfortune and decided to use hatchets to carry out the punishment, since they each had one of their own. Galarza took his down from the rack, noticed that it had a broken handle, and began to repair it with wood glue while Carvajal went home to get his. They sharpened them, drilled holes in the handle, and attached straps, and one of the two, Galarza or Carvajal, Carvajal or Galarza, said:

"This is ready for chopping down eucalyptus trees."

Then, realizing they didn't even have enough money for another drink, they headed over to La Comercial, a pawnshop, with a nickel-plated ratchet brace that might get them a good loan. They asked for a hundred pesos, and were given fifty. Carvajal signed the receipt with Galarza's name. From there they went to drink a shot of *aguardiente*, one more in another bar, and returning to the workshop they found that María Arrubla had sent Galarza a tray of food. They polished it off between the two of them, sharing the portions of rice and boiled potatoes, sharing the fragrant coriander broth, and sharing the cutlery, and at half past eleven they went to look for the general.

What was Uribe Uribe doing at that moment, while his murderers were spying on his front door? It would be ascertained later that he spent a few minutes in his study, going over the documents he needed to take to the senate session. Had he looked out the window? Had his gaze swept over the two poncho-clad figures lying in wait for him like hunters at the edge of a forest? As for Galarza and Carvajal, what would they have seen at that moment? Who would have seen General Uribe first? Who would have given the other the heads-up? The assassins had gone into the shop at the corner and, supposing the general was having lunch in his house, decided they had time for a couple of beers; just after one, they walked a few meters in the direction of Carrera Séptima, and stopped when they reached the gateway to the novitiate to get a better view of the door from there. But they didn't see him leave; they didn't see the instant the door opened. When they saw Uribe Uribe walking down the street, he was already passing right in front of them. "There goes my man," said Galarza, or maybe it was Carvajal.

They followed him. Carvajal was walking just behind the general, four or five meters away on the sidewalk, and Galarza down the middle of the road, facing straight ahead so as not to arouse suspicion. They were still like that when the general turned north on Séptima and crossed over to the western sidewalk, the one on the Capitol side. The assassins were still concerned with keeping the same formation, and one has to wonder what would have happened if Uribe Uribe had turned around—thinking he heard a noise, for example—and surprised the man who was following him so closely, who might not have been able to keep walking that closely without giving himself away somehow. But that did not happen: Uribe Uribe didn't turn around. He continued along the sidewalk in front of the atrium of the Capitol. Carvajal would later declare that at that moment he had intended to signal to Galarza that they should desist with the attack. "I said to myself: If he turns and looks at me, I'll motion to him that we should turn back," he explained. But Galarza didn't turn around, didn't look at him, didn't feel his eyes on him: if he had, would General Uribe's life have been spared? A suspender came loose from one of Carvajal's socks, and he knelt down for a minute to fix it (an observer would later describe his dark, hairless skin). Right after that the attack began.

It was Carvajal who stepped down onto the road, quickened his pace, and, at the moment of overtaking the general, did something to catch his attention. Some say he whistled and others that he called him by his title. According to the version that initially prevailed, he burst out with a complaint: "You're the one who screwed us up," he said. At that instant, when the general stopped to respond to the shout or answer the accusation or perhaps just surprised, Galarza approached from behind and delivered the first blow to the head, with enough force that Uribe fell to his knees. The first screams rang out (some calling for the police, others just horrified), a cart stopped on the tramway tracks, and then the witnesses, already aware of what was happening, already aware of being witnesses, saw Carvajal approach the fallen man—"as if to look at his face," one of them said—raise his small hand, and strike more than once, with such force that the sound of the hatchet crashing against the skull was perfectly audible, the delicate noise of bones breaking. "Now they can kill me," Carvajal was heard to say. "I've done my duty to that son of a bitch."

"Murderers! Murderers! They killed General Uribe!" The shouts began to ring out from corner to corner, as if fleeing the scene of the crime, like the expanding rings a stone makes when it falls into still water. Desperate, those who had seen what happened tried to find help. "Police! Police!" somebody screamed, and somebody else cried: "Officer! Officer!" This was María del Carmen Rey, a passerby who later testified to having felt actual vertigo: "Not one police officer turned up," she would say.

Uribe Uribe's hair and face were covered in blood. Someone had leaned him up against the Capitol atrium, and many would later boast of having wiped away the blood with their handkerchiefs, or of being the owners of handkerchiefs that had wiped away the wounded man's blood. Carvajal looked at him, looked at Uribe, and the witnesses looked at him looking, and in his look was contempt, but a serene contempt. Nevertheless, he appeared disoriented. At first, after dealing the blow to the general, he went north, toward the Plaza de Bolívar, but then he turned around and came back toward the victim, as if to strike him again. One of those present confronted him: "What's going on?" Carvajal hesitated and turned to walk away again, but the expression on his face, according to the witness, was one of "defiance," of "satisfied rage." He did not put up any resistance when Habacuc Osorio Arias, a police officer, apprehended him and twisted his arm to take away the bloodied hatchet, and those who saw said he didn't even seem worried about his fate.

Galarza, meanwhile, escaped to the south and turned west on Novena, as if going around the back of the Capitol, but he was already being pursued at a certain distance by several witnesses and some army officers. Those pursuing him saw him stop to speak briefly with a worker by the name of Andrés Santos (he asked him if he had a job and Santos said no; Santos asked him if he had a job, and Galarza said no). They saw him then keep walking toward the Santa Clara Church and stop in front of the wall to read, or pretend to read, the notices posted there. Officer José Antonio Pinilla, alerted by the witnesses, caught up to him then, and right there, in front of the wall covered in papers, seized and began to search him. Galarza, according to Officer Pinilla, had in his left hand a hatchet with "blood on the handle and on the flat part of the head that can be used as a hammer," and in his pockets, a small knife and a wallet with documents in it. While Pinilla was frisking him, a man approached Galarza and punched him in the face, breaking his nose, and Galarza would later try to use that unforeseen attack to justify the blood that was smeared on the handle of his hatchet. Why, if he had a hatchet in his hand, did he not try to defend himself? asked the prosecutor. Galarza replied with another strange sentence, the strangeness of which nobody observed.

"Because I never use that," he said, "because I haven't been a murderer."

Meanwhile, Carvajal had already been sent to the police station, and Officer Osorio, who had detained him, was helping General Uribe to stand up. The general was holding a blood-soaked handkerchief to his head as if he were afraid it would fall to the ground, and, with his gaze lost among the trails of blood running down his face, he tried to walk, but his legs would not obey. Officer Osorio and some of the witnesses lifted him onto a cart to take him back to his house, jogging alongside as if they wanted to prevent the wounded man from arriving alone at his destination or as if something important might start without them.

At that very same moment, on the opposite side of the Plaza de Bolívar, Dr. Luis Zea—one of the country's most reputable surgeons, a skilled taster of French wines, and a reader of poetry able to recite Victor Hugo and Whitman—was on his way to his office, and as he passed in front of the Capitol saw the crowd that had gathered on the east side of the building. For the rest of his life, Dr. Zea would tell how he heard a stranger say that General Uribe Uribe had been murdered, how he rushed to Uribe's house, how he was praying silently that the rumors were not true, how he made his way through the bystanders and crossed the threshold and ran up the steps (tripping on the last one) and found the wounded man in the room off the front hall, lying on a cot, surrounded by family and strangers and barely aware of what was happening to him.

They had ripped his clothes open, tearing the fine fabric that was now no more than a long scab, leaving his torso naked. The general's head was propped up by a pile of pillows and his expression distorted by the contusions; his face, drained of blood, was pale and hardened, and contrasted with the dark red of the liquid bathing it and gave him the frightening look of a wax statue. Dr. Zea noted the presence of some colleagues he respected and calmed down as he did so; then he requested gauze, boiling water, and cotton, and he proceeded to clean the wounds and inspect the extent of the damage the way an explorer enters a jungle not knowing what dangers lurk therein. He put his hands into the curly hair, which did not stop dripping blood, to apply the first cotton compress. His fingers found a circular wound that went as far as the cranium, and he realized the blade had sliced cleanly through the soft tissue, as if cutting the flesh of a fruit. He carried on examining the head by touch, trying not to allow his nervous fingers to get caught in the locks of hair sticky with coagulated blood, and then, getting near the crown, above the right parietal bone, he found the wound that was bleeding the most: the major wound.

Dr. Zea washed his hands with boiled water, put a layer of sterile cotton over the wound, and began to cut off the hair. Uribe shook, tried to sit up, mumbled incoherently. "But man!" he said. "What's this? Leave me! Leave me alone!" In the middle of his struggle against nobody, he lost consciousness and fell back against the pillows. Someone thought he'd died, and a stifled cry from a corner filled the room. Dr. José María Lombana Barreneche took his pulse. "He's still with us," he said quietly, as if not wanting to drown out the murmur escaping the wounded man's dry half-opened lips. Then the general came to again, shuddered again, shouted again. "Leave me alone! What is this? What is this? Leave me!" Dr. Zea prepared to explore the major wound. He found that the blade had broken the cranium horizontally, and thought the attacker, instead of attacking from the front, had taken the time to choose one of the sides, the better to injure him. He would have to trepan. But there, in the general's rooms, there were no instruments to carry out the operation, and he had to send to the medical center for them.

The wait was a torment. Dr. José Tomás Henao took the general's pulse so frequently that Uribe got annoyed, but his tone of angry complaint had the content of official documents: "Honorable sir, I do not share your opinion," Uribe said. Carlos Adolfo Urueta, the general's son-in-law, had retired to one of the adjoining rooms to let the doctors work and to console his wife, who must have heard the attentive silence that had fallen over the house. From outside, from the street, arrived cheers of *Long live Uribe*, and in the patio of the house strangers paced nervously, but the second floor was quiet. So Urueta went to the room where Uribe was, and on his way he noticed that the police commissioner had arrived, General Salomón Correal with his luxuriant mustache, acting as if he owned the house; he was talking to those present, trying perhaps to anticipate the reactions of a furious or frustrated crowd. Urueta was not pleased by Correal's presence, among other reasons, because he knew General Uribe would not have liked it, but he preferred not to say anything at that moment: Correal, after all, was the authority. He unknotted his tie and went into the room. He suggested, in a tearful voice, that they give the general ice chips with brandy. The general reacted as if he'd suddenly recovered his lucidity: "Not brandy," he said. "Water, pure water, to quench my thirst." They brought him water in an earthenware jar. They gave him injections of saline solution. They prepared him for surgery.

At ten past three the envoys from the medical center arrived. They set up an operating table, awkward and square like an overloaded mule, while Dr. Zea washed his hands again. The chloroformist Helí

Bahamón put the general to sleep; Dr. Rafael Ucrós shaved his head around the injury with a straight razor. *"Viva Rafael Uribe!"* shouted the crowd from Eleventh Street, and Dr. Zea separated the soft tissues and exposed the lesion to the cranium, and the crowd answered from the Plaza de Bolívar, *"Viva!"* and the doctor extracted a splinter and with his fingers separated the cerebral substance, viscous and warm, and ascertained that the blade of the weapon had penetrated more than an inch into the meninges. The wound kept filling up with blood, which made the operation difficult. "But where is all the blood coming from?" someone asked. *"Viva General Uribe Uribe!"* they shouted from Sixth Street. "Here it is, here it is," said Dr. Zea when he found the cut in the superior sagittal sinus. "Put some gauze on, more gauze," said Dr. Henao, and outside they shouted: *"Viva!"* While the practitioners applied injections of strychnine and camphor to the tired body, the general complained in words nobody understood, let out whistles as if he were singing, or called for his wife, who on one of those occasions approached, her face and neck drenched with tears, and asked the wounded man what he wanted. The general replied with the frankness of the dying: "How should I know." Minutes later, Dr. Putnam asked him if he felt any pain, and the general was up to a snide remark:

"Imagine if I didn't."

Surrounded by bandages and gauze, in the hustle and bustle of injections, neither Dr. Zea nor the rest of the doctors noticed that night had fallen. They looked at the clock on the wall only when Julián Uribe, the general's brother, looked in to say the priests had arrived. They were two Jesuits with gentle manners who stayed with the general for more than an hour, despite the journalist Joaquín Achury trying to point out that Uribe would not be in agreement: after all, he had denounced the Church's excesses till he was blue in the face and had refused its indulgences. "I'm just a doctor," said Zea, "and these matters are not my concern. Besides, the general is unconscious." As soon as he said it, Uribe began to shout refusals: "No, no!" he said. And also: "You! You people!" The words ended in a bloody spew of vomit. A cold sweat drenched his forehead and neck. "He's reaching the end," someone said. Dr. Zea moved the bottles of hot water to check the general's temperature, and then his pulse, which had absented itself from his forearms and was now only detectable in his carotid arteries. The crowd outside was no longer shouting. And then Zea saw the wounded man open his eyes, press his head against the pillow, and repeat the same phrase three times in a terrified voice: *"Lo último!"* he said. "The end! The end!"

General Rafael Uribe Uribe, fifty-five years of age, senator of the Republic, leader of the Liberal Party, and veteran of four civil wars, died at two in the morning on Friday, October 16. The windows were open in spite of the cold of the Bogotá night, and some sisters of charity had knelt to pray in a corner, beside a collection of four seashells the general had brought back from one of his trips, while two indigenous women, more diligent, began to wash the corpse. The water they poured over his head washed down over his neck, converted into a pink solution, and formed delicate pools in his eyes, which one of the women dried with light taps with a cloth, while she cried and passed her sleeve over her living eyes: a macabre echo of the other eyes, dead but also wet. Clean and with his head wrapped in bandages, the general was placed in an open coffin, and the coffin in the center of the main hall. Over the hours that followed, relatives came to see him for the last time and weep for him with those special tears wept for a murder victim: those shocked tears but also tears of pure rage, of impotence and pained surprise, those tears that are also shed against all those who could have prevented the crime and did not, against those who knew the murder victim was at risk and did not want to warn him, maybe believing that to speak of bad things is to invoke them, opening a door for them in our lives, perhaps allowing them to enter.

THE MEDICAL EXAMINERS arrived mid-morning on October 16, just when a young artist was making a clay mask of General Uribe. Those in charge of the autopsy were two doctors, Ricardo Fajardo Vega and Julio Manrique, and three assistants from the coroner's office; they all took notes, wrote down words like *posterior biparietal zone* and *scalp wound*, took out a measuring tape and wrote *Oblique direction. Twelve centimeters.* Then they cut the scalp open from one ear to the other, separated the cranial vault, and found the segment where the hatchet had destroyed the bone. Dr. Fajardo ordered the wound be measured (the result was eight and a half centimeters long by four and a half wide), and Julio Manrique requested scissors to slice the meninges, cut the medulla with a scalpel, and extracted General Uribe's brain, with both hands, as if he were lifting a dying pigeon off the ground. He placed it on the scales. "Fifteen hundred grams," he said. The medical examiners then reconstructed the cranium and began to examine the body. The abdomen and intestines were perfectly healthy and the lungs had not a single tubercle: to judge by the tone of the tissues, anyone would think the general hadn't smoked a single cigarette in his entire life. Everyone agreed that he should have lived for another thirty years.

At dawn on the seventeenth, the assassins were taken to identify the corpse. The wake was held at the Salón de Grados, a huge pile of colonial stone on Carrera Sexta that had been a religious cloister and an incipient university, and in which Francisco de Paula Santander had spent months incarcerated while he was on trial for his part in the conspiracy that led to the attempted murder of Bolívar in 1828. For the funeral chapel, the police had arranged two corridors, one an entrance and the other an exit, so the crowd could circulate without danger or disorder, and members of the army in parade uniforms arrived to escort or perhaps protect the casket. Past the catafalque streamed people of all races, of all social classes, of all occupations, who wanted no more than to leave the general their inconsolable sorrow, take a look at an illustrious dead man out of morbid curiosity, or argue, with anyone who'd listen, about their version of the crime and their theory of the reasons for the assassination. And that's where, accompanied by a police officer and a detective, Leovigildo Galarza and Jesús Carvajal arrived.

By that time there were few people left in the hall, but the ones still there would have been enough to provoke a real catastrophe: at any moment the general's supporters, wounded men with a desire for revenge, could have jumped the assassins and lynched them in front of everybody. But nothing happened in the Salón de Grados; the assassins were not victims of any attack, any blows, any hanging, any tearing of their clothes, any dragging down the city streets, or any humiliation whatsoever. They arrived at the side of the body of their victim and cast their slippery gazes over the dead face as if they were any other two visitors. By then, their responsibility for the crime was already an established fact, since the officers who arrested them recognized them without hesitation in police lineups—the ponchos, the straw hats—and immediately supplied the corroborating evidence: the hatchets with holes in the handles and straps in the holes, and the general's recently dried blood on the blades. And nevertheless there, in the Salón de Grados, in front of the lifeless body of their victim, the two assassins responded to the detective's questions, denying their responsibility for the events.

Yes, they had met the general.

No, they didn't know what had caused his death.

No, they had not attacked him.

No, they didn't know who might have attacked him.

After the legal recognition, the detective and police officer led the murderers to the exit. The officer walked on the left, holding the arm of one of the assassins, and the detective did the same, walking on the right. They were so distracted, said a witness, that the murderers could have run away: it was as if no one was looking after them: it was as if they trusted them.

It was the most lavish funeral the country had seen in a long time. Someone later wrote, with that grandiloquence so characteristic of Bogotá, that the city had dressed as Rome to bid farewell to its Julius Caesar. (The simile was not a fortunate one: as someone else replied in the newspapers on the following days, Julius Caesar was assassinated for being a tyrant.) The articles in the press would speak of a ceremony with pennants and flags and words from the archbishop, and then a funeral march surrounding the casket to carry it to the cemetery, and then carriages with wreaths passing in strict order: first the president, then the apostolic delegation, then those of congress and the supreme court of justice, then the dead man's party. There were so many wreaths that the plaza filled with the smell of flowers, and the scent followed the cortège down the Calle Real and then along Florián. From the adjacent streets more and more people came to join the retinue; someone said that during those moments Uribe was more important than Bolívar. From all the balconies, black-clad women and children watched, sad children faithfully following the instruction of sadness. At the cemetery, nine orators, from senators and congressmen to journalists and soldiers, delivered eulogies at the tops of their voices, and thus the people of Bogotá discovered that the country had *left aside party hatreds* and *wept with a single cry for the memory of the great sac-rificed man* and that *before the casket men's passions fell silent*. But the truth was very different: beneath the calm surface, the silenced passions and unanimous weeping, the close relatives of the Uribe family began to realize that very strange things were going on around them.

First of all, there was the annoying matter of the investigation. It had been started, as it should, on the day after the crime; it had fallen, according to legal procedures, to the top municipal inspector, a lawyer who had previously worked as a public prosecutor and whose aptitude, therefore, was well proven. But as soon as he began to work, he received notice that the case no longer fell within his jurisdiction: the president of the Republic had personally requested Salomón Correal, the police commissioner, to take charge of it. Since when could the president assign whomever he wished to a criminal investigation? How was it possible, furthermore, that he should assign the investigation to a man who did not have the education or the knowledge or the experience to carry out the sort of investigation required? But the most disturbing thing was that there was no record of the presidential decision anywhere. It was not written in any document, did not appear in any official letter, there was no tangible proof of it. It did not exist.

The police commissioner, Salomón Correal, was a man of recognized Conservative sympathies and authoritarian temperament. His reputation had followed him since the beginning of the century, when he participated in the intrigues that a group of Conservatives carried out in order to withdraw the government from the legitimate president, the octogenarian Manuel Sanclemente, and replace him with one more in line with their thinking. Legends and truth blended in people's memories, but one terrible version told that Correal, as prefect of the town of Guaduas, had arrested Sanclemente, had tied him to a chair, had insulted and beaten him as if he were a thief picked up off the street rather than a president in his eighties, and had then locked him in a glass case and left that case out under the midday sun, all to force him to resign from power. When they went to take him out of the glass case, the walls of which had steamed up under the violence of the heat, the elderly Sanclemente had fainted from exhaustion or dehydration, but never gratified his torturers with his resignation. Rumors of this ruthlessness had spread all around the country, and when Sanclemente died, two years after the macabre events, people agreed that he had not died a natural death: the humiliations and pain inflicted by his enemies had killed him. And among his enemies, Salomón Correal.

So his presence in the proceedings did not inspire any confidence among General Uribe's followers. Everything Correal did was surrounded by obscurity: as soon as he received the order from the president to take charge of the case, he assigned the head of the police investigations department the task of collecting statements from witnesses to the crime; three days later, however, he had dismissed him with worrying efficiency and without giving him the right to the slightest protest. The head of investigations was called Lubín Bonilla, and he was a civil servant recognized for his integrity and also for his stubbornness, so his dismissal seemed difficult to justify. But Salomón Correal accused him of "underhandedly divulging insidious rumors against the government, which he later repeated in a telegram." And he took him off the case.

The telegram Correal referred to in his version was already the talk of Bogotá society. Shortly after his dismissal, Bonilla had sent it to an acquaintance; this person, without warning or asking permission, had it published in a newspaper. The telegram contained an accusation that was not to be taken lightly—WHEN LIGHT BEGAN TO SHINE, TOOK ME OFF INVESTIGATION—and in Bogotá people wondered if Bonilla had been on the verge of receiving some important revelation. Here and there, in casual conversations that had been repeated and distorted, Bonilla complained that they'd taken him off the case just when he was going to arrange a face-to-face meeting between the two assassins; he had also been heard to say that Señor Correal had interfered in the investigation, imposing his presence during the interrogations in spite of the law forbidding it, and even holding a finger to his lips when a question was asked, as if instructing the assassin to keep quiet. But these weren't the most serious rumors circulating around the police commissioner, for by the time of the dismissal of Bonilla, the Uribe family had found out about a very grave matter from a mysterious witness: a man called Alfredo García.

He was just over thirty, with disheveled clothes and straight hair, and a gold tooth gleamed in his otherwise toothless mouth. Along with other of the general's sympathizers, Alfredo García had gone to his house the night of his agony, and from the start made himself comfortable on the landing of the stairway, speaking quietly and discussing with the rest what had just happened. They all had their own speculations about the crime and its culprits; they said them out loud and the house was filling with conjectures. Señor Tomás Silva, family friend of the Uribes', owner of a shop that had sold boots to the general on more than one occasion, was passing the stairs when he heard García say this sentence to no one in particular:

"If they knew who Galarza's and Carvajal's comrades are in this incident, it would be something else altogether."

Tomás Silva interrogated him immediately: "What do you mean? What do you know?"

"You have to tell everything you know to the police," they told him.

They went to see the investigating official. The officer listened with interest, but told them that so late at night no statements could be taken, that they should return the next day. That's what they did: the next morning, very early, García and Silva returned to the police station. The commissioner was waiting for them in the entrance hall.

"I already know what you've come to tell me," he told them. He patted Silva on the shoulder: "We have to talk about this matter." And then: "Wait for me and we'll talk."

He went inside the building and left them alone. Silva and García thought he'd gone to get some paper, or to find a secretary to take a statement, and they waited for him to return. They waited for ten, twenty minutes, an hour, two hours. But General Correal never came back out. At eleven o'clock at night, García and Silva realized that General Correal, for reasons no one understood, had preferred not to receive their statement.

For a few days they wondered what to do. Finally, a lawyer suggested that Tomás Silva should bring two witnesses and put the statement down in writing. Silva convened Señor García and two citizens called Vásquez and Espinosa at his shoe shop. Once they were there, he brought out a loose-leaf notebook and a pen and placed them on the counter. He said (but it was more like an order) to García:

"Now then, write down what you saw."

It was this: The evening before the crime, García was passing Galarza's carpentry workshop, after having gone for a soft drink in the shop next door, when he saw the two assassins, Galarza and Carvajal, talking to a group of men in elegant suits, with bowler hats on their heads. It was dark and García did not register the faces of the men in the group, but it did seem odd that such well-dressed people should be conversing with two workers at that hour of the night. As he passed the group, García could hear Galarza. "If you give us what we're asking for, we'll do it," he said. "If not, there's nothing to talk about." "Keep your voice down," one of the gentlemen demanded, "there's somebody eavesdropping over there." They all went inside Galarza's place and closed the door. García was more curious than sleepy, and waited for almost an hour leaning against the house of Señor Francisco Borda, walking up and down the street, freezing to death. When he finally saw them come out, he hid behind the corner and from there heard the polite voice of one of the gentlemen: "All set, then." "No worries," answered Galarza or maybe Carvajal. "We're going to do this really well." And Carvajal or maybe Galarza added: "You gentlemen will see this very well done." The witness read out loud what he'd just written and then put his signature to it with more arabesques than necessary. But none of this interested Correal. He never found out who the men who spoke with the assassins that night were; he never investigated the validity of García's testimony.

That disregard soon reached the ears of Julián Uribe, the general's older brother. He was a man with a long neck and a straight mustache, and he'd always acted more like a second father than a companion. On his relaxed brow there was something serene that the general had never had, as if rather than two years he was two lifetimes older. From the beginning he got involved in the criminal proceedings, following them closely, taking an interest in their particulars, and he also had his own worries, his own qualms about the way everything had been carried out. At the beginning of the month of November, he had gone to Salomón Correal's office. He took with him a document written in his own hand: a draft detailing certain information he had obtained himself after several days of investigation. Since he himself had compiled that material, he himself had put it down in writing and he wanted to hand it personally to the police commissioner, because it seemed to him to be of sufficient significance and because he had realized he could not trust messengers.

It contained the statements of twelve witnesses. With varying degrees of precision and various anecdotes, the twelve described a sort of outing or visit to the Tequendama Falls by General Uribe's murderers. The falls, a dramatic mountain gorge where the Bogotá River throws itself over a cliff, was an important local tourist destination, and there was nothing to reproach in a group of workers spending a day off there: in fact, the artisan associations that existed in Bogotá often programmed excursions, and the falls, with its spectacular cascades that took the breath away from the most jaded viewers, with its always misty air that gave the tree-covered mountainside a fairy-tale atmosphere, was the first choice of many groups. But that outing, which according to witnesses' versions had taken place in the month of June, had not been an outing like any other, for the assassins—according to the witnesses' versions—were not alone: they went with a man from a higher social class, wearing a dark poncho and a fine woven straw hat, who had paid out of his own pocket to hire two sprung carriages and had also provided the thousand pesos for a picnic for ten people. It was Pedro León Acosta.

And that changed everything.

Pedro León Acosta was a sinister man, one of the most sinister in a time and country not lacking in sinister men. His left eyelid drooped slightly, which made his gaze seem at once doubting and disquieting, and his pointed ears gave him the look of a perverse goblin: a goblin who was also a capable rider and quite a good shot. His family, with long-standing Conservative and Catholic traditions, owned vast rural estates. But Pedro León Acosta did not inspire respect, but the fear that in every good family the lost sheep inspire, those sons who have not only done damage to the world, but have broken their parents' hearts. When a family like the Acostas produces a son like Pedro León, that accident strikes us as more frightful, for there is something gratuitously evil in such a twist of fate: almost evidence that God had forgotten them. What the people of Bogotá had not yet forgotten, however, was that the man who dressed in an elegant poncho and hat to ride out on horseback to inspect his properties, that man who was always armed even if he was only going to meet street dogs along the way, was not like the rest of the lost sheep of good families that God had abandoned. No, he was not like the rest: eight years earlier, he had tried to kill a president of the Republic of Colombia.

AT THE BEGINNING OF 1905, Pedro León Acosta and his brother Miguel had joined up with the three Ortega brothers, sons of another Conservative family, to conspire against President Rafael Reyes, who they saw as too weak in the face of Liberal posturing. The plans were the fruit of long resentment. They mistrusted Reyes because he had once said his duty was to govern on behalf of the whole country, not just for his party, and the conspirators were not prepared to allow such a concession to the enemy. But the most intolerable thing was his reconciliation with General Rafael Uribe Uribe, an atheist who had risen up in arms against the party and demanded the revocation of the concordat with the Catholic Church. In the war of 1895, President Reyes had defeated him; now, it was said, he was going to allow him to form part of the government. What good was it to win wars in the name of God and Colombia if you then handed the country over to the vanquished?

On an evening that would later be recounted the way legends are told, twenty Conservative men on horseback gathered before the valley of Sopó, and there, in front of the gigantic mountain sleeping like a beast, making the sign of the cross with thumb and index finger of their right hands and holding a glass of champagne in the left, they swore to overthrow Reyes and drank a toast to the success of the enterprise. They did not count on their plans being found out, but that's what happened: they were found out. Nevertheless, the consequences were not what they might have feared; the heads of their two families were also friends of President Reyes. That earned the conspirators certain privileges: the president, who had heard rumors of the conspiracy, summoned them all to the Presidential Palace—the fathers, the sons, and the parish priest— and asked them, the way one speaks to naughty children, to abandon their plans. To placate the conspirators, he offered to put Acosta in charge of the national police and send his brother as government representative to a military school in Chile. In spite of the cordiality with which Acosta received the offers, in spite of the smiles and the embraces with which the meeting ended, in December President Reyes found out that the conspiracy was still going on. General Luis Suárez Castillo, commander of the army, carried out a series of arrests. But neither the Acostas nor the Ortegas—the sons of his friends—went to prison.

In 1906, at the beginning of February, the intelligence services brought President Reyes confirmation of the rumors: the attack would occur between the tenth and twelfth of that month. Reyes refused to limit his excursions or to increase his corps of bodyguards; on the tenth, at around eleven in the morning, he picked up his daughter Sofía at the Palacio de San Carlos and headed north with her along their usual route toward the north end of Bogotá. The carriage was almost completely closed: even though Sofía suffered from motion sickness, this time she'd insisted they only open the front, to protect her father from the wind that could give him a chill. They went down to the Plaza de Bolívar and then headed north along Calles Florián and Real. As they passed the Nieves church, the president looked up to the heavens, removed his hat, and recited a prayer. At the corner of the San Diego Park he noticed three horsemen moving in a way that suggested they were waiting for someone, and noticed that the riders also noticed him. He thought they were assassins; he thought, as well, that getting out of the carriage to confront them would only facilitate the task of assassinating him. So they kept going. When they arrived at the Magdalena quinta, in the area called Barro Colorado, he realized it was already half past eleven and time to return to the Palacio. He gave the order to the coachman; when the carriage began to turn around to take them back the way they'd come, he found that the three riders had followed them there. One stopped in front of the carriage. The other two, from behind, swept aside their ponchos, pulled out their pistols, and opened fire.

"Shoot back at them," Reyes shouted to his only bodyguard, Captain Faustino Pomar. And he said to the driver: "Get a move on, Vargas! Run over him!" Bernardino Vargas, the coachman, whipped the horses and the carriage lurched; seeing what was coming on top of him, the man who had blocked their way moved aside, went around the carriage, and began to fire. The president counted five shots and was disconcerted that none had wounded the attackers. "Cowards!" shouted Sofía. "Murderers!" Captain Pomar kept shooting until he ran out of bullets; then they realized the attackers were escaping, galloping north. President Reyes made sure Sofía wasn't hurt, but discovered that they'd come very close: the landau had several holes in it, and there was one in the brim of his daughter's hat. "God has saved us," said the president: minutes before he had said a brief but heartfelt prayer to the Holy Sacrament of the Nieves church, and now heaven repaid him with a miracle. The next thing was to head to a telegraph office and begin to issue orders. The president had telegrams sent to La Calera, Puente, and Cajicá: all the towns the attackers might pass through in their flight. The hunt had begun.

On February 28 the following edict was published:

The Commissioner General of the National Police cites and summons Roberto González, Marco A. Salgar, Fernando Aguilar and Pedro León Acosta to present themselves at the Commissioner's Office of the Directorate or at the Commissioner's house, in terms of the distance from the place where they are now, to respond to the charges against them concerning the attack on the tenth of the present month against his Excellency Señor Presidente and his daughter Señorita Sofía Reyes de Valencia.

If they do so, their willingness to appear will be taken into consideration, but if not, they will face the full rigor of the law.

Any individual who hides, corresponds with, supplies knowledge or news or food to the aforementioned, shall be subject to Court Martial and judged as accomplice, auxiliary or accessory. However, any person who gives notice of their whereabouts or refuge, or brings in those summoned, will receive a reward of 100,000 pesos for each of the first three named and $200,000 for Pedro León Acosta, and it is promised that the name of the informant will be kept secret.

Once the attackers were identified, and a juicy reward offered, it was only a matter of time before they fell. A certain Emeterio Pedraza, seemingly a close friend of the three assailants, denounced them at the beginning of March and collected the reward. González, Salgar, and Aguilar were captured and brought before a court-martial, which designated the attack an aggravated assault by a "gang of criminals" and sentenced the condemned men "to be shot by firing squad in the same place where they committed their crime."

Never had an execution been documented so exhaustively. There they would remain, in a well-known photo, the bodies of the three assailants plus the instigator Juan Ortiz, who had been seen with the three assailants the Saturday before the attack, toasting with *aguardiente* in the Bodega de San Diego. Yes, there they all were, seated on wooden stools and already dead, their hands tied behind their backs and their bodies splayed, and one of them, at least, with his eyes covered by a white blindfold. In another photo you can see the rest of the conspirators, part of whose sentence was to witness the execution. How many would have looked away? How many would have wished for a white blindfold covering their own eyes? Would any of them have seen the death of the others? Would he have briefly thought *I could have been that man who is now dead* or maybe *Now a man dies and it's not me*? We cannot know with certainty, but there they are: also seated on stools and surrounded by police, in a scene that could have been part of a public fiesta, of a theatrical performance in the middle of the street. There are all those who conspired against the president. All, that is, except one. Pedro León Acosta was not there. He had slipped through the police net.

How was it possible? It was possible because Pedro León Acosta was not short of friends among the powerful people of Bogotá, many of whom shared his antagonism toward soft or cowardly Conservatives, all those who were handing the country over to the atheist Liberals. The very day of the attack Colonel Abelardo Mesa had called to tell him that he was being sought, and in a matter of hours Acosta had ridden down Thirteenth Street and left the city across the western fields. He couldn't hide at El Salitre, because he found the gate closed with an unbreakable lock, but he ended up reaching the hills of the San Bernardo estate and disappearing among the trees, where they would never think to look for him. It was one of the coldest and dampest spots in those mountains, and Pedro León Acosta had to stay there while moods calmed down in Bogotá. He found a cave in the mountains: it was true that to get into it he had to drag himself like a beast, and it was true that the back of the cave was the darkest place he'd ever known, but it was far from any path and from any habitation, and there he would be safe.

During those days, not falling ill seemed like a miracle; later, hidden in a hut others had built for him, he paid close attention to the information that reached him, and knew how many men they'd sent out to find him and also knew the price on his head. He realized he'd begun to distrust everyone. Traveling alone and at night, he managed to reach his home; his intention was to see his wife one last time, eat a hot meal, and rest a little beneath a woolen blanket before resuming his long flight. But the visit gave him another idea. He rummaged around in his wife's wardrobe; he found an ample dress that wasn't too tight. Disguised as a woman, always traveling at night, he reached the Magdalena River, boarded a United Fruit Company freighter that was sailing for Panama, and in a matter of days he had reached the place that would be his refuge—his exile, he said—until the end of Reyes's term of office: San José de Costa Rica.

Nothing more was heard of him.

Years later, when President Rafael Reyes handed over power, forgiveness and forgetfulness (or a mixture of the two) gradually extended to and benefited his old enemies. When Pedro León Acosta secretly returned to the country in 1909, he realized that his former sins had become legends: they were something he could boast of in public. And he did: he tended to say, sometimes in person and sometimes in print, that he had never regretted conspiring against General Reyes, and that it had been the cowardice of others who hadn't followed him, as well as the more than likely disloyalty of those who would have betrayed him if he'd stayed in Colombia, that forced him to leave. By 1914 not only was he not a fugitive, but many Colombians, from all walks of life and not necessarily with similar political affiliations, regarded him with respect: with the respect reserved since the beginning of time for conspirators who get away with it.

AT THE END OF NOVEMBER, Julián Uribe met with Carlos Adolfo Urueta, the late General Uribe's son-in-law, to make a decision about that worrying situation. Correal was manipulating the proceedings and no one seemed to care; Pedro León Acosta had been seen in the company of Galarza and Carvajal and this lead had not been followed up, nor had any investigation been carried out, and of the twelve witnesses who said they had seen Pedro León Acosta with General Uribe's assassins, only two had been asked to testify. One of them, who had initially been sure he'd recognized Galarza from the photos in the newspapers, retracted this in his new statement without any explanation, and only remembered having spoken of tradesmen in general, not having identified them specifically. The other, who lived near Tequendama station and rented carriages for a living, confirmed that Acosta had been one of his customers, and had taken the carriage he'd hired to Tequendama Falls, but said nothing of his companions. For Julián Uribe, all of that proved an obvious fact: even if the witnesses could not or did not want to identify Galarza and Carvajal, it had been proven that Pedro León Acosta had been in that place in the company of a group of tradesmen, and there was more than a probable indication that Galarza and Carvajal could have been among them. Was it not simply logical to carry on inquiring along these lines, confirming the identity of all the members of the group and finding out if it was true, as the other ten witnesses said, that the assassins had been there? But none of that had been done. It was as if the prosecutor of the case, the famous Alejandro Rodríguez Forero, wanted to avoid their testimony being taken into consideration in the indictment: as if he wanted to pretend they didn't exist. And on that November evening, Julián Uribe and Carlos Adolfo Urueta decided that, in light of the circumstance, there was only one option left to them: to conduct their own investigation.

But who could take charge of it? Who would be bold enough to confront Salomón Correal and Rodríguez Forero, and shout to the four winds that the nation's authorities were carrying out the most famous criminal case in Colombian history with irresponsibility and negligence? Who would be rash enough to accept this job? Who would be, as well as rash, loyal enough to the memory of General Uribe to get involved in such a mess? It had to be a convinced Liberal; it had to be a lawyer, who knew legal procedure and investigation techniques; it had to be a sympathizer and even unconditional supporter of General Uribe, and much better if it were also a friend of his. It was Carlos Adolfo Urueta who said it first; but when the name floated in the air of the room, they both felt that it seemed to have always been there: Marco Tulio Anzola.

Anzola was twenty-three years old at that moment. He was a young lawyer, but one with a well-established professional reputation since his days as a civil servant in public works. He was, more than anything else, a bold nonconformist, and he had been friends with General Uribe in recent years—or rather General Uribe had been his mentor and his patron and his godfather, had taken him under his wing and gotten him his first positions. He had dark hair already receding far too much for his age, an undistinguished mustache, and eyes that didn't seem particularly bright at first glance, but Julián Uribe had not the slightest doubt he was the man for this mission.

So, at the beginning of December, on a night as cold as Bogotá nights get when the sky is clear, Julián Uribe and Carlos Adolfo Urueta arrived at Marco Tulio Anzola's house with a briefcase full of papers. Over the course of an hour they told him about Alfredo García, about the well-dressed men who had visited the assassins on the eve of the crime, about the witnesses who had told them about the trip to Tequendama Falls, about Pedro León Acosta and the brief Julián Uribe had drawn up to explain his suspicions to General Salomón Correal, the police commissioner. They told him that various events had convinced them that the investigation into General Uribe's murder was being manipulated to prevent any version getting into the case file that didn't corroborate Prosecutor Rodríguez Forero's version: that Galarza and Carvajal had acted alone. But they believed this was not so, and they believed they had gathered sufficient evidence to cast doubt on the official investigation.

"We wish to request that you, young Anzola, carry out a parallel investigation," Julián Uribe finally said. "To follow up Alfredo García's leads. To follow the Tequendama Falls leads. To follow up with Ana Rosa Díez."

"Who is Ana Rosa Díez?" asked Anzola.

She was a very poor young woman who had been washing Alfredo García's clothes for the last few months. But that wasn't the important thing: the important thing was that she lived with Eloísa Barragán, Galarza's mother. Shortly after having written his testimony in Tomás Silva's loose-leaf notebook, García brought Señorita Díez to the cobbler's shop and asked her to repeat what she had just told him. Ana Rosa obeyed. Several days earlier, she told Silva, in the house where she was living, a Jesuit priest knocked on the door and asked to see the mother of Leovigildo Galarza. When Ana Rosa Díez told him the lady was not at home, the priest took out a card, scribbled a few words on it, and asked Ana Rosa to give it to her. And what did the card say? asked Tomás Silva. That he would have to see with his own eyes, said Ana Rosa Díez. And where was the card? asked Silva. She could bring it to the shoe shop, said Ana Rosa Díez: she would try to take it without the lady noticing. But four days later, when Ana Rosa Díez finally came to show him the card, he'd gone out. The cobbler's employees saw the card, but Ana Rosa did not want to leave it there. She took it with her and said she would bring it back later. And she never came back.

"We'll simply have to go and find her," said Anzola.

"That's just the problem," said Julián Uribe. "Señorita Díez disappeared."

"What do you mean disappeared?"

"She's not there anymore. She's not at Galarza's mother's house. She's nowhere. She's disappeared off the face of the earth."

"And what do the police say?" asked Anzola.

"The police can't find her either," said Carlos Adolfo Urueta.

"But you gentlemen don't believe—"

"We," Julián Uribe interrupted him, "no longer know what to believe."

It was at that moment when he felt that the brother of General Uribe, his mentor and *maestro*, was about to repeat his request. And Anzola could not allow it to be said in the future that he had had to be begged to find out the truth about the general's murder. He looked at Julián Uribe and said:

"It will be an honor."

"Does that mean you're going to help us?" asked Julián Uribe.

"Yes," said Anzola. "And also that it will be an honor to do so."

The next morning, very early, when the cold air of Bogotá still burns the nostrils, he left his house and walked the dozen blocks to the scene of the crime. The Plaza de Bolívar was calm. Anzola approached the Capitol from the north, passing in front of the cathedral and then in front of the Jesuit college, and noted the presence of several police officers in the area. He arrived at the exact spot where two months earlier Rafael Uribe Uribe had leaned against the low stone wall, with his head bleeding profusely, while the assassins were each arrested separately, a short distance away. He was able to recognize the spot because when he looked up toward the eastern wall of the Capitol, above which a timid sun was beginning to shine, he saw a marble plaque as small as a bathroom window. He thought the plaque seemed too discreet, he thought the plaque seemed to want to go unnoticed, he thought it seemed embarrassed by what it said or maybe (Anzola thought then) by what it didn't say:

TO RAFAEL URIBE URIBE.

THE CONGRESS OF COLOMBIA.

15 OCTOBER 1914

Anzola thought that this Congress didn't deserve to have had General Uribe. Even the country, this country where threatening another with death was routine and where these routine threats were not infrequently carried out, was undeserving of the battles General Uribe had waged for its fate and its future. Then he crouched down in front of the stone wall, just as they'd told him the general had fallen after the attack, and tried to see the world from there: Ninth Street, the Jesuit college, the cathedral, all standing out against the blue background of the morning sky. He looked along the wall for the mark, he'd been told, one of the assassin's hatchets had left on the stone, but didn't find it. He looked for traces of blood, a stain or the silhouette of a stain, and not only did he not find anything, but he felt stupid for believing he might have found something. But deep down it didn't matter. He was content with himself, proud of the mission with which he'd been entrusted, sure that this imminent investigation would be the most important thing he'd done with his life. He could not have thought that he had just been thrown overboard, with that honorable decision, everything that until then had appeared in his head when he thought of his future.

"AND THERE'S where it all begins, Vásquez," said Carballo. At around midday he had emerged from his monster's cave, after a murmur of running water heard through the walls, in a clean shirt and with his thin hair stuck to his temples; and like that, walking through his apartment in white socks, he'd started to talk as if picking up a conversation that had been going on for centuries. "Yes, that's how it all begins. This whole monumental confusion, that nobody in this country of ours knows, this forgetful and credulous country, all this disorder that I've devoted more time to than to my own self, begins there, at the end of 1914, with that young man called Anzola: a mystery of history, a phantasm who emerged from the shadows with the crime and five years later had disappeared back into them, a man who was leading a normal and maybe happy life, and who had an obligation land on his shoulders: that of bringing to light a conspiracy. It is the noblest task a person can carry out, Vásquez: to thwart a lie the size of the world. To confront people who wouldn't think twice before doing him harm. And to run risks, always running risks. Searching for the truth is not a hobby, Vásquez, it's not something one does because one is idle. It was not a hobby for Anzola and it hasn't been for me. This is not clowning around. So get ready for what you're going to see here, with me, in these upcoming days and between these four walls. Because this story is going to change more than one of your ideas. What happened to Anzola over the next few years transformed his whole life, so don't expect to go through this and come out unscathed. Nobody comes out of here unscathed. Nobody, nobody, not you or anybody else."

VI

THE INVESTIGATION

During the last days of 1914 and the first of the following year, while the city tried to celebrate the birth of Jesus at the same time as it mourned the death of General Uribe, Marco Tulio Anzola devoted his time and energy to finding out as much as he could about the witnesses to the events: those who saw the crime, those who didn't see it but were nearby, those who'd said important words that the prosecutor decided to ignore. The first thing he noticed was predictable: neither the prosecutor Rodríguez Forero nor the police commissioner, Salomón Correal, seemed too pleased that a fresh-faced young man was starting to stick his nose into such a delicate procedure. But Anzola started asking questions and saw that people answered them. He moved around and about the city, wrote letters and received replies, and thus gradually discovered various worrying things. The first was the nickname the people in the street had invented for Salomón

Correal: General Hatchet. He was called that everywhere, always carefully, to not be heard by officers or friends of the police commissioner; and even though a popular nickname had no importance within the investigation Anzola was carrying out, it was also true that the people have a reason for why they say what they say, and it's also true, as Julián Uribe once said, that the voice of the people is the voice of God.

"General Hatchet," Anzola repeated. "I don't know whether the voice of the people is the voice of God, but at least they don't mince their words."

Strange things kept happening with the proceedings. In spite of the prosecutor knowing what the witness Alfredo García had seen in Galarza's carpentry shop the night before the crime, in spite of knowing about the document that had been drawn up and signed on the counter of Tomás Silva's cobbler's shop, he still had not called García in to make an official statement that would have legal validity in the trial. Why not? Yes, it was true what Julián Uribe had said: sometimes it seemed as if the prosecutor was determined to prevent or hinder any version of the crime other than that of two lone assassins, or the admittance into the preliminary investigation of any bit of information that might complicate the simplest story. Tomás Silva went to look for him on every third day, almost accosting him in the street when he saw him, begging him in vain to take that statement. The prosecutor answered evasively; he said he hadn't received any document from García; he said he'd already asked for it. And the days went by without his investigating who those six well-dressed men talking to the assassins on the night of October 14 might have been.

Meanwhile, one question bothered Anzola: Where was Ana Rosa Díez? What had happened to the alleged card that an alleged Jesuit priest had allegedly left for Galarza's mother? What significance could that piece of paper have, such that Ana Rosa Díez had tried to hand it over to Tomás Silva? And how was that significance related to the woman's disappearance? Anzola looked for her everywhere. He went to Señora Barragán's house, and did not find her. He spoke to Eloísa Barragán, Galarza's mother, who struck him as a more astute woman than she let on, and could only find out that Ana Rosa Díez had gone without giving notice, like a thief, and she'd left owing two weeks' rent. Her room had been let out immediately, of course, but the new tenant was not in at the moment, and Anzola could not look inside the room. He then thought of looking for her at Galarza's place, at number 205A Sixteenth Street, but when he got there, three days before Christmas, he found a municipal inspector finishing up an eviction. Galarza's belongings and those of his concubine, María Arrubla, had ended up in the street: their furniture was still there, cases and the sad spectacle of clothing strewn on the curb, waiting for someone to pick it up. Anzola would later find out that the eviction process had turned up an important find. Behind some wooden boxes, well hidden, the third municipal inspector had found a sharpened hatchet and, a few meters from the hatchet, a wooden handle with a braided cord. It was an identical tool to the ones used by the assassins to attack General Uribe. The strange thing was that the police officers who had searched Galarza's room exhaustively on the afternoon of the crime hadn't found it then.

"It's new," the municipal inspector said to Anzola. "Never been used."

"It's sharp," said Anzola.

"Very sharp," said the municipal inspector. "Strange that it should be here. This is not a carpentry tool."

"*Desjarretadoras,*" said Anzola.

"What?"

"That's what they're called," said Anzola. "And no, the strange thing is not that it's here. The strange thing is that it's never been used."

It was from that day on that Anzola began to suffer from two obsessions: first, that the crime had been planned for much longer than the assassins claimed, who still insisted on having made the decision the night before, after meeting in the *chicha* bar; second, that the third hatchet must belong to a third attacker, someone who, for reasons impossible to guess, had never come to use it. Had there been another attacker prepared to assault General Uribe that day?

Anzola began to speak of the third man whenever he interrogated anybody, trying to reconstruct the moment of the crime through new witnesses or a new reading of the existing testimony. He realized that the scene of the crime changed the way our memories changed: with each new day, with each new conversation, with each minuscule discovery, the images that appeared in his mind became diaphanous, and men appeared in places on Carrera Séptima that had been empty before, and then on Ninth Street some silhouette that he had thought fixed would disappear. He began to notice that people looked at him out of the corners of their eyes: the people of Bogotá began to hear about the job the murdered general's family had entrusted to him. "That's him," he heard someone say behind his back one afternoon, in the Café Windsor. "Who knows why they give grown-ups' jobs to children." And a third concluded: "Well, I don't think that boy will make it to the New Year." When Anzola turned around, all he saw were people reading newspapers. It was as if nobody had been speaking.

He did make it to the New Year. He spent those days (the holiday that goes from one year to the next) going over witness statements, trying to find a reference, even if indirect, to an aggressor other than Galarza or Carvajal. Witnesses spoke of the attack, of the assassins, of the victim; they spoke of those who called for help, and of those who helped. But Anzola couldn't get anything clear. At the beginning of January, however, his investigations led him to two men whose statements hadn't been taken by anyone before, in spite of the importance of what they had to say.

They approached him, and not the other way around. Anzola was walking up the street when a man in a bow tie came up and started walking beside him. He said his name was José Antonio Lema and that he'd been trying to make himself heard by the prosecutors of the Uribe case, but without success. "I haven't come to tell you what I saw," Lema told him, "but what another person saw. I hope you believe me." The other person was a certain Tomás Cárdenas, an employee of the Senate, who was coming out of the Capitol shortly before the crime, and managed to see everything. "Everything?" said Anzola. "Yes, everything," said Lema. Cárdenas had told him and other friends in a café, and he had done so with such clarity that it was impossible not to take him at his word. "And what was it that he saw?" said Anzola. Lema answered: "That there was someone else with the two assassins."

"Oh, really?" said Anzola. "And who was it?"

"Cárdenas didn't recognize him," said Lema. "He was the first to strike the general. Cárdenas saw the weapon, although from a distance, and he thought it was a knuckle-duster. He went to tell the police, but they wouldn't take his statement."

"What did they say?"

"That this information wasn't useful," said Lema. "That it distorted the matter."

In the middle of February, Señor Tomás Cárdenas confirmed all that Lema had told him. He told Anzola that on the day of the crime, at about one in the afternoon, he was looking at the posters on the wall beside El Oso Blanco when he saw General Uribe (although at that moment he didn't know it was General Uribe) walking along the eastern sidewalk of the Capitol. Then he saw that he wasn't alone: a man with a mustache, in a black suit and bowler hat, was following very closely behind him. The man in the hat picked up his pace behind General Uribe, raised his hand, and punched him hard in the face. Cárdenas saw something shiny on his raised fist and he thought it was a knuckle-duster.

"And you tried to give this information to the police?" asked Anzola.

"Yes," said Cárdenas, "but they wouldn't take it. They said it would skew the matter."

The image of the man with the knuckle-duster would not leave Anzola. His presence did not appear in the first reports of the crime: he was like a phantom. Was he the man who was supposed to have had the third hatchet, the one discovered among Galarza's stuff? And why, if that were the case, had he decided to change weapons before the attack? In any case, one thing was confirmed regarding the man with the knuckle-duster: even though it was not possible to know his identity, it was possible to know he was neither Galarza nor Carvajal: that he was, therefore, a third man.

When he got home, Anzola shut himself up in the dining room to review the autopsy. A blow from a fist wearing a knuckle-duster was not the same as a hatchet blow, and there must be evidence of that difference in the forensic exam: unless, of course, Cárdenas had lied, or thought he saw something he didn't see, or imposed on the scene his own anxieties. But no: there, in the autopsy, in black and white, was the possible mark of a knuckle-duster on the skin and the bones of General Uribe. *On the face,* read Anzola, *at the level of the left inferior orbital fissure, there is an oblique wound, 4 centimeters in length, in the skin and part of the soft tissues, and it has the characteristics of a wound inflicted with a sharp object. Over the left frontal region is an abrasion of the skin, with ecchymosis, in a circular shape, and a diameter of 3 centimeters; this lesion was caused by blunt trauma. In the right malar region, there is a wound on the skin a centimeter and a half in diameter, caused by blunt trauma, and a similar lesion on the right cheek. On the side of the nose is an abrasion of the skin a centimeter long caused by blunt trauma.* Each time the word *blunt* appeared, Anzola thought of the knuckle-duster, of a hand wearing one crashing into General Uribe's face, preparing him for other beasts to arrive with their hatchets and finish the job, to butcher the victim.

Here it was: here was the proof that someone else had attacked the general, for the wounds caused by a blunt instrument could in no way have been produced by one of the hatchets the assassins Galarza and Carvajal were carrying. Anzola could have felt vindicated, but he felt sad. He felt alone.

To keep from running the risk of making mistaken judgments, he went to see Dr. Luis Zea, one of the doctors who had tried to save General Uribe's life. In the consultation room, while he waited, Anzola examined the skeleton, the diagrams on the walls, the glass case, and the beveled glass of the doors, which played colorful games with the white light. He didn't know Luis Zea well, but Julián Uribe had spoken of him in such favorable terms that Anzola felt he was in the presence of a friend. No: an ally. The world was beginning to divide itself between those who were with him and those who were against him. On one side, those who were searching for the truth; on the other, those who wanted to hide it, bury it. He also felt that the world around him was behaving in unfathomable ways.

Around that time, a newspaper published an advertisement by the Di Domenico brothers, Italians who showed foreign films in the Salón Olympia. The Di Domenico company offered to pay one hundred francs for a script concerning the life of General Uribe. Anzola couldn't imagine the result of that announcement, but something about it smelled fishy to him. Here he was, trying to find out the truth about an object of national mourning, and meanwhile in the newspapers people were offering money to someone who would invent a story about the same man.

"Everything is up for sale in this country," he said to Dr. Zea when he arrived at his surgery. "Even the death of its illustrious leaders."

To his surprise, the doctor was very well aware of the advertisement in the newspaper, and furthermore informed him of a surprising revelation: the Di Domenico brothers had been present the day of the attack. Not on the street, the doctor clarified, but in Uribe's actual house, at the time when the general was fighting for his life (struggling between life and death, said Dr. Zea) under the surgical instruments of the doctors who were trying to save him. "They were there?" Anzola exclaimed. And the doctor said yes, that there they had been mixing with the people with their black box that took images of uncertain purpose. Dr. Zea then asked if Anzola liked cinematography, and he had to confess that he'd only gone to see a projection once. Then he tried to return to that revelation that had felt upsetting: "They, the Di Domenico brothers, had been in the general's house during his agony?" he asked again, and Dr. Zea again replied: "Yes, they had been there." "Doing what?" Anzola asked, and Dr. Zea shrugged:

"Who knows."

Then Anzola explained the reason for his visit. He pronounced the words *ecchymosis* and *blunt* and *knuckle-duster*. Dr. Zea listened to him politely, but didn't seem to be granting him much consideration. *He thinks I'm not worthy,* Anzola said to himself. *He sees me as a child, a child with a grown-up job.* And then, without looking at him, the doctor said in a low voice that yes, Anzola was right.

"Explain it to me, Doctor," said Anzola.

"It's very simple, to tell you the truth. There is no way those injuries on his face could have been caused by the hatchets."

"Not even by the side edge?" asked Anzola. "I don't know what the other side is called, the part that's not sharpened. Not even with that part of the hatchet?"

"It seems improbable to me," said Zea. "The assassins' hatchets weighed some eight hundred grams. Such a thing could not cause these wounds." His finger traced the lines of the autopsy. "Look, look here. There are four lesions on the face, in a very small space of the face. Each lesion has a very small diameter in and of itself. No, my dear friend, this has a name of its own. This would be a punch if the aggressor were a super-powerful man. A monster or a giant. But there were no monsters or giants in the Plaza de Bolívar that day, isn't that right?"

"That's right."

"So then there's no other option. This is a blow from a knuckle-duster." Anzola must have regarded him with skepticism, because then Dr. Zea added: "If you're not convinced, go and see the coroners. Maybe they could show you the general's bones. If you're one of those who needs to touch everything before you can believe anything."

"The general's bones?"

"Well, the forensic team had to keep the cranial vault. The top piece of the skull, which has to be removed to examine the brain. In the general's case, to examine the injury to the meninges. It was broken, of course: there was the hole made by the fatal hatchet blow. A piece of broken bone in the cranial vault. That's where a person's life escapes." He remained silent for an instant. "I was there when they took it, I helped them do all that. And one of them must have kept it."

"But is that allowed?"

"It's practically a commandment, my dear friend. Read the autopsy: you'll find that the fatal blow was that one. And it was just one, as far as I remember: the one that broke the skull and opened the meninges. None of the other wounds would have killed him, is that not right?

Only the one that penetrated his cerebral mass, that is the only one that finally caused General Uribe's death. And therefore, that part of the body is kept for future investigations. It's like a witness, you see? That part, the cranial vault and its segment broken by the hatchet blow, is the witness. That's why it must be conserved. And I think Dr. Manrique took charge of it."

"But what do they put in the dead person's head?" asked Anzola. "What do they fill it with?"

"My dear Anzola, please do me the favor of not asking silly questions," said Zea. "Instead let me write you a couple of letters of recommendation. That's what I can do to help you, which is why you're here. I want to know as much as you do what happened that day."

AND THAT'S WHAT HAPPENED. With Zea's letters in hand, Anzola arrived one rainy morning at the office of Julio Manrique, professor of pathology at the Faculty of Medicine and coroner for the Department of Cundinamarca. The doctor had a short, pointed beard, and blue eyes that resembled those of a shy boy and immediately inspired an illusion of trust. At forty-odd years of age, Manrique was already a medical eminence in Bogotá: he had studied surgery in Paris and sensory organs in New York, researched leprosy in Great Britain and Norway, and worked in the San Juan de Dios infirmary with patients affected with ophthalmic disorders. His achievements surprised nobody, however, because Dr. Manrique was the fourth of a dynasty of illustrious physicians: his grandfather had been a doctor; his father had been a doctor; and his brother was a doctor, a sort of surgical legend in the country, a man with magical hands who had founded clinics, presided over university departments, and had time to be a parliamentarian in Bogotá and later minister plenipotentiary in France and Spain.

"Do you know what happened to me that day?" he asked Anzola. "Everyone in Bogotá knows what happened to me that day. Do you know?" Anzola said no: he didn't know.

"You don't know?" said Manrique.

"I don't know," said Anzola.

The day of the autopsy, Dr. Julio Manrique told him, he had arrived at General Uribe's house in the company of Dr. Ricardo Fajardo Vega and three assistants. One of them, a young man who was just starting out, could not contain his emotion and burst into tears. Manrique understood fundamentally—because opening up the head of a man like General Rafael Uribe Uribe is not something you do every day—but could not allow that kind of attitude and ended up evicting the young man from the room. "Come back when you've calmed down," he said. And meanwhile he cut the skin, made use of the saw, separated the cranial vault, examined the cerebral mass, and together with Dr. Fajardo extracted the brain, weighed it and noted down its weight, and stopped for a moment to think, as everybody would have thought, of what had occurred in that brain during the last few years. The assistants helped to cut open the general's abdomen and remove his viscera and examine them; they helped to break the sternum to examine the heart and lungs. And in the end, when they began to close up the body and he was preparing to reconstruct the head, the expelled young man came in and said, I beg your pardon, Dr. Manrique, but someone needs you outside. Without looking at him, with something like involuntary contempt, the doctor responded: "Well, tell them that I'm busy." And he added a question that was more of an admonition or simply a complaint: "Or have you not noticed what it is we're doing here?"

"It's just that it's urgent, Doctor," said the youngster.

"So is this," said the doctor. "And furthermore it's important."

"They've brought you some news," said the youngster.

That's how the doctor learned that his brother had died. After his diplomatic jobs, Juan Evangelista Manrique had continued to practice medicine in Paris. For two years he was a sort of great-uncle to Colombians who lived in France: attending them, consoling them, seeing them fall ill and, in a few cases, die. But then the war broke out. When Germany invaded the neutral territory of Belgium and their army headed for Paris, Juan Evangelista Manrique, and his wife and her sister, chose to pack their things and take refuge, like so many others who could afford it, in Spanish territory. He crossed the northern border and settled in San Sebastián. That was the last his brother Julio knew of him: a letter that mentioned the fall of Longwy, which he called the gateway to Paris, and then the capture of the fortifications of Liège. "They are barbarous," his brother wrote of the German army. Now this news reached Julio: Juan Evangelista had fallen ill with bronchial pneumonia, most likely during the border crossing, and his weak heart had further complicated his fragility. His lungs had ceased to respond on the night of the thirteenth. Juan Evangelista did not know that at the moment of his death, in his distant city, someone was planning the assassination of General Uribe, whom he greatly admired. Nor could he have imagined that his brother Julio would learn of his death while, with an artisan's skill, he sewed up the general's head.

"The Bogotá newspapers published the information," said Julio Manrique. "But who's going to care about the death of a doctor on another continent, when here one of the most important men of recent decades has just been hacked to death?"

"And you in the middle of doing his autopsy," said Anzola.

"Right in the middle," said Manrique. He remained silent for a moment, looking in on his own recondite sadness. Then he spoke again. "So you want to see General Uribe's remains."

"It's about the autopsy," said Anzola.

"What about the autopsy?"

"The autopsy talks about a blow with a blunt object, not a sharp one," said Anzola. "A blow the hatchets could not have caused."

"Oh, I see. Yes, I see where you want to go with this," said Manrique. "What I'm going to show you, my esteemed Anzola, won't help you. But I'm going to show it to you anyway. So you won't say later that I wasted your time."

Dr. Manrique stood up and opened a cabinet. He took out the cranial vault and set it down on his wooden desk. The bone was smaller than Anzola had expected, and it was clean, clean as though it had never been covered by the skin and the flesh of a man. Anzola thought it looked more like a bowl for drinking *chicha* in the countryside than the remains of a military leader who had changed the course of history. Then he was ashamed of that thought.

On the front of the cranial vault the three initials were engraved: *R. U. U.*

"Is that always done?" Anzola asked.

"Always," Dr. Manrique told him. "So they don't get lost or mixed up. Touch it, don't be shy."

Anzola obeyed. He brushed a finger along the edge of the wound, where the bone broken by the hatchet blow was no longer smooth but rough, and then he touched the inside, as if visiting ruins, and he felt that you could cut something with the edge of a broken skull. "This wound was done by a hatchet," said Manrique. "The wounds with the blunt object affected the right cheek, if I'm not mistaken, and part of the eye socket. That is, everything below this line." With these words he lifted the cranial vault and drew in the air an imaginary border, as if there, in the space, began the rest of General Uribe's cranium. "They were wounds that don't leave a mark on the bones. But if they had left one, that bone's buried. With the rest of the general, I mean."

"They're not here," said Anzola.

"I'm afraid not," said Manrique. "But if it's any consolation, I saw them."

"That's not much use to me."

"No, of course not," said Manrique. And after a silence: "May I ask you something?"

"Go ahead, Doctor."

"Why are you doing this?"

Anzola looked at the skull. "Because I want to know," he said. "Because someone I respect asked me to. I don't know, Doctor. Because of what could happen if nobody does these things. I know it's difficult to understand."

"It seems very simple to me," said Manrique. "And very admirable, if you don't mind my saying so."

On his way out, Anzola realized he wasn't disappointed. He left empty-handed, it's true, but he also left with the sensation of having touched a piece of the mystery. It was a falsified sensation, of course: falsified by the contact with a dead man's bones, falsified by the curious solemnity of the moment, falsified by the sudden and fleeting contact between that violent moment and a great moment of another violence, a distant violence, a war occurring right now thousands of kilometers away that had come to touch us. That made him stupidly emotional. He looked at his hands, rubbed his fingers that had been on the fragment of cranium, its peaceful terra-cotta landscape. But no, it was not peaceful: something violent had occurred on it. The cranial vault that had been perforated with a trepan, the piece of bone detached where, as the doctor had said, a life had slipped out. Anzola thought that few people had seen what he had seen. It was like a religious experience, yes, it was like the proximity to a relic. Like religious experiences, it was profoundly incommunicable: a void opened up between him and everyone else, he thought, just for having seen what he'd seen, for having touched what he'd touched.

He went to the Café Windsor, ordered a coffee with brandy, noticed people looking at him. It seemed as if they were talking about him and later he was able to confirm it. But he didn't care and it surprised him that he didn't care.

THE NEXT PERSON who came to speak to him—yes: now people were approaching him, telling him stories—was Mercedes Grau. The day of the crime, Señorita Grau had been waiting for a tram on the corner by La Torre de Londres, on Ninth Street. While she was waiting, an elegant man who was standing a few meters away, and seemed to be waiting for something, caught her attention. He looked familiar, though she couldn't remember where she had seen him before. The man was wearing fine patent leather ankle boots, fancy black trousers with white stripes, and a light gray poncho. Yes, it was the same man Mercedes Grau had seen on other occasions: she recognized the mustache and the small eyes, and she noticed, by the clear tone of his skin, that the man was freshly shaven. Then she remembered: she had seen him several times in the cathedral, attending Mass, and she'd even seen him once at a cinematographic gathering at the Salón Olympia (maybe *The Count of Monte Cristo*, maybe *The Three Musketeers*, maybe one of those shorts the Di Domenico brothers had filmed in other cities: she didn't remember for certain). She was wondering whether she ought to acknowledge him with some gesture, not to be rude, when the elegant man turned to another, clearly a tradesman or a worker, and said:

"Here comes General Uribe."

Mercedes Grau looked in the direction the elegant man had indicated and saw that, in effect, General Rafael Uribe Uribe was coming down Ninth Street. The artisan, who until that moment occupied the corner of the San Bartolomé building, watched him walk past toward Carrera Séptima, so close that he almost had to get out of his way, and began to follow him. He moved his hands under his old poncho, said Mercedes Grau, and took short steps. The elegant man, for his part, did not move: it was as if he were nailed to the pavement of the sidewalk. The tradesman followed General Uribe, who had crossed Carrera Séptima and began to walk along the sidewalk by the Capitol, beside the stone wall; that was when Mercedes Grau noticed that farther on, at the corner of the same wall, another man appeared, also in an untidy poncho and also with the look of a tradesman. He brought a hand out from under his poncho and leaped on General Uribe, delivering two blows to the head so the general fell back against the stone wall. "Oh, he broke his neck," she heard someone say. The man who had been following the general from the beginning moved in then and hit him again. Someone else shouted: "Police!" And at that moment the first attacker, who had fled but without hurrying toward the south, walked past her, past Mercedes Grau, and she, in terror, could only exclaim: "How they kill people in Bogotá!"

"That's how it's done," the attacker replied.

Mercedes Grau did not feel able to look him in the eye, but she did manage to see his weapon—a knife, maybe; no, a small machete—shining under his black poncho. And then the attacker approached or made as if to approach the elegant man, the one in the patent leather boots, who when the attacker was closer spoke to him in a horrible voice, a voice Mercedes Grau would never forget: a calm voice that seemed to come out of a mouth that wasn't moving: a voice that gave Mercedes Grau shivers each time she summoned it up in her head.

"How'd it go?" said the man. "Did you kill him?"

Without looking at him, or looking at him out of the corner of his eye, the attacker said:

"Yes, I killed him."

And then he turned the corner heading west, as if to pass behind the Capitol. The man in the patent leather ankle boots, however, began to walk up Ninth Street, toward the hills. Mercedes Grau took a couple of steps into the street to keep him in view; she saw him meet another man halfway up the block, more thickset than him but well dressed, wearing a felt hat. The one in the patent leather boots did not greet him the way you greet someone you run into in the street, but the two came together as if one had been waiting for the other. And they carried on walking up the street, passing in front of the Uribe family home and under the balcony of the novitiate, while the general, lying on the sidewalk, bled to death in full view, among cries, shouts for help, and people running up the avenue.

Anzola wondered: Who was the man in the patent leather boots? Who could have asked Galarza if *he'd killed him yet* and, hearing the affirmative reply, walked away from the site of the attack? Neither the police nor the prosecutor had been interested in discovering the identity of that man. Since the day of the attack Mercedes Grau had thought she'd seen him several times, but had never been able to find out who he was. She saw him or thought she saw him from a distance in the procession following General Uribe to the cemetery; she saw him or thought she saw him in the delegation that affixed the commemoration plaque on the eastern wall of the Capitol. But on both occasions she was alone, with no one to ask, and the man disappeared as quickly as he had appeared. Had she imagined him? The imagination can do these things, Anzola knew that, and imaginations in Bogotá were feverish in those days, like frenetic, ferocious, uncontrolled animals. Whatever the case, Mercedes Grau had not imagined the man in the patent leather boots. That, at least, was a tiny certainty. That man was real, had a real voice and real ankle boots, and was the proof that Galarza and Carvajal had not acted alone: that this was something bigger, much bigger, than Salomón Correal and Prosecutor Rodríguez Forero wanted to believe. No, thought Anzola, Leovigildo Galarza and Jesús Carvajal were not solitary assassins. The crime against his mentor General Rafael Uribe Uribe, whose broken cranium he'd held in his hands and caressed with his fingers, had not been the improvised work of a couple of disgruntled unemployed tradesmen. It was something else. A third attacker had participated, who did not carry a hatchet but wore a knuckle-duster, and an observer, better dressed than the assassins and well shaven, who had advised Carvajal when their victim was approaching and who had asked Galarza about the result of their mission. Anzola thought of a *plot* and then he thought *conspiracy* and the words resonated uncomfortably in his head, like an insult from someone who loves us, and made him close his eyes.

ANZOLA BEGAN to notice that all over the country there had been a phenomenon of prophets or visionaries, diviners or witches, who predicted the crime against the general several days in advance. In Simijaca, a hundred thirty-five kilometers from Bogotá, five witnesses said that Julio Machado had announced the assassination of General Uribe forty days before it happened. After his prophecy came true, the clairvoyant Machado met a certain Delfín Delgado: "Remember what I said?" he asked. "Do you remember?" In Tena, sixty-six kilometers from Bogotá, a certain Eugenio Galarza said he was a first cousin of General Uribe's assassin, and had known months ahead of the criminal plans. "I didn't want to take part because I'm from a good family," he said. Later, when he had to reaffirm what he'd said, he admitted that he'd lied about being related to the assassin, whom he knew of only by name, and denied all the rest. No, he had not confessed his previous knowledge of the crime to anybody. The witnesses had misunderstood, probably, because he'd been drunk that day.

The most notorious of those fortune-tellers was named Aurelio Cancino. He was a mechanic by profession; at the beginning of August 1914, he'd begun to work for the Franco-Belgian Industrial Company, and in the weeks before General Uribe's assassination he had been part of a team of engineers and workers contracted to install an electrical plant in La Cómoda, near Suaita, in the Department of Santander: some two hundred and seventy kilometers from Bogotá. Seventeen days before the crime, his coworkers heard him say that General Uribe Uribe had at most twenty days to live. "I know it and I guarantee it," he said. After the assassination was committed they heard him speak harshly of the general: "If it had come down to me to kill him," it was said that Cancino said, "I would have killed him and I would have drunk his blood." He also said he knew Galarza and Carvajal, and knew very well what association they belonged to. Cancino talked freely about it. "I am also a member, and it's a great honor. I could have been drawn. That's why I came out here. So I wouldn't get drawn." A draw? someone asked. What draw are you talking about? The association, said Cancino, had some four hundred members and the sponsorship of some very grand people, and it was these people who'd drawn the names of Galarza and Carvajal. But he could assure anyone, without fear of being mistaken, that the two assassins would say nothing about the crime. "They're under orders not to say anything else," were Cancino's words, according to witnesses. The same coworkers who had heard the prophecy met with Cancino later to confirm the crime in the national press, and Cancino received them with a smile and a satisfied exclamation:

"What did I tell you, señores!"

In March, Cancino arrived in Bogotá to give his version of these declarations to the second judge of the circuit court. It was a wonder of simplicity and economy: he denied it all. He didn't remember having said those words; he remembered the get-together with his workmates, but not what they discussed. He justified his lack of memory with the argument of inebriation. Several witnesses said they'd heard his predictions and his satisfaction at seeing them fulfilled, but he denied it all and his singular voice weighed as much as the several that accused him in chorus. He said they'd misinterpreted him, that he'd expressed himself awkwardly, that at no moment had he predicted the crime against General Uribe, much less boasted about his prediction coming true. If they asked him who had said that if General Uribe were resuscitated, he would kill him again, Cancino replied: "I don't know." If they asked him who had claimed to be capable of killing General Uribe and drinking his blood, Cancino said: "I don't know." He denied knowing Galarza when he was not in front of him, and later, sitting across from him, remembered that yes, he had lived next door to him two months before the assassination, that he'd met him and his friend Carvajal in the Puerto Colombia *chicha* bar, that he'd often heard them talk about their activities in the association they belonged to. What association was that? he was asked. The Recreational Association, said Cancino, a large group that had been organizing picnics and outings for tradesmen for many years. They asked him if the Recreational Association also devoted itself to political activity, and he replied with an emphatic no, but adding a clarification that seemed pertinent: "I don't understand politics." Without anyone asking him, he added that the association, to his loyal knowledge and understanding, did not devote itself to religious activities either. But the most striking thing was that he denied ever being a member of the association. "What I said," said Cancino, "was that Galarza and Carvajal had a carpentry shop in Bogotá, and an association that they called Recreational met there, but I never knew what for." "They met in the assassins' carpentry shop?" asked the judge. Cancino confirmed it and then said: "To my loyal knowledge and understanding." The judge then called the witnesses. In front of them, Aurelio Cancino maintained his version of events: he was drunk, they'd misinterpreted him, he had never said those things. The witnesses, for their part, maintained theirs.

It seemed the matter would stay like that, but then a superior judge summoned Cancino to return, this time to give a statement in front of Prosecutor Alejandro Rodríguez Forero. For many hours he was asked the same questions he'd been asked before; he defended the same replies. But then Cancino began to lose his composure. He said there was a conspiracy against him, that the witnesses had made an agreement to get him sent to jail. The judge pressed him, asked him again about the witnesses' statements, pointed out the contradictions in what he had said, asked him how it was possible that five distinct individuals were able to give the same version of his words. Then what nobody expected happened: Cancino admitted having talked to his coworkers after the crime.

"What did you tell them?" asked the judge.

"I bet them I could say who had killed Uribe Uribe."

"And who did you say had killed Uribe Uribe?" asked the judge.

"General Pedro León Acosta," said Cancino. "He was the one who sent the assassins."

"And on what do you base that statement?" asked the judge.

And Cancino replied: "Well, that's what the *Gil Blas* said."

The *Gil Blas*. A sensationalist newspaper that printed irresponsible rumors and the toughest satire, and did not respect the sacred values of religion or the dignity of high-born members of society, that had published images of children run over by trams and corpses dismembered after a political dispute. A tabloid with neither dignity nor shame: Cancino hurled his reckless accusations based on reading such a rag.

The judge and prosecutor immediately rejected them.

THE CABLES that arrived from Europe filled the newspapers with news of the Great War. In Bogotá society the majority prayed at Mass for the triumph of France, and people who had never heard of Reims tore at their clothes over the destruction of its cathedral, and people who didn't know where the Ardennes were were of the opinion that the *Boche* had behaved like savages there. There were those who followed with admiration the advances of the German army, and others who praised Germanic civilization and said something of their temperament would do us good, see if we might finally save ourselves from the harmful influence of so many blacks and so many Indians. In the middle of May, a vague rumor became news and then a sort of legend: a Colombian had died fighting in the ranks of the French Foreign Legion. Nothing would ever have been known, beyond the curiosity that the fact awoke among newspaper readers, if the dead man had not been a favored son of the bourgeoisie of the capital city. But he was; and during a few days, while Anzola was carrying out his investigations, his death in the Battle of Artois, where the Second Regimental Combat Team of the First Foreign Regiment had the mission of taking control of the White Works, taking Hill 140 and holding it, was the favorite topic of conversation in all the cafés, and all of society's salons and at all upper-class dining tables.

Was that what the people of Bogotá needed to emerge for some days or weeks from the atmosphere of claustrophobia and contained paranoia that the murder of Rafael Uribe Uribe had provoked? In any case, the death of Hernando de Bengoechea (as well as the short life that preceded it) occupied people's attention, and was told in obituaries, celebrated in poems published in magazines, expounded upon in scattered memoirs by his friends. In *La Patria*, Joaquín Achury spoke of the pain the death of Hernando had caused his sister Elvira, who appeared in a chronicle praising those who give their lives "not for a nation, but for an entire civilization." In London his disappearance was noted in the magazine *Hispania* by the diplomat and writer Santiago Pérez Triana. In Paris, Léon-Paul Fargue, a good friend of the dead young man, devoted intense pages to him and published his Colombian friend's poems as a posthumous homage. And the people of Bogotá discovered that Hernando de Bengoechea was a great poet; yes, sir, at just twenty-six years of age he had already become a great poet, and would have inherited José Asunción Silva's mantle if a heroic death had not taken him so young.

Marco Tulio Anzola took an interest in the story of the poet soldier. During those days in mid-1915 he thought of him often; he began to follow what was published about him the way one follows a novel published in installments. He didn't really know where this exotic interest, like that of a collector, came from: maybe it was just strange that a Colombian dying far away should be so newsworthy, given that here so many died every day without anyone taking any notice; maybe it was a generational matter, for Hernando de Bengoechea was just two years older than he was, and Anzola could not help thinking the absurd thought we all think at least once in our lives: *It could have been me.* In another life or in a parallel life, Anzola could have been Bengoechea. With a tiny change of fortune, with a minimal displacement of causes and fates, the young man fallen on the fields of France could have been him, Anzola, and not Hernando de Bengoechea. If his father had been a successful businessman of a moneyed family, if he'd studied at Yale and found business opportunities in Paris, if he'd settled there the way so many other Latin Americans had at the end of the century, maybe Anzola would have been born in Paris as Bengoechea had been, maybe he'd speak French and Spanish with equal fluency, maybe he would have read Flaubert and Baudelaire as Bengoechea had read them, maybe he would write essays for Parisian Spanish-language magazines: the *Revue de l'Amérique Latine,* for example, where all Bengoechea's essays appeared, writings about Impressionist art, Russian ballet, Nicaraguan poetry written in Parisian boulevards, or German operas played by fantastical orchestras with Firmin Touche playing saxophone. Anzola went on talking to witnesses who sent him to other witnesses, he went on receiving confused statements that tried to clarify, he went on interviewing people of unknown standing who said they'd seen such and such an enemy of General Uribe in such and such a compromising circumstance, and meanwhile Anzola was thinking about Bengoechea, reading about Bengoechea, pitying Bengoechea's parents who would perhaps be regretting the moment they decided to stay in Paris, and then wondering where in Bogotá the rest of the Bengoechea family lived and pitying them as well.

In those days he spoke with two nuns, who swore they'd seen Galarza and Carvajal watching General Uribe's house from the ground floor of the novitiate in the days before the crime (they gave him another piece of evidence, consequently, that the crime had not been improvised the night before it happened). Anzola found out that for Bengoechea his Colombian nationality had been a decision: at the age of twenty-one, obliged to choose one or the other of his two nations, he'd chosen that of his parents, that of his mother tongue. The newspapers held him up as an insuperable example of patriotism, and when they found out that he'd also been a devout Catholic, their admiration knew no bounds. In *La Unidad*, a columnist known as Miguel de Maistre sang the highest praises of the dead soldier, for it must not have been easy to keep his faith in that country of unbelievers, in that republic of atheism that had declared war on Catholics. The article referred extensively to the French law of 1905, which decreed the separation of Church and State, and said that path led peoples to hell. It also referred to the encyclical *Vehementer Nos*, in which Pope Pius X condemned that subversive law and accused it of denying the supernatural order of things. And it ended by saying that *also among us there were those who attempted to deny the role of the eternal Holy Mother Church, violate the traditional values of our people and unilaterally abrogate the Concordat, source of our perseverance and guardian of our consciences*, and for that *God, who does not punish with clubs or whips, had made of them a lamentable example.*

Anzola read this with terrified fascination. In the space of a few lines, this Miguel de Maistre had managed to go from praising the soldier killed in France to a tacit diatribe against the general assassinated in Bogotá. Yes, *La Unidad*'s column was speaking of Rafael Uribe Uribe, and Anzola had to read it again to make sure there were no more hidden allusions, as if suddenly the death of young Bengoechea had become for the columnist a mere pretext for other things. And who was this Miguel de Maistre? He wasn't the first nor would he be the last to justify the general's assassination in some way: similar opinions had appeared in other newspapers, which had treated the general brutally in the months leading up to his death, and now allowed themselves the odd ambiguous commentary on the ways God has of writing straight on twisted lines. For Anzola, all that rhetoric was sadly familiar. Weeks before the death of the soldier Bengoechea, he had heard the tale of a bootblack in the Plaza de Bolívar, an adolescent called Cortés who had wanted to talk about what he'd seen and heard on October 15. When the assassins attacked the general, the bootblack was working on the shoes of a client at the corner of the atrium of the Capitol, in front of Enrique Leytón's café. The client, a fat, short man, with a big, red nose and black, curly hair, stood up enthusiastically.

"That's how to kill that swine," he said, passing a gloved hand over his frock coat. "Not with a club, not with whips or bullets, but with a hatchet as he should be killed."

The boy Cortés watched him run away toward the Capitol, forgetting, in his sudden haste, that he had only had one shoe shined.

He never found out who that man was who'd demonstrated such satisfaction at the assassination of General Uribe. But it didn't really matter: there were many like him, Anzola thought, in Bogotá: many who had cheered, considering that the murder of General Uribe was not a crime, but a punishment; many like that columnist Miguel de Maistre who condoned the assassination or tolerated it in a more or less covert way. How alone General Uribe had been in his final days! How this dishonest city had turned its back on him! Anzola remembered the procession that had carried General Uribe's coffin to its burial and thought: All liars, all hypocrites. Then he felt unfair, for it was true that in that crowd there were also others, those who had defended Uribe or had accompanied him silently and, what was saddest, without his knowledge. Those who had looked after him on October 15, holding his wounded head, mopping up his blood with their handkerchiefs, and later keeping the handkerchiefs the way they keep relics; those who had prayed for him in the entrance hall of his house; those who in the months since had sought out Anzola to give him some information or share a suspicion that might allow him to proceed toward the light amid the mud of lies and distortions. Yes, they existed as well, and Anzola owed to them the little he had managed to figure out so far. He owed this to the witnesses, yes: to Mercedes Grau, to Lema and Cárdenas, to the bootblack, to the doctors Zea and Manrique. There were also other witnesses later, whose names he would finally forget, in the still-distant future when all this could be forgotten. They were voices, voices that had spoken to him or would speak to him of the crime against General Uribe, friendly or selfish or crude or rough voices, precise or forgetful voices, voices like an army marching through Bogotá to confront another army: one of lies, distortion, and concealment.

ONE OF THOSE VOICES, one of the most important, was that of Alfredo García, the man who had seen six well-dressed strangers talking to Galarza and Carvajal on the eve of the crime, the man who had heard the assassins say that they were *going to do this very well* and that *you gentlemen were going to see this very well done.* Tomás Silva, the shoemaker who had taken García's testimony when no authorities wanted to take it, arrived at Anzola's office one day. This happened in the month of October, while the Third Battle of Artois was raging and the German army, the Austro-Hungarian army, and the Bulgarian army joined forces to invade Serbia. The shoemaker Silva was worried, but not about what was happening in Europe. "He wants to sell," he said.

"Who?" asked Anzola. "Who wants to sell what?"

"García, the witness. He's a decent guy, but poor. And now he's telling me that he can't wait any longer. That if the prosecution is not interested in what he has to tell, maybe Pedro León Acosta will be interested."

"I don't understand," said Anzola.

"The guy's broke," said Tomás Silva. "He can't afford to buy food. I've given him five and ten pesos now and then to get by on, Dr. Anzola, and my employees have fixed his shoes free of charge. And now he thinks that Pedro León Acosta can pay him for his testimony. 'With Dr. Acosta I can do better than with the indictment,' he told me. Like that, in those words: 'I can do better.' The guy is desperate, and desperate men do things like that."

"And why Acosta?" asked Anzola. "Why would Pedro León Acosta pay him to tell what he knows?"

"I'm wondering the same thing," said Tomás Silva. "But we've been begging the prosecutor to take García's statement for a year. We've spent a year asking for the draft statement that García wrote in my presence to be incorporated into the case file. None of that has been done, and I don't even know where that draft is."

"Yes," said Anzola. "But why Acosta?"

The name of General Pedro León Acosta began to appear too many times in the investigation. To Anzola it was more obvious every day that he was involved in some way. And there were good reasons to believe it: was Acosta not one of the surviving conspirators against Rafael Reyes? His past was that of a violent man, and one does not undo one's past, thought Anzola; his past was always with him, and someone who has tried to kill once will try to kill again. It was true there was no proof, but there were strong indications. Acosta had been seen with the assassins at Tequendama Falls, even though the prosecutor had decided not to carry out the investigations necessary to confirm it. And now Alfredo García had reasons to think that man would be willing to pay for his testimony. Anzola thought about this and then he thought: No, he wouldn't pay for his testimony; he thought: He'd pay him for his silence. And then, as if in a dream, he saw Pedro León Acosta standing outside a carpentry shop on the night of October 14, surrounded by others like him, accomplices and conspirators, and he saw him telling the assassins, *All set, then,* and he saw the assassins answering him that they were *going to do this very well* and then, *You gentlemen are going to see this very well done.*

"Acosta was there," Anzola said to Tomás Silva. "Acosta was one of them."

"I think so too," said Tomás Silva.

"And Alfredo García must think so too."

"He wants Acosta to pay him not to say anything."

"No," said Anzola. "*He knows* Acosta will pay him not to say anything. It occurs to me that wouldn't be the first time."

"Do you think he already offered him money?"

"I think we have to do this as soon as possible," said Anzola. "We find García, take him to see Prosecutor Rodríguez, and we chain ourselves to the door until they take his statement."

"And if they won't take it?" said Tomás Silva.

"They have to take it," said Anzola.

"And if they won't?"

"First we have to get him there," said Anzola. "Then we'll see."

The next day they went to the house on Sixteenth Street where Alfredo García rented a large room. They didn't find him. They tried again two days later, and had no luck again. Almost a week later, the morning the cables announced that the United Kingdom had declared war on Bulgaria, was the third time. They knocked insistently on the door, shouted Alfredo García's name, and a police officer who was doing his rounds approached to ask if there was some problem. While they explained to the officer that there was no problem, that they were looking for Alfredo García, a neighbor came out (stuck her head out the window and then the rest of her body, a voluminous body) and told them she knew Alfredo García and could assure them he was absent.

"What do you mean by absent?" said Anzola.

"That he's not here, Doctor," said the woman. "That we haven't seen him in these parts for several days."

Anzola kicked the door violently and the woman's hands flew to her mouth.

A YEAR HAD PASSED since the crime. In the salons they were giving speeches in memory of General Rafael Uribe Uribe; in the streets there were processions of people who sometimes waved white handkerchiefs and prayed in low voices, and sometimes shouted slogans at the tops of their lungs and promised justice and vengeance. All over the city speeches were delivered that lamented General Uribe's departure, missed his civic leadership and his moral strength, saw a profound truth contained in his controversial positions, and complained that other people, his enemies, had not been able to see it. On the green balconies there were new geraniums and on the doors, black ribbons tied to the knockers or the bolt.

Anzola participated in one of these demonstrations of collective pain. He did so out of a sense of duty, but not with pleasure: he walked from the basilica to the cemetery with hundreds of others dressed in dark colors, repeating the same route they'd covered a year earlier, the day of the funeral. A year, thought Anzola, and there had been no answer yet to the thousands of questions everyone asked, that he asked, that he had asked of others. Anzola had been entrusted with the responsibility of answering them and he was failing and his failure was still secret, and that was more humiliating or painful. Another witness had vanished. After the disappearance of Ana Rosa Díez, now it was Alfredo García who had been erased from the face of the earth. Witnesses disappeared from under his nose, or someone compelled them to disappear, and he could do nothing about it. Anzola felt incompetent, like an impostor; he felt that the job was too big for him, that he had gone to play a game with grown-ups without being ready for it. He felt confronted by forces beyond his control, that he didn't even so much as suspect, and he also felt that he wasn't fighting against them on a level playing field. He looked at his black gloves as he walked. That was how, empty-handed, he would arrive to visit the Uribe family later, with empty hands he would embrace the widow, greet the brother. Nothing yet? Julián Uribe would ask him, and Anzola would reply: Nothing yet.

He felt ashamed: walking along the wide avenue toward the west, moving with difficulty and in silence in the midst of the waves of people that were like a funeral cortège though the body was no longer there, brushing up against other living bodies or other mourners or sympathizers of the victim, Anzola felt that he was letting down General Uribe's brother or that he was demonstrating that he was unworthy of his confidence. That pained him. He realized that what Julián Uribe thought of him mattered: it mattered to him the way the opinion of our elders matters to us when they have something to teach us or they are dignified or experienced. He wanted to get out of that mob and hide at home, without any noise, to feel more acutely in solitude his frustration and exhaustion. The mourners' heels resounded on the ground, passing over cobbled streets and others that were still unpaved, sometimes stepping in puddles of dirty water, trying not to step in dog shit. Anzola, for his part, also concentrated on not stepping on anyone else's foot. The people around him (sleeves touching sleeves) didn't allow him to know exactly where he was putting his feet. He looked up, saw in the gray sky ahead of the cortège and behind, to the east, a large cloud shaped like a dead rat above the hills. He knew that later it would rain.

The procession ended in front of the mausoleum. There the general's remains were interred (except for one part of his skull, of course, called the cranial vault, which Anzola had held in his hands and touched and caressed). The crowd had squeezed through the cemetery gate and now filled the available space in front of the monument, and its movements and murmurs filled the cold air. There were speeches that Anzola half listened to and quickly forgot. The orators took turns in front of the mausoleum, standing on tiptoe for more emphasis and shaking one open hand while holding wrinkled pages in the other, and the crowd received their words with respect and sometimes responded to them soberly and then began to withdraw in silence. Anzola watched them go. He looked at the white stone of the mausoleum, that unshadowed white that still conserved the sheen of new things, and thought that it would not be long before it was sullied as all monuments to all the dead of this country eventually were. Then a sustained murmur ran through the crowd, and Anzola looked up and saw a woman wearing a tunic who climbed up onto the pedestal of the mausoleum and began to wave a Colombian flag. Before the act could strike him as ridiculous or banal, Anzola realized that up ahead, in the front rows, were the Di Domenico brothers, who pointed their black box at the woman in the tunic. One of them (it might have been Francisco but also Vincenzo: Anzola didn't know them and couldn't tell them apart) moved his face close to the black box while turning a handle with his right hand; the other directed those present, requesting space, pushing them aside with his hands as if they were an unruly mob, to keep them from interfering with their activities, as if the crowd were the intruders, those who had come to grieve for the general, not them, who had come to record their laments with their annoying, incomprehensible machine.

Yes, thought Anzola, that's what the Di Domenico brothers had come to do. They were collecting images; undoubtedly they had collected some of the procession, and who could know what other things they had captured with their apparatus. Did this have something to do with the advertisement in the newspaper? Had the Di Domenico brothers found a writer prepared to recount General Uribe's life? Anzola could not know and did not feel like approaching to ask: the presence of the Italians there, in the midst of the people's sadness, struck him as impertinent and rude, mercenary and opportunistic. The woman in the tunic walked from one side of the mausoleum to the other, waving the flag, but there was no emotion on her face and no words came out of her mouth. What was her role? What was the aim of her presence there, on top of the mausoleum, dressed the way actresses dress in the theater? Anzola could not know it at that moment, but he would find out days later, at the end of November, when the Di Domenico brothers announced with much publicity the projection in the Salón Olympia of their most recent cinematographic work: *The Drama of October 15.*

ON THE WALLS of the city, large advertising posters promoted the premiere. The people of Bogotá were used to being viewed from those rectangles of paper by bullfighters or acrobats or circus clowns, but finding themselves confronted with the likeness of Rafael Uribe Uribe, who many knew only from solemn portraits published in the newspapers, seemed too close to sacrilege. The general's widow refused to attend the projection; Julián Uribe, however, had no fear of using his surname to obtain the best seats at the premiere, and at his side sat Urueta and Anzola. Nothing like this had ever been done before. The posters announced a *Great event*, the *First showing of moments never before seen on the screen*, and the town criers promised an *homage to the great leader murdered by criminal hands*, and a *reconstruction of the final minutes of a leader*. Some in the audience remembered that the Di Domenico brothers had already shown a cinematographic film about the death of the patriot Antonio Ricaurte in San Mateo, but that had happened more than a century ago, whereas the assassination of General Uribe was still in the news and still causing tension and clashes and serious disputes among friends. The Salón Olympia was full before half the line had gone in. Police officers had to be called to control those who didn't manage to get in. Those outside were frustrated and those inside couldn't believe their good luck, but neither group really knew what to expect. Nor could the Di Domenico brothers, who observed with satisfaction the marvelous spectacle of the theater filling up, have anticipated what would happen.

The film opened with the image of Rafael Uribe Uribe (his broad forehead, his pointed mustache, his impeccable tie) surrounded by two branches that resembled laurels. The people applauded; from somewhere in the room came timid booing, for not even Uribe's enemies had deprived themselves of attending the event. By then, without giving the audience time to grow accustomed to anything, the general's body appeared on the screen, surrounded by doctors who were performing the last surgery. Anzola could not believe it. Something in the images seemed out of place, like a piece of furniture moved without permission, but he couldn't manage to identify the discordance: there were the doctors, moving around the general and brandishing implements that on screen looked white, not shiny, and there was the dying body of General Uribe Uribe, ignorant that the efforts being made to save his life were futile. Then Anzola understood that the images did not correspond to reality, but had been falsified, staged in the way plays are staged in a theater.

It was all a slap in the face. How had the doctors lent themselves to such a farce? But were those the real doctors operating on the screen, or actors? The noise of the voices raised at the grotesque spectacle echoed off the wooden walls of the Olympia. People seemed indignant about the indiscretion of the images, but no one left: in a sort of collective hypnosis, the audience in the hall drank in every indiscreet image, passing from the failed surgery to the coffin coming out of the basilica, to the crowds that surrounded the dead man on the day of the funeral to the carriages with wreaths of gray flowers and skinny horses. On the screen mute speeches were delivered by Uribe's sympathizers, and his brother Julián gave a start when he saw himself speaking on the screen the day of the funeral. The images registered the relatives approaching the coffin to say good-bye to the deceased, registered the men in black hats and sad mustaches, registered the open mouths that emitted no sound whatsoever, registered the salvos the army shot that did not resound inside the Salón Olympia: they were like fleeting clear stains on the gray screen. The people who had been made indignant by the exhibition of the general's dying body seemed to calm down. Anzola, however, had become more anxious than before. In the rainy image of the projection there was a presence that made him uncomfortable: among the notables in the front rows, standing, making a gesture of respect like all the other mourners of the assassinated general, was Pedro León Acosta.

Yes, there was Acosta: his head uncovered, the black three-piece suit, eyes looking up at the sky. He was beside a priest whose antagonism toward General Uribe had never been secret; Anzola remembered that he was Spanish, but his memory could not summon up his exact name. The camera picked up Acosta's unmoved face for two or three brief seconds, but that space of time was long enough for Anzola to recognize him. The general's brother also recognized him, because he glanced at Anzola with complicity and melancholy, a disappointed look in which there was less camaraderie than obscure resentment. There, in the theater, surrounded by alert ears and attentive eyes spying on them, they couldn't say what they would have liked to: that many things had happened since that October 15, and that General Acosta, who on the day of the funeral had accompanied the coffin like one more mourner, one year later had now become one of the main suspects in the case. Anzola saw Julián Uribe lean over to Urueta and say something in his ear. He knew without proof that they were talking of that same thing: of the presence of Acosta among those who had bid farewell to General Uribe, and how that simple image had transformed with the passing of this year. The image of the funeral turned into the scene of the crime: there was the eastern wall of the Capitol, the sidewalk where the general had fallen, the stone wall he'd leaned against. The camera registered the Plaza de Bolívar with its park and wrought-iron fence and its passersby who looked (who looked at us, thought Anzola) with curiosity. Then the assassins appeared.

"This cannot be," exclaimed Julián Uribe. But it was: on the screen the Panóptico had materialized, the jail where Leovigildo Galarza and Jesús Carvajal were awaiting the result of the case that was proceeding against them, and the camera showed them talking to each other, laughing unheard but satisfied guffaws, arguing with other prisoners like cronies in a bar. Now the assassins appeared posing for the camera, first in their adjoining cells and then out of them, in the prison yard. The strangest thing was their outfits: both were impeccably dressed, as if they'd been expecting the cinematographers. Anzola knew that the prison had refused to allow journalists or photographers in to see them:

How had the Di Domenicos managed to get them to strike these poses? Some of the images seemed to be taken without the assassins realizing, but in others Galarza and Carvajal looked at the camera (their sleepy eyes like an affront) and in others they raised their arms to hit an imaginary victim with an imaginary hatchet, as if the men behind the camera had asked them how the crime had happened. "This is an outrage," said Julián Uribe between his teeth. "Shameless scoundrels!" shouted Urueta, losing his composure for an instant, and Anzola didn't know if he meant the assassins or the impresarios of the motion picture. One thing was certain: everything had gone the opposite of the way the Italians had hoped. They had wanted to ingratiate themselves with the Bogotá public through a re-creation of a traumatic event, but what might have been an homage had turned into a slap in the face, and what could have been a memorial to a great man had turned into an insult to his memory.

"Cynics!" shouted Urueta. "Shameful!" From the back they heard worse insults, in angrier tones. Anzola turned around to look for the faces of the Italians, but couldn't see them above the furious heads, the irascible raised fists. On the screen, the assassins knelt looking at the camera and clasped their hands together, asking for forgiveness for the crime they'd committed, but they did not look repentant, only cheeky and unconcerned. Another wave of catcalling swept through the theater. Someone threw a shoe at the screen, and the shoe bounced off and fell onto the platform like a dead bird. Anzola feared things could get out of hand and began to look for the nearest exit, maybe on the left side, beside the lower boxes, maybe through a door that led out to the gardens. On the screen there was a sudden blackness, and it was followed by images that Anzola recognized immediately: they were of the procession the other day. Little more than a month had passed since the homages paid to the general on the first anniversary of his death, and already those homages were up there, moving magically and clumsily on the screen. Anzola wondered if he'd see himself. He didn't, but he recognized the mausoleum he'd visited and was shocked at how much things changed when they were part of a film; on top of the mausoleum, the woman in the white tunic, the same one he'd seen with his own eyes, waved for long tedious seconds the colorless flag of Colombia. He understood that it was meant to be an allegory: liberty (or perhaps the nation) manifest on top of the tomb of its deceased defender. The idea seemed infantile to him and its execution mediocre, but he didn't say anything to anybody. Then the screen went black again. In the middle of a luminous jumble of crazed bubbles and random scratches, the projection finished, and the Salón Olympia filled with the noise of people standing up from their seats.

When Anzola emerged onto the street, he could still hear jeering. People surrounded Julián Uribe and Carlos Adolfo Urueta to show their indignation, and Anzola took advantage of the moment to walk on without having to give voice to his own. He went along the edge of the gardens and crossed the street and began to walk in the direction of home, but taking a long meandering route, to give himself more time alone. For a few moments the murmur of the crowd carried on simmering behind him. That was when he noticed that the same people had been walking in front of him since he left the theater. They were four men in fine ponchos and top hats, and they were talking animatedly about the projection they'd all just seen. Anzola was not in the mood to listen to other people's conversations; when he tried to overtake them, however, he glanced their way, in case there was an acquaintance among them he should greet out of politeness, and he felt a stab of panic as he recognized Pedro León Acosta, who seemed to recognize him in turn, raising two fingers to the brim of his hat and nodding in greeting, but in such a way that his polite greeting was

charged with hatred, more hatred than Anzola had ever seen on anyone's face, a terrible and frightening hatred because it was displayed so
calmly, because it was the hatred of someone who controlled it and
managed it at will. *He knows who I am,* thought Anzola, *he knows who
I am and what I'm doing.* He also thought, with the certainty of a sealed
fate, that this man was perfectly capable of hurting him, that his hand
wouldn't shake nor would any scruples trouble him, and furthermore
he had the necessary means at his disposal. In a second he imagined
the dead bodies of Ana Rosa Díez and Alfredo García, thrown to the
muddy bottom of the Bogotá River or tossed pitilessly over the Tequendama Falls, and wondered if a similar fate awaited him.

Anzola stopped walking. Pedro León Acosta was no longer looking
at him: he had turned back to his companions, and they had walked a
few meters away from Anzola when they burst out, in a sort of infernal chorus, into loud laughter. At that instant Anzola noticed that Pedro León Acosta was wearing patent leather ankle boots.

Anzola, standing in the middle of the street like a lost dog, let
him go.

THAT AFTERNOON, when he reached home, he opened his drawers
and looked for the newspapers from the day of the crime. He had kept
them carefully, first as a sort of commemoration or ritual superstition,
later as documents or memoranda of the task he was carrying out, and
over time he had developed a taste for rereading them. The first he
found was the four-page edition that *La Republicana* distributed the
very evening of October 15. The headlines took up three noisy lines:
half of the front page. First line: "General Uribe Uribe." Second line:
"Cowardly Attack on Way into Senate." Third line: "Assailants Taken
into Custody—Society Outraged and Suffering." Under that began

the text of the editorial, titled "Our Protest," and in the middle of the text a box emphasized something that still moved Anzola: "Attempted Assassination of Gen. Uribe Uribe." What a simple world he could still see in that page: a world where Uribe had not yet died, where his attack was just an attempt and not an accomplished murder, where the assailants had already been captured and society was outraged . . . How different was the world today, with the general dead and cold in his tomb, with those responsible for the crime hidden among rumors and confusion, and the assassins being paid in dollars to appear in the Di Domenico film.

Anzola took out the loose-leaf notebook he'd been using to take notes on the investigation. He looked for a blank page and began to write an opinion piece—an article with the tone of opinion pieces—on the negligence of the prosecutor Alejandro Rodríguez Forero, and the police commissioner, Salomón Correal. But every phrase came out as an accusation, and before passing to the next sentence Anzola realized he had no proof. Halfway through he lost his enthusiasm and began to play on the paper. He began to write delirious versions of the formulaic interrogations of the court. "It is true and I attest that the prosecutor is hiding information, has looked the other way when important facts were presented to him, and allowed a key witness to disappear out of pure lack of interest. It is true and I establish that we, the friends of General Uribe, have pursued the authorities ad nauseam, urging them to investigate the clues that could lead them to the true culprits, and we have come up against an insuperable wall of concealment and corruption." No, it was not true: none of this could he actually establish. It was certain, very certain, but he could not establish it, and thus he put it in writing: "All this is true, but I cannot prove it."

He sat back in his chair, shook his Waterman fountain pen, and continued:

"It is true but I cannot attest to the fact that the assassins Galarza and Carvajal did not act alone, and that this thesis is a tall tale of the conspirators. It is true but I cannot establish that Pedro León Acosta, the same man who tried to assassinate President Reyes and was pardoned, led and financed an association of tradesmen, along with other rich leaders of the Conservative world, all of them sworn enemies of Liberalism. It is true but I cannot attest to the fact that they had some sort of lottery in that association to choose who would carry out that long-standing Conservative wish: the disappearance of Rafael Uribe Uribe. It is true but I cannot establish that on the night of October 14 Alfredo García saw a group of influential Conservative figures talking to the assassins in their carpentry shop, and it is true but I cannot establish that one of them was Pedro León Acosta, who that night contracted with the assassins for General Uribe's fatal destiny. It is true but I cannot establish—if only I could establish—that Pedro León Acosta was present at the scene of the crime on the fifteenth, freshly shaved and wearing a new poncho and patent leather ankle boots, which Señorita Grau saw and remembered. It is true but I cannot establish that after the attack he approached one of the assassins and said: "How'd it go? Did you kill him?" It is true but I cannot attest to the fact that the assassin replied: "Yes, I killed him." It is true but I cannot establish that in this whole cloud of dust there are very powerful people involved who might go up as far as the president of the Republic, who has remained as mute as a sphinx on this subject. It is true, it is a truth like a cathedral, that Pedro León Acosta did not act alone, that General Hatchet is not alone, that the corrupt prosecutor is not alone. But who pulls the strings? I cannot establish, a thousand times I cannot establish! What I can establish, what is true and what I do attest, is that the conspirators have every possibility of getting away with it. What is true and I do attest to the fact, what I can establish every day, what I can attest to even when I'm asleep and dreaming, is that God has forgotten us."

Then he scrunched up the paper into a ball, put it on the logs in the fireplace, and went to look for something to light the fire with before it was time to pray a novena.

THE FRENCH REPORTED more than eight thousand dead on the opposing side at Ypres and Armentières. The British cabinet was in crisis over the war's calamities. The Germans had reached the heart of Russia and had taken control of Poland, and in the Balkans they had erased Serbia from the map and opened a communication route with Turkey.

Anzola read this news and felt that he too was losing a war, and then the thought struck him as unworthy and frivolous (although each person suffers by the measure of their own experience). But it was true, deep down. The investigation was not going anywhere: Anzola had reached the impregnable conviction that the assassination of Rafael Uribe Uribe had been a conspiracy of gigantic proportions, but his conviction had come up against the now obvious complicity of the prosecutor Rodríguez Forero, and there was no way to achieve anything. The whole situation had affected him. The Salón Olympia had canceled, by order of the censors, any further showings of *The Drama of October 15*; the film had been officially banned, and some said that the authorities had gone so far as to burn it; and Anzola thought that one could clearly see there the hand of the conspirators, who had made a crucial piece of evidence against the true authors of the crime disappear. But when he aired his paranoia in public—even if it were just the reduced and private public composed of his acquaintances and family members—he received the same answer: "You're mad."

Or: "What an imagination."

Or: "You see enemies where there aren't any."

They told him he seemed different: more severe, quieter, more closed in on himself. He spent his days going over the dossier of the Uribe case, studying it until his eyes hurt or he felt a weight on the nape of his neck as if he were carrying a sleeping child, and he eventually knew by heart the witnesses' statements and felt uncomfortably as if he'd known and lived with them. He frequently visited Julián Uribe Uribe to speak with him of his frustration and impotence. The general's brother had become Anzola's protector and adviser, someone who invites the illusion of providing us shelter, dissipating our disillusion, filling us with confidence. But this time he received him with an undecipherable expression.

"Do you remember Lubín Bonilla?" he asked.

Lubín Bonilla, yes: the former head of the police investigations. The man who'd been put in charge of the case the very day of the general's assassination, and later, brusquely dismissed by Salomón Correal, accused of divulging rumors against the government. Bonilla, for his part, had always maintained that his dismissal had been due precisely to his efficiency: in a few short days of investigation he had come too close to certain uncomfortable truths. "I burned myself like a moth," he had told Julián Uribe. "By getting too close to the light."

"I remember perfectly," said Anzola.

"Well, General Bonilla sought me out this morning after Mass," said Julián Uribe. "And I think you're going to want to speak with him."

"General Bonilla is in Bogotá? I thought they'd transferred him to Arauca. To get rid of him."

"Well, he's here. I don't know whether he's only recently arrived or if he's been here for a while. But he came back with an urge to say things, and I told him he should say them to you."

"And how can I speak to him?"

"He's going to be taking tea at La Gata Golosa," said Julián Uribe. "If you stop in there, you're sure to find him."

It was past five when he reached Avenida de la República, but General Bonilla was still there, sitting alone at one of the most discreet tables, far from the windows as well as the large mirror. Bonilla seemed younger than he actually was. He had small ears and black hair so rigid it seemed painted on, and his low eyebrows imposed on his face, on the bones of his face, a certain angular discipline that Anzola liked. The cutlery lay on the table in perfect symmetry. One arrived to speak with Bonilla and immediately felt a kind of order: order in the person, on the table, in the whole place. "How are you, General?" said Anzola.

"Here I am," said Bonilla. He raised his tired face, looked at Anzola. "*Caramba*. They told me you were young, but I never imagined you'd be so young. It must be true, as they say, that youth knows nothing of danger."

"I didn't know you were in the city," said Anzola. "Hadn't they sent you somewhere?"

"I was away for a while, yes," he said. "But not because they sent me somewhere. I left because I thought they were going to do something to me."

Over the past few months, Lubín Bonilla had been truly tormented. Days after fleeing Bogotá, looking over his shoulder and keeping an eye on every corner, he had arrived in San Luis, in Cauca, and even way out there the public prosecutor went looking for him. One day a telegram arrived at the mayor's office demanding he present himself in Bogotá as soon as the required travel time would allow. "That order is illegal," Bonilla told the mayor. "I am not a delinquent. If the prosecutor wants my testimony, he has to request that you take my statement." Three days later he learned that a new communication came in, ordering his capture.

"They wanted to imprison you?" said Anzola.

"By order of the governor," said Bonilla. "Effective immediately."

"And what did you do?"

He went into hiding, what else could he do. He left town in the middle of the night and without taking his medications; a colleague helped him recover them, or what was left of them, by ruses and wiles. Bonilla had never led the life of a fugitive, but there, in the mountains, he had to do so: while his friends tried to discover what crime was being attributed to him and what consequences his eventual surrender might have, he spent several nights sleeping out in the open, sheltering from the rain under trees and against rocks, eating and drinking thanks to others who took risks to help him, and once in a while finding a borrowed bed in which to spend a few hours without the fear of being awoken by vermin. One night he was close to being captured by one of the foot patrols sent out by Puno Buenaventura, a police chief famous for his pitiless methods; the barking of some dogs saved him, but didn't give him time to take his only blanket. Barefoot, almost naked, appealing to the charity of farmers to put something in his stomach, he arrived through the mountainous jungle at Ibagué. There he discovered that General Hatchet had offered a reward of three hundred thousand pesos to whoever caught him and handed him over. Then he was certain: if they wanted to jail him, it was not to accuse him of any crime, but so that he'd be found dead one morning at the hands of a hungry hit man.

That's why he'd returned to Bogotá. He had heard that Anzola was carrying out a personal investigation for General Uribe's family. Was that so?

"At the request of Don Julián," said Anzola.

"Well," said Bonilla. "And tell me, have you already talked to Eduardo de Toro?"

"Eduardo de Toro?"

"The one who was in charge of the detective college that day. The one who was with Salomón Correal when news of the attack arrived."

"You weren't with him?" asked Anzola.

"I arrived later," said Bonilla. "But I learned things afterward. Or rather: he informed me of them."

"Things like what?"

"Like about the cells, for example. Galarza and Carvajal were put in separate cells, and kept incommunicado, as is logical. Well, Salomón Correal changed their cells as soon as he could. Put them in cells next to each other, with only a thin wall between them. It's as if he had given them written authorization to speak to each other and agree on their lies. And the assassins took advantage of it, Señor Anzola, they're not that stupid. Each time one of the assassins went into an interrogation, it was as if he'd memorized a lesson. And I would call them back in and ask more questions, often the same ones over again. The first evening was exhausting. We were all tired. There was a lot of nervousness in the air, it was really unbearable. Galarza and Carvajal were nervous, in spite of the fact that they'd come in willingly. They asked to go to the lavatory every hour or so and the guards let them go in together. To urinate together! Forgive me. The doors to the cells were open and so were those to the yard. They could have escaped if they'd wanted to. And with all that as well they were nervous, as if they couldn't stand so much questioning. And at the end of the first day, after an especially tough interrogation, Carvajal grew furious. They took him back to the cell and he said: 'If they keep grilling me, I'll denounce them.' He said it loudly, so everyone would hear."

It was the day after those interrogations when the rumor reached Lubín Bonilla that elegantly dressed and well-shod persons had been seen in Galarza's carpentry shop in the days leading up to the crime. It was said there were meetings held there; people talked about an association of tradesmen and a police officer who guarded the entrance, allowed certain people in and turned others away. Bonilla insisted on finding out what was true in all that, for that officer, if he actually existed, could maybe give useful testimony. He appealed to Salomón Correal, because only the police commissioner could authorize the information Bonilla was seeking: the names and numbers of all the officers who had served in that sector on the nights before October 15. "He fobbed me off," said Bonilla. "What would I need that for, that was not where we needed to be looking." But Bonilla insisted. "This was the afternoon of the Friday, I think. On the Saturday, first thing in the morning, I was informed of my dismissal."

"You hit a nerve with those meetings," said Anzola.

"I think so," said Bonilla. "People of distinction meeting with tradesmen at night . . . That doesn't happen in Bogotá, unless there's a very good reason."

"And you never found out who went to those meetings?"

"No. But I did find out that General Pedro León Acosta was seen with the assassins outside of Bogotá."

"At Tequendama Falls," said Anzola. "That was on June 14. Yes, I heard about that too."

"I was referring to a different outing. Four or five days before the crime."

"He was also seen with the assassins then?"

"In the Hotel Bogotacito. I even went there to confirm it, and they confirmed it. Later the witnesses retracted." So Lubín Bonilla had continued investigating on his own account, in spite of being taken off the case. No wonder Correal felt threatened, thought Anzola, for Bonilla was one of those detectives by temperament as well as occupation: *bloodhounds*, they call them now. Outside night was falling; Anzola raised his eyes and saw that a black butterfly had landed in the corner of the ceiling, right above their heads. Or maybe it had been there since the beginning.

"And what does Eduardo de Toro have to do with all of this?" said Anzola.

"Oh, yes," said Bonilla. "Señor Toro."

Some days after the crime, perhaps a couple of weeks, Bonilla ran into Toro coming out of the police station. "Don't even think of going in," said Toro. "You are persona non grata in this building." It was starting to drizzle, so Bonilla asked Toro if he could buy him a coffee with brandy somewhere to ask him a few questions. He just wanted to confirm a few bits of information about the day of the crime. A short while later the two of them were sitting in El Oso Blanco.

"Just as you and I are seated here," said Bonilla. "I took out my notebook and pencil and prepared to read off a few questions I'd jotted down. But I didn't even get to the first one."

Eduardo de Toro advised him not to keep attracting Salomón Correal's attention: to stop contradicting him, to suspend his illegal investigations. "They're not illegal," said Bonilla. "It doesn't matter what you think they are," said Toro. "The man has you in his sights." And then immediately he began to tell him of Father Berestain's visits to the police over the past few months. Rufino Berestain, one of the city's most influential Jesuits, was the police chaplain; and so it was not strange that he should visit occasionally, said Bonilla. "Occasionally, no," said Toro. "I get the impression that Father Berestain spends more time at the police station than in his parish. He comes, speaks to Correal, they shut themselves away to talk for a whole hour sometimes. I am a good Catholic," said Toro, "but I've never liked that holy father. And after what happened recently, even less." On October 15, from early in the morning, Eduardo de Toro had seen Father Berestain at the police station. He was pacing back and forth, and came out into the corridors of the upper floors asking questions nobody understood very well, but which had the obvious objective of obtaining information about what was going on out in the street.

"Or about what hadn't happened yet," Bonilla said to Anzola.

After the crime, Father Berestain's conduct had bothered a lot of people. The country was in mourning, the city was grieving for Rafael Uribe Uribe, and within the city there were those, people like Eduardo de Toro, who had followed the general or admired him or simply condemned that barbarous act. However, Father Berestain imposed his will: he managed, with the weight of his authority, to have some spiritual exercises take place that had been planned some time previously.

"I was there," said Eduardo de Toro. "I felt obliged, as the whole police corps did, to attend Father Rufino's spiritual exercises."

For several days officers and detectives and Jesuit priests met in the Casa de Cajigas. It was the old Nineteenth Street tannery, which now, under the administration and management of the Society of Jesus, served as a place for retreats and reflection. That weekend, the house, which ordinarily received generous quantities of guests, was full to overflowing. In his final sermon, before the crème de la crème of the police force and two steps away from Commissioner Salomón Correal, Rufino Berestain asked the officers to remember the deceased friar Ezequiel Moreno Díaz, Bishop of Pasto, whom God had called to his side more than eight years earlier. He mentioned, almost in passing, General Uribe Uribe, assassinated a few days earlier, and said that today he thought it more valuable to concentrate on the sacred memory of a servant of God on the eighth anniversary of his death than on the profane memory of an enemy of the Church, even though his body was just newly in the ground. Ezequiel Moreno, said Father Berestain: What was left of that wise and brave, God-fearing man, who had come to these lands from the mother country to bring a message of resistance to the blows of atheist Liberalism? His message remains, my sons, and that legacy fell to them. Its protection fell to them; its defense was up to them. Now that the nation's faith was weakening before the attacks of the friends of Satan, it was well to remember the saints like Brother Ezequiel, who had left the world of the living as he had passed through it: with the brave intransigence of a true shepherd of souls. Eight years, eight years had passed since his death, and the words of his last will and testament still lived, and they would live forever. Did the illustrious members of our police corps know the last will of Brother Ezequiel? They can all be summed up in one, a very simple and sadly forgotten one: Liberalism is a sin, enemy of Jesus Christ and the ruin of nations. Do they know what the saintly man requested? That they put that phrase in the hall where his lifeless body lay and also in the temple during his funeral. That's what he left as a testament, or in exchange for his testament: the request for a sign with that eternal truth. *Liberalism is a sin.*

When the exercises were finished, before the men began to leave for their houses, Habacuc Arias, one of the first officers who had arrived at the scene of the crime beside the Capitol that day, dared to suggest that they also pray for the soul of General Uribe. Maybe he hadn't been present during the sermon, maybe his ignorance didn't allow him to understand what he was requesting: but he did request it. Rufino

Berestain stood up and new shadows appeared on the harshness of his face. He looked at the officer with cold, clear eyes that no one had ever seen and that Eduardo de Toro, for his part, would never forget in what remained of his life. And then he spat out:

"That brute should be rotting in hell."

VII

WHO ARE THEY?

Walking through the city the morning after his encounter with Lubín Bonilla, Anzola held against his chest a leather-bound notebook that Bonilla had placed on top of the tablecloth after finishing his tale. "Here are names and addresses, and some more or less legible notes," he'd said to him. "It would be an honor if they could be of some use." He pointed out two or three names that he should seek out immediately to try to get statements. One of them was Señor Francisco Soto, which Bonilla had underlined twice.

Señor Soto lived in a large two-story corner house with balconies and geraniums spilling through the railings. It was the house of well-to-do people. A servant opened the door and led him into a living room to the left of an interior patio framed by terra-cotta flowerpots, and Anzola caught sight of a barefoot child who was playing a game tossing coins against a corridor wall. Francisco Soto greeted him with surprise: he was a young man, but he was accustomed to being advised beforehand by those who wanted to see him. He had just returned from a long business trip, he explained, an exhausting trip that had taken him from Caracas to Havana, from Havana to New York, and upon returning to Bogotá he had preferred not to let the newspapers announce his arrival. Many of his friends didn't even know of his presence in the city yet. How had Señor Anzola found out?

"It was General Lubín Bonilla," said Anzola. "He was the one who spoke to me about you."

"Ah, General Bonilla," said Soto. "That gentleman's sharper than hunger."

"He told me he'd met you more than a year ago, after the assassination of General Uribe."

"A couple of weeks after, more or less," said Soto. "I had gone to the office of Alberto Sicard, the lawyer. We began to talk about his detective college, which he was thinking of founding back then. I introduced myself and he recognized my name. He took out a notebook and said he'd been wanting to talk to me for some time."

"About the general's murder?"

"He had heard that I had certain information," said Soto. "I don't know how he knew and I still don't know. A bloodhound, that General Bonilla. Did he set up his detective school in the end?"

"Yes, he did," said Anzola. "What information was it? Something to do with the Jesuits?"

Soto half closed his eyes. "How do you know?" But he didn't let Anzola answer. "Yes, that was it. I told him someone else had seen what I saw. Or that I knew of someone who had seen that, but I didn't tell him it had been me. I didn't want any problems. He said we'd meet on another day in a different place, where no police would see us." He paused. "But we never managed to see each other, because a few days later, when I left on a trip, he still hadn't come to find me."

"And to this day."

"Yes," said Francisco Soto. "And I haven't spoken of this to anybody, or almost anybody. I don't know how you found out."

"And what was it you saw?"

On the night of October 13, two nights before the crime against General Uribe, Francisco Soto was walking down Ninth Street with his friend Carlos Enrique Duarte. It was late and the street was deserted. They passed beneath the balcony of the novitiate and Francisco Soto pointed to the house on the opposite corner. "General Uribe lives there," he told his friend. His friend didn't say anything. They kept walking in the direction of the Capitol, but before they reached the corner of Carrera Séptima they saw two people, one in a felt hat, the other in a straw one, come out of a small door.

"The San Bartolomé building has a little door that opens onto Ninth Street, a sort of back door," Soto told Anzola. "That's where they came out. The one in the felt hat I recognized immediately: it was Leovigildo Galarza. I couldn't see the other person very well, but it was a taller person who looked better dressed."

He'd met Galarza at El Meeting bar, back in 1909; his friend Carlos Enrique Duarte also knew him: Galarza had done some carpentry jobs for his mother a few months earlier. They both thought it odd to see Galarza at this hour of the night, in the company of a man not of his class, coming out of the Jesuit college by the back door. But they didn't mention it again until Galarza's photo appeared in the newspapers. "Galarza killed General Uribe!" Duarte said to Francisco Soto the Friday of that week. "It was him!" he said, and repeated, "It was him!"

They didn't go to the police immediately. The day of the funeral,

Soto and Duarte formed part of the mourning crowd that accompanied General Uribe from the basilica to the Central Cemetery, and realizing then the magnitude of what had happened, and watching from afar the priests who were walking with the victim's family, they spoke of the possibility that the Jesuits had known about the crime. The public and vocal antipathy they professed for the assassinated general was a secret to no one; Francisco Soto had seen, as had everyone in Bogotá, the violent campaign to discredit him over the past few years from the pages of *La Unidad* and those of *Sansón Carrasco*, their two favorite megaphones (Francisco Soto said: their two mercenaries); and having seen one of the assassins coming out of the San Bartolomé seemed like too much of a coincidence. He and his friend Duarte remembered that Father Rufino Berestain, Bogotá's highest-ranking Jesuit and also its most implacable, was the chaplain of the police force. (The Rasputin of the police force, said Francisco Soto. Duarte did not laugh at his joke.) And right there, walking as part of the black-clothed procession bidding farewell to the deceased, they said to each other that it would be best to keep quiet, because a crime involving the police and the Jesuits was a crime that was best not to get involved in. Later they were pleased, as over the course of the weekend a rumor began to circulate that anyone coming forward with information was being arrested. They saw this later with their own eyes: people they knew, people whose good reputations went without saying, had to spend hours or a night in jail, like delinquents, for committing the error of saying what they saw.

"Those poor folks didn't know there are things you see but don't say," said Francisco Soto. "Especially these days."

"But now you can say them," said Anzola. "Now we need you to tell these things. If people like you don't talk, the ones who did this are going to get away with it."

"Have you been to see them?"

"Who?"

"The murderers. Have you gone to the Panóptico?"

He had. Last December, shortly after arriving from his long business trip, he thought that he hadn't entered that building since his father was a prisoner. "Your father was a prisoner in the Panóptico?" asked Anzola. Yes, said Soto: that was after the last war. His father, Don Teófilo Soto, was a militant Liberal, on the losing side of that odious war like the thousands of losers who filled the prisons of Colombia. Don Teófilo raised his son on war stories: stories of heroism when Francisco was a boy, stories of pain and failure and truncated hopes as he was growing up.

"Well, I realized I'd never visited the prison as an adult," said Francisco Soto. "And I thought I should."

He arrived at the Panóptico on a sunny morning. In the yard, prisoners were basking in the light. Soto walked through, looking left and right, asking questions of the guards, putting up with the smell of urine and rotting food. He realized it had all changed since the war, but also that he couldn't pinpoint exactly what had changed. Maybe, he thought, what had changed was him, who had come to visit his father as a boy, and now he was a man and the spaces of the prison, its corridors and walls, its rooms seen from outside, seemed smaller. The whole place now seemed less impressive than it had back then; but of course, then it had also been a place of fear and anguish, because nobody had explained to the boy that his father was not going to die locked up there, that he wasn't witnessing his final days. So Francisco Soto went along, passing through that place of sadness like a tourist in a museum, when he recognized, sitting in their cells, General Uribe's assassins.

"There were Galarza and Carvajal," he said.

Galarza recognized him. He shook his hand but without standing up, and looking not at his eyes, but at his tie or the buttons on his vest: "How are you, Señor Soto." He asked the assassins, without crouching down, how they were, if they were being well treated, if they were bored.

"Now you see, Doctor," said Galarza. "They get us into these things and then they won't even look at us."

BEFORE THE YEAR ENDED, the mysterious Alfredo García, that disappeared witness, had written a letter from Barranquilla, on the Caribbean coast, announcing his definitive trip to Costa Rica, signing himself *Alfredo García A*. Anzola and others commented that it was strange that the initial of his second surname should be *A*, for he had never used it in his signature before; but they didn't dwell on it, because in any case that defector was no use to them now. But in February, the Medellín newspaper *Etcétera* published a strange letter. It was signed by Alfredo García, but the initial of his second surname had changed. "García B.," Anzola read, and a crease appeared on his brow as if the text contained a discourtesy or an insult. The letter, furthermore, was dated from Bogotá, which meant that Alfredo García had not ended up traveling to Costa Rica. Had he changed plans? Was it possible that he was in Bogotá clandestinely? Or had the announcement of the trip been to throw off the investigators, proof that García had not been paid just to disappear but also to confuse those seeking justice? The contents of the letter were explosive: its author denounced the suspicious behavior of certain individuals related to the Uribe crime, and did so in terms that left not the least shadow of a doubt. The letter was like the ruling Anzola would have written if he had been a judge. It was, as Julián Uribe said, a dream come true.

The author of the letter began by accusing General Pedro León Acosta: "I saw that man on October 11, 1914, at the Hotel Bogotacito, owned by Señor Benjamín Velandia, around half past eleven in the morning, in the company of Galarza and Carvajal. The three of them, after a few short words that I could not hear, continued to Tequendama Falls." He immediately involved the Jesuits: "On the thirteenth of the same month I saw, with my own eyes, at around ten at night, Pedro León Acosta and his companions Galarza and Carvajal, enter the college of San Bartolomé through a small door the convent has at the back on Ninth Street." He even went so far as to mention the famous card that Ana Rosa Díez had wanted to hand to Tomás Silva before she disappeared off the face of the earth: "Later I heard from a Señora Rosa, close friend of Galarza's mother, that she had received a card from a friar whose name I cannot yet say." Alfredo García then allowed himself the liberty of paraphrasing the card, as if he had seen it. "The card referred to says more or less the following: 'The reverend father recommends to you, in a very special way, to this lady, that she remain at home for some time, while we figure out how to organize certain things.'" And he finished by referring to General Hatchet: "I also know positively that Galarza's mother went to see General Salomón Correal and said he should see about looking out for her well-being and her life; that they had her son in prison, and he was the only one who took care of her; that it was not fair that she was having a rough time. Señor Correal answered that she shouldn't worry, that he would go and talk with some gentlemen so they would give her a monthly sum of money, by a third hand, to attend to her necessities."

The *Etcétera* revelations in Medellín shook the proceedings in Bogotá. The public prosecutor began to move as he hadn't moved in the year and a half since the crime. Pedro León Acosta wrote to the court to request they find out who the author of the letter was; the prosecutor summoned Acosta, Galarza, and Carvajal to testify; finally, he decided to search desperately for Alfredo García, and in order to find him began to send communiqués to various cities. One afternoon toward the end of February, the newspaper was passed from hand to hand in Julián Uribe Uribe's house while the *almojábanas* got cold and a thin skin formed on top of the hot chocolate. Tomás Silva and Carlos Adolfo Urueta were present, having been called to celebrate the incident as if it were the conviction of the real murderers. "It's all here," said Tomás Silva. And Julián Uribe ran excitedly around the dining table saying yes, finally, here it all was. The page of *Etcétera*, thought Anzola, had arrived at the Uribe house the way news of the end of the war would have arrived at French households.

And yes, he had shared the enthusiasm of all those present at first, but as the hours went by he began to fall into a disenchantment that nobody could really understand and he himself, much as he tried, could not explain. Something in the letter grated: it was too perfect, too pertinent, too useful, too opportune. "Precisely, here it all is," he said. "All that we needed, all that we would have liked to prove. Here are Acosta and the assassins at the falls, here are Acosta and the assassins coming out of San Bartolomé, here's the Jesuit's card that no one could find a year and a half ago, here's proof that Correal helped the assassins in hidden ways. Yes, here it all is."

"And what is the problem?" asked Silva.

"I don't know," said Anzola. "But these things don't happen just like that."

"Everything happens somehow," said Silva.

"Yes," said Anzola. "But nothing happens like this."

"You're beginning to worry me, esteemed Anzola," said Silva. "You're so used to looking for enemies everywhere that now you can't realize it when a treasure falls out of the sky."

"This is no treasure."

"Be careful, that's all I'm saying. Because this way you won't even believe in Our Lord Jesus when he comes to save you on the Day of Judgment."

Anzola tried to put his skepticism into words. After the crime, Alfredo García had remained in Bogotá for more than a year, waiting in vain for the prosecutor to take his statement; in all that time, he had never mentioned what he saw on the night of October 13, in spite of the importance of the incident. He had never mentioned Salomón Correal, in spite of being aware of the suspicions that floated around the police commissioner since he refused to take his statement. Never had he mentioned the Jesuit's card and never had he revealed that he could paraphrase its contents, in spite of having shared Anzola's and Silva's worries over Ana Rosa Díez's disappearance. "Why not?" said Anzola. "Why didn't he tell us any of this? Why was he with us for a year and a half talking about the crime, talking about all these things, without mentioning these precise things? Why just now, when we've collected testimonies telling of Galarza coming out of the Jesuits' building with a mysterious man? Why now, when the complicity of the Jesuits and General Hatchet has begun to be obvious? Why does he now say yes, he knew, that he also saw and also knew? By what gift of fortune do we receive everything we would need so that the prosecutor will finally arrive at the truth about the assassination in a single document? Why does what García mentions in his letter correspond almost exactly to what we have been discovering from other sources these days? And why the change in initial? Now his second surname begins with *B* but on the draft it began with *C* and in the letter from Barranquilla it began with *A*. Why?"

"Could it be a different person?" Urueta said timidly.

"It's not a different person." Anzola was suddenly irritated, and he came very close to being insolent or rude to his elders. "It's clear that it's the same person. Unless by pure coincidence there are three homonyms in one. Unless the three of them know the same things about the crime against General Uribe. No, I think they are the same person, and I think that person is playing along with this game. I think someone got Alfredo García out of Bogotá by paying him a large sum. They bought him, as we feared, and now they're making sure they get their money's worth. They make him write letters that mislead us. They make him sign with different initials. And they make him confess in a letter all that can implicate the Conservatives and Jesuits in the crime."

"But it's absurd, Anzola, listen to what you're saying," said Silva. "Why would they do that? Why would the conspirators want to point themselves out?"

"Look who's pointing at them," said Anzola.

"A witness," said Silva.

"A disappeared or escaped witness," said Anzola. "A man who writes a letter to a newspaper and mistakes his own initial. That document has no credibility for a judge, because there's no one to take responsibility for it. Where is the denouncer? No one knows. Is he in Barranquilla? Is he in Bogotá? Is he in Medellín? He has no face, and a witness who does not show his face might as well not exist. No, what this letter does is screw us." Julián Uribe raised an eyebrow. "With a single stroke of a pen, the conspirators just discredited all of our accusations. The participation of the Jesuits, Salomón Correal, Pedro León Acosta, has all now turned into a cheap rumor. A confused letter sent by an escaped witness, whose whereabouts are unknown and who changes his second surname every time he signs a piece of paper: no, this does not produce the least conviction, and no judge in his right mind would give it the slightest credibility. This is what they want, to take credibility away from any accusation we make, turn it into the absurd rumor from a lost madman. And they are succeeding, it seems clear to me. They are beating us even before the battle starts. Do you want me to make a prediction? The prosecutor is going to move heaven and earth to look for the accuser, to turn this into a great spectacle of pursuing a hidden truth. Within a few weeks or months he'll declare that he didn't find him. That in spite of all his efforts, he did not find the accuser, and then the accusations are going to turn into the words of a madman. The Society of Jesus involved in the crime! Absurd. General Acosta and the police commissioner involved in the crime! Absurd. Of course, they'll say, what can we expect from an anonymous accuser who signs with a borrowed name and doesn't dare to emerge from his cowardly burrow. No, they'll say, these accusations are no more than the odious product of a feverish mind. We cannot, they'll say, take them seriously." He paused and then said: "It's a masterstroke. If it weren't the work of our enemies, I'd find it easy to admire."

Later, as Anzola said good-bye to the gathering, he noticed they were looking at him differently. Was it pity he saw in their eyes, was it mistrust or worry? They looked at him the way people look at a delirious relative: with the same tense mouths, the same grieving eyes. When he left, Anzola thought he'd lost something that afternoon. He walked two or three blocks through the city watching the shadows made by the yellow light on the paving stones. Thinking of Alfredo García A., of Alfredo García B., and of Alfredo García C., remembering the man he'd met in Bogotá and whose conscience the conspirators had devoured, he told himself he was confronting a powerful machine, and a shiver ran down his spine. Was he capable of confronting those monsters? Then he wondered: Was this fear he was feeling? A small group of men looked at him as he turned into the Plaza de Bolívar, and Anzola was convinced they were talking about him. They began to move toward the corner, and then a burst of laughter erupted from the group that sounded at once hollow and deep in the empty plaza, like a stone falling into a pool. Anzola had an idea. In minutes he was back at Julián Uribe's house, where the diners were sitting in the same places as when he left, and where the pitying eyes looked at him in the same way they had before.

"Dr. Uribe, Dr. Urueta," said Anzola, "I have a favor to ask you." And before they could answer, he added: "I want you to put me in prison."

THAT'S HOW HE BEGAN to work in the Panóptico. His former occupation as a functionary in public works was helpful: using it as a pretext, Uribe and Urueta pulled some strings to get Anzola an administrative post in Bogotá's main prison. No one ever knew what his tasks were, apart from wandering idly through the building work taking place in the jail; but no one asked and for several months Anzola was able to enter the building of cold stone where Galarza and Carvajal lived alongside criminals and delinquents from all over the country, and saw a tired hatred in the faces of the prisoners and also saw the defeat that wasted away the flesh of the cheeks and drew shadows under the eyes. Yes, the salary at the Panóptico was considerably lower than that of an inspector of public works, but Anzola didn't mind tightening his belt for a time: what mattered to him was his investigation, which by then was much more than a commission or even a job: it was a vocation, something that gave structure and reason to his days. He looked for Galarza and Carvajal. He observed them from afar, trying not to be seen by them, and when he got home in the evenings, he made notes of his finds. He realized that his conduct imitated or repeated that of the assassins before the crime, the vigilance of observing prey, the satisfaction of carrying it out without the prey noticing anything; he understood or seemed to understand the intoxicating power of someone observing someone else and thinking of causing him harm. From a certain moment on he began to discover a new attitude that might just be curiosity but could also be something more disturbing. What did the assassins think during the day? he wondered when he saw them. Did they remember their victim? Did they dream of him? What was it like to kill a man? One afternoon he asked a guard to point out to him a prisoner convicted of homicide and approached him later, cautiously, as someone might approach a circus beast.

"Do you dream of your victims?" he asked.

"Yes," the murderer told him. "But only when I'm awake."

Anzola had never heard a more perfect definition of guilt, and didn't ask him anything else on the subject. But as the days wore on that prisoner led him to another, and this one to yet another, until he ended up having sincere dialogues with a man called Zalamea who had seen him prowling around Galarza's and Carvajal's cells. "Your Honor is a detective?" the man had asked him. Anzola said no, that he was there to carry out some work on behalf of the Ministry of Public Works. But he couldn't avoid a mistaken interest—a bit morbid, he had to admit—in General Uribe's assassins.

"More interesting is what's happening to them," the man said.

"What do you mean?"

"They do whatever they like," said Zalamea. "It's as if they were free men."

This Zalamea was a man of some education, that was obvious, and for that reason he dared to complain to the guards about the injustice of treatment in the prison. He was in prison, he claimed, for reasons of debt, but he never gave any explanations or further details; he did explain, however, his surprise at seeing Galarza and Carvajal receiving special treatment that verged on illegal. It was Zalamea who told An-zola of some letters that the guard Pedraza took out clandestinely for the assassins; it was Zalamea who spoke of an incident in which a Je-suit priest came personally to collect some sealed envelopes the assassins were sending out into the world. "Are you sure he was a Jesuit?" asked Anzola.

"Father Tenorio," said Zalamea.

"Rafael Tenorio?"

"That's the one," said Zalamea. "Do you know him?"

Anzola knew him, yes, but not by sight. Julián Uribe had discovered an uncomfortable fact about him: it seems that Father Tenorio had been a chaplain in the Conservative army in the last war, and in that capacity had once met a soldier by the name of Carvajal who offered to assassinate General Uribe and thus end the war the easiest way. After the crime, when the photo of Carvajal appeared in the newspapers, Father Tenorio told the anecdote to a certain Eduardo Esguerra, a Conservative and frequent visitor to the chaplain. "It's the same man," said Tenorio. But months later, when he was finally inter-rogated about the matter by the prosecutor, he retracted. "Comparing the portrait with my memories," he said, "I can assure you they are not one and the same." And this was the man who visited the assassins? This was the priest who served as their private mailman?

"Galarza and Carvajal receive him in the chapel, they talk like friends," said Zalamea. "I've seen them with my own eyes." He paused and then added: "But it's been like this the whole time. Father Tenorio visits them a lot. He brings them gifts. They are spoiled, I should say."

"What gifts?" asked Anzola.

"I've seen packages," said Zalamea. "Books, newspapers. But I don't know any more than that."

Zalamea told him about a conversation he'd had with the assassins one day, during the hour they were allowed out in the yard. When he asked them why they'd gotten involved in such a mess, one of the two, Carvajal or Galarza, replied with ease: "If we hadn't killed him, someone else would have killed him." They were very sure they wouldn't spend more than four years in prison, despite having committed a crime normally sentenced with twenty-five, and Zalamea believed this arrogance somehow came from their impunity. On a certain occasion, he told him, the guards had found the hammers, chisels, and files that another prisoner had been using to try to escape, hidden in their cells, and that offense, which would have resulted in grave punishments for any other prisoner, had no consequences for them whatsoever.

"They didn't do anything to them?"

"They didn't even tell them off," said Zalamea. "That's why I tell you, they're sacred bodies, these two. They're even making a living as cinema artists."

He was referring to the Di Domenico brothers' film, for which the assassins had posed here, in these corridors, in front of these cells. From the beginning a rumor had spread that the appearance of the assassins in *The Drama of October 15* had been remunerated; now Zalamea was confirming it out loud.

"So they paid them?" asked Anzola.

"Yes, they got paid," said Zalamea. "Fifty pesos each. Look how well they dress. Look at the things they wangle. And not to mention what they have in their cells."

For several days, monotonous days of long hours, that his imposture made all seem the same, Anzola was waiting for a convenient opportunity to get into the assassins' cells and see what he could find. It wasn't easy, however, because Galarza and Carvajal had different routines from the rest of the inmates: they weren't obliged to attend the instruction sessions, for example, or to get up at the cruel hour imposed on the rest of them. Sometimes they had lunch with what the inmates called the community, sharing everyone's food at the same time everyone else ate, but sometimes they were allowed to receive elaborate dishes from outside that their women brought, and sometimes they bragged openly about eating as if they were in a restaurant, and people had seen how they had food brought to them in their cells. Those privileges, Anzola noted, had earned them the antipathy not to say frank resentment of the community. The other indicted men looked at them from afar, the way people look at intruders, and changed the subject and even their way of standing when one of the two approached. He even heard that Galarza and Carvajal lent money within the prison, and at high interest rates; that the neediest inmates sold them chains or rings or bottles of *aguardiente*, and they paid good prices; that sometimes they ordered raw food from outside and sold it inside the prison to inmates who didn't have those permissions. He also noticed that the general's assassins didn't go to Mass at the same time as the rest: they had a sort of preferential place in the Panóptico's chapel, so they could receive their services at different times, shutting themselves in there alone with the priest. Anzola had an idea. The following Sunday he went to the prison at an early hour. At midday a bald priest arrived, went to the assassins' cells, and took them to the chapel. Anzola saw his opportunity.

Galarza's and Carvajal's cells were not only more spacious than the rest: they were another type of room. They were separated by a mere partition wall, so thin that it would not have even kept them from talking to each other at night. Anzola chose the one on the left, without knowing which of the two it belonged to, and he was astonished. On the floor, a rug and a calfskin warmed up the place. A bare lightbulb floated above and threw domestic shadows across a painting of the Sacred Heart of Jesus; at the back, a tap dripped rhythmically. A cell with running water and electric light, thought Anzola, what kind of people were keeping watch over the assassins? The two beds placed symmetrically in the two cells were each made up with two woolen blankets, four pillows with pillowcases, and a cushion with an embroidered cover. There was no grime in the corners. On a wooden tabletop, in a disorderly pile, there seemed to be more than the necessary books and papers, as if the carpenters who assassinated General Uribe didn't live there, but rather some poor student. No, thought Anzola, not a student but a seminarian: beside the wall, under a picture of the Virgin of Carmen, leaned a padded stool like the ones for kneeling on to pray.

Anzola saw missals and novenas to read at Christmas, he saw a leather-bound Bible, saw pamphlets and noticed one especially: *The Yes and the No*. It was the first time that he had seen it, but he had heard people talking about the book on several occasions, and always with the same indignation. In 1911, years after Father Ezequiel Moreno maintained that Liberalism was a sin, General Uribe had responded with a brilliant pamphlet, full of his best rhetorical weapons and precise ideas: *How Colombian Political Liberalism Is Not a Sin*. The opuscule was a scandal: in it Uribe asserted that the Liberal Party was as Catholic as the other party, as respectful of the family and social institutions that informed Colombian life as the other, and then went on to encourage Colombian Liberals to confront, denounce, and condemn the abuses of the clergy. That, however, was not the worst of it: after the Colombian Church forbade the reading of the book, Uribe had committed the gravest affront of all: appealing to the Holy See. For priests, this was the definitive slap in the face; and *The Yes and the No*, which occupied such a special place in the assassins' belongings, was their reply. The author hid behind an impenetrable pseudonym: Ariston Men Hydor. Anzola took out Lubín Bonilla's notebook and noted down, on the last page, the title, the author, and the name of the press: Cruzada Católica. It was the same press that published the newspaper

La Sociedad, the pages of which had declared General Uribe an immoral force and established, beyond all doubt, that the war of 1899 had been God's punishment against the acolytes of Satan. Anzola opened the pamphlet at random and read that Uribe Uribe was the enemy of religion, of conservative principles, and of the nation. But then a convict passed the open door howling and startled him, and Anzola left the cell without looking at anyone, in case he might encounter the eyes of the assassins in the long corridor.

The next morning, before arriving at his simulated or pretend job, Anzola passed by the offices of the Catholic Crusade printing press. He wanted to buy a copy of *The Yes and the No*; he also wanted to find out about its author. But he didn't have any success at that: nobody, in the whole press, knew who the man was who hid behind that strange foreign name. A certain Marco A. Restrepo, a Jesuit priest, had brought the manuscript to the press, but the truth about its author could only be found in the accounts. Anzola asked if he could see them, but they explained that they were looked after by the Curia and they told him, in more elegant words, that the canons would sooner cut off one of their own arms than show them to a man of his reputation. Nevertheless, leaving with a copy of the pamphlet under his arm produced the absurd sensation of a small victory.

He read it over the course of the day, during the meal breaks he took in solitude and in moments of rest, and forced himself to reach the end, despite every paragraph of the book being a grotesque lie, a distortion of evidence and calumny, a gob of spit from the pen of Ariston Men Hydor that sullied the memory of General Uribe as it had previously sullied his living image. One paragraph especially caught his attention. In it the author reminded his readers of General Rafael Uribe Uribe's unpardonable sins as a senator of the Republic of Colombia. And what were those sins? Not having attended the session in which they discussed the consecration of Colombia to the Sacred Heart of Jesus; having abandoned the senate chamber when they debated whether the country should join the Catholic world celebrations of the fiftieth anniversary of the dogma of the Immaculate Conception. Yes, thought Anzola, that's why this country of fanatics hated him to death: for not modeling Colombian laws with the clay of their superstitions, for not entrusting the uncertain future of the country to the distant magic of a rotten theology. A Conservative congressman, seeing Uribe retire from the chamber when they were about to vote on the support of the festivities, reputedly cracked a joke that several others applauded.

"The general is like the devil," he said. "He runs away when he hears the name of the Virgin."

Enemy of the Catholic religion. Culprit of the civil wars. Murderer of Colombians. The accusations were familiar. Anzola had heard them a thousand times, a thousand times he had read them in the pages of newspapers, but now, reading the pamphlet, he noted something more. It was an echo, a vague flavor, and it took him a few minutes to arrive at this private revelation: the voice of Ariston Men Hydor was singularly similar to that of the author who, under the pseudonym El Campesino, had viciously attacked General Uribe from the pages of *El Republicano*. They were opinion pieces that Anzola had read and regretted for years; he'd followed the polemics they provoked; he'd discussed their implications with other Liberals. The Campesino also blamed Uribe for having sent thousands of young men to their deaths during the war of 1899; the Campesino also accused Uribe of desiring the disappearance of the Church, the destruction of the family, and the elimination of private property, of wanting to hand the country over to atheist socialism. The Campesino accused Uribe of seeking with his writings the deterioration of all morals and the discrediting of the faith that was the sustenance of the good life. Who was this man? If Anzola's intuition was correct, the Campesino and Ariston Men Hydor were the same person: two different pseudonyms and one true libeler. But how to confirm it?

He tried visiting *El Republicano*'s printing press. He spoke with staff writers and a machine operator. A young reporter with a patch over one eye came out to meet him. "Not here," he said, and took his arm to lead him outside. While they walked around the block, the young man introduced himself as Luis Zamudio, told him he'd been a reporter for the newspaper at the time when the Campesino's editorials appeared, he expressed his admiration and respect and desire that he would soon arrive at the truth about the Uribe crime. Then he said he didn't know who the author of the articles against the general was.

"They arrived already typed," he said. "They were not written here in the office."

"The editor in chief didn't write them?"

"No, definitely not," said Zamudio. "We used to say the Jesuits wrote them. Though you didn't have to be a genius to figure that out."

"But who brought them?"

"Sometimes Father Velasco, the Franciscan superior. He would close the door to talk to the editor. Sometimes Father Tenorio. The Jesuit, I don't know if you know him."

"Yes, I know him," said Anzola. "And you don't think they could have been him?"

"The Campesino?"

"Yes."

"Oh, that I wouldn't know. The articles arrived typed, as I said. Impossible to know whose hand had written them. What I do know is that they didn't come from the newspaper." And then: "I am ashamed, Señor Anzola."

"Of what?"

"That this newspaper has turned that way. Of what they did to the general, of that rude campaign they waged against him," said Zamudio. They were arriving back at the printer's door. "Can I ask you something?"

"Go ahead."

"Why so much interest in the Campesino? The campaign against Uribe came from everywhere. Why especially the Campesino?"

Anzola felt an explosion of fellow feeling: he remembered what it was like to confide in someone and, furthermore, to feel that someone confided in him; the feeling seduced him (perhaps a blend of vulnerability and nostalgia) and he was about to explain the whole situation to that unknown journalist with a damaged eye. He almost told him of Ariston Men Hydor and *The Yes and the No*; he almost told him the authors of the pamphlet and the columns were, in his opinion, the same person, and that he'd found that pamphlet among the assassins' belongings, in one of their private cells; he almost explained that, in his opinion, the assassins had received that pamphlet from those who ordered the assassination, that they gave it to them to strengthen their resolve, nourish their hatred of Uribe, neutralize their guilt, and prevent their repentance. Anzola had gotten it into his head, therefore, that the discovery of this hidden identity would throw new light on those responsible, and there, on the narrow sidewalk, he was about to explain this to the reporter. But he reconsidered in time. This Zamudio, after all, was still working for *El Republicano*, was he not? Who could know what secret intentions drove his loquacity? What invisible strings had guided him around the block? How was it possible to confirm that he hadn't been sent on a secret mission by Salomón Correal or Rodríguez Forero?

Anzola glanced at all the corners, to make sure no one was watching them. He said good-bye to the reporter and went on his way.

———

AT THE END OF MAY, what Anzola had predicted with respect to the mysterious letter published in *Etcétera* happened. Prosecutor Rodríguez Forero, with a great fuss, ordered heaven and earth to be searched for the witness Alfredo García, who had written those fearful accusations. He wrote to Barranquilla, where the first letter had come from, addressing himself to the mayor of the city in peremptory tones; but he did so without the minimal astuteness of describing García physically, which meant his request could not be fulfilled. The mayor of Barranquilla replied with a request for a description of the individual being sought, but in spite of the information being on record, he received no response. The prosecutor's office then sent a mass telegram to all the mayors in the Republic: YOU ARE REQUESTED TO ESTABLISH AND INFORM BY TELEGRAM IMMEDIATELY IF ALFREDO GARCÍA A. RESIDES IN YOUR JURISDICTION. There was no favorable reply. When Anzola learned the contents of the telegram, he headed for Julián Uribe's house without wasting any time. "Why García A.?" he said to the general's brother. "Why not García B., why not García C., if the prosecutor knew of the confusion over the initials? Now we know why the criminals asked him to sign in three different ways: so later he could be searched for and not found, so they could seem to make an effort without running the risk of having their efforts succeed. I was right. I was right and you didn't believe me." Julián Uribe had to admit it.

On the morning of the twenty-eighth, Anzola was working at the Panóptico when one of the guards—the one called Pedraza, who seemed to be a Salomón Correal plant and helped the assassins have dealings with the outside world—came to tell him that someone was waiting for him out front. When he went out, the street still wet from the recent rain, and Anzola found Tomás Silva holding a copy of the edition of *El Tiempo* where the prosecutor had published an edict. He unfolded it, straightened it with a flick of his wrists, and read: "Alejandro Rodríguez Forero, prosecutor of the criminal proceedings against those responsible for the death of General Uribe Uribe, cites and summons the author of the letter . . ." He didn't need to say more. Anzola understood immediately: the prosecutor was publicly requesting the witness to come forward and declare what he knew about the crime; he assured him his rights would be guaranteed; but if he did not come forward, he would be viewed as an accessory.

Anzola walked a few steps and then sat down on one of the benches overlooking the avenue, under the trees with their dusty leaves. He saw two noisy automobiles go past, he saw ladies in hats in the backseats of the automobiles, he saw a horse shitting as it walked north, toward Barro Colorado. "There it is, they did it," he said. "They're magicians, my dear Silva, we can't beat them. García isn't going to come forward: his absence is already paid for and assured. Tell me something, Tomás: How much does it cost to make a man disappear without taking his life? How much does it cost to transform him into a writer of absurd letters, and then into a ghost, and then a fiction, and then an instrument to discredit an entire investigation? That's what Alfredo García is now: an invention of ours to tarnish the good name of the distinguished people of this country. All his accusations, everything he wrote in that letter, has now and forever been turned into the ravings of an accessory. With this maneuver, Pedro León Acosta's presence at Tequendama Falls has just become worthless. The assassins having been seen coming out of the Jesuit convent's door has just become worthless. I can't do anything against this. Not me, not anybody. It makes me sick, but what can one do? What can be done against such a mighty force, capable of making Ana Rosa Díez disappear off the face of the earth, making Alfredo García write what he doesn't know and then turn the truth into a lie, turn what happened into what has no longer happened? I thought only God could bring about such miracles, but it turns out that's not the case, that others have this power too. Yes, I feel sick, that's what one feels, that's what I feel. And what can be done? Vomit, Silva. Vomit all that one has inside, and try not to let the vomit splash anybody."

No one spoke again of the witness Alfredo García: this marked his disappearance from the trial and also from the world. Sometimes it occurred to Anzola to think of him, wonder where he would be, whether in Barranquilla or in Costa Rica or in Mexico City, or perhaps buried a couple of meters underground with a machete wound in his neck, with two bullets at point-blank range in his back. At the end of September a rumor began to circulate that Alejandro Rodríguez Forero was coming to the end of gathering testimony and carrying out investigations, and some people, who had no reason to lie, said that he had begun to write the *Vista Fiscal*, his Prosecutor's Indictment. Anzola heard the rumors and only thought: *Alfredo García's testimony will not be in that Vista. They have achieved that. They have kept it out.*

The second anniversary of the crime was approaching, and Anzola realized it had been a long time since he had visited the site. (He had grown used to calling it that, the *site*, in his monologues and dreams and ravings.) He went one morning. He was on his way somewhere else, but as he passed the Santa Clara Church he allowed himself this detour. Entering the Plaza de Bolívar from behind the Capitol, he had to pass the exact spot where an officer and a civilian had arrested Leovigildo Galarza, confiscating a blood-covered hatchet from him. "I never use that," Galarza had said later, during his first interrogation, "because I haven't been a murderer." Anzola shivered, as if one of those gusts of icy wind that knock down foreigners had blown in, as if for an instant the entire city had turned into the *site*, every street and every wall had become a witness to Uribe's murder or a crime scene.

Anzola turned the corner. He was still twenty paces or so from the sidewalk when he noticed a new presence in the familiar landscape; as he approached, without taking his eyes off it, he saw that it was a marble plaque that someone had put up in the past few months so the people of Bogotá would never forget the tragedy. He read:

> HERE, AT THIS TRAGIC SITE, ON OCTOBER 15, 1914,
>
> THE DISTINGUISHED GENTLEMAN, DOCTOR AND GENERAL
>
> RAFAEL URIBE URIBE, BELOVED SON OF COLOMBIA
>
> AND HONORED THROUGHOUT LATIN AMERICA,
>
> WAS TREACHEROUSLY SACRIFICED
>
> BY THE AX BLOWS OF TWO SINISTER VILLAINS.

Who would have put it there? For whom? It was obviously not for these lazy passersby who walked by without looking at it. *Two sinister villains,* read Anzola, and suddenly he felt deceived. No, it wasn't two, it was many more: in this, the plaque was complicit with the conspiracy. Furthermore, the word *tragic* was a lie, the word *sacrificed* was affected, the word *ax* was an imprecision, and the word *beloved* was hypocrisy. Yes, thought Anzola, this whole plaque was a great marble impostor, probably placed here by orders of the general's enemies, so dexterous in the art of distortion, of false leads and concealment in broad daylight. *Written in stone,* wasn't that how people referred to an eternal truth, something that was true until the end of time? This plaque, with its appearance of an inoffensive memorial, was in reality the consecration of the conspirators, one more step in the imposition of that reality in which two half-drunk carpenters kill the general because the government hasn't given them work. That plaque was part of the irrevocable absolution of the great wolves of the pack. Anzola then imagined an absurd scene in which he lifted the plaque and, there beneath it, on the wall, found the names Salomón Correal and Pedro León Acosta and Rufino Berestain. Then he had this revelation: that this marble plaque announced, in thirty-eight words, what the prosecutor would say in many more in his *Vista Fiscal*, as if they were tilling the soil in which to sow the seed of the lie. He read it again, took out Lubín Bonilla's notebook, and copied the thirty-eight words, and with each stroke thought he wouldn't even have to read the *Vista Fiscal*, for he already knew what it would say. It would say *honor of Latin America*, it would say *distinguished gentleman*, and it would say, especially, *sacrificed by two sinister villains*.

Two lone wolves. Two assassins with no accomplices.

THE *VISTA FISCAL*, the prosecutor's pretrial statement, the document that would declare before the law who was accused in the Uribe case, was published in November by the National Printing Bureau. It was a leather-bound book of three hundred and thirty pages of small print and legal technicalities, but people devoured it as if it were a popular novel. "It's out, it's out," you heard people saying on the street corners, and the newspaper vendors announced it even though they didn't have it to sell. On the afternoon of the same day, Julián Uribe called an urgent meeting, not at his house, but at 111 Ninth Street: the general's house, where his widow still lived, where his study and his library remained as he had left them and where his ghost was present in a thousand ways: on those steps his coffin had come down, in that spacious salon where they had kept watch over him, in those windows through which had entered, the night of his death, the disconsolate wailing of his followers. In the general's study were Julián Uribe and Carlos Adolfo Urueta, both standing, both overcome with sadness and indignation.

"Have you heard?" Urueta asked Anzola as soon as he saw him come in.

Anzola had procured a copy from the offices of *El Liberal* and turned immediately to the last pages. He read with his heart clenched the vindication of his worst fears. After declaring the criminal case open against Jesús Carvajal and Leovigildo Galarza, the prosecutor concluded that there was no proof of responsibility against any other suspects. Anzola read the list of the innocent, all those people the law would take no action against. It began with the name Aurelio Cancino, that worker at the Franco-Belgian plant who predicted the crime against General Uribe weeks before it happened and whose prophetic talent, nonetheless, was never of interest to the investigators. He revised one by one the almost fifty names on the list, and eventually found the only one that truly interested him: *Pedro León Acosta* occupied the last place in that inventory of infamy. It was as if they had wanted to play a joke on him, thought Anzola, for the name of Acosta, placed at the end of the paragraph, served as an obscene bridge to the next paragraph, where the innocence was declared, beyond any doubt, of Salomón Correal. And now Anzola had arrived at the general's house, and his brother was looking at him with eyes sunk in sadness while Carlos Adolfo Urueta asked him: "You saw it?"

"I saw it," said Anzola.

"Acosta, innocent," said Urueta, shaking the book like a preacher. "Correal, innocent."

"And not a word about the Jesuits," said Julián Uribe.

"Not a one," said Urueta. "As if they didn't exist. As if you hadn't established all that you established. Unless, of course, it was all your imagination."

"I didn't imagine it," said Anzola. "I know the Jesuits visit the assassins and are mixed up in this. I know there is a pamphlet writer hidden behind the name Ariston Men Hydor, and that it is the same one who signed his editorials, horrible articles against General Uribe, as the Campesino."

"And who is that man?"

"I don't know," said Anzola.

"You don't, do you?" said Julián Uribe. "You have circumstantial evidence, Anzola, just circumstantial. There's Acosta over here, Correal over there, the priest Berestain a little farther back . . . I want to believe you, but you still haven't explained how all the things you discovered are related. Beyond your imagination, or rather, your theory. And if you haven't explained it to me, how are we going to explain it to the judge when the trial begins? I want to believe you, Anzola, but the judge is not going to want to, because what you maintain is not going to be to anyone's liking. With this *Vista Fiscal* we've run out of time. The law is the law: only the suspects in the *Vista* will go to trial. The ones who are not in the *Vista* might as well not exist. And you know that as well as I do, don't you?"

"It's true."

"The trial is going to begin within the year, more or less. We have a year to tell the judge why the *Vista Fiscal* is a lie. We have a year to convince him that this book is wrong. To put it a better way: the one who has a year is you, my esteemed Anzola. You have a year not to let us down, and not to fail my brother's memory. You have a year to demonstrate that we were not wrong when we assigned you to this delicate operation. Many things are at risk, Anzola, many things that go beyond justice in the particular case of my brother. If what you say is true and there is a conspiracy, the future of this country depends on the conspirators not getting away with it. One who kills with impunity kills again. Whoever organized this will do it again. How are you going to prevent it?"

Anzola remained silent.

"Tell me, Anzola," Julián Uribe went on. "How are you going to convince the judge that this book is a distortion of the truth, or rather that the truth is elsewhere and that we have found it?"

"I am going to write as well," said Anzola. He pronounced the words with such certainty, that in that instant he had the illusion of having decided this some time ago. "I am going to tell everything. And then let the heavens fall."

THE FIRST of his articles came out five days later.

The vile murder of Rafael Uribe Uribe, eminent Liberal leader and moral beacon of the Republic, has gone unpunished before the trial of the accused has even begun. We can draw no other conclusion from the unfortunate *Vista Fiscal* from Dr. Alejandro Rodríguez Forero, whom we had thought more upright and honest, or at least more diligent and rigorous. But his document is the sad proof of the power that those behind the crime, who still remain in the shadows, have over the entire citizenry; if they can wish for and achieve the death of a personage as illustrious as General Uribe, if they can organize and perpetrate in broad daylight a cowardly and treacherous attack such as the one our leader suffered on October 15, 1914, we must accept that none of us is safe; that the powerful decide from the shadows who lives and who dies in this godforsaken country.

The *Vista Fiscal* is a formidable document, not for its probability or its justice, but for the talent with which it manages to mask the truth and hide those responsible for the aforementioned crime. So obvious was the twisted will of the Prosecutor from the very beginning of the investigations, that the victim's brother, Dr. Julián Uribe Uribe, found himself obliged by suspicion, which is sometimes a good adviser, to commission us to carry out a parallel investigation into the events. At the time we took on the task with honor, the honor that was possible for having known and admired the work of General Uribe and having been hurt by his death; little could we imagine that we would come up against this web of plots, falsifications, immorality, and lies. For months we have spared no time or expense to bring to light the truth of what happened, against the somber interests that have distorted the facts and obstructed the investigations. And today, from the pages of this valiant newspaper, we dare to raise an accusing finger, just as the illustrious Émile Zola did in recent and similarly tough times, and say: We accuse.

We accuse General Salomón Correal, police commissioner, of having appropriated the Uribe case without the necessary authority, and even of having lied about a supposed personal order from the President of the Republic. We accuse General Correal of having pursued and harassed the detectives who deludedly thought, as in the case of General Lubín Bonilla, that their duty was to find the murderers of Rafael Uribe Uribe, not hide them behind a smoke screen. We accuse General Correal of having refused to receive evidence that implicated individuals other than the named assassins, when he prevented a valuable witness, with the complicity of the Prosecutor, from giving a statement. We accuse General Correal of hiding evidence, as when he received a bundle of papers found at the house of one of the assassins and, in front of his subordinates, chose a few, put them in his pocket, and returned the rest, leaving to posterity the question of what information those now disappeared documents contained. We accuse him of having allowed the assassins to communicate freely with each other since their arrest; we accuse him of indicating to them with his finger when they should remain silent and when they should answer the investigators' questions; we accuse him of having arranged for the assassins to have only a thin partition wall between their cells in the Panóptico, so they could reach agreement on their lies and their strategies; we accuse him of having assigned each of the assassins a personal orderly who cooks for them whatever they want, makes their beds in the morning, and removes their waste at night, and allowing each of them to receive unusual quantities of food from the market, according to some prisoners, around six pounds of meat. We accuse him, finally, of using his power, which is not small, to extend to the assassins benefits that no other prisoner in Colombia has a right to expect. Why? Because only these assassins might speak up against those truly guilty of the crime against Rafael Uribe Uribe; because only these assassins are the owners of a silence worth its weight in gold.

General Correal's behavior is surrounded by suspicions under any dispassionate gaze, to any free intelligence whose intention is none other than finding the truth. Not so for Prosecutor Rodríguez Forero, who has been his accomplice since the dawning of these proceedings, and whose conduct, rather than that of an upright civil servant, has been that of a slave who obeys his masters. Thus, he has refused to pursue the possible truth in the declarations of so many witnesses who saw General Pedro León Acosta in the company of the assassins at Tequendama Falls; he has refused to even consider the possibility that General Pedro León Acosta was the man who was seen the night before the crime speaking to the assassins at the door of the carpentry shop. He has refused, in fact, to involve General Pedro León Acosta, in spite of the thousand indications that implicate him in the criminal activities. The public Prosecutor, faced with the testimony of dozens of witnesses, has preferred to take the word of the suspect, who has denied he was even present in Bogotá on the days preceding the tragic moment. Readers of *La Patria* will remember, since it was a very public event, that General Pedro León Acosta was the same man who attempted to assassinate General Rafael Reyes, President of the Republic, one ill-fated day. Is it his word the Prosecutor chooses to believe over that of others? What does this tell us about a civil servant like Prosecutor Rodríguez Forero, supposed representative of the interests of the community, when he gives full credit to the word of a coup attempter and discounts that of citizens with blameless pasts?

Today, only deliberate myopia or bad faith can deny the evidence that General Pedro León Acosta had more responsibility in the assassination of Rafael Uribe Uribe than the *Vista Fiscal* assigns him. Only corruption or indolence can maintain without blushing that the police commissioner is free of all guilt and innocent of all negligence. And only ignorance or amnesia can avoid the fact that the two sinister men have something in common: they each once tried to murder a president of Colombia. Salomón Correal, torturing the elderly Dr. Manuel María Sanclemente; Pedro León Acosta, attacking in cowardly fashion General Rafael Reyes. What more proof is needed of their complicity and their identical purposes?

But there is a third point in this triangle of evil, readers of *La Patria*, good Colombians, a third point that must be sought among the Society of Jesus. Scandal, shout the readers, blasphemy? No: simply, the audacity to put in black and white certain truths that hurt us all and few of us accept.

We must look at the evidence. Who were the men who held meetings behind closed doors with the police commissioner? The Jesuits, represented by Father Rufino Berestain. Who were those who used the pulpit to insult and attack the memory of the assassinated general just a few weeks after the fateful day, who desired that his soul should rot in hell? Once again, the Jesuits; once again, represented by the Basque Berestain, Machiavellian Rasputin of the Colombian police. Where did the assassins emerge from on October 13, 1914, according to testimonies we have been able to gather? From the Jesuit college, that has a little door on Ninth Street. Who visits and accompanies the assassins in the Panóptico, who brings them gifts of books that libel and dismiss General Uribe, undoubtedly to strengthen their resolve and convince them that the Catholic faith condones and even celebrates their horrendous crime? The Jesuits. The Jesuits. The Jesuits.

Launching these difficult contentions from the tribune of the free press, we do not pretend to establish criminal responsibilities, which is what the justice system of our country should be concerning itself with. We will settle, however, for denouncing the faults and errors in a *Vista Fiscal* that seems designed more to cover up than to elucidate. Dr. Rodríguez Forero's *Vista Fiscal* states his opinion that there are no other people responsible for the murder of General Uribe Uribe than the two confessed assassins who are awaiting trial in jail; but common sense and diligent investigation suggest a wider fan of complicity that involves high-ranking members of our society. In the days that follow, if God gives us life and the pages of this heroic paper lends us space, we will reveal what we have been able to find out in the course of our own investigations, unspoiled by any spurious interest or thirst for vengeance. We seek only the answer to our legitimate questions. Do the Colombian people not have a right to leave behind deceit, conspiracy, and lies? Do they not have a right to know the truth about who rules their destiny? Who are the true masterminds behind General Uribe Uribe's death?

Who are they?

When Marco Tulio Anzola read his own article published in the pages of *La Patria*, he thought that now it was certain: there was no turning back. Over the next few months, with some frequency, he sent the newspaper the results of his investigations, or rather gave written shape to what resided in disorder within the unfathomable universe of his notes and documents. He did so fully aware not simply of publishing indignant columns, but excerpts from a future book: a book that would have to be a valiant response to the *Vista Fiscal*, his demonstration that Julián Uribe had not been mistaken in entrusting him with this task: a book that would be, yes, his *J'accuse*. He didn't publish those articles under a pseudonym, as the Campesino or Ariston Men Hydor did with his diatribes and false accusations against Uribe Uribe, but used his own name in proud capital letters, and he was flattered that hurried readers would stop him in the street and praise his courage. Word went around that those scandalous articles were part of a book in progress, and there was respect in the eyes and voices of his few readers and sometimes admiration. Anzola had never known vanity till then, the terrible vanity of being brave.

That was when he started to see suspicious people on every corner. It all began one morning, when he looked out the window to see if it was raining and saw, instead of rain, two men who seemed to be watching his house. He saw them again—at least, he saw what he thought were the same two men, but then later he wouldn't have been able to confirm it, even if his life depended on it—as he came out of his office one Friday night. He didn't tell anybody about it, certainly not Julián Uribe: he didn't want to be one of those men who is always looking over his shoulder. General Uribe, he thought, had not looked over his shoulder that day, he had not been one of those men. What right had Anzola to harbor fears that the great general had disdained?

Nevertheless, he did write a letter to the minister of government. He reminded him of his responsibility to safeguard the rights of citizens; he told him of the interest he'd taken in the clarification of the crime against General Uribe; he told him that, as part of this "perfectly legitimate" task, he had begun to publish a series of columns in *La Patria* demonstrating the errors committed by those responsible for the proceedings. Since then, he explained in his letter, he had been the victim of a "covert but no less dangerous persecution on the part of unknown individuals," and he requested the minister to send officers or detectives to arrest those individuals. "This does not mean the undersigned is requesting personal protection," wrote Anzola, "but is simply proposing an efficient and opportune support from the authorities when the case should present itself."

A month later he received a reply. More than a negative, it was a taunt: "As soon as what the correspondent says happens, the National Police will provide whatever help might be necessary." Anzola saw in the disdainful sarcasm the stamp of Salomón Correal. Meanwhile, a

newspaper published an elaborate cartoon in which a ferocious Anzola, with aquiline nose and prominent teeth, stood beside the figures
of Uribe Uribe and Death with a scythe; on the other side of the frame
was Salomón Correal, serenely holding a Christian cross. The caption
said: *Cowards attack in gangs.* The cartoon appeared on a Monday; the
next day, Anzola attended a speech given by followers of Marco Fidel
Suárez, a white-bearded grammarian who had begun to sound like a
Conservative candidate for the next year's presidential elections. The
meeting took place in the Parque de la Independencia, among tired
trees and low houses that protected no one from the wind that blew
down from the eastern mountains. There was Anzola, standing in the
middle of the anonymous crowd, waiting for the first speaker to take
the stage, when someone recognized him.

"You're that atheist," a man in a dark poncho said to his face.

And before Anzola knew it, a catcalling had started up. "Atheist!"
mouths he didn't see shouted at him. "Atheist!" Anzola attempted to
defend himself: "I am Catholic!" he shouted absurdly. "I go to church!"
Behind the threatening faces, beyond the gold teeth that shone in slan-
derous mouths, the treetops had begun to tremble. He remembered
what had happened to General Uribe shortly before his death: in a park
like this one or perhaps right here, during a speech by Ricardo Tirado
or Fabio Lozano, a furious crowd had shouted at him, had surrounded
him, and was on the verge of striking him when his companions
opened a black umbrella as a shield and almost carried him through
the air.

Around the same time he wrote to Ignacio Piñeres, director general
of penitentiaries, to request he order and carry out a search of the assassins' cells. Would there be evidence there, valuable clues, compromising documents that would allow him to back up his accusations?
Anzola thought it possible, at least judging from what he'd been able

to see when he'd been on his secret mission inside the Panóptico; but for it to be useful an inspection would have to be carried out in full compliance with the law and, at the same time, without the assassins' knowledge. It wasn't difficult to convince the official: on March 14, at around half past nine in the morning, Anzola and Piñeres arrived at the front door of the Panóptico. They were accompanied by the director of prisons, a young man called Rueda, who spoke and moved as if he were holding something between his buttocks, and whose piercing voice took some getting used to. Piñeres and Anzola, however, got along from the start. He seemed diligent and disposed to help. When they arrived in front of Galarza's and Carvajal's cells, he stepped forward to take charge; he informed the assassins, who regarded him disdainfully from their beds, what was going to happen; and asked them, in a firm but not impolite tone, to stand up and wait in the corridor. Galarza came out first, barefoot, and Anzola saw his hairless feet and dirty toenails, except for his left big toe, which was violet as if he had stubbed it; Carvajal took a little longer, and when he finally emerged he took a quick look around, sweeping his gaze over the cell as if wanting to make sure nothing compromising or incriminating was lying around there. The assassins leaned against the wall in the corridor, without looking at each other. On their mouths, on those pale, thin lips their sparse mustaches did nothing to hide, there was a hostile but at the same time serene expression, as if all that was going on was happening to others. Galarza, fixing his slanting eyes on Anzola's necktie, said:

"Aren't you the one who used to work here?"

"Yes," said Anzola.

"And didn't you get fired?"

"No, I wasn't fired," said Anzola. "I was transferred, promoted. They didn't fire me."

"They told us you'd been fired."

"Who?"

"People."

"Well, it's not true. They didn't fire me. They promoted me. They transferred me."

Galarza said: "Ah."

Then the search began. For three and a half hours, the two civil servants went through the two adjacent cells looking and touching and separating and describing, and then noting down everything they found in a loose-leaf notebook. In Carvajal's room, which they saw first, they found a three-piece serge suit in good condition, a new jacket and well-pressed trousers, three foreign-made shirts, and a box full of very good undershirts and shorts. They found a rope ten arms-lengths long, a metal hoop, a saw, and three needles. They found a box with chocolates and *pandeyucas*, a wallet with money in it and a key ring without keys, and a quantity of letters, books, and notebooks that Anzola looked through while Piñeres and Rueda moved around the spacious rooms, coming out of one and going into the other under the impassive gaze of the assassins. In Galarza's room they found woolen blankets, three pairs of almost new boots, a suit of green cloth in per-fect condition, four pairs of trousers, two fedoras, half a dozen recently purchased collars, one box of ties and another of good-quality under-pants. After revising the inventory, Piñeres summed up the situation in seven words:

"These wretches dress better than I do."

Meanwhile, Anzola leafed through the assassins' books and note-books as if the revealed truth were in them, and transcribed his finds. When he had finished doing that, shortly before one, he went out into the corridor; but instead of speaking to the assassins, he crossed the yard and confronted a guard with a phrase that could have been a question, but came out sounding like an accusation:

"You people advised them we were coming."

"No, sir," said a broken voice. "It was last night that the general was here, I didn't do anything."

The guard he'd questioned was called Carlos Riaño. From his statement they found out that the previous night, shortly before midnight, Salomón Correal had arrived at the Panóptico along with one of his most trusted men, Officer Guillermo Gamba. The warden of the Panóptico accompanied them in person to the assassins' cells, and then left them alone with them. The meeting lasted half an hour, but neither the guard nor the warden nor any of the prisoners knew what they talked about.

"And who advised Correal?" said Anzola. "The only ones who knew about this were you lot and us. And it wasn't us."

"The general has ears everywhere, sir," said Riaño. "Especially when it comes to Carvajal and Galarza. There is nothing that happens around here he doesn't find out about. Each time those two have a fight, either the general shows up or Father Tenorio appears. I swear, it's as if they could see everything in the Panóptico."

It seemed that Galarza and Carvajal, he told them, had been behaving for several months like a mismatched married couple. Only the intervention of Correal or the priest allowed them to reconcile. The last incident had happened just a few days earlier: Riaño was in the room next to the assassins, playing chess with a few other guards, or watching them play on the wooden board. Then they heard the first shouts. Carvajal told the other one that it was his fault they were stuck in here, that it was because he'd gotten involved with those people and he didn't know why he'd listened to him, when everything was so good before. And Galarza began spitting insults. "Shut up, you son of a bitch," he said. "And let's see you loosen that tongue so I can slit your throat." Carvajal responded with the screams of an offended woman that he wasn't scared, but it was obvious the opposite was true. It was at that moment that Galarza went to get his knife and, in full view of everybody, put it in the pocket of his trousers. Carvajal ran to hide in the lavatory.

"And Correal found out about all this?"

"I don't know if he found out, but the next day Father Tenorio arrived, took them to the chapel, and closed the door. That's what always happens. And from there, from the chapel, they come out as if nothing ever happened," said Riaño. And then he added: "They do say that confession eases the burdens of the soul."

"So they say," said Anzola. And then he asked: "Did they take anything away last night? Correal and his subordinates, I mean. Did they remove anything from the cells?"

"Not that I saw," said Riaño.

Anzola made certain recommendations to the director general of penitentiaries: that they take the rope and tools away from the assassins, to prevent them from harming themselves or harming others, or trying to escape, and that they also confiscate the fedoras, for the assassins could use them to disguise themselves in the case of someone letting them out. All this was done. When he got home, Anzola was satisfied and at the same time worried: for he had verified firsthand what he knew from the testimonies: that General Hatchet and the Jesuits had become, for all practical purposes, the godfathers or protectors of the assassins. Did they so fear what they could say? *Confession eases the burdens of the soul,* the guard Riaño had said, and Anzola thought no: it wasn't the confessions of the assassins, but the promises of their superiors. The reason for that nocturnal visit was the same as the one the books full of libelous allegations against Uribe Uribe had arrived at the cells, and the pamphlets declaring him an enemy of God and of the Church. Anzola wrote: *Stiffen the assassins' resolve.* He wrote: *Quieten their consciences.* He also wrote: *Assure them they will not go to hell.*

Some days after the search, a package arrived for the assassins, care of the prison chaplain. When they opened it, they found two new pairs of ankle boots and a bundle of underwear. Carvajal chose the yellow leather boots, and Galarza had the white canvas ones, and they divided the new undershirts and underpants between them. The guard Riaño told Anzola all this. He also told him that one day, in the afternoon, he'd seen the assassins return to their cells carrying two piles of good clothes. He didn't know who or where they came from, but he said that Galarza put his bundle away in the trunk without looking at it, as if he didn't need it, but Carvajal started unfolding his new garments and holding them up to take a better look at them, and then noticed Riaño watching him, shoved it all in his trunk, and slammed the lid down insolently. Anzola listened to this testimony, and there was so much envy and resentment he detected in the words, the contempt for these inmates who lived better than their guards was so obvious, that he had a vexing illumination. He thought that all it would take was the offer of a couple of coins for Galarza and Carvajal to die one night in their sleep, with their throats cut, bleeding over the embroidered edges of their fine cushions.

Some days ago, accompanied by the Director General of Penitentiaries, we went to the Panóptico with the aim of carrying out a surprise search of the cells of Jesús Carvajal and Leovigildo Galarza. How surprised we were to realize that General Salomón Correal, police commissioner, had mysteriously found out about our visit, and had himself visited the assassins on the eve of our arrival just before midnight. Readers of *La Patria* will wonder, as we wondered ourselves, what the police commissioner has to do at such hours in the cells of the self-confessed assassins of General Rafael Uribe Uribe. One doesn't need to be Sherlock Holmes to suspect that the intentions of someone who receives information from spies and acts secretly and nocturnally were not honorable ones.

But now we'll leave aside the accusations, which are many and very sinister, against the man whom the people in their wisdom have baptized General Hatchet. We wish to present to the public certain findings fortune offered us on the aforementioned visit, and let the public assign the value their consciences dictate. The first is a notebook belonging to Jesús Carvajal, from which someone had torn out seven pages before our visit, without our being able to discover what information they contained. But the accomplice's hands could not tear out all the pages, and sufficient information was found on other pages. For example, this note from the first of June 1916: "I bought from José García Lozano a woolen blanket for four hundred and fifty pesos ($450) cash." The most obtuse mind, faced with such proof, would wonder: How does a prisoner get hold of such a generous sum? As the sadly famous *Vista Fiscal* states, Galarza and Carvajal were so poor at the moment of the crime that they'd been forced to pawn a carpenter's brace for fifty pesos. Now, by what we've been able to investigate, they spend hundreds of pesos on clothing and amenities, and they have money to lend to other prisoners as usurers. What a mysterious change of fortune! But none of this has been judged worthy of attention by the Prosecutor Rodríguez.

Let us observe now what has happened in these past couple of years to those around the assassins. Galarza's mother has held several interviews with the police commissioner; according to testimony the Prosecutor has not wanted to take into consideration, during one of these interviews she declared her worry about the fact that her son, who supported and cared for her, was in jail; General Correal asked her not to worry and assured her he would find a way to get money to her. María Arrubla, Galarza's concubine, went from living a life of poverty to hiring servants and hosting picnics for her neighbors. Señorita Arrubla was detained for a time in the Good Shepherd women's prison, while her judicial situation was clarified; and there, according to witnesses, she enjoyed unusual privileges, being put in charge of the rest of the inmates and receiving a liter of milk daily and a food basket that no one else had a right to. One witness has stated: "I swear that before the assassination of General Uribe Uribe, María Arrubla dressed poorly, in chintz dresses and *alpargatas*, and that afterward I saw her wearing ankle boots, with silk shawls and tweed skirts, and she also started using two surnames." Does this situation not deserve any investigation on the part of the Prosecutor? We will surprise no one if we state that none has been carried out.

Carvajal's relatives have had similar luck. In the aforementioned notebook we found the following annotation: "On May 19 Alejandro left Bogotá, heading for Tolima." The subject mentioned is Alejandro Carvajal, the brother of the assassin Jesús, who was present at the scene of the crime—mysterious coincidence, which the Prosecutor has not wished to explore—to protect him from the possible fury of the crowd. Having made our own inquiries, the ones the Prosecutor could not or did not wish to make, we discovered that the assassin's brother, once solemnly poor, is now a prosperous merchant in Ibagué, operating under the name of Alejandro Barbosa. Readers can judge for themselves whether there isn't something profoundly suspicious in such a sudden change of fortune, and whether someone who changes their name does not wish, of necessity, to conceal and hide.

And despite all of this, the Prosecutor in his *Vista* rejects the probable motive of financial gain in the case of the Rafael Uribe Uribe crime. The clues and the testimony swarmed around him from the beginning of the proceedings, but the Prosecutor has made superhuman efforts not to find out. Why? Because if he should come to admit that the assassins acted in pursuit of profit, he would ipso facto have to look for the source of that money and ask who was paying it. To shape his fable of the crime, his *Vista* had to ignore any clue that would lead him down other paths; now we know it was not simple negligence, but unmistakable will to conceal the real culprits: the black hands that, with bloodstained money, contracted and paid for the assassination of a man and split in two the history of a people. We continue to ask: Who are those black hands?

Who are they?

IN THE MIDDLE OF JULY, Julián Uribe sent for Anzola. "I have another testimony," he told him, "but it is not just any other. If this doesn't convince the judge, then nothing will."

And now Anzola was here, sitting in Julián Uribe's drawing room, just as he so often had in recent years, sometimes feeling himself in an oasis of peace while, outside, a country was collapsing into war, sometimes feeling like a plotter confronting from this secret place the other plot, the murderous plot of the powerful. Outside, a light rain had begun to fall and the wind was driving it against the beveled glass. In one chair, the nearest to the front window, sat Julián Uribe, smoking a thick cigar the glowing tip of which drew shapes in the shadows; across from Anzola, sitting on the edge of the velvet cushions of matching wicker chairs, were Adela Garavito and her father. General Elías Garavito was a man with a dense gray beard and shaved chin, as was more common in earlier times. He was also an old member of the Colombian Guard, who had known and admired General Uribe. It was he who spoke first.

"Tell him, my dear," he whispered. "Tell him what we know."

His daughter was a shy and religious woman in her forties, with long black skirts and chaste manners, who went to Mass much more than her Liberal father would have liked. It was a good while before she dared to look Anzola in the eye, but in this way, avoiding his gaze, speaking more to the carpet than to her interlocutor, she told him out loud things that someone more worldly, more spirited, or more coura-geous would have kept to themselves out of fear.

Her tale took place on October 15, 1914.

"The day of the crime," said Anzola.

"For me," said Señorita Adela, "the day of Saint Teresa of Ávila."

After going to the nine o'clock Mass at the Chapel of the Sagrario, Señorita Adela was returning home, walking up Ninth Street, where she thought she recognized General Salomón Correal, who was mak-ing another police officer enter the entrance hall of a house that looked abandoned. The lady took a couple of steps and saw that it was indeed Correal, for she knew him well; the other wore a sword and jacket, but she couldn't identify him. She had never seen him before.

"Were they in the house next door?" asked Anzola. "Next to Gen-eral Uribe's house, I mean?"

"Yes," said Señorita Adela. "It was from there that they signaled to the others."

"Who?" asked Anzola.

From the entrance of the neighboring house, after bringing in the police officer with him, Correal leaned out, looked toward the corner of Carrera Quinta, and began to wave one arm. At the corner, a few steps up from General Uribe's door, there were two men who looked poor, both wearing ponchos and straw hats. Even from a distance, Señorita Adela could tell that the whole situation was abnormal: the men on the corner seemed worried, and seemed to be looking at each other wondering what they should do. Trying at the same time not to seem impertinent or nosy, Señorita Adela carried on walking up the street, until she passed the two tradesmen. That was when she noticed they were hiding something under their ponchos.

"Both of them?" asked Anzola. "Are you sure?"

"My daughter neither lies nor exaggerates," said General Garavito.

"I didn't mean to suggest that she would," said Anzola. "I'm just asking if she's sure. It's been two years."

"As sure as God exists," said Adela Garavito. "Both had their hands hidden under their ponchos and were moving something. Both had something hidden."

"The hatchets," said Anzola.

"That I don't know," said the señorita. "But they were nervous, that could be seen from a mile away."

At that moment she crossed paths with Señora Etelvina Posse, who was in such a rush she didn't stop to say hello though they knew each other well. "She didn't even notice it was me," said Adela Garavito. Doña Etelvina had never been in her good books: people said she was too friendly with Correal, and that her husband, however, hated the police commissioner; they also said that Correal had recruited her into the secret police, an army of citizens who informed on other citizens. Adela Garavito turned around covertly, and saw Doña Etelvina stop and speak to General Correal. She couldn't hear what they said, because she had turned the corner by then, but when she got home, half a block farther south, she told her father what she'd seen.

In the afternoon, the news reached them: General Uribe had been attacked with hatchets by two tradesmen. General Garavito ran out into the street to see what he could find out and arrived at General Uribe's house, but in the chaos of the entrance hall couldn't find any relatives. He spoke to two or three Liberals he recognized, but everybody was as disoriented as he was, so his instinct was to return home to be with his family in these moments when the world seemed about to end. He barged into his daughter's room without knocking, not caring if she saw the tears in his eyes. He did not have to explain what he meant when he sat down on her bed, pushing aside the cushions, and spoke as if someone might be listening in.

"Do not repeat what you told me this morning," he said. "They might go so far as to poison us."

She obeyed. Days later she ran into Doña Etelvina Posse again, but this time she did stop to chat and Doña Etelvina ended up showing her the newspaper she was carrying, open at the photos of Galarza and Carvajal.

"I recognize them," said Adela Garavito. "They're the same ones who were standing there, at the corner, the day they killed him."

Her words took Doña Etelvina by surprise. "It was as if she'd suddenly understood she'd been wrong about me," said Adela Garavito. "It was as if she'd believed I was with her, or with those who were happy about the death of General Uribe. It hadn't occurred to her that I wasn't one of them. Her face changed."

"Standing where?" asked Doña Etelvina.

"There, at the corner of General Uribe's house," said Adela. "And General Correal was signaling them from the neighbor's house. It seemed odd."

"Salomón wasn't here that day," she said.

"Of course he was," said Adela Garavito. "I saw him with my own eyes."

"Well, I didn't see anything."

"And he wasn't alone," said Adela. "There was someone with him, they were signaling to the assassins."

Without looking at her, Doña Etelvina handed her the newspaper.

"Here, child, I've already read it," she said, and began to walk away. "Excuse me."

"Who else have you told this to?" asked Julián Uribe.

"Nobody else," said General Garavito. "Everyone was saying in those days that the police were mistreating people who went in to give witness statements. That they were harassed, intimidated. And I knew several of them: people who went to tell what they'd seen and ended up spending two or three nights in jail. So I ordered Adelita not to say anything, and she has obeyed me."

Julián Uribe stood up and walked to the center of the room. In the half darkness of six o'clock in the evening, his figure seemed to stretch.

"And you would testify?" he asked.

Adela Garavito looked at her father and saw in his face something that Anzola could not see.

"If it will do any good," she said.

"It would be enormously useful," said Anzola. Then he spoke to the father instead of the daughter, even though he was answering something she had said. "I'll organize it all, General. The day after tomorrow I'll bring the judge to take the señorita's testimony. And yours too, if you don't mind."

"I don't mind," said the general. "A gentleman's word is a gentleman's word, with or without witnesses."

"If only it were that simple," said Anzola.

Anzola left Julián Uribe's house in a state of exaltation that he had not felt for a long time. He knew the optimism would last a matter of hours, but he nevertheless allowed himself those brief instants that were like an antidote to despondency. Night was falling but not all the streetlamps had been lit yet. Lights from the houses, however, were reflecting in the puddles and the cobblestones still shiny with the recent rain. The wind began to pick up. Anzola felt his hair blown around and had to fold his arms across his chest to keep the gusts of wind from opening his overcoat; it wouldn't do to catch pneumonia at this critical moment. People must have been feeling the same cold and the same discomfort, for everyone had gone inside much earlier than usual, so Anzola's footsteps echoed on the paving stones the way an intruder's do through an empty house. That's what he was thinking about when he sensed another presence in the street.

Looking back over his shoulder, Anzola saw two men in ponchos. Was it his imagination, or were the ponchos waving as if the men were hiding something? He sped up and the sound of his steps bounced off the whitewashed walls. He turned the corner and as he did so found himself taking long strides, almost leaping, to get away from the men in ponchos without their noticing. The men turned the corner, too, and again Anzola looked over his shoulder, and again saw something under the ponchos, and wondered if what he thought he saw could be true: that one of the ponchos was blown up like the wing of a manta ray and allowed him to see, for a fleeting instant, the silver flash of a metal blade in the light of the street. Now suspecting he was in danger, he walked even faster, and the echo of his steps imitated his racing heart. He felt his chest was soaked in sweat. He saw in the depths of the night a light shining on the cobblestones, and advanced toward it and came to a *chicha* bar open and full of people. As he went in he glanced back at the street, but there was no one there: no men in ponchos or anybody else. Anzola felt the warmth all of a sudden, the warmth of other people's breath. His ears were throbbing. Perhaps for that reason he was slow to answer the question:

"What can I get for you, sir?"

ONE MORNING, before going out, he found that someone had left him an envelope. It was a cutting from the previous day's *Gil Blas*, which Anzola had not seen: not because of being shut up with the difficult company of the three thousand pages of the criminal dossier, but because he thought the *Gil Blas* as irresponsible and reckless as his ideological enemies. The cutting had been torn out by hand, not with scissors, so in one corner a couple of letters were missing, but that didn't make it indecipherable. It was a letter: a letter from a prisoner in the Panóptico addressed to the editor of the newspaper and in which he declared, publicly, having been a victim of torture by Salomón Correal's police force. The prisoner was a certain Valentín González, about whom Anzola knew nothing apart from the information contained in the page from the *Gil Blas*: that he was in the Panóptico accused of the theft of the Nieves monstrance. Anzola remembered the case: the monstrance had disappeared from the church of Nuestra Señora de las Nieves one day in July of the previous year; a week later, after the arrest and liberation of a Spanish citizen, a priest, and an opera singer, the police had found, in a dark corner of the church, under the statue of San Luis, part of the loot. There was the pedestal of the monstrance, some crumbs of the host, a handkerchief, cigarette butts, and footprints: the unmistakable trace of the thief. The police made six arrests; declared that they were solving the crime and society could rest easy. Like many, Anzola had wondered at the time how it was possible that so many necessary clues should be found inside the very church where the robbery had occurred eight days before, as if in all that time no one had even passed by to sweep the floor. Now, the matter was briefly back in his hands.

"For nine days," wrote the accused Valentín González, "I was held in a tiny cell and not allowed any food, not even bread, and without any covers of any kind; I was taken from that filthy place every night, from one to three in the morning, only to be led to an office off the patio, shivering with cold and starving to death, and there, in that office, I was subjected to the stocks torture, which consisted of tying me up by my big toes together with rifles strapped around my neck and knees." After these torments, the superintendent in charge, Manuel Basto, had him taken back to the tiny cell, and upon arriving there the prisoner would find that officers had doused it with urine and shit water. One day, overcome by the pain, hunger, cold, and humiliations, Valentín González asked his jailers to kill him once and for all.

"That wouldn't be any fun," they told him. "We do have to, but little by little."

And to that, apparently, they devoted their days. Valentín González spoke of the assaults of the secret police, who frequently took him out of his cell, tied his hands, threw sawdust in his eyes, and punched him and tripped him, while the loud laughter of the other officers echoed around the yard. After several days of that routine they took him out of the tiny cell and put him in a dungeon, where he was held incommunicado for two days. Now, according to what he said, his fingers were covered in wounds from the tortures, and the dampness of the dungeon had left him with cruelly painful rheumatism. "I asked, insistently but futilely, that they bring me a doctor," he wrote in his letter. "Señor Basto didn't think it was advisable for anyone to find out about my situation." And he finished by saying that anyone could come to the Panóptico to confirm the truth of these accusations: there were the scars on his fingers, for anyone who wanted to see them. He didn't declare himself innocent of the theft of the monstrance, Anzola noted. That didn't matter to him: what mattered was that the outside world should know of his suffering.

Anzola read the cutting and then reread it. The first thing he thought was that all was not lost if these things still happened: if anonymous citizens, good people, took the time and trouble to compile and send the necessary proof to denounce in the court of public opinion the true face of the police, to divest Salomón Correal of his masks. If only everyone on his side would do the same, all those looking for the truth about the crime! If the conspirators felt the pressure of public indignation! Oh, yes, how grateful he was for the anonymous shadow who had left this envelope for him perhaps running grave risks, perhaps hiding from the secret police . . . That's what Anzola was thinking when he retrieved the envelope, to see if he could find some clue to the identity of his benefactor, and instead found a piece of yellowing paper he hadn't noticed at first. He read the few handwritten words feeling like the victim of a childish prank, but not just any childish prank, rather one in which the other boy has a machete in his hand and a liquid darkness in his eyes.

> Doctor Anzola: so you can see the kinds of things that
> can happen to you if you don't stop looking for what you
> haven't lost.

Later he would realize that much more had happened in this moment than was apparent. The first thing was fear; the second, and he hadn't foreseen it, the fear of his own fear. What if he gave in? What if he let himself be defeated by the threat, by the prospect of physical pain and a violent death? What would be left of all these efforts, of putting others at risk and taking risks himself, of looking for a confused idea of truth and justice in the mud of conspiracy? All this had changed brutally on the night in 1914 when Julián Uribe and Carlos Adolfo Urueta came to visit him to ask him a favor. The world was simpler then, but only for him: for General Uribe the written threats had turned into a real attack that had taken his life. There were two ways to think about this: one was that it would be a foolish man who, knowing firsthand the possible consequences of an action, continued with its execution; the other was that yielding to the threats would be to dishonor the memory of the assassinated general. Anzola did not save the threatening note with his documents, but threw it on the fire. The cutting from *Gil Blas*, however, he put on his desk with the intention of transcribing it later. Although he didn't realize it, this simple action already contained his hidden decision to carry on. Some weeks later, a casual encounter decreed it irremediably.

Anzola attended a conference on the European war organized by a group called Friends of the Entente, which gathered more than three hundred people in the Salón Olympia. For two long hours he listened to people talking about what was happening in Europe now that this war had been going on for three years: this hell that had devoured strong countries, and in its five million dead one could see the decimation of an entire generation. He heard talks about the French ambassadors in the United States, about the latest battles in Ypres, about the miles of trenches the Germans had won on the Belgian border, and heard a Spanish citizen say that the Liberals were making efforts to bring Spain into the war as well, so that later they would not be ashamed for having stayed out of the struggle against barbarism. He didn't know who revealed that up in the front rows were the relatives of the soldier Hernando de Bengoechea; or maybe it wasn't necessary for anyone to tell him, because each of the speakers in turn was looking at them from the platform, praising the young soldier's bravery and the outstanding quality of his poems. Then the audience burst into applause; in the front rows two silhouettes stood up, and then the entire theater stood up, and Anzola found himself feeling moved.

When the conference was over, he walked toward the front, against the direction of the audience trying to leave the theater. He wanted to meet Bengoechea's family, shake their hands and hear what their voices sounded like, and he was not disappointed to find that it was not the whole family, but just Elvira, the soldier's sister, who had attended the conference with Diego Suárez Costa and a chaperone. Suárez, it seemed, had been the soldier's greatest Colombian friend; Anzola didn't understand whether he was passing through Bogotá or lived here, but wasn't overly interested either, because his attention was focused on Elvira. She was a young woman with large eyes and a thick chignon and at her throat she wore a brooch of the French flag. "I would have liked to know your brother," Anzola said to her when they were introduced. He took her hand, lifting it like a fallen handkerchief, and brought his closed lips near to her fingers without touching them. "Marco Tulio Anzola," he added.

"Oh, yes," she said. "You're the one who writes those things that have us so worried."

"Forgive me," he began. "I don't—"

"My brother would have liked to know you as well," Elvira interrupted him. "At least, that's what they say in my family."

They speak of me, thought Anzola. And also: *He would have liked to know me.*

He remembered that brief dialogue absurdly in the months that followed, while he was sinking all his time and energy into writing the final version of his book. Sometimes he thought that the words of the young Elvira contained a vindication; other times he thought they were a demand. Sometimes, while he was writing a paragraph denouncing Salomón Correal or Pedro León Acosta, he thought that at his age Hernando de Bengoechea was already dead, but his mere twenty-six years had been enough to write pages that are now applauded publicly and to die a heroic death in defense of eternal values. And he, thought Anzola, what had he done in his twenty-six years? And this book that he was writing, this book that was not poetry but vulgar prose, this book the only intention of which was to denounce a murderous plot with no more embellishments than the precision of the law and the crude rhetoric of common sense, could it effectively bring on his death? Was Anzola digging his own grave, paragraph after paragraph, article after article, testimony after dense testimony? On each handwritten page, each draft that Anzola filled with his sloping calligraphy, exploded a subversive revelation or he made a denunciation that was like a bomb or a torpedo. Yes, thought Anzola, that was how it was: the manuscript was a submarine and certain paragraphs were torpedoes aimed at the ocean liner of Colombian power, ready to open a big hole below the waterline so they'd all sink in the sea never to be seen again.

To test the force of what he was writing, he kept publishing columns in *La Patria*, but by this time they weren't made up of material he would later transform into the book, but with whole fragments of the definitive manuscript. He took out pages to show them to the people who were on his side, sometimes to ask a witness to confirm their version of events, sometimes so that a more skilled professional—a criminologist more qualified than he was, an expert on procedural law—could correct a vulnerable theory or a misinterpretation of the law. In an article in the press, Rodríguez Forero had declared that the

Uribe family was angry about the work of Señor Anzola—they judged him to be a hopeless mythomaniac, and disapproved of the course his investigation had taken. And when Anzola went to see Julián Uribe, he found him looking embarrassed and unable to meet his gaze when he gave him the news.

"The family has just named their lawyer for the trial," he said. "I want you to know it had nothing to do with me."

"Who is it?" asked Anzola.

"Pedro Alejo Rodríguez," said Julián Uribe. "And no, I don't understand it either."

Something incomprehensible had happened. Pedro Alejo Rodríguez, a young lawyer, was the son of Prosecutor Alejandro Rodríguez Forero. Naming him as legal representative of the Uribe family in the trial of the general's assassins was not a clumsy mistake: it was a formal commitment to suicide. But that was the news brought by the general's brother, who obviously had not wanted to be the messenger: Pedro Alejo Rodríguez was officially the lawyer of the victim's family, in spite of being the son of one of the conspirators, or someone who had put all the means within his reach at the disposal of the conspirators. No, it was not possible that Julián Uribe had fallen into such a vulgar trap. Anzola held his head in his hands, but dignity prevented him from saying all that he wished to.

"So it's true," he said. "They no longer trust me."

"I don't know exactly how this happened, my dear Anzola," said Uribe. "It was up to Doña Tulia. Who knows what they'll have told the poor woman."

"Widows should never decide anything ever," said Anzola.

"Careful, my friend," said Uribe. "That widow is my sister-in-law. And she is still owed our respect."

"Well, with all due respect, that widow just ruined everything," said Anzola. "What do the children think?"

"I don't know."

"And Dr. Urueta? He entrusted me with this just as you did. He has a right . . ."

"Dr. Urueta is in Washington."

"What? And what is he doing there?"

"They appointed him to the legation," said Uribe. "And he went, what else was he going to do."

"Well, that doesn't matter. A minister can just as easily disagree with this."

Julián Uribe began to grow impatient. "As I said, I am as surprised as you are. But it's also true that we do not know the young Rodríguez. We have no reason to expect the worst."

"But we do, Dr. Uribe, we do," said Anzola. "The worst and then some."

The news left him so upset that he shut himself away for three weeks to finish his book, to keep the disappointment and disillusionment from making him give up on it. He was about to do so: Why risk his reputation and even his life on an endeavor that could no longer count on the admiration, or even the simple solidarity, of General Uribe's family? Nonetheless, he kept on writing, allowing the schedule of his days to become inverted, sleeping late and working through the nights, with bad light and aching eyes. The criminal dossier with its three thousand pages of irrefutable facts accompanied him, and also the *Vista Fiscal* with its three hundred thirty of lies and distortions. He no longer felt indignation by then, and he had even forgotten the reason he had accepted this job one distant evening, when he wrote, in the early hours of a September morning, the word

Conclusions, which on paper seemed longer than usual. And underneath it:

1st. That Leovigildo Galarza and Jesús Carvajal are, solely, in the assassination of the Liberal caudillo, General Uribe Uribe, the material instruments of the deed.

2nd. That the assassination of the great patriot was concocted by the group of Conservative Carlists who count among their victims President of the Republic Dr. Manuel María Sanclemente, who made an attempt on the life of President of the Republic General Rafael Reyes, and who will surely continue their series of crimes against all those who in their superior conditions place themselves in the situation to direct the country toward democracy; and

3rd. That the soul of this grim and sinister group is the so-called Society of Jesuit Priests.

Then he wrote the words THE END, in six well-spaced, capital letters, so thick that the delicate tip of his Waterman scratched the paper. He thought it would not be worth wasting his time offering it to the National Printing Press, which wouldn't take it if the Pope himself ordered them to. So he decided he would take the book, as soon as he could, to Tipografía Gómez and pay for the print run out of his own pocket. He went to bed, but his excitement kept him from falling asleep. The next morning, at first light, he grabbed a new sheet of paper and wrote the title:

Who Are They?

He put it all in a leather briefcase and went out into the recently awakened city. It was cold and the wind was biting. Anzola took a deep breath and felt the cold air burning his nostrils and prompting a teardrop in his eye. Everything seemed normal. But nothing was anymore. He was completing the job assigned to him three years ago by the Uribe family, and now the family no longer supported him; he was raising an accusatory finger against all those who were powerful in this country, and no one could assure him they weren't going to do him harm. He could still change his mind, switch directions at the next corner, walk around the block, sit down and drink a hot chocolate, and forget all about this, go back to his old life and live in peace. But he carried on, thinking about what the people who watched him pass would see: a solitary, but not completely defeated, young man, already without illusions, dragging his feet. Would the fatal decision he was carrying within be visible on the outside? And if somebody were able to recognize it, would they try to dissuade him? But they would not succeed, no. He had to resist, had to carry on, and thus one day he would be able to say he had fulfilled the promise he had made to Julián Uribe: he had written his book, he had told everything, and now all that was left for him to do was to sit down and wait for the heavens to fall on his head.

Anzola stopped at a corner while a Ford passed. A young woman in a hat looked up shyly, and her gaze went through Anzola as if he were invisible.

VIII

THE TRIAL

Marco Tulio Anzola published his subversive book without knowing that ninety-seven years later, in a small, dark apartment of that city that had forgotten him, two readers would meet to talk about the author as if he were alive and about what he related in that book as if it had just happened, and that they would do so furthermore with his book in their hands. I couldn't know if it had been Carballo's intention from the start to show me the book, because the relationship between the two—the object and its reader—was at a level of intimacy I've never seen and perhaps never felt. I couldn't know whether there were fears or uncertainties in his mind at the moment of placing the book in my hands, or whether he was doing so because he considered me worthy of that trust. We had been talking about Anzola, about the job Julián Uribe and Carlos Adolfo Urueta had entrusted him with; I asked Carballo how he had come to know all that he was telling me, where that information could be found. In reply, he stood up and went to his room, not to his bookshelves: it was obvious he had been rereading the book recently and it was next to his bed. He brought it back in and held it out to me with both hands.

"What happens is that you have to read it twenty times," he said. "Otherwise, nobody could unlock its secrets."

"Twenty times?"

"Or thirty, or forty," said Carballo. "This book is not like any old book. One must be worthy of it."

It was a venerable-smelling, leather-bound volume and with embossed letters on the spine. *Assassination of General Rafael Uribe Uribe*, it said on the first page; then, Carlos Carballo's signature; beneath the signature, the title that, more than a title, was a declaration of paranoia: *Who Are They?* This line was missing the opening upside-down question mark, a punctuation mark that exists only in the Spanish language, and only since a distant day in the eighteenth century when the Royal Academy made it compulsory; beside the final, closing question mark was the inked-in silhouette of a hand: *a black hand*, I thought, whose index finger was *pointing*.

"This is the denunciation of a conspiracy?" I asked. "Not terribly subtle, our Señor Anzola, truth be told."

But Carballo didn't find my comment funny. "This book was in every library in Bogotá," he told me coldly. "They all bought it: some for the altar, some for the bonfire. But in 1917 everybody had this book in their hand at one moment or another. I wonder when you'll be able to do something similar."

"A scandalous book?" I asked.

"A valuable book," he said. "A book with a noble aim." And then: "Although that's not a word anyone of your generation uses."

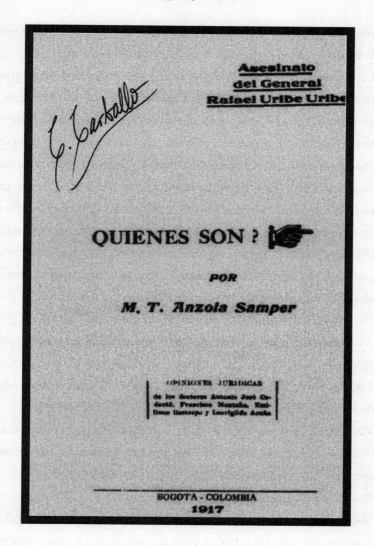

I decided to ignore the attack. "And what is that aim, if one might know?"

"Well, no, you cannot know," said Carballo, "until you have certain information in your head. First you have to read this book and understand it well. In other words, move through it like a fish in the water.

I'm not saying you have to read it twenty times the way I have. But four or five, at least. Until you understand it, I should say."

I opened *Who Are They?* and flipped through pages without disguising my boredom. There were three hundred pages of cramped type. I read: *For those of us worthy of the honor of being friends with General Uribe Uribe and having professed the most sincere affection for such an exemplary patrician, it brings utmost satisfaction to pay a heartfelt tribute to his memory.* There was everything that repelled me: the pomposity, the grandiloquence, the affected phrases Colombians adore and I detest more than the worst vices of the human species. I looked, out of an old habit, at the last page, where certain readers tend to jot down notes or impressions, and found only the date 1945, a trace of one of the many readers the book might have had in almost a century of useful life.

"You want me to read this book four or five times?" I said.

"To understand it," said Carballo. "Otherwise, there's no way to continue."

"Well, maybe I don't want to continue, then," I said. "I don't have time for this, Carlos. This is your obsession, not mine."

Carballo, sitting with his legs apart, elbows resting on his knees, and fingers interlaced, hung his head and I could have sworn I heard a sigh. "It's yours too," he said then.

"No. It's not mine."

"It's yours too, Vásquez," he insisted. "Believe me, it's yours too."

I remember him then letting his gaze hang for an instant on the back wall, on the picture of Borges or beyond, on the darkened window covered by a white lace curtain, and then saying: "Wait a second. I'll be right back." I remember him disappearing behind the other door, the one that wasn't the one to his room, and I also remember this: a long time passed, more time than I would have thought necessary to look for and find a precious object the location of which, presumably, one never forgets. Then I speculated that Carballo had repented of the whole thing—of having invited me to his house, of having let me back into his life to write the book that I, although he didn't know it, would never write—and I imagined him thinking of plausible excuses not to show me what he was going to show me. But when he came back out, he was carrying an orange cloth that I arbitrarily associated with his garish scarves. The cloth was covering an object with an ambiguous or irregular outline (or were its unpredictable folds what prevented me from making out the precise shape of the object). Carballo sat down on the green sofa, began to unfold the cloth point by point, and uncovered its content, and it took me a brief instant to understand that what I was seeing under the intense light was a bone, a human bone, the top part of a skull. "Well, here it is," he said. The cranium, clean and shiny under the white light that poured down from the ceiling, was broken: there was a loose piece of bone. But my attention fixed immediately on the three dark letters that seemed etched onto the frontal bone: *R. U. U.*

I DON'T REMEMBER if there was a certain reticence on my part, if my understanding took a bit of effort to realize what I was witnessing, and I don't remember what I said, if I actually said anything, while Carballo showed me the object, with pride but also with nerve and at the same time with obvious preoccupation, handling it and letting me handle it as if it were not unique and irreplaceable, as if its damage (if it fell on the floor or hit something) would not have represented an irreparable loss to the world. As I came to accept the miracle, I could think only that this formerly living part of a formerly living body had been the part through which the life had escaped that body, and when Carballo separated the broken bit of bone carefully and handed it to me so that I could hold it between two fearful fingers and hold it up to the light and examine it from both sides, as if it were a precious gem, a single phrase ran through my head: *Rafael Uribe Uribe died right through here.*

And Carballo, as if he had guessed my thoughts (and in the transformed atmosphere of the apartment, under the phantasmal light from the neon tube, I was not entirely able to rule out that possibility), said:

"Through here his life went out, through this hole. Incredible, no? You should be proud, Vásquez," he joked, "because very few people in the world have seen this. And most of them are dead. The person who gave it to me is dead, for example."

"Dr. Luis Ángel Benavides."

"May he rest in peace."

"He left it to you?"

"The *maestro* used this in his classes. I was not only his student: I was his confidant in his final years, the person who kept him company. I was his support and also I'm the one who understands these things. I'm the one who knows how to use them. I'm the one who will benefit from them. So yes, he left it to me. Don't be so surprised."

"What do you mean, *these things*?" I asked. "What do you mean, *use them*, Carlos? Is there something else? Did Dr. Benavides leave you other things?" And then: "And also, how did the doctor come to have this? How did something like this end up in his hands, if he hadn't even been born yet when Uribe was killed?"

I saw him think; I could almost hear the mechanism in his head weighing risks, making estimates about my loyalty, trying to read on my face what I would or would not do with particular bits of information.

"I think we better go step by step," he finally said, "haste makes waste. Let's not bite off more than we can chew."

"But I don't get it. This is wonderful, Carlos, don't misunderstand me. Holding this in my hand, being able to touch it . . . I'll never be able to thank you enough for allowing me this. But I don't understand how this fits in with our project."

"You're really grateful?"

"Infinitely," I said.

It was perhaps the most genuine word I had pronounced up till then. That's what I felt: holding those remains in my hands, letting my living fingers pass over that bone, was provoking emotions I hadn't felt since that night in 2005 when I saw Gaitán's vertebra in Benavides's house, but this time the direct contact with the relic was enriched by my own experience, by the nine years that had gone by since then. So there, sitting in that room with daylight beginning to creep in through the window, holding in my timid hands the remains of Uribe Uribe's skull, I felt that life had led me to this moment along paths impossible to trace; but I felt, at the same time, that something was escaping me, like someone standing too close to a painting to see clearly what's happening in it.

"Well, this changes things," I said. "I'll take the book, read it as soon as I can, and come back so we can talk."

"Impossible," said Carballo. "This book doesn't leave my apartment."

"So then what? I come and read it here, as though it were a public library?"

"Why does that seem so absurd to you?" said Carballo. "I get home every day at five in the morning. We meet here, you read while I sleep, and *then* we talk. I'm sorry, but it's the only way. Because this book, I repeat, does not leave my apartment."

I was going to protest, but good sense intervened in time: what this man was offering me, believing that he was obliging me and that I was accepting reluctantly, was to spend hours in his apartment, in solitude and free from his watchful gaze, while he slept. He was offering me the possibility to scrutinize with impunity every visible corner of the place in search of the lost vertebra. It would have been stupid to refuse.

"Shall we start tomorrow?" I asked.

"If you're up to it," said Carballo.

"I'm up to it," I said. "But I have another doubt."

"Tell me."

"What is in Uribe's head instead of this? Why does the autopsy say they reconstructed it?"

"Well, reconstruct doesn't mean they put the cranial vault back in its place," said Carballo. "This became clear to me from visiting Maestro Benavides so often. Let's say there's a bone bank, for example. When you take bones from a corpse for the bone bank, you reconstruct the cadaver with burlap or a broomstick. Look, when I started spending time with the *maestro*, many years ago, I found out many things I had no idea about. For example, I discovered that in operating rooms there are freezers with saved cranial vaults. Just like this one, yes. A patient with craniocephalic trauma, for example, has a piece of his skull removed, so the brain can expand and the patient won't die, and that piece is saved. Sometimes it can't be stored in the freezer for whatever reason. Then the piece of cranium will be stored in the abdomen, which protects the human tissues and avoids infection. The patient can have a piece of his cranium removed and his head will still retain its shape, because there is a layer that remains. Nobody's going to touch that man's head to see if it's hard. You can take out the bone and just leave the skin. I imagine that's how Uribe will be, down in his tomb, interred in the Central Cemetery."

When I got home, I closed the blinds in my bedroom (neither my wife nor my daughters were home: luckily, since I didn't have the energy or mental clarity to explain to anybody what had just happened to me), and suddenly all the sleepless night's exhaustion fell on me at once. I put in the blue earplugs I use when I'm writing and climbed into bed. I had a moment of fear that, in spite of my exhaustion, I would have a hard time getting to sleep given my overly stimulated state. But in seconds I had lost consciousness, and slept deeply, slept as I hadn't slept in daylight hours since I was a teenager, sunk in a sleep that was not unlike sleep under anesthesia: a place where there is no perception of time or space, a *no place* where we are not even someone who knows we're asleep, where only upon waking do we begin to understand how much our body was demanding its rest. A dreamless sleep from which at first it's hard to emerge: and there is disorientation, and a sensation of solitude, and a certain melancholy; and we want to find when we open our eyes someone to hold us and remind us with a kiss where we are, the life we're leading, how fortunate we are that it's this life, and not another, that we're lucky enough to have.

That night I phoned Dr. Benavides. When I told him what I'd seen in Carballo's house, a deathly silence came down the line.

"The cranial vault," said Benavides finally. "He has it."

"You knew it existed?"

Another silence. In the background, behind the static, I could hear cutlery and crockery. Benavides had been eating with his family, I supposed, and I had interrupted him. It didn't seem to matter.

"My father brought it home a few times. I was a child then, I would have been about seven or eight. My father showed me the cranial vault, explained things to me. He let me hold it, turn it over, look at it from all angles, turn it around. And Carballo has it?"

"Well, yes. I'm sorry," I said, without really knowing why.

"With the letters, right? The initials on the frontal bone."

"Yes," I said. "The initials are there: *R. U. U.* There they are."

"I remember it perfectly," said Benavides. There was no noise anymore: he must have gone into another room and closed the door, away from the racket of the family dining room. "Those letters fascinated me, it seemed fantastic that they should be on someone's forehead. My father thought that was very funny. He'd tell me: 'We all have them. We all come with our initials engraved on our foreheads.' I'd spend hours in front of the bathroom mirror, standing on a wooden step stool to get closer to the light, holding my hair aside with one hand and touching my forehead with the other to see if I could manage to feel the initials. *F.B.* I searched for them with my fingertip, rubbing it over my forehead looking for the *F* and the *B*, the *F* and the *B*. Then I'd go and complain to him. I'd say: 'Papá, I can't find them.' And he'd touch my forehead, or more accurately, he'd caress me, and say: 'Well, there they are, I can feel them.' And then he'd pass his hand over his own forehead and put a concentrated look on his face, profound concentration, and he'd tell me: 'Yes, yes, here they are as well: *L.A.B.* Look, see if you can feel them.' And I'd try and I couldn't feel them on him either, it was very frustrating. I feel like I'm reliving it: putting a concentrated look on his face, too, as I touched him, feeling his small son's fingers touching his forehead. I've done the same thing with my children, Vásquez. I imagine you know what I'm talking about."

I had never heard such nostalgia in his voice. It seemed as if he'd grown sad, because his clear voice sounded a touch liquid, but I thought it would be impertinent not to mention futile to ask: if it were true, Benavides would never have confessed it to me. But my revelation about Uribe Uribe's cranial vault had awakened a sleeping memory and, with it, his emotions. Childhood memories are the most powerful ones, perhaps because in those days everything is a rupture or an upheaval: every discovery forces us to relocate ourselves in the known world and each show of affection fills our body: the child lives in flesh and blood, without filters or shields or defense mechanisms, fighting however he can with whatever steamrolls over him. Yes, I wanted to say to Benavides, I know what he's talking about, I have also let my forehead be touched by my daughters, by my daughters' hands, by those long fingers they inherited from me. Although they have never held the remains of any of the murdered men of this country, which they've also inherited. There are many, and there will undoubtedly be many more in the years of their lives; and one can therefore imagine that one day fate might provide them with what it provided me: the strange privilege of having in their hands the ruins of a man.

"Yes," I said. "I know what you're talking about."

"You do, don't you?" said Benavides.

And I told him: "Yes."

There was another silence on the line. Benavides broke it by saying: "Bring it to me, please."

"All right," I said.

"That cranial vault is mine as well, just like the vertebra, just like the X-ray."

"But you told me the opposite, Francisco. That these things were not yours, that they were everybody's, that they were going to a museum. You're not changing your mind?"

"Bring it all to me, please. Promise?"

"It won't be easy," I said. "But I promise I'll try."

"Will you promise me, Vásquez?"

"Yes, Francisco. I promise."

"Well, I hope you'll fulfill that promise," said Benavides, and he suddenly turned very, very serious. "Look," he added, "the remains of a dead human body shouldn't be lying around just anywhere. Human remains are potent weapons, and anyone could use them for things that neither you nor I could imagine. We can't allow them to be in the wrong hands."

I said of course, I understood. And then I didn't say anything else.

It was three days, three days in reverse that I followed the same unlikely routine. I woke up at four in the morning, left my house at half past four, and arrived at Eighteenth Street at five or a few minutes before five—a time when this inhospitable city seems friendlier, because the scant traffic produces the illusion that human beings are in charge—and there was Carballo, drinking a weak coffee in spite of his intention to go to sleep in a few minutes. He left me alone with the Marco Tulio Anzola book and I read the way I tend to read when I'm working on one of my own books: with my black notebook open beside it and a fine-leaded pencil on top of the notebook. I took notes and organized chronologies, struggling with the chaos of the book, taming its crude indignation, and little by little among the chronologies and notes a profile of the indignant author began to come to life, that bold young man who had defied the most powerful men in the country. Anzola caused me to feel both fascination and mistrust at once; his bravery was indisputable, however it seemed obvious that the accusations in his book were not all well founded, for no judicious reader could find in the Jesuits of *Who Are They?* the responsibility he attributed to them (that Berestain, for example, was an intolerant and unpleasant guy, but nothing in Anzola's book demonstrated that he was a murderer). At midday the murmur of the water pipes started up, and after a while Carballo would emerge from his room, ready to start his day, always in white socks and sometimes with a cravat already tied at his throat. He told me things that weren't in Anzola's book; he showed me other documents. And thus, one afternoon at a time, I ended up finding out about what happened after the publication of *Who Are They?* or, I should say, *due* to its publication.

The book came out in November 1917. The responses of Anzola's enemies soon followed, and in many cases were tougher than he himself—even when most dismayed—could have predicted. At the same time, Anzola began to realize that many of those who were attacking him had not read the book. They were mere hit men of the printed word, sent by powerful men to discredit his book and his personality, although sometimes they acted in their own name, sad figures moved by envy and resentment. In *El Nuevo Tiempo* they went so far as to make this confession without the slightest shame: "We do not have to sully our gaze with the contents of this work to know it is the fruit of an overheated imagination and an aimless education," wrote a columnist who signed as Aramis. The Conservative press in general called him an anarchist, moral assassin, and salaried defamer; in long prominent articles, implausible pseudonyms called him an enemy of the Catholic Church, a paladin of immorality, and even a messenger of the devil. Anzola was consoled by the thought that the same charges had been leveled against General Uribe, and kept awake nights wondering how he would have responded to one or another especially painful or unjust affront. "Some who pretend to be Christians," the man who signed his articles Miguel de Maistre wrote in *La Sociedad*, "have given themselves the mission on this earth of staining the good name of the Holy Mother Church, attacking representatives of God among us with immoral libels, and in doing so attacking every single upstanding man, every single one of our chaste women, every single one of our innocent children. From pages that have been factors in our internecine wars sowing discord, these messengers of evil aim for the conversion of the country to atheistic socialism. But they will find that the warriors of God are more numerous than they think; and that we are prepared to defend our faith, if the time comes, with the blessed force of arms." During the following weeks, Anzola had to endure a Bogotá writer calling his book a "mere criminalist novel" and him, an "exaggerated detective"; he had to endure whispering whenever he entered a café; he learned to avoid crowds in which he would find himself unprotected.

At the beginning of December a workers' demonstration was organized in the Plaza de Bolívar; Anzola had to take a long detour to get home, for the memory of what had been about to happen to him in another plaza was still vivid. He had never felt so alone. He knew his name was on everyone's lips but noticed how they all avoided his gaze. At Christmas he received a parcel from Julián Uribe, and when he opened it he found a small box of Equitativa chocolates and a card that said "Happy Holidays," and that was the first sign that the family had not exiled him from their lives. So he let the days pass, going from his home to his office, from his office to his home. Inspecting the building works in the extensive city, between Christmas and New Year's, he had to revise the repairs to a bridge over the San Francisco River. They explained that a woman had fallen from the bridge in the past and smashed up her face on the slippery stones. Anzola listened to these explanations, but he didn't pay attention to or sympathize with them, because he was thinking about the latest lie that had been told about him in the press, about the last time an article had spat a gob of ink at him. That's what occupied him during the first weeks of 1918: the observation of what was happening to him, a real defamation campaign the only objective of which was that Anzola would not reach the date of the trial in one piece.

Or at least that's what I imagined. When I spoke to Carballo, he agreed: yes, that's how it must have been. "Yes, it's true that one part of the city had declared war on him, and it was the most powerful part," he told me. "Neither you nor I can imagine what the boy must have been going through." Carballo called him a boy, as if he were his son, or the son of someone he knew, and every time he did so I remembered Anzola's age: when the book was published he was either twenty-six years old, or just about to turn twenty-six. In the month of November of my twenty-sixth year I was arriving in Barcelona, after publishing two novels that had given me a sensation of disorientation first and then failure, and I was preparing to start over again, start a new life in a new country, start to try to be a writer for the second time. Anzola, for his part, had not only published a book that had turned him into the most troublesome man in a country where troublesome men tend to suffer various kinds of retaliation, but he was also preparing to be a witness in the trial of the most notorious crime in recent history. *The crime of the century*, many called it, in spite of the fact that the century was still just getting under way and had already offered us several candidates for that dubious honor. They would say the same of the Gaitán crime, but also, years later, that of Lara Bonilla and that of Luis Carlos Galán. My country has been bountiful that way.

"The crime of the century," Carballo said, laughing, at some point. "They had no idea what was coming."

———

THE TRIAL AGAINST Leovigildo Galarza and Jesús Carvajal, accused of the assassination of General Rafael Uribe Uribe, began in the month of May 1918. It came preceded by the denunciations of Anzola, who had not settled for just publishing *Who Are They?* but had announced his intention of bringing thirty-six witnesses to the trial and revealing, according to what he said in the press, unknown details about the crime against General Uribe. The lawyer for the plaintiff, Pedro Alejo Rodríguez, asked that those testimonies be declared inadmissible and that Anzola be barred from participating in the trial in any way.

"Pedro Alejo Rodríguez," I said. "Oh, yes, the son of the public prosecutor who had brought the pretrial proceedings. The son of the enemy, to put it a better way."

"Exactly," said Carballo. "He asked that Anzola not be permitted to take part in the trial, even as a witness. And the judge agreed."

But Anzola was not intimidated. On the appointed day, he left his house at midday and headed to the Salón de Grados, the authority of which was so great and so old that no one thought it odd to be trying the general's murderers in the same space where they had held his wake four years earlier. He carried a bundle of papers under his arm, and never, the entire way there, did he stop wishing he'd brought them in a briefcase. He walked the long blocks under a drizzle too faint to get anyone wet, feeling at each step that he was dragging his fearful feet over the paving stones, but also that not showing up would be giving in or giving up. Before reaching Carrera Sexta, the clamor of the crowd filled the street like the buzzing of a swarm of tropical bees. Anzola went down Tenth Street; he passed in front of the window through which Simón Bolívar escaped the conspirators—men who murdered one of his guards before finding his room empty and his bed still warm—and carried on walking with his eyes on the ground, to make sure he didn't trip, until he reached the end of the wall. He stopped. Among the documents he carried was a copy of *Who Are They?* Anzola didn't know whether it had been a mistake to bring it. He took a deep breath, quickly crossed himself. And then turning the corner was like entering the arena, confronting the beasts and feeling that a large gate was closing behind him.

"There he is!" someone shouted. "There's the one who wrote that book!"

Anzola felt the eyes in the crowd as one, a single monster with a single eye that had detected him. "Go away!" a furious chorus shouted. "Go away! Go away!" Other voices came from elsewhere, closer to Ninth Street, as if from the nuns' balconies: "Let him in! Let him come in!" Anzola made his way through the crowd, meeting the gazes of some of them so they wouldn't sense his anxiety, and arrived at the thick wooden door with its large solid iron knockers and sacred air. Beneath the sculpted stone coat of arms, one of the two police officers guarding the entrance stepped in front of him: "Banned," he said.

"And why is that?" asked Anzola.

"Judge's orders."

Then Anzola cleared his throat and said to the police officer, so that everyone could hear:

"The people who should be in there are not inside."

The crowd began to shout. "Slanderer! Atheist!" From beneath the nuns' balconies, others were still saying he should be let in, and they were doing so in such a belligerent tone that Anzola feared for a moment becoming the cause of pitched battle. The efforts of those faceless voices were futile, in any case, for the policemen's orders were clear. Anzola could not enter.

"But the next day," said Carballo, "he had better luck."

"What changed?" I asked.

"Nothing and everything," said Carballo. He sat thinking about something. "Have you been in, Vásquez? Have you gone inside the place where the Salón de Grados used to be?"

"Never," I said.

"Oh, well then, I suggest we take a walk," he said. "Nobody says we're obliged to stay in this apartment all the time."

We went outside and began to walk south along Carrera Quinta. I asked Carballo again what had changed, what had happened so that Anzola was allowed into court the day after he was forbidden from doing so.

"The press," said Carballo. "All the journalists protested Anzola's exclusion. All the day's editorials came out in favor of the author of *Who Are They?* and his right to present his thirty-six witnesses. And the people joined the protest. There was such a scandal that Judge Garzón, against all expectations, found himself forced to recant. I don't know: maybe thinking the whole thing could blow up if he insisted on refusing him entry." We were crossing Avenida Jiménez and we passed by Aventino's billiards bar, where I had spent so many idle hours, and we came to the wall of Fourteenth Street, in front of which Ricardo Laverde was murdered one afternoon in 1996, then we turned right and continued south along Carrera Sexta. "The next day Anzola returned to the Salón de Grados. The newspapers covered every day of the trial, transcribing the interrogations and then giving their opinions on them, and that's how we can know in some detail what went on. One newspaper talked about Anzola: it described him arriving with a bundle of papers under his arm. Books, notebooks, loose papers. I don't have any of that now, but other times I've come here bringing it all with me, to go in and study the scene and try to see what my boy would have seen at that moment."

My boy, Carballo had said. We were walking up to the corner of Tenth Street, where the stone pile begins that a century ago housed the Salón de Grados, and only then did a revelation hit me that should have arisen much earlier: the intense relationship between Carballo and Anzola, or rather the profound link Carballo felt for that other conspiracy hunter. *My boy.* I watched him without his awareness while I walked behind him on the narrow sidewalk. He must believe in reincarnations, I thought mockingly, which I later regretted. Then we arrived at the imposing carved stone arch and huge wooden door, and crossed the dark entrance to emerge into a bright courtyard, one of those courtyards with rose bushes and a carved fountain in the middle, and I thought that Carballo must have felt or wanted to feel what Anzola had felt at the time, walking through those corridors with their solemn colonnades: for example, entering the spacious nave with its high ceilings where the hearings took place; for example, listening to the noise of the crowds that reached him from the galleries like a chorus of things shaken during a tremor.

"It was here?" I asked.

"It was here," said Carballo.

It was a space big enough to hold hundreds of people on wooden benches. That's why it was called the Salón de Grados, of course, the graduation hall: because long ago it had been the most important part of a university that operated there. Carballo told me about the photos that came out in the press during those days. From the door of the cold enclosure, he explained where Anzola would have sat, and he said that at the back, on an imposing throne above which a canopy darkened the space below, Dr. Julio C. Garzón, second superior court justice of Bogotá, would have sat. The jury accompanied him, and above their four heads hung a wooden crucifix whose Christ was as big as a five-year-old child. In front of them, at a different table, sheltered behind a stack of papers four hands high, was the court registrar. The day Anzola entered for the first time to testify, he learned that Pedro León Acosta had fought with clubs and bare knuckles with a citizen who accused him in the middle of the street of having had something to do with the crime. The fight had been so violent that a police officer had to break it up, and would have taken them to spend the night in a cell had he not noticed in time that one of them was an illustrious man.

"I imagine Anzola thinking: *My book did that.* I imagine him looking up, seeing how he was being insulted or applauded from the galleries, and thinking that his book had done that. In any case, he must have seen the public prosecutor Rodríguez Forero sitting as if he were just one more onlooker. Most likely Rodríguez Forero had sat there, in the gallery, because he was no longer participating in the trial. He had written the *Vista Fiscal* and published it, but then he had been replaced in his prosecutor's duties by someone else. And his son was acting for the Uribe family, another reason he couldn't participate, right. He would have had to recuse himself."

"And where would the assassins have been?"

"There, look."

I looked where Carballo was pointing. I could practically see Galarza and Carvajal sitting against a side wall, on a bench with no back, surrounded by police officers. They attended without showing any interest in what was going on, as if nothing was going to happen to them, and what showed on their faces, instead, was the paucity of their understanding. They both wore scarves knotted around their necks, so thick that their faces were obscured every time they tilted their heads. Galarza was bald, as if he'd recently had his head shaved, and Carvajal had in his eyes the liquid gaze of a very tired man. He turned every once in a while to see the time on the clock hanging on the otherwise bare wall. Regarding the expression of his entire body, a journalist wrote that he wasn't tired, he was bored.

As soon as the judge declared the court in session, the Uribe family lawyer asked for the floor. Pedro Alejo Rodríguez's forehead was too wide and his receding hairline had already made deep inroads on his temples in spite of his barely thirty years of age, and his heavily lidded eyes always seemed dozy, and his high voice sounded like the whining of a spoiled child. He pointed a finger at Carvajal and Galarza, and said:

"These are the murderers. We are not going to talk about anybody else here or accuse anybody else."

People began to whistle; hands banged against the wood.

"Silence in the court," said the judge.

"The jury is here to rule on the responsibility of Galarza and Carvajal," Rodríguez continued. "In reality, justice has nothing to do with any other individuals. We prepared ourselves for this trial, but then this man turned up in the court."

He pointed at Anzola. Murmurs came from the upper gallery. "Get him out!" someone shouted.

"Silence," said the judge.

"This gentleman," said Rodríguez, "turned up at court and asked to be called to testify here. And not just him, but thirty-six more witnesses. But Señor Anzola is not just any witness: he is the author of a tract in which implications are leveled at persons other than Galarza and Carvajal. And it is very likely, Your Honor, that he has come here to make those same accusations. Well then, we shall hear the witnesses, as required by law. And their testimonies will lead us to one of two conclusions: either the new evidence will be perfect in the face of the law, or it will be mere suspicion that should not be taken into consideration, as it will not lead to any conclusions. We, for our part, shall comply with the wishes of the general's family." He picked up one of his folders and took out a piece of paper. "This," he said, "is a letter sent to us from Washington by Dr. Carlos Adolfo Urueta, the general's son-in-law. It says: 'You know what our desire has been in relation to the investigation. That everything possible be brought to light, but without futile scandals and most of all without the general's name being taken as an instrument of defamation against anybody.' And that, Your Honor, is what we shall do as the prosecution."

"Very well," said the judge. He rang a bell that Anzola had not seen until that moment. "Let the witness approach."

"Anzola stood and walked up there," said Carballo, pointing with one finger. "All the way up there. The newspapers talk about the quantity of papers he had. He dropped them and picked them up. He was nervous, of course. His enemies were present: Alejandro Rodríguez Forero, Pedro León Acosta."

"Acosta was here?"

"In the front row," said Carballo. "The one who wasn't here was Salomón Correal."

"Why not?"

"He didn't need to be," said Carballo. "He'd sent his spies. In fact, all police officers were Correal's spies."

"Señor Anzola," said the judge. "Do you swear before God to answer with the truth all that you are asked, as far as you know it, in the knowledge that if you say something untrue you can be punished with years in prison?"

"Yes," said Anzola. "I swear. But I warn you that I am no orator. I request the public's patience if I bore them or say something terrible. I have been an eyewitness to some of the things I am here to declare. Regarding others, I am here as a referential witness."

"Let the record show what he has just said," said Rodríguez.

"Record it all," said Anzola. "Because what I shall say here, I shall not retract."

"The facts," said the prosecutor. "Let us look at the facts."

"That's where I'm going," said Anzola. "Here I am going to show that the former prosecutor, Señor Alejandro Rodríguez Forero, mutilated the criminal dossier to favor the theory that Galarza and Carvajal acted alone. I beg the plaintiff's prosecutor, Don Pedro Alejo Rodríguez, to turn to the *Vista Fiscal*. And I suggest the former prosecutor, since he's with us here, does so as well and follows along. So he won't get bored."

A burst of laughter erupted in the gallery.

"The facts, Señor Anzola," said the prosecutor.

"I am going to demonstrate a fact here: that Prosecutor Rodríguez Forero adulterated the dossier."

"Counsel demands proof, Señor Anzola," said Rodríguez Forero's son. "Present it right now."

"With great pleasure," said Anzola. "Señor registrar, open the criminal dossier to page 1,214. Señor plaintiff's counsel, open your father's *Vista* to page 270. This refers to a meeting in the carpentry shop of the assassin Galarza fifteen days before the crime. A police officer of Salomón Correal's force stood guard. The meeting is of high importance, because of the need to determine who attended it. Well then, in the dossier we read: 'Fifteen days before the crime . . .' We look to see what Señor Rodríguez Forero puts in the *Vista*: 'Days before the crime . . .' So now it's no longer exactly fifteen days, but a vague date. And I ask: When does a prosecutor prefer vagueness to precision? And I, Your Honor, reply: When precision would put certain persons in an awkward situation, and he is trying to avoid that at all costs. This is an adulteration!"

Anzola awaited applause and the applause arrived.

"But no!" said Rodríguez. "Adulteration is removing something that figures in the proceedings or changing it with evil intent. The only thing here is an abridgment. The prosecutor can, when summing up the facts of a criminal dossier, change some words for others."

"Can he?" said Anzola sarcastically.

"Of course he can. The prosecutor did not adulterate anything, because these words are not in quotes."

"But it's not just this one," said Anzola. "There are many more mutilations."

"Cite them all," said Rodríguez.

"A man named Alejandrino Robayo was also in the assassin's carpentry shop that night. In the criminal dossier, Robayo names the persons who were there with him, and includes a certain Celestino Castillo. But read the *Vista*, Señor registrar, read it: there the name of the man with him has disappeared, and instead it says: 'A companion he was with at that moment . . .' Of course, Castillo's name has been eliminated. Why? Because he was one of Salomón Correal's men!"

Rodríguez gesticulated. "Señor registrar," he said, "please tell us whether that passage is in quotes."

The registrar said: "I see no quotes."

"Therefore, there is no adulteration."

Anzola turned to the gallery. "I am talking to the plaintiff's counsel about the truth, and he talks to me of quotation marks!"

The galleries erupted. The noise was deafening, but above the voices accusing him, above the open jaws of his enemies Anzola heard someone call him by name and say: "Don't worry! The people are here ready to defend you." The words were the backing he needed. Anzola raised his voice.

"I declare," he exclaimed, "the prosecutor Rodríguez Forero is an accessory."

People were standing in the galleries, fists raised, and open mouths vociferating. Anzola felt that he was in a position to provoke a riot, right there and right then, and for the first time he knew what General Uribe must have felt when giving speeches: the power over the crowd and the terrible possibility of using it. The police constables had taken up their positions in front of the galleries to preserve order, and that was seen by those who supported Anzola as a threat. "Come on!" they shouted. "Go ahead and shoot, and you'll see the people know how to defend themselves!" The judge tried to raise his voice over the uproar, the racket of hands banging on the wooden benches. "Order!" he shouted. From a corner came a shout: "Death to the assassins!" "Death to Acosta!" came from the other side. And the judge kept ringing his little metal bell and shouting: "The session is suspended! Court is adjourned!"

"And the trial was adjourned," Carballo told me. "So you can see what the atmosphere was like. And what happened on the first day of Anzola's testimony kept happening on subsequent days. The uproar. The protests. The applause. The galleries divided between hostility and support, the atmosphere of an uprising about to break out . . . And Anzola there, giving his testimony. And later, when he started to call his witnesses, the atmosphere did not improve."

"He called his witnesses? But that can't happen in a trial, Carlos."

"Yes, I know," said Carballo. "You're a lawyer too, I almost forgot. Well, yes, it was possible if the judge allowed it. Somewhere I have the number of the law and the article, in which it states that the judge is allowed to direct the debate as he sees fit. I don't know if this is still possible, but at that time it was. And Anzola was not just any witness, because he'd written the book, because he'd announced his own thirty-six witnesses, and because he had the press on his side, or he seemed to. So they allowed him to bring them and talk to them, interrogate them, even though he was not representing either side. It was exceptional, but this whole trial was exceptional, and it was an attempt to prevent riots. So Anzola brought two guards from the Panóptico who spoke of the privileged living conditions Galarza and Carvajal enjoyed in prison and the murderers' relationship with Salomón Correal. One of them told of a day, when he was on inspection duty, when he saw Galarza's wife arrive to visit him. At a moment when they thought they were unobserved, the woman gave Galarza a piece of paper. He hid it in his boot. After she left, the guard ordered Galarza to show it to him."

"And what did the paper say?" the judge asked the witness.

"The words were these," said the witness. *"I spoke with the doctor, who told me that everything was fine in the street. But remember that you two are not the only ones responsible. Don't be so stupid as to keep taking the rap when there are others responsible."*

"The galleries shouted at those revelations, and there were several every day," said Carballo. "And Anzola kept interrogating his witnesses and having them say in the trial everything they'd said in his book. But he realized very early that he was going to need much more than the pages of *Who Are They?* to convince the jury."

Adela Garavito, the religious daughter, said she had seen Salomón Correal beside General Uribe Uribe's house on the morning of the crime; immediately Officer Adolfo Cuéllar, Correal's secretary, declared that the general had spent the whole morning in his office, and the public applauded with excitement. Ana Beltrán, who said she was the mother of Carvajal's daughter, spoke of a meeting at Galarza's carpentry shop, and assured the court that they spoke there of killing Uribe Uribe; the judge immediately led her to confess that she had another daughter by another man, and the public laughed at her and her words magically lost all value. A witness called Villar, who had been a prisoner in the Panóptico, declared that Anzola had offered to reward him if he would testify in his favor, and even said that all Anzola's witnesses in this trial would have been bribed. "I'm almost sure of it," he said, "though I can't prove it." He didn't need to prove it: the galleries shouted that all this was a farce. Villar was slandering him, but the galleries shouted that Anzola was a slanderer.

"And the worst thing," said Carballo, "is that it was all for naught. The three members of the jury had one obligation: to try Galarza and Carvajal. The law was very clear: those accused in the *Vista Fiscal* were the ones to be tried. Nobody else. So the jury couldn't make any decisions about those pointed out by the book: they would have had to start a whole different trial for that. What happened in the Salón de Grados was a trial in the court of public opinion, and Anzola knew it very well, and had come to accept it. His task was just one: to demonstrate that Correal, Acosta, and the Jesuits had some responsibility for the crime, and then let public opinion take care of the rest. He couldn't do more. He carried on. And he began to pay the price."

"What do you mean?"

"Come with me, Vásquez." Carballo made me follow him down a corridor that bordered the old cloister. From the center of the courtyard we could hear the constant murmur of water, and rosebushes flourished between us and the fountain: it was a place that looked like a fairy-tale setting, and as in so many fables, horrible things had happened there. We arrived at a door. "This was the room for the witnesses during the hearing," Carballo informed me. "They kept them here before they were called, so nobody could talk to them. Do you know what happened here?" But it was a rhetorical question: of course I didn't know; of course he was going to explain it to me. "What happened here was at first just a scandal, but for Anzola it had terrible consequences later. It was six or seven days into the hearings, I don't remember exactly. One day Anzola arrived at the Salón de Grados earlier than usual, because he wanted to talk to some of those attending the trial: journalists, sympathizers, a captain who wasn't a witness but could be called as one. But the police constable wouldn't let him."

"Orders of the judge," he said.

"This is unheard of," said Anzola. "I cannot speak to people?"

"The judge decreed that you should go to the witness room," said the constable. "This way, Señor Anzola, I'll take you."

"No," said Anzola. "I'm not going of my own free will."

To the astonishment of those present, the police constable grabbed his arm and tried to drag him. Anzola dug his heels in, and the constable had to call two more officers. In the struggle, Anzola fell to the floor, and the officers picked him up and shoved him, while he shouted, asking if there weren't any Liberals around to defend him. "They're taking me prisoner because I've tried to demonstrate Correal's guilt!" he was saying. The police pushed him up against a wall and, when they searched him, found his revolver. Anzola was kept locked up in the witness room, next to the entrance hall, while the officers took the revolver to show it to the judge. Later he would hear that they'd accused him of taking out the revolver to shoot them. In front of the judge, when they finally called him, Anzola accused the officers of insulting and punching him, and also launched another accusation: he said the police officers who had dared to testify against Correal were suffering retaliation by their own corps.

"More than retaliation!" Anzola exclaimed. "It is a real repression!"

"Anzola had brought a letter from one of the retaliated-against officers," said Carballo. "He tried to read it out, but the judge forbade it, saying he was not a prosecutor, but a witness. Then, before they could stop him, Anzola strode over to where the journalists were, handed them the letter, and asked them to publish it. The former prosecutor

Rodríguez Forero stood up to protest and people shouted with him. 'He's trying to censor us!' Anzola said, and could barely hear his own words. The judge ordered the room cleared. The officers carried out the order: they suddenly seemed to have multiplied, but the people in the galleries so stubbornly refused to leave that the officers ended up raising their weapons. They started doling out blows with their rifle butts, and the newspapers recount that at that moment, in the middle of the shouts, someone was heard to say: 'They're expelling us because things are beginning to come to light.' That's what Anzola must have thought as well, because that afternoon he had planned to call an extremely important witness. He must have thought: They found out, our enemies found out, and that's why they're attacking me, that's why they're adjourning the hearing. But no, the hearing was adjourned for only fifteen minutes, fifteen minutes were scarcely enough to calm spirits and avert the possibility of a catastrophe. Broken bones and bloody rifle butts could have happened, but didn't happen. Fifteen minutes and the testimonies resumed. And Anzola, the witness Anzola, called another witness to testify. He was a young worker, in a brown suit and black scarf. He was called Francisco Sánchez, although his name doesn't matter. What matters is what he was asked: whether it was true that Emilio Beltrán had proposed killing General Uribe."

"Emilio Beltrán," I said. "Rings a bell, but I don't remember who he was."

"Yes, he's mentioned a couple of times in *Who Are They?* But when his book was published, Anzola didn't yet know what he now knew."

Emilio Beltrán was one of Carvajal's drinking buddies. They saw each other frequently in *chicha* bars, drunk most of the time, or playing poker in El Molino Rojo. For a few months Beltrán was Carvajal's tenant, business was going so badly for him; nevertheless, when he gave his statement, he denied all of this: that he knew Carvajal,

413

that he'd been his tenant, that he'd played cards with him, that he'd been in Galarza's carpentry shop the morning of the crime.

"It's true," said Francisco Sánchez. "I was a friend of Emilio Beltrán and that friendship ended when he suggested I help him to kill General Uribe."

"When was that?" asked the judge.

"I don't remember the date. But I do remember what he said: that if we went along with this business, our luck was going to change."

"Why did you not alert the authorities?"

"Because I didn't want to betray a friend. But I did advise him not to get involved. I told him I wasn't an Uribe follower, but I wasn't going to get involved in that business, and he shouldn't either. I asked him how he could do that to his *mamá*."

"And why do you think he made that suggestion to you?"

"Because he knew I wasn't with Uribe, I guess. One day he invited me to his workshop and said: 'Things are really bad. We're really screwed, and it's all General Uribe's fault. Help me get rid of him and you'll see.' That's what he told me."

"Did he speak to you about anybody else involved in the plot?"

"I could tell there were others involved, by how sure he was of what he said. But he didn't mention anybody by name."

"Did he offer you money?"

"He didn't offer it, but I understood that I would get some. And I did notice the change in his situation after the assassination. He was much better off. Before he was a carpenter, now he's a rich man."

Anzola intervened then. "That's true," he said. "Beltrán now owns his own house and carpentry business. How did that happen? That's what the public prosecutor, father of the present counsel here, did not want to investigate."

Pedro Alejo Rodríguez shrugged his shoulders: "This is not the time . . ."

"Your Honor," said Anzola, "I request that Señor Emilio Beltrán should please be called to the stand."

"Beltrán was extremely elegant," said Carballo. "Even the reporter from *El Tiempo* wondered how a carpenter could afford to dress in a brand-new suit and elegant hat."

He looked nervous. The judge turned to Sánchez to ask him if he confirmed everything he'd just said about his friend Beltrán.

"Yes," said Sánchez. "I confirm it."

"It's not true," said Beltrán.

"Remember, man," Sánchez said. "You told me that day when I went to your house to get some pieces of wood."

"I don't remember."

"Of course you do, man, think back," said Sánchez. "That day I went to your house, just before the San Juanito holiday."

"Has the witness been to your house?" asked the judge.

"Two or three times," said Beltrán.

"Well then, remember, there's no reason to deny it. Remember when you suggested we should kill General Uribe."

"I don't remember that," said Beltrán. "That's a slander this man has been making against me for days."

"Beltrán, is it true that you used to work at Galarza's carpentry shop?" asked Anzola.

"That's true."

"And at that time, you were in a bad situation?"

"Yes, sir. In a bad situation."

"And now how are you?"

"Now I'm in a worse situation."

"But it's very strange that in that time you had no money and now you're a property owner."

Beltrán didn't say anything. Anzola asked him about the events of October 15. The interrogation was an hour of torture, because Beltrán insisted on responding in monosyllables, and his monosyllables, most of the time, were forgetful ones. Nothing was brought to light: there were long exchanges about when the assassins came in and out, about hatchets being sharpened and how to repair broken handles, about commentaries made while hatchets were sharpened, about places where the assassins had lunch, and about the ratchet brace they pawned.

"However, it was clear," said Carballo.

"I don't understand," I said.

"Don't you see?" said Carballo. "But it's as clear as water: there, sitting on the bench, was the third attacker."

"The one with the knuckle-duster?" I asked.

"Exactly," said Carballo. "The one who was going to use the third hatchet, the one they found by accident. He didn't use it, he used the knuckle-duster. And there he was."

"But did Anzola manage to prove that?"

"No," said Carballo. "But what he did manage was almost as good."

At the end of his declaration, Anzola felt he had enough circumstantial evidence to maintain in public that Emilio Beltrán's complicity was proven. "He was close friends with Galarza and Carvajal," he said. "He lived with them, made threatening statements against General Uribe, and finally proposed to another man that he help to assassinate the general." And he concluded: "This man should be confined to prison. To order the imprisonment of an individual requires corpus delicti, concrete evidence of a crime, and serious circumstantial evidence. In our case we have corpus delicti and there is very serious evidence linking Beltrán to the crime." Anzola then addressed

Dr. Murillo, the assassins' defense lawyer. "Do you not think Beltrán should be confined to prison?" In other words: Why should your clients be in prison and this man free? Did the lawyer not think Beltrán should be in the same place as Galarza and Carvajal? The gallery applauded when Murillo said yes. And then Anzola lifted his face, as if he were addressing the high ceilings and the roof beams, and said in a victorious voice:

"By all of what has been said, we have arrived at the conclusion that there does indeed exist a third accused. The *Vista Fiscal* is therefore demolished."

"The public exploded as if it were a village holiday," said Carballo. "Imagine, Vásquez, imagine what it was like: Anzola had just demonstrated that the *Vista Fiscal* was a defective document. That was half the victory. Until now, the true culprits had been safe because the *Vista Fiscal* declared them innocent and left them out of the trial. But if the *Vista Fiscal* was not entirely reliable, then what was left of that immunity? In other words: Acosta and Correal had hidden behind the shield of the *Vista Fiscal*. But Anzola had just taken their shield away. Now anything could happen. And Anzola began to put all his determination into ensuring that it did. He was extremely excited, my boy was extremely excited. And do you know what? I think that's why he screwed it up in the end. He felt he had it all in hand. Something went wrong for him then and he lost control. I have to say the same thing would have happened to me."

ANZOLA'S DOWNFALL HAPPENED in the following way.

After his victory against the *Vista Fiscal*, Anzola must have felt the path was clear for him to go after those accused in his book: Pedro León Acosta, Salomón Correal, and the Jesuits. He decided to begin

with Acosta, since the publication of *Who Are They?* had brought him
an interesting encounter. In the month of February, according to what
Carballo had been able to find out, an Italian named Veronesi had approached Anzola to tell him three things: first, that he'd read his book;
second, that he was merely a guest in the great nation of Colombia and
didn't want to get into trouble with anybody; third, that this had not
prevented him from hearing the things people said about the Uribe
Uribe assassination. And one of those people worked for him. Her
name was Dolores Vásquez and she had seen something important.
Maybe Señor Anzola would consider it important too.

Dolores Vásquez was an old woman who wore a dark shawl, had a
thin voice and calm manners, one of those women who seem to live at
a certain resigned distance from the world and observe the evil of men.
She had been working for the Italian off and on for several years and
lived close to the Puerto Colombia, the *chicha* bar where the assassins
had met the night before the crime. We can imagine that Anzola
would have been pleased to have discovered her. Since long before
publishing his book, he had suspected that the assassins had met in
that bar many other times, and other people had met with them there
to talk about killing General Uribe, but he hadn't been able to gather
testimony to prove it. Dolores Vásquez told him about well-dressed
men who met with the assassins in the Puerto Colombia, and among
them she frequently mentioned one in particular who wore a top hat
and overcoat, and who showed up there shortly before the crime looking for Galarza. Anzola, it seems, asked her if it had been General
Pedro León Acosta, and she said she didn't know the general. Anzola
found an old newspaper photo, from the time of the attempt against
President Rafael Reyes, and took it to Veronesi's shop, and she looked
at the yellowed cutting and said she wasn't sure, but maybe she'd recognize him if she saw him with her own eyes. Anzola decided he

would bring about such an encounter, and that it would happen in the Salón de Grados.

But the day Dolores Vásquez was to recognize Pedro León Acosta, something happened. According to a version published in the Bogotá press, Anzola was waiting to be allowed into the Salón de Grados when a man with gloves and a cane approached him. "Congratulations," he said scornfully. "You are now reaping the fruits of your labors." It turned out that Pedro León Acosta's mother had just died. People blamed him, but that wasn't the worst thing; the worst was that the court registrar began the session by reading a telegram that Acosta had sent to one of his close friends:

ONLY THE AGONY OF MY MOTHER, WHO THIS MORNING AT

IO A.M. MADE HER FINAL FAREWELL, LEAVING US IN SUPREME

PAIN, COULD EXEMPT ME FROM FULFILLING MY PUBLIC

DUTY. SHOW THIS TO THE JUDGE.

So Acosta was not in court when Dolores Vásquez was called to testify. Anzola's frustration must have been unbearable. Nowhere are his emotions recorded, but I can imagine his anticipation when arriving at the Salón de Grados, perhaps believing that day would mark the beginning of the end for the real culprits—their definitive and indisputable unmasking—and that this country's justice system would have no choice but to confront the powerful, as he had; thinking, finally, that today would be the culmination of his last four years of difficulties and sacrifices, and that destiny, which does not tend to record its debts, would pay him what he was owed for having taken so much of his time in exchange for turning him into a pariah in his own city. But no: destiny had not wanted to play it that way. Or maybe, Anzola must have thought, the ones who hadn't wanted it were his enemies.

(That, in any case, was what Carballo believed: that the information had filtered out, they found out that Dolores Vásquez was going to testify, they knew who Dolores Vásquez was and what she might say, and the puppet masters of the world had pulled their strings so that Pedro León Acosta would not show up. Slightly embarrassed, because he was the one who had done all the investigating and had all the documents, I told him that nobody fakes their mother's death to get out of attending a hearing at such a notorious trial. "These people are capable of that and much worse," said Carballo.)

Anzola's frustration was increased by the fact that Dolores Vásquez turned out to be a formidable witness, the kind that seduces the public and disarms the opposition. She said that for months before the assassination she had been working every night at Señor Veronesi's shop, on Ninth Street by the Nuñez bridge. In those days she lived in an alleyway adjoining the Puerto Colombia *chicha* bar and three doors down from the room where Jesús Carvajal was then living. The night of October 1, at around eleven, she finished her cleaning duties at Señor Veronesi's shop, locked the door, and headed for home. When she arrived at the alley she met a neighbor who lived in the same building; and the two of them were standing there, waiting together for someone to open their door, when Dolores Vásquez saw a man in an elegant overcoat and a top hat who walked briskly and knocked on Carvajal's door. He was accompanied by a boy who was carrying a shapeless package under his arm. Carvajal's door opened and the two men, the man in the top hat and his assistant or whatever he was, stepped quickly inside.

"Did you recognize the man in the top hat?"

"No, sir."

"Could you identify him if you saw him?"

"I think so, sir."

"Good. Let's move on to something else. You knew Carvajal?"

"Yes, sir," said the woman. "I knew him from seeing him in the Puerto Colombia."

"And what did you do that night?"

"I told my neighbor what I'd just seen and he went up to Carvajal's house. Later he told me he'd heard several voices."

"That is to say, that there were other people."

"Yes, sir. A large meeting, according to my neighbor."

"And what was the meeting about?"

"My neighbor didn't tell me. He told me he couldn't hear what they were talking about, but they were important people. And I thought it strange that important people would go inside a tradesman's house, almost at midnight, as if not wanting to be seen."

"Please, Your Honor," said the plaintiff's counsel, "can the witness please abstain from interpretations."

"The witness is describing a behavior that struck her as suspicious," said Anzola. "She has every right to do so."

"Let the witness continue," said the judge.

"Where were you on the eve of the assassination of General Uribe?" asked Anzola.

"You mean October 14?" asked the woman.

"Yes, the night of October 14."

"Oh, yes. I was working at Señor Veronesi's shop."

"And what did you see there?"

"I saw a group of about fifteen tradesmen come in and order a round of drinks. We were suspicious. And when a man saw that we weren't pouring, he pulled a roll of bills out of his pocket and said: 'See, I do have cash. I'm going to pay, see. Do me the favor of serving us what we ordered.' I took a good look at him, because it seemed odd for a tradesman to have so much cash. And when all those boys were leaving, I said to the patrolman to check to see if anybody had been robbed, because I'd seen all that cash. The officer left with him and after a while came back and told me: 'I left him there in the carpentry shop. Don't worry, señora. They won't rob anyone.'"

"Could you please repeat that? Where did the patrolman leave him?"

"In the carpentry shop."

"And the next day, what happened?"

"The next day General Uribe was killed. And three or four days later I saw the photos in the papers of the assassins, and I was really surprised to realize that one of them was Carvajal. And his partner was the same one who I'd seen: the one with all the cash in the shop."

The newspapers the next day agreed: Anzola was winning small battles. Seeing it all a century later, I can interpret what happened next as the proof that his enemies were noticing the same thing. Well, the next day (it was a Friday) Anzola arrived at the hearing and he found a different public. The galleries of the Salón de Grados, which in previous sessions had harbored as many of Anzola's friends as enemies, the galleries whose applause and booing had been evenly distributed, from one day to the next came to be occupied only by those the press had started calling anti-Anzolistas. They were all men, all capable of deafening whistles, all quick to raise their fists and snarl menacingly, all capable, by way of the simple gesture of stretching a hand in Anzola's direction, pointing at him with one finger while spitting an incomprehensible insult, of filling the place with a hitherto unheard-of hatred. They were disguised policemen. They were united by the same clandestine condition: three-quarters of the public was now composed of members of General Correal's secret police. They had taken over the enclosure: they were intimidating, frightening, and distracting.

And then the witness Luis Rendón took the stand. His should have been a testimony like so many others in those days: the declaration of a prisoner in the Panóptico about the privileges conceded to Galarza and Carvajal by the guards. Rendón, a man with slanting eyes, had caught his lover with another man, who he'd murdered, and then he'd attacked her in the course of his hearing, during a face-to-face encounter that could not have gone worse. For these crimes he had been sentenced to eighteen years in prison, but he acted as though he'd been sentenced to life: he was violent and unkempt, and more than once he had been sent into solitary confinement for immoral conduct or insulting the authorities. And this was the man Anzola had chosen to continue demonstrating, to the jury, General Correal's corruption.

After a series of insipid exchanges, Carvajal's lawyer asked Rendón about the meal plan of the accused. Rendón spoke of the meat and lard they were brought from outside; of the candles they were given to light their cells until whatever time they wished; of the money Galarza and Carvajal gave to other prisoners for various reasons, which were not always clear. Then he said that Galarza and Carvajal behaved well in prison, that they almost never left their cells, and that in any case there was an order from the management: anyone offending them would receive serious punishment. "They are protected," said Rendón.

Then, in an attempt to discredit the testimony, the registrar read out his sentence for murder. A voice shouted from the back of the gallery:

"And Anzola defends him."

It was a taunt, of course: an allusion to the witnesses Anzola had brought from the prison on previous days. He defended himself as well as he could, trying not to give in to the provocation.

"That's not what this is about, gentlemen," he said. "It's not about defending witnesses who have been charged with more or less serious crimes. What does that matter? What does it matter that a witness has committed a crime if he's telling the truth? Do you people want me, for a crime hatched in the Puerto Colombia *chicha* bar, to call witnesses from the diplomatic corps? You want me to summon ministers from their offices to testify about what goes on inside the Panóptico? No: when we come to talk about the moment of the crime itself, I will bring ministers who were present there. For now, I have to appeal to the criminal underworld. And I will even bring the backroom girls from the *chichería* if I think they might bring me closer to the truth."

Those on his side applauded shyly.

"Anzola, do me the favor of not making speeches here," said the judge.

And then it happened. Now, as I write, I wonder what could have gone through Marco Tulio Anzola's head to make him say what he said next, what dirty trick his emotions could have played on him to make him lose control of his own rhetoric.

"I have to go back over all the incidents that have been seen here," he said, "so that the public will understand their consequences. I have to demonstrate that Pedro León Acosta was at Tequendama Falls four times, not two, as he said here. I have to tell you about the gentleman in the top hat who went to find Galarza in the Puerto Colombia. Because I should tell you, sirs, that I now have very precise information on who that man is."

As soon as he pronounced the words he knew he should not have done so. That's what I believe, because it's not possible that he mightn't have known, it's not possible that he wouldn't have realized that he'd just lied: for he did not have any precise information on the man in the top hat. It seems to me that in his head there was some kind of swap: so many years of working with the witness statements, so many years of studying the facts of the crime to the extent of writing a book about them, had allowed him to confide in his instinct; and his instinct, since Dolores Vásquez talked to him about the man she'd seen in a top hat, had put Pedro León Acosta in his mind. Who else could it be? Anzola would have thought. He was magically, superstitiously, sure that the man in the top hat who had gone to look for Galarza in the Puerto Colombia, who had visited Carvajal in his house after eleven at night, was the same man who the disappeared witness Alfredo García had seen that night at the door to the carpentry shop, and the same man as well who on the day of the crime had been seen by Mercedes Grau elegantly dressed, with striped trousers and patent leather ankle boots, and asking one of the assassins: "How'd it go? Did you kill him?" But that unproven certainty had just played a dirty trick on him. In any case, he had just fallen into a trap, and the fact that he'd laid the trap for himself made it no less serious.

"Let's have the name!" furious voices shouted from the gallery. "The name, Anzola!"

Others joined in the chorus: "The name, if you're capable."

"Señor Anzola, say the name of that individual immediately," said the prosecutor. "Under penalty of being charged with concealing evidence."

"You are required, Señor Anzola," said the judge, "to specify the charges you have just made, within three days."

"Please, Your Honor," replied Anzola, "clear the galleries."

"I ask the galleries to keep their composure," said the lawyer Murillo. "So the judge will not lose patience."

Anzola, I think, had to know at that moment that he could not keep quiet: his silence was now the silence of defeat. He needed a smoke screen, a distraction, so he did what he did best: he protested. He complained that the whole trial seemed designed to hinder his cause. He complained that the testimonies that helped it were left inconclusive; he was allowed to interrogate witnesses only when the judge wished to allow it; now he wanted to force him to reveal his cards—publicly confess an identity that was better kept secret—and thus lose the small advantage he had been able to gain. In contrast, the judge had refused to order the presence of Salomón Correal, to counteract what witnesses had said against him face-to-face. "Why?" Anzola asked, and immediately answered his own question: "Because that would harm the police commissioner."

But his strategy did not succeed. Rodríguez Forero's son, who until then had remained still and silent in his chair, stood up.

"Your Honor," he said, "the private prosecution demands Señor Anzola name the famous gentleman in the top hat right this moment, and requests you to oblige him to do so."

"Oblige him!" shouted the galleries.

"You cannot oblige me to do that," said Anzola. "Until I finish an investigation that I am carrying out, I am not going to give it and you cannot oblige me. You're not going to take away my evidence to then bring in hired policemen to contradict it. Very pretty that."

"Out!" roared a voice from the gallery.

"Señor Anzola," said the prosecutor, "you have an obligation to respect us. You cannot come here to offend us with charges like these."

"You are a witness," said Carvajal's lawyer. "As a witness, you must supply the name if you know it. Otherwise, you will face trial as an accessory after the fact."

"You will have the name," said Anzola, "the day I bring my evidence to the courtroom."

"If you don't want to give the name in public, you must give it to the judge privately."

"I shall not give it to anyone. And nobody can force me to."

The uproar from the galleries was so great, and there was so much hostility, that the judge decreed a ten-minute recess. Anzola did not leave: the courtyard with the fountain and the brick arcades were full of men who would not hesitate for a second, not a fraction of a second, before hurting him if the occasion presented itself. It was not impossible that among the public that day were the men in ponchos who, as he recounted in his book, had followed him threateningly through the streets. What would he have been thinking at that moment? It is possible that he might have seen, as if in cinematic images, the whole path that remained to be covered in this stubborn labor. It remained for Pedro León Acosta to return to court to be identified; it remained for him to call for the testimonies that placed the Jesuits center stage. Many pages of his book remained to be gone through, many of the thirty-six witnesses he had recruited had yet to be called.

Then the judge came out. To the surprise of all, he did not even take his seat. He waved his bell, waited for silence, and crossed himself lengthily while looking up at the crucifix.

"Everything that has happened here today is a mockery," he said. "And as I cannot continue to permit Señor Anzola to mock everyone, I have decided to set him a deadline. Señor Anzola has four days, until next Tuesday, to present all the rest of his witnesses and make all the rest of his statements. After that point, he will no longer be allowed to speak."

"You cannot do that," said Anzola.

"Of course I can," said the judge.

"I am speaking here by virtue of a decree of yours, sir. I might not know much about the law, but I know that judicial decrees are the law in a trial. So you cannot come in here now and tell me for how long I can speak."

"You are speaking here because I have a discretionary power to direct the debates," replied the judge. "And when I want to I can, discretionarily, order you to be silent."

"Shut him up!" shouted the galleries.

"I don't care about those who shout," said Anzola. "Tomorrow I will publish in the newspaper the list of those making such a ruckus. They are civil servants and police officers who have left their posts to come here and insult me, and they do so under orders from Correal."

"You will please restrict yourself to the charges you have come to make," said Judge Garzón. "And know that if you do not respect me, I am going to fine you."

"Before that, let's clarify the time period you've imposed."

"No, sir. Bring your charges. Then I shall summon the witnesses that are confirmed."

"I have huge evidence against people you cannot even imagine," said Anzola. "But I will not say their names yet, so they don't bring false witnesses here to contradict them. I shall assert my evidence to an impartial judge. What I have on Emilio Beltrán, on the man in the top hat, and on all the rest."

"Fraud!" they shouted at him.

The prosecutor demanded of Anzola, once more and in the name of the people, the full name of the so-often-mentioned man in the top hat.

"If you do not give it," he said, "I am going to ask the judge to fine you."

The judge did not wait to be asked.

"Under a fine of ten gold pesos," he said, "tell us the name of that gentleman in the top hat who you believe to be involved in the murder of General Uribe."

"If I do not give it," answered Anzola, "it is the fault of all of you here." He realized he had to strain his throat if he wanted to be heard over all the shouting, the insults, the hands banging on the railings; he also realized that he was losing control over the development of the hearing. "I cannot give that name because I do not have confidence that the evidence I have against him will be followed up. As for the fine, I shall pay it with great pleasure. But first I shall have to demonstrate to the country who the accessories to the real assassins of General Uribe were. Your Honor, issue a judicial decree that will allow me to give my sworn statement before an impartial judge, and then I shall bring my evidence!"

It was a desperate gesture. I know it, though I'm not sure he knew it. To whom was he going to take what he hadn't been able to demonstrate there? Then the prosecutor stood up. He said the charges leveled by Anzola were extremely grave; that Anzola had complained a lot about the thuggishness of the rest of them even though no one had kept him from talking about whatever he liked there. And this was true. He said there should be a demand that he be required to present all his evidence immediately; not doing so suggested that Anzola, far from searching for things to come to light in this trial, was seeking confusion, by all means possible. This also could seem true. He said that Señor Anzola had not brought, up to that moment, a single piece of concrete evidence. And that was incontrovertibly true. He said that Anzola had wanted to display himself here as a standard bearer of justice, and instead he had brought about a farce. And the public shouted, insulted him, and had begun to threaten him: how they loved that word, *farce*, how many times had it been thrown in his face during the hearings. And everything the prosecutor said was true. Had Anzola wondered if he was right? Had he come to doubt his own certainties?

"If Anzola does not present his evidence," said the prosecutor, "His Honor will be obligated to expel him from the hearings. If he does not present it, he cannot allege that he was not allowed to speak, much less that there is a cover-up going on in this trial."

The chronicles recount that Judge Garzón leaned over to the three jurors and shielded his mouth while talking to them, and the jurors shielded their mouths while answering him. When he sat back in his seat, he announced:

"In accordance with the jury, it has been decided to submit you, Señor Anzola, to an interrogation. You are required to articulate all the charges against people you believe to be involved in the assassination of General Uribe. You are also required to say their names."

"I cannot," said Anzola.

"You are required to say the names of those you consider responsible."

"I cannot," said Anzola.

"For the last time, will you or will you not give the names?"

"I cannot give them," said Anzola.

"Very well, then. Your presence here is useless. Your intervention here is concluded. You can no longer speak."

The hearing ended like a street demonstration, seized with a similar clenched violence, the same sensation of a lit fuse. Another identical demonstration awaited Anzola outside, on the pavement of Carrera Sexta, and it was so ferocious that the journalist Joaquín Achury tried to block his way and advise him not to go out. "Wait a moment," it seems he said, "wait for them to go. Do yourself a favor." But Anzola didn't listen to him. When he went through the big wooden door, an avalanche of threats hit him: they were going to kill him, he was a son of a bitch, and they were going to kill him. Bastard, they shouted from the corners; son of a whore, they called him, and others said he was a traitor, and others, finally, accused him of having robbed and murdered and bribed. He lowered his head so their spit would not land on his face; a squad of police surrounded him, which was the only reason the furious crowd did not pounce on him and tear him apart with their bare hands. One of those hands managed to reach over the officers and punch him between the shoulders, and another knocked his hat off with a slap that would have hurt if it had caught him on the face. Among his aggressors were many of those who had cheered him a week earlier: Would Anzola have recognized them? Like that, surrounded by police, in the middle of that hallucinatory violence, without taking part in any decisions about his movements, he reached the Plaza de Bolívar. The journalist Achury, from afar, saw a car appear out of nowhere and a door open, and saw Anzola shoved into it and heard a voice order:

"Take him home. And don't stop, don't stop no matter what."

There are no witnesses to what happened next. We can only deduce it from the next news we have about Anzola: his arrest and imprisonment. It must have been immediate, for the following morning found him already in the police jail cells; it is reasonable to suppose that the car that had orders to take him home actually took him straight to police headquarters. I imagine Anzola in those seconds prior to his arrest: I imagine him thinking he's about to arrive home and take refuge in his bed, under the wool blankets, and suddenly realizing that he wasn't in front of his house, but in front of police headquarters. Two policemen come up on either side of him on the sidewalk, seize him, and begin dragging him inside the building. A third, whose face Anzola never manages to see, tells him he's under arrest.

"Under what charges?" shouts Anzola, trying to resist. "What are the charges?"

"Disrespecting authority," a rude voice tells him. "And trying to use a firearm against a police constable."

That's how it could have happened. The charges under which the arrest was made were a week old: they stemmed from the incident in the corridors of the Salón de Grados, when a police constable had tried to take Anzola by force to the witness room. The only one injured in the incident had been Anzola, who fell to the floor and was shoved down the corridor. But now they were charging him over that;

and, most absurdly, they accused him of having tried to use his revolver, when the police constable had removed it from him during the search. This was their revenge; this was the revenge of the whole police force, of every officer discredited by the statements of his witnesses. This was Correal, yes, Salomón Correal, explaining to him that you do not mess with the police of this country.

I DON'T KNOW how many days Anzola spent in jail, because there's no record of it, but I do know that the trial went on without him in the Salón de Grados, that place where Anzola was now unwelcome, where his name was disgraced. I don't know if any of the officers guarding him might have done him the favor of telling him how the hearings were going, or if he received visits from anyone—Julián Uribe, for example—who could have brought him recent newspapers as a form of information charity. If he could have seen them, he would have known what they thought of him in that world, the outside world, the world to which he had sought to restore a little bit of justice (perhaps clumsily, perhaps believing that he could prove in practice the convictions he had acquired in the most private part of his soul). Under the headline "Impressions of the Trial," the reporter for a newspaper had written some paragraphs that were like a broken mirror: Anzola could have seen himself there during the days of his imprisonment, feeling reflected but at the same time distorted or incomplete, while obscure nameless forces decided—slowly, sullenly—how to dispose of his life.

> Señor Anzola Samper has stopped attending the hearings of the trial of the assassins of General Uribe Uribe. For thirteen days he was the figure of such a sensational

cause; thirteen sessions were taken up with hearing his witnesses and carrying out the confrontations he demanded,
and after all of that this anxious young man finished off
his performance himself by refusing to lay charges and
make frank accusations. He presented himself before the
jury as an exponent of the truth and the light, and he retired from it wrapped in shadows, refusing to give the
names of those responsible he claims to know, clearly refusing to make the terrible accusations we all expected to
hear from his lips. After that refusal his presence in court
no longer made any sense, and he no longer had anything
to do there.

Let's see him, let's try to see him. In the mornings, very early, a tired
and irritable officer wakes Anzola up, grumpy from having been on
guard duty all night. He takes him to the lavatory—allows him to
enter alone—and waits for him on the other side of a half-open door
with a disabled latch, and Anzola has to do contortions to crouch over
a stinking hole in the floor without losing his balance. Luckily, the
scant food and the effects of disgust have unregulated his stomach's
habits, so that he has gone three days without relieving himself. Sometimes he is allowed to wash his hands, but not always. His clothes begin to smell of urine and rancid sweat, and he is getting used to his
own stink when the same officer who arrested him shows up, hands
him a paper package tied with string, and says: "Be grateful you have
friends." It is a change of clothes. Nobody tells him who brought it;
Anzola buries his face in it and inhales deeply: he has never felt such
pleasure at rubbing recently ironed cloth against his skin. When he
changes, the starched collar rubs against the back of his neck all day.

He doesn't care. When night falls, he has a painful rash, but he notices that concentrating on that banal discomfort keeps him from thinking too much about his disgrace.

During the thirteen days of his intense intervention, Señor Anzola did not manage to prove anything; his witnesses insinuated suspicions of certain facts, magnified some details, or destroyed some legends as unsustainable as those related to General Pedro León Acosta, who perhaps in this whole trial has done nothing but atone for his participation in the February 10 attack, since only because of it could he be implicated in a crime in which not the slightest nor the furthest blame could be proven against him. The big witnesses, those who saw General Correal, accompanied by another man, conversing with the assassins three hours before the crime, in broad daylight, on the doorstep of the illustrious victim and giving them instructions there, had no other difficulty than that of saying things that were purely and simply implausible, because those statements indicated in General Correal, more than his complicity, a monumental stupidity, a flippancy so enormous, such lack of foresight, that are simply not credible in the most oblivious illiterate, let alone in a Police Commissioner. It could be affirmed as axiomatic that precisely if General Correal had participated in some way in the horrendous crime, he would never have allowed himself to be seen conversing publicly in the street with the assassins the day of the crime and in front of the victim's house. That is elemental and obvious.

After a few days—three, maybe four—they move him to the Pan-óptico. It can't be said his jailers lack a sense of humor: his cell is a few doors down from the ones previously occupied by the assassins Galarza and Carvajal, who had now been transferred, awaiting their sentence. A couple of times they allow him to go to the chapel alone to pray. As soon as he closes the wooden door, he kneels down on the cold stone floor, and in the semidarkness his lips try to form the Our Father, but then his mind interrupts: Anzola thinks that the assassins did the same thing with the Jesuit priests. Yes, the ones who came to visit them, to demand their restraint and recommend readings; the ones who left no trace apart from a few articles written under pseudonyms and a few rumors, what somebody said that somebody heard that somebody said. They had remained in the shadows, those priests, they had come out of the plot against Uribe victorious . . . but who are they? Anzola has not even seen their faces: he could not even recognize them if he ran into them in the street.

At night it was cold; Anzola wraps himself in his blanket and draws his knees up to his chest, and has enormous trouble falling asleep, perhaps for having spent the day inactive: reading the papers, taking pointless notes out of long habit, commenting on what, according to the newspapers, they're saying in the Salón de Grados. They call him disloyal, a liar, a slanderer, and the public applauds, happy to be rid of him, yes, happy to have dismissed him. Anzola, meanwhile, goes out into the yard at the same time as the rest of the prisoners, receives the same food as the rest of the prisoners, and uses the lavatory at the same times. Sometimes he visits the construction projects he supervised during his fictitious employment; sometimes he talks with other prisoners. One of them, that man called Zalamea who gave him generous information about the assassins and their privileges, approaches him one morning and talks to him the way one talks to a child: "Oh, my dear friend, it could only occur to you," he says. "Only to you could such a thing occur."

But the new culprits? They appeared clearly nowhere. It is a simple and very easy labor to suggest, in any sort of matter, vague and sinister complicities; the popular spirit is very fertile soil for those kinds of seeds; in it suspicion catches, even the most absurd, marvelously fast; but that wasn't what was expected of Señor Anzola, but proof and concrete accusations, and the country was left waiting. We felt, as we listened to Señor Anzola, the sensation that he, deep down in his spirit, did not know for certain more than the judge, the prosecutor, and the great public knew. That is why he could barely manage a few hours in civic awareness; his apparition as an audacious, decisive, brave accuser seduced many and attracted the attention of all, but his fall was irremediable, because the pedestal he perched upon was made of nothing but vagueness, and in the light of debate it came undone. The anguished intensity of the first sessions became an amusing farce in the last ones, and people who had begun by feeling the chilly breath of Nemesis above their heads, ended up smiling or yawning.

When Anzola is released, after a series of judicial maneuvers and called-in favors on the part of Julián Uribe, the first thing he does is go home and take a hot bath, so long that his servant has to leave two extra jugs by the bathroom door. When he comes out Anzola notices, with surprise, that his briefcase has been returned: it is lying beside his office chair, like a pet dog. It stays there for the following days, without Anzola picking it up or organizing its contents: the briefcase is a memento of his failure, an archive of wasted years. He spends some days shut up at home, a prisoner of the hatred of the citizens of Bogotá, without even looking out the window to see the cobbled street, for he fears encountering a finger pointing at him or a contemptuous sneer. But the first time he goes out, forcing himself to recover his life, almost on his way into the drugstore to buy some pills, he runs into Señorita Adela Garavito. He greets her by raising a hand to his hat and takes a step toward her, but Adela Garavito dissuades him. "You made us look like liars," she says in a tone of voice that has gone through repugnance and now settled comfortably into bitterness and resentment. "Señorita, I . . ." Anzola tries, but she cuts off his justification. "Do not come near my house," she said, "or my *papá* will shoot you." She speeds up, as if Anzola had leprosy, and disappears around the nearest corner. Marco Tulio Anzola no longer feels capable of going as far as the drugstore.

And meanwhile the speeches are still going on in the Salón de Grados, the eternal long-winded spiels that appeared in the newspapers, taking up sixteen columns of tightly packed type, the orators of which all seem to have a secret objective: to sink Marco Tulio Anzola in the mire of opprobrium. In the speeches of the prosecutor and the assassins' lawyers, Anzola is a fanatic Liberal with an irrepressible desire for vengeance or a shyster longing for fleeting glory, and in any case irresponsible, an attacker of other people's reputations, a pyromaniac loose on the altars of the nation, and a violator of the sacred values of truth, justice, and honor. For a week Bogotá is a bonfire ready to burn Anzola, everyone's enemy. The speeches—with which the lawyers of one side and the other are closing the trial—call him a coward, a vulgar backstabber, an opportunist whose pettiness hides him from the gaze of honorable men. Once or twice during the course of a night of insomnia (or when a dog wakes him from his light and disturbed sleep), Anzola wonders, as has tended to occur to him lately, if they're not right.

When the trial finished in the Salón de Grados, the court registrar turned to the three members of the jury, who sat up straight in their seats, and read out two questions: "Is the accused Leovigildo Galarza guilty of having willfully and premeditatedly brought about the death of Señor General Rafael Uribe Uribe, by way of the injuries caused by a sharp and offensive instrument, on Carrera Séptima of this city, block 10, on October 15, 1914? Is the accused Leovigildo Galarza guilty of having committed the offense mentioned in the previous question, with the following circumstances, or some or part of them: (1) with previous subterfuge, (2) with malice aforethought, treacherously and sure of having caught the victim off guard, defenseless, and unprepared?" He then read the same thing over again, but exchanging the name of Leovigildo Galarza for that of Jesús Carvajal. The jury unanimously answered yes. Yes to everything. Yes in both cases.

On June 25, 1918, in the afternoon, Judge Garzón read out the sentences against Jesús Carvajal and Leovigildo Galarza. For the assassination of General Rafael Uribe Uribe they were condemned to twenty years in prison, deprivation of their political rights, and a fine of eight thousand gold pesos, plus the court costs. The galleries exploded in applause, in cries of "Long live the prosecutor" and "Death to Anzola and his book." Commenting on the sentence, and using the same words the judge had employed to do so, a newspaper said:

> This verdict will not satisfy those who have wanted to use
> the crime to bring serious charges against their political

rivals. It will not satisfy those who have wanted to ventilate partisan passions through the abuse of the pain of a whole people. This verdict will, however, satisfy genuine patriots, as some, in attempting to stain the flag of the parties with a great man's blood, also threatened to stain that of the nation with dishonor. This verdict, Colombians, returns honor to all of you, gives you the gift of justice, frees you of an uncertain past, and makes you a gift of a future in peace.

IX

THE SHAPE OF THE RUINS

I don't know when I started to realize that my country's past was incomprehensible and obscure to me, a real shadowy terrain, nor can I remember the precise moment when all that I'd believed so trustworthy and predictable—the place where I'd grown up, whose language I speak and customs I know, the place whose past I was taught in school and in university, whose present I have become accustomed to interpreting and pretending I understand—began to turn into a place of shadows out of which jumped horrible creatures as soon as we dropped our guard. With time I have come to think that this is the true reason why writers write about the places of childhood and adolescence and even their early youth: you don't write about what you know and understand, and much less do you write because you know and understand, but because you understand that all your knowledge and comprehension is false, a mirage and an illusion, so your books are not, could not be, more than elaborate displays of disorientation: extensive and multifarious declarations of perplexity. *All that I thought was so clear,* you then think, *now turns out to be full of duplicities and hidden intentions, like a friend who betrays us.* To that revelation, which is always annoying and often frankly painful, the writer responds in the only way one knows how: with a book. And that's how you try to mitigate your disconcertion, reduce the space between what you don't know and what can be known, and most of all resolve your profound disagreement with that unpredictable reality. "Out of the quarrel with others we make rhetoric," wrote Yeats. "Out of the quarrel with ourselves we make poetry." And what happens when both quarrels arise at the same time, when fighting with the world is a reflection or a transfiguration of the subterranean but constant confrontation you have with yourself? Then you write a book like the one I'm writing now, and blindly trust that the book will mean something to somebody else.

It is possible that these ideas were in my head that day, the day of the revelations. It was the last day of February, a Friday; I arrived at Carballo's apartment at lunchtime, when that night owl would be, I calculated, already showered and ready to begin his convoluted routine. And so it was: I found him dressed, not with the care he usually put into his outfits and accessories, but in a loose and comfortable gray sweatsuit that had seen better days. He looked ready to go out for a run, like one of those old men who has suffered a pre–heart attack and gets obsessed too late with exercise, so they never look at ease in their sports clothes: they look like intruders, impostors, actors disguised for a role they detest. That's how Carlos Carballo looked that day. Was it his appearance that made me perceive a kind of melancholy in the air, or was it the melancholy that had dictated and in some way produced his appearance? I saw him, for the first time, looking really tired; I thought that the work of remembering tires us out, even when we're concerned with pasts not our own (when we're concerned with our pasts, it not only tires us out, but wears us the way water wears away a rock). That's what I thought when I arrived: that Carballo was tired from looking so hard, for my information and benefit, at this country's hidden past. When I put my empty black knapsack on the floor, beside a tower of detective novels, and sat down like a diligent understudy, I could not have imagined that the most memorable day of all those we'd shared was about to begin. I could not have imagined that we were going to spend that February 28 very far from the present, plunged into another day in a remote year, watching the terrifying spectacle of a man who remembers what hurts and stings him, and not doing so because he wants to, but because he has no other choice.

By that point I had lost track of how many hours I'd spent stuck in *Who Are They?*, scrutinizing its pages, questioning its conclusions, telling myself on occasion that it was all false, that things like this could not have happened in my city, and the proof was that nobody knew about or talked about them: that this foolish denunciation had not survived. And then I thought: It's true precisely because it hadn't survived, because history has proved a thousand times its extraordinary capacity to hide uncomfortable versions or to change the language with which things are told, so that terrible and inhumane things end up turning into the most normal, or desirable, or even laudable thing in the world. And then I would think again: It hasn't survived, nobody talks about it, it has sunk into oblivion and therefore it's false, for history, which has its own rules, filters and selects like the natural selection of species, and that's how the versions that try to distort the truth, lie to us, or deceive us, get left behind, and only the ones that stand up to our questioning, our skepticism as citizens, survive. And then I didn't know what to think anymore, for the fact that Anzola had disappeared into the cesspool of Colombian history would not stop tormenting me. The man who had been at the center of the news for a month, appearing every day on the front pages of the papers and seeing his words published there on a daily basis; the man who for the previous four years divided the citizenry with the promise (some said with *the threat*) of his investigation and his book, disappears from the public stage as of June 1918. After he went to prison, the media do not mention him again. There is no news of him, his name is not mentioned except to denigrate him, and after the ruling he's not even mentioned for that. The only thing Carballo had been able to find after years of following the trail of that young man, the only miserable crumb of information that had crossed his path, was a mysterious bibliographical note in the Library of Congress in Washington, D.C. It dated from 1947 and this was the information:

SAMPER, MARCO TULIO ANZOLA, 1892– ©, New York. *Secrets of Roulette and Its Technical Tricks: Revelations of a Croupier*, 32 p., illus.

Everything in those lines seemed strange to Carballo and also seemed strange to me: the alphabetical classification of the author (listed under his second surname, rather than his first), the length of the work (a short illustrated booklet), and finally, its unpredictable subject (I couldn't imagine the author of *Who Are They?* writing a manual for compulsive gamblers). In our last conversation we spent a long time speculating about that old discovery. I asked if he hadn't tried, but really truly tried, with the force of an obsession, to find *Secrets of Roulette*; I asked if he'd really hunted for it, even though the revelations of a croupier had nothing to do with Rafael Uribe Uribe or Jorge Eliécer Gaitán or with the violence or the politics or the political violence of our sad country. In short: even though it was of no use.

"Of course I have," he answered. "For a time I looked for that damned little book over land and sea. I called all the bibliophiles I know and asked for help contacting all the rare- and secondhand-book dealers. And of course I called the Library of Congress. And nothing. The book does not exist. It's not in the Library, and it's supposed to have a copy of everything with pages in this stinking world. But that doesn't mean it hasn't been of any use to me."

"What do you mean?"

"I began asking myself about the place of publication," said Carballo. "New York. Why New York? I had always thought Anzola's disappearance was too total, too perfect. Nobody disappears like that. Or rather: there is only one way to disappear so completely from the Colombian media after having been so much of a presence."

"Leave Colombia."

"Yes. And it's logical, no? What would you have done? If you'd written a book like *Who Are They?*, if you'd participated in the most notorious trial in history, and if your book and your participation in the trial had turned you, in your early twenties, into the most hated man in Colombia . . . You would have left too, Vásquez, and so would I, I would have left too. I thought of that and then I thought: And where would a young man like Anzola go? Somewhere where he knows someone, where he has some contacts at least. And then I remembered that Carlos Adolfo Urueta was a diplomat in Washington. I thought: The United States. Anzola went to the United States. I still think that's what happened."

"Oh, you're not sure?"

"A hundred percent sure, no," said Carballo. "But it's logical, isn't it? And anyway, it doesn't matter."

"Why doesn't it matter?" I said. I had begun listening to his reasoning expecting a revelation: *Now he'll tell me he followed the lead,* I even thought, *he'll tell me he found his trail in New York, and he'll surprise me.* I didn't hide my disappointment. "What do you mean it doesn't matter, Carlos? There's a story there, don't you think? There's a hole in the story. Wouldn't you like to fill it? Wouldn't you like to know what happened to Anzola?"

"I'd like to, but it doesn't matter to me. They're two different things."

"You don't care?"

"Well, no," said Carballo. "I can imagine the situation very well: Anzola left the country the way so many people leave Colombia when they speak a truly troublesome truth. He became uncomfortable and he had to leave: just like so many. If we started making lists, we'd never finish. Well, Anzola is an old example, not the oldest, but one of them. And that's that, we don't have to keep wondering about it. I believe that's how it was and that's enough for me, because Anzola's life doesn't really matter to me. Or to put it a better way, what matters is his book, understand? What matters to me is that he wrote his book. So a reader would find it, right? That's when things begin to happen."

I can't say at that moment I noticed that last phrase, the profound significance of which would have been impossible for me to guess or foresee in the moment I heard it. I took it as a cliché, maybe; maybe I believed that Carballo was revealing the miracles of encounter between any reader and any book. I didn't think he had in mind a particular reader when he pronounced those words, or a specific book, nor did I think the imaginary and even abstract encounter might occur in a definite place and on a concrete date. But that's how it was. I then asked an innocent question, more out of courtesy than genuine curiosity:

"Carlos, don't you think Anzola's departure might have any simpler explanations?"

Carballo passed a hand over his new beard. "Like what," he said curtly.

"Maybe Anzola didn't leave because he was persecuted. Maybe he left Colombia simply because he failed."

He half closed his eyes and a scornful look appeared on his face. I didn't care. I told him what I thought was an incontrovertible truth: that beyond what had happened in reality, beyond the accusations he'd made in his book, the fact was that Marco Tulio Anzola had not been able to demonstrate anything in that trial. And then Carballo got angrier than I'd ever seen him.

"What do you mean?" he said, standing up. "What do you mean Anzola didn't prove anything? Are the witnesses not there?"

"Don't blow up at me, Carlos," I said. "The witnesses are there, but they don't prove anything. The book is very convincing, and I would love to give in to a three-hundred-page conspiracy theory. But what matters isn't the theory of the book, but what happened at the trial, and the trial was a failure. A total failure: a spectacular and even humiliating failure. A disappointment, in other words, a betrayal of all the people who supported Anzola. The poor guy had nothing more than clues about the men he accused: that Correal was seen here, that Pedro León Acosta was seen there. Both those characters strike me as fairly evil, but that doesn't mean they did what Anzola said in his book. Agreed: Acosta tried to murder a president a few years earlier. Agreed: Correal mistreated and even tortured another. But that's not proof of anything, except of their pasts. And what can you tell me about the Jesuits? Against the Jesuits, who are also accused in the book, there is nothing, absolutely nothing in the trial. They're not even mentioned."

"Because Anzola didn't get that far!" shouted Carballo. "Because they kicked him out before he could get to the Jesuits!"

"Fine, that makes it easy. 'Yes, they're guilty, but it's just that I was going to prove it later.' That's not serious."

"I can't believe it," said Carballo, lowering his voice.

"Well, apparently," I said sarcastically, "neither could the jury."

"And what about Father Berestain's meetings with Correal? What about the witness statements of the people who saw the murderers come out of the San Bartolomé door?"

"They remain just that, Carlos: meetings and witness statements. But Anzola didn't prove that it led to anything."

"And what about Berestain's words? When he hoped Uribe was rotting in hell. What about that?"

"Oh, Carlos, please," I said. "In this country people wish hell for each other with astonishing ease. Everybody does it all the time. That doesn't mean anything concrete, don't tell me you haven't noticed."

Carballo sat back down. His face and his expression (crossing his arms, the way his knees buckled) were suffused with an intense disappointment. I told him I was very sorry for speaking to him like that, but the facts were very clear: the book is one thing and the trial is something else. I brought up the subject of the Jesuits again: Anzola hadn't even mentioned them once during the whole trial, at least as far as he had told me. "Or did he?" I asked. "Did he produce any evidence against the Jesuits at the trial?"

A tiny voice said: "No."

"So then?"

"So they win."

"What?"

"You are doing exactly what the whole country has done for a century, Vásquez. Since he didn't win the case, since there was no ruling against those Anzola accused, then what Anzola said was a big lie. Well, yours is a very poor truth, my friend, because the truth of the courts is sometimes very different from the truth of life. You say that Anzola didn't manage to prove anything and therefore his book is unbelievable. But have you asked yourself why he didn't manage to prove anything in the trial? Is it not obvious that the whole trial was manipulated so that Anzola could not prove what he had? Is it not obvious that they silenced him in a very subtle way, with all the appearance of legality?"

"But Carlos, they let him say everything he wanted to. They let him call as many witnesses as he wanted. How did they silence him?"

"You are repeating what they said in the newspapers, I don't know if you realize it."

"I am perfectly well aware," I told him. "And let me tell you something: the commentator in *El Tiempo* is completely right. I don't know who he was, it's a shame he didn't sign his commentary, but he's right. He's right when he says that Anzola wasn't able to prove anything against either Correal or Acosta. He's right when he says that it's very easy to ignite suspicion but what is necessary is to prove it. Why didn't Anzola say who the man in the top hat was? Do you really believe that he knew who it was, Carlos? If he knew, why not come out with the name right there, in front of everybody? You don't believe that if he didn't say it was because he didn't know it? Tell me, Carlos, tell me sincerely: Don't you think that Anzola was bluffing?"

"No, he wasn't bluffing," said Carballo. "This is not a poker game."

"He doesn't clarify anything about the Jesuits' publications. He doesn't clarify anything about the associations where they supposedly drew lots to see who would assassinate a man. Who can believe him? Tell me, Carlos, who is Ariston Men Hydor and that Campesino who wrote against General Uribe? Bogotá was not a city of millions back then: it was a small town. Nobody could hide that well, I imagine. So, why can't he prove anything against a couple of fanatical columnists whose only cover is a pseudonym, two libelous madmen like those who exist all over social media? The answer: Because they're nothing more than madmen, fanatics, and mudslingers. And as for the associations, does that really happen? Are there really groups financed by rich people who choose assassins by drawing lots and order the death of anyone who annoys them? Where does Anzola show proof of that?"

"They win," he muttered, or that's what I thought I heard.

"I don't know who *they* are," I said. "But it's not that they win, it's that this is the truth we have available now. There isn't enough evidence to change it."

Carballo remained silent. He drew his feet up on the sofa and curled up like a frightened puppy. And then, with a voice that blended defeat and stubbornness, he began to speak. He did so without looking at me, as if thinking out loud. However, he was not thinking out loud: he was talking to me: he wasn't talking to anybody but me.

"But there are other truths, Vásquez," he said. "There are truths that do not come out in the papers. There are truths that are no less true due to the fact that nobody knows them. Maybe they happened in a strange place where journalists and historians can't go. And what do we do with them? Where can we give them space to exist? Do we let them rot, only because they weren't able to be born into life correctly, or because they let bigger forces win? There are weak truths, Vásquez, truths as fragile as a premature baby, truths that can't be defended in the world of proven facts, newspapers, and history books. Truths that exist even though they might have collapsed in a trial or even though people's memories forget them. Or are you going to tell me that known history is the only version of things? No, please, don't be so naive. What you call history is no more than the winning story,

Vásquez. Someone made that story win, and not any of the others, and that's why we believe it today. Or rather: we believe it because it got written down, because it wasn't lost in the endless hole of words that only get said, or even worse, that aren't even spoken, but are only thought. The journalist shows up, the twentieth-century historian shows up, and they put something in writing: it might be the Uribe crime, it might be men landing on the moon, it might be whatever you like: the atomic bomb or the Spanish Civil War or the secession of Panama. And that's the truth, but it's only true because *it happened in a place that can be told and someone told it in concrete words.* And I repeat: There are truths that don't happen in those places, truths that nobody writes down because they're invisible. There are millions of things that happen in special places, and I repeat: they are places that are not within the reach of historians or journalists. They are not invented places, Vásquez, they are not fictions, they are very real: as real as anything told in the newspapers. But they don't survive. They stay there, without anybody to tell them. And that's unfair. It's unfair and it's sad."

And that's when he began to speak of his father. He did so without fuss or sentimentalism, perhaps with a bit of melancholy, but he told a complex story without stumbling, and this allowed me to perceive that one of two things was true: either he'd told this story many times or he'd waited his whole life to tell it. I decided on the second, and it turned out that I was right.

I've corrected the few instances in which Carballo's prodigious memory misfired or mixed something up, and I've completed his tale with information necessary to understand or appreciate it better. Apart from that, I've tried to remember that my task was that of a notary, because it is more than likely I'll never come across a similar story again in my life. My job, very difficult and simple at the same time, is to do it justice or at least not misappropriate it.

The story is as follows.

CÉSAR CARBALLO WAS BORN in a house in the neighborhood of La Perseverancia, in eastern Bogotá, eleven or twelve blocks north of the street where his son would live (and where he would tell me all this) many years later. In that year, 1924, his mother, Rosa María Peña, worked as a laundress for people who lived in the rich neigborhoods, which she would get to by walking down the hill, crossing Carrera Séptima and then the railway line, and walking a few blocks north: those neighborhoods she could see from the flat rooftops of her street on clear mornings, when she'd chat with the women from her block, helping each other to hang up wet clothes on pita-fiber cords, which scratched the more delicate material. César's father was the only cobbler in that neighborhood inhabited mostly by tradesmen: mechanics and bricklayers and carpenters. Barely into his teens, Benjamín Carballo had begun to learn the trade in the shoemaking shop of Don Alcides Malagón, an old man who looked like he'd been born when the city had and seemed to have every intention of dying with it. When old man Malagón died, Benjamín Carballo was twenty-two years old, with a wife and a lot of common sense, so he took over the shoe shop without asking himself too many questions. Later he was glad of it, because as the years went by he became convinced that the art of making shoes was just that, an art, and there was no more dignity in sculpting a statue than in making a shoe to fit: in exploring the irregularities of a foot, taking a plaster mold that was precise and clean, constructing the lasts, reproducing in them the characteristic features of the living model, for no two feet are the same, and drying the leather over the lasts, so they don't lose their precise relationship. He had devoted his whole life to learning his trade; he hoped his son César would learn it from him.

He had good reasons to wish for that, because César handled the calipers and curved ruler like a professional, and he could trace perfect patterns by the age of ten. The problem—the problem for his father, who would have liked to have him as a helper eight hours a day—is that he was also an excellent pupil. His school was a place with badly patched roofs where classes couldn't be held when it rained, where there weren't enough notebooks to go around and books were a luxury item, but it was presided over by a woman with an indisputable vocation who noticed the boy's potential very early on. The teacher, who knew very well how things worked in this neighborhood, persuaded Rosa María to let the boy finish his studies, but she did so much earlier than they would have begun to consider taking him out of school to help the family. Rosa María paid attention to the teacher. César would always talk about how hard his parents worked so that neither he nor his little brother would have to drop out of school. It was there, in a dirt-floored classroom, where César Carballo first saw Jorge Eliécer Gaitán.

At the time, Gaitán had only been mayor of Bogotá for a few months, but he had already been all over the city, seeing and being seen, cultivating his image as a man of the people. He was thirty-three years old at that point and had an extraordinary appetite for power and a fabled résumé: he came from humble origins, son of a schoolteacher and a secondhand-book dealer, but he had spent fifteen years shaking up the political world with the most ferocious eloquence anyone had heard in these parts since Rafael Uribe Uribe. At eighteen he had given such a fiery speech in support of a Liberal candidate that his enemies shot at him from the crowd; the bullet passed under his gesticulating arm, and

Gaitán kept the jacket with the bullet hole and took it as a gift to his candidate.

In Rome, during the doctoral studies he took with Maestro Enrico Ferri, he had discovered and admired and learned the ways Mussolini had of hypnotizing crowds of thousands of people. He had a natural talent for improvisation, but taught himself a virtuoso handling of pauses and silences, and found a mysterious alchemy between the language of the street and the most high-toned rhetoric. The result was an orator capable of defeating any antagonist on a public platform, for Colombian politicians, convinced that they did not have to seduce their audiences, but simply intimidate them, began their speeches by mentioning Pallas Athena or Cicero or Demosthenes, and then Gaitán showed up and started firing his ferocious phrases with an archer's precision, and everything changed. Gaitán went into a trance; the whole audience seemed ready to follow him to that place he was talking from. Sometimes it didn't seem to matter what Gaitán was saying: what mattered was that it was him who was saying it. This was what his audiences felt, with their fraying hats and smell of old sweat. He was one of their own, but nobody (much less one of their own) had ever talked to them like that.

With that same tremendous oratory he had launched one of the toughest congressional debates a Colombian president had ever had to endure. In 1928, after a failed strike, the army had killed an indeterminate or secret number of banana plantation workers in the Caribbean region of the country. Gaitán denounced that event, which everyone knew very well; but when he did so it seemed as if the massacre had just taken place or the country was actually seeing it for the first time. Later someone referred to the moment when the orator, this Indian with slicked-back hair whom the high-class congressmen were mocking, devoured the chamber with a disturbing speech and finished his words with dramatic effect: taking out and showing everyone a skull, a bare human skull, the skull of one of the victims of the banana worker massacre. It was the skull of a child.

Seven years later, the agitator turned mayor visited a public school. The whole of La Perseverancia neighborhood was paralyzed by his visit. They saw him arrive on foot, with his double-breasted suit and fedora, and walk up the steep, dusty streets from Carrera Quinta, at a good pace, without sweating or fretting, surrounded by a committee who very soon mixed in with the curious and the needy onlookers. They heard him congratulate the teacher on her labor, heard him remind the throng that his own mother was a schoolteacher, heard him say that there was no more beautiful or nobler profession in the world than that of educator. They heard him promise the creation of school cafeterias, because children learn better on full stomachs. They heard him ask a boy why he'd come to school barefoot and heard him promise that shoes would be free and obligatory for public school pupils. Among those listening to his improvised speech was the shoemaker Benjamín Carballo, who had never heard a politician speak of shoes, and who spent the rest of the day and week and month remembering how his son César had interrupted the mayor's words to shout an offer in his changing adolescent voice: "My *papá* can make them!" Gaitán smiled but didn't say anything. Afterward, when his visit was finished, he crossed paths with César at the door of the school. Almost without looking at him, he said: "The shoemaker's kid." And he headed on down the hill.

César Carballo would later say that was the moment he began to be a Gaitanista. He saw himself in Gaitán as if in a mirror; as the years went on, Gaitán became his model, the pattern on which to trace the design of his life. If a man from Las Cruces, a neighborhood not very different from La Perseverancia, had managed to become a congressman and

mayor, why could he not follow a similar path with the sole force of discipline and study? César Carballo wanted to study law, like Gaitán, at
the National University, like Gaitán. But when he finished school reality
came crashing down on him with its full weight: there was no money to
send him to university. He was sixteen years old.

In January 1941, less than a year after Gaitán was named minister
of education, César Carballo woke up very early one morning, put on
a clean shirt, and walked to the offices of the ministry, on Carrera
Sexta at Tenth Street. He asked for Gaitán and was told he wasn't in.
He went back an hour later and asked for him again, and they told
him again that he wasn't in. He looked around—three children with
their mothers, a young man with books under his arm, an older man
with glasses and a cane—and he realized that he wasn't the only one
who'd asked to see the minister with the obvious intention of asking
him for a favor. Then he had a hunch: he walked around the block and
stationed himself beside the back door, thinking that Gaitán, when he
came out, would leave that way so he wouldn't have to fight his way
through so many people's requests. At one in the afternoon he saw
him leave, approached him, and said: "I'm the shoemaker's kid." He
gabbled out that he wanted to go to university, needed a grant, and had
heard that Minister Gaitán could award him one. Gaitán was walking
with two well-dressed gentlemen; César Carballo saw a sarcastic smile
on their faces and thought he was wasting his time. "I am a Liberal,"
he said, without really knowing what good that would do him. Gaitán
looked at his companions, looked at him, and said: "That doesn't matter. Hunger isn't liberal or conservative. The urge to get ahead isn't,
either." He looked at his watch and added: "Come back later and we'll
see what we can do."

That's what César did. Gaitán received him in his office, offered
him a coffee, and treated him like a son, or at least that's what César

would tell everyone for the rest of his life. He would also say that he'd seen the law degree from the National and had been enthralled, thinking one day he'd have one like it, but the real impression came from one of the other frames adorning the office wall: a photo of a twenty-five-year-old Gaitán standing beside his teacher, the great criminal law specialist Enrico Ferri. The photo was personally dedicated by Maestro Ferri to his student Jorge Gaitán, who had written a distinguished and much-admired thesis in Rome. César asked what his thesis had been on and Gaitán explained in three incomprehensible sentences. Of course César, a humble tradesman's son, not yet of age, had no way of understanding what premeditation was at that moment, much less how mitigating circumstances could be related to it, but Gaitán's phrases sounded like spells, and the very fact that the great man had tried to explain them to him allowed him to overcome the next disappointment: there were no grants left. But César Carballo saw Gaitán make a real effort: he saw him call his secretary, ask if the deadline had passed, and hear that it had, yes, Doctor, the deadline had passed; then he heard him ask his secretary whether any of the most recent grantees had not taken up their awards, as often happened, and in such a case whether we could give that grant to this lad, and heard the secretary say no, Doctor, there were no unclaimed grants this year, they'd all been accepted already. And then Gaitán said: "You see, young man. I'm very sorry. If you come back next year, before the deadline, I'll make personally sure you get your grant."

But a conspiracy of fate crossed César Carballo's path. When Gaitán, five weeks after meeting him there, left the ministry of education prematurely, César saw just another obstacle: he said to himself that life had never made things easy for him, that he was capable of winning a grant with or without the help of a politician, and he would apply in November and the following year he would be starting his new life. But he did not apply. One afternoon in May, just before he turned sixteen, César arrived at the workshop and found his father lying on the floor, among papers with sketches on them and with his measuring tape still around his neck. Apparently, he'd just taken a customer's foot size and was calculating the pattern, but the customer had left when the heart attack overcame him, and in any case everyone agreed there was little he could have done. César Carballo took over the shop and, of course, the support of his little brother. The job took up all his time and almost all his attention. Any idea about studying at university was unworkable now. César Carballo forgot those hopes, or filed them away in a deep part of his conscience and devoted himself to his lasts and forms and the leather he bought from a saddler on Eighth Street, down the road from the observatory. The next few years went by like that.

It might have been a sad fate, but César Carballo did not have time to think about it. He made sure not to feel sorry for himself, as well. When he could close the workshop at five instead of six, he would go to one of the cafés on Avenida Jiménez and read the papers and listen to the law and med school students talk about politics as if nothing else existed in the world. In those moments he felt alive. He spent all day in the workshop, but one of the few advantages of not being twenty yet was a blameless bachelorhood. Nobody was waiting for César anywhere, no woman complained of his absences or the smell of cigarettes or the few too many beers he'd allow himself two or three times a month, if things were going well. In the cafés he'd grab the waitresses and get slapped for it, and he could sit for hours behind the domino players and watch their matches, as long as he was careful not to bump the table and knock over their pieces, and he saw famous writers from afar in El Molino and found out that the figures on the wall were those of the characters from *Don Quixote* and heard the famous writers talk about *Don Quixote* with wide-eyed students and realized none of that interested him. Not that *Don Quixote* didn't interest him: made-up stories didn't interest him. Nor was he interested in the poetry he heard from the bohemian tables of the Café Automático, under the caricature someone had done of the poet León de Greiff, although he came to recognize words from hearing them so often, and occasionally, trying to get a girl to go to bed with him, he would come out with some lines he'd go on reciting all his life.

> *This rose was witness*
> *To this, which if not love,*
> *No other love could be.*
> *This rose was witness*
> *When you gave yourself to me!*

No: the only thing that interested him was politics. As the months went by he started taking his friends from the neighborhood on these excursions, and sometimes they would get together with older men, tradesmen in their thirties or forties (mechanics, bricklayers, carpenters), who went to the more working-class cafés to take, they said, the country's temperature.

And that's how César Carballo began to find out that the country had a fever. The war in Europe was arriving in Colombia: it wasn't so much because the price of coffee was lower than it had ever been, or the shortage of building materials that was sweeping away the construction business and the builders with it, but also that the Conservatives were talking about the triumph of fascism and complaining that, by backing the United States, the Liberal government had forced them to bet on the losing horse. They all believed that Germany was going to win the war and that would be good for the country: because they were all Franco supporters, by conviction or contagion, and the Axis victory would also be Franco's victory, and Franco's victory would also be the victory of the right wing of the Conservative Party. For César Carballo and his comrades from La Perseverancia, these Conservatives were the enemy. They had to fight against them: because the triumph of the Conservative Party in Colombia would be not just a return to the dark days of the past, but the invasion of European fascism.

But then, like a bad rumor, a series of new ideas began running through the poor neighborhoods of Bogotá. Jorge Eliécer Gaitán was traveling the country giving speeches that the paper wasn't reporting on, but were transmitted by word of mouth like a secret gospel. In them he was saying strange things like that hunger was neither conservative nor liberal, and neither was malaria; that there was a national country, that of the people, and a political country, that of the ruling class; and that the common enemy of all of them, the architect of the injustices and disasters overwhelming Colombian workers, was a two-headed serpent: one head was called the oligarchy and the other was imperialism. In February 1944, when Gaitán gathered his most fervent supporters at the Bar Cecilia and officially launched his political campaign for the '46 presidential election, César Carballo and his comrades from La Perseverancia were there, in the front row, drinking in their leader's words and promising they'd do whatever needed to be done, they'd even give their lives if necessary, so that Gaitán would become the president of Colombia.

The week began to revolve around the Cultural Fridays. These were the speeches Gaitán gave in the Municipal Theater: he would stand, with nowhere to rest his empty hands, in front of a square microphone that broadcast his words over the radio, and raise his fist and fill the place with an electricity nobody had ever felt before. César Carballo lived for those speeches; every moment he didn't spend in his cobbler's workshop, or training the neighbor's son, who had started to work for him, Carballo was thinking about what Gaitán had said at the Municipal Theater the previous Friday and anticipating what he'd say on the next.

And when the day arrived, he'd leave on foot at three in the afternoon, to make sure he got in, and stand in line for the four hours until the doors opened. It was time he could ill afford to be away from his obligations at the workshop, and his mother began to complain. "I know you're going to see the chief, son," she said. "I know it's important. But I don't know why you have to leave so early like this, dropping everything, as if this family wasn't running a business. As if we didn't have a radio in the house, son. What would your father say if he hadn't left us?" How could he explain to his mother what he felt in Gaitán's presence? He couldn't, so he just told her: "If I don't go now, I won't get in, *madrecita*." And it was true: the theater filled with the leader's followers, every seat upstairs and down but also all the spaces in the aisles. The mysterious solidarity that united them was something César would not have exchanged for anything in the world; besides, not getting in meant possibly missing an unrepeatable event, like when the theater's speakers weren't working and Gaitán, with a gesture of impatience and irritation, thrust the microphone out of his way, took a deep breath, and belted out a forty-minute speech at the top of his lungs, with the naked force of his supernatural throat and such clear diction that even the poor souls in the very last row at the back of the balcony caught each and every one of his words.

What happened after the Municipal speeches was just as important. After the moment of magic ended, they'd all meet on the overflowing sidewalks of the Carrera Séptima, and the comrades from La Perseverancia would go to one of the downtown cafés to talk about what they'd just heard. They couldn't all go, of course, because many of them had to be at work at first light; and many others weren't all that interested in politics. But Carballo was always there, walking the nocturnal streets in the now biting cold, surrounded by young men like himself, in whose company he felt invulnerable. The police didn't do anything to them, because in those days almost all the officers were Liberals and many of them clandestine Gaitanistas, but sometimes they'd exchange a couple of words with a haughty Conservative, and in moments like those Carballo believed himself capable of rare bravery. Then they'd burst into a café or a *chicha* bar as if they were taking over the place, and everybody knew that attitude wouldn't have been possible before Gaitán: their leader had given them this new pride, and thanks to him they felt that this city, for which they'd worked for generations, belonged to them as well. There, during those long nights of beer and *aguardiente* in El Inca or El Gato Negro or the Bar Cecilia or the Colombia, it seemed for hours as if it were true, or they seemed to be living in a parallel and phantasmagorical city owned by all of them. In those moments César Carballo received a true sentimental education. Now that I'm trying to reconstruct those days, I cannot belittle what went on in those covens that I'll call *tertulias* because that's what their members called them.

There were chaotic discussions that might finish at two or three in the morning, with shouts and tables knocked over by clumsy drunks. In those days, the Gaitanistas began to organize themselves better: the city was divided into neighborhoods and the neighborhoods into zones and the zones into committees. The café and *chicha* bar *tertulias*, that started off with people from the La Perseverancia committee, would be joined as the night went on by people from other committees, almost always from bordering neighborhoods but sometimes from farther away: men of all ages for whom, just as for Carballo, the Cultural Fridays didn't end when the *jefe* stepped away from the microphone and drove away from the Municipal Theater in his classy car. But sometimes some stray bohemians would show up as well, poets or novelists or cartoonists, newspaper columnists, chroniclers from the police beat who'd just covered some bloody crime, photographers who accompanied those chroniclers and whose tired eyes had already seen all there was to see as far as mankind's evil went. And, most of all, there were students, those from the National and those from the Free University or the bourgeois rebels from the Rosario who showed up around midnight after studying law or medicine in other cafés, or after talking about Franco and Mussolini, Stalin and Roosevelt, Churchill and Hitler in other *tertulias*, or after visiting brothels in groups to get insulting discounts in places that already paid starvation wages.

Carballo felt an immediate sympathy toward the students, in spite of their representing all that he had been denied. He saw them arrive, loud and satisfied, bulging with political enthusiasm and confused urges to change the world from their café table (which in those days was the size of the known universe), waving their hands as if possessed and exchanging books between emptied bottles. Most of them were Liberals, because the Gaitanista committees took great care to frequent cafés where others like them predominated, but there were also recently converted communists who arrived with Marxist booklets from the bargain bins of Bogotá bookshops, and even a small group of three or four melancholy anarchists—all dressed in black, all looking like alley cats—who usually occupied a corner table in the Gran Vía and stayed there for hours and hours without talking to anyone else.

Carballo would leave those *tertulias* with his head bursting with ideas and with documents that seared his hands, and he later wrote down, in the margins of the shoe shop account books, the titles he'd managed to retain. He read voraciously in those days: borrowed books, stolen books, books bought from secondhand stalls. He felt a certain superstitious reverence for them: books had saved Gaitán, and might also save him. He, like Gaitán, had been born into a narrow life, with scant possibilities and mediocre luck. Books—those books he knew and ended up reading in cafés and *tertulias*, thanks to luckier students— were the escape tunnel.

In the years that followed, Gaitán's movement was organized with the speed of a conspiracy. La Perseverancia owed much, perhaps un- knowingly, to the shoemaker's son's enthusiasm; César Carballo was the most active member of their committee. At night, after his mother went to sleep and he'd finished up any overdue jobs, he would go out to put up posters in his neighborhood and others nearby. Sometimes he got into more or less violent arguments with owners of houses who didn't want Gaitán's posters on their walls or on the lampposts of their street. César learned to take with him the better-known bandits, thugs, or ex-convicts, so people's objections disappeared as if by magic. The streets of La Perseverancia got covered with posters on yellowing pa- per, often written by Carballo, announcing the next speech at the Mu- nicipal Theater ("Bring the family," they commanded) or the chief's visit to some conservative neighborhood (and the people went with him, just so the locals would know that Gaitán was never defenseless).

The committee received or gave itself a resonant nickname: Los Empolvados, which came from how dust-covered they were when they came down from the mountains into the city, but they later found out that outside their own neighborhood they were known as Reds. The meetings were held in a different house each time; members fought for the honor of receiving the Gaitanistas; in bare, cold kitchens that smelled of butane, a sweat-stained hat would be passed to collect a few coins.

In that time, the Liberal Party was split: on one side, Gabriel Turbay, son of the eternal political class; on the other, Gaitán. In the committee meetings, it was César Carballo who had the idea of walking down Carrera Séptima with construction ladders and fumigation pumps full of formic acid, stopping beneath each post to spray the luxurious cloth banners of the candidate Turbay. The next morning they were rags, and all of Bogotá saw them. The success of the operation was total. César Carballo was not yet twenty-two years old, but he was already one of the most respected men on the committee. He was growing stronger in his neighborhood and Gaitanism was growing stronger all over Colombia. At the same time, under the new mandate of President Ospina, the violence in the countryside was worsening.

The rumors could barely be believed. News of the Conservative police excesses began arriving in Bogotá, of how they were harassing and persecuting Liberals and their families as hadn't been seen since the war of 1899. One day they heard about a young Liberal who, in the central square of Tunja, had been carved up with machetes for not responding to shouts of *Long live the president*, and the next day they heard about a group of policemen in Guatavita that had arrived at a Liberal house in the middle of the night, shooting dead seven inhabitants and setting fire to the furniture. An eight-year-old child escaped out the kitchen door: they caught up with him in an overgrown ditch, and chopped off his right hand with a machete and left him there to bleed to death, but the child survived to tell what had happened. Similar victims of similar atrocities told similar stories in every corner of the country. None of that bothered the government too much: they were isolated cases, said their spokesmen, the police was simply responding to provocations. But the Liberals of Bogotá, and in particular Gaitán's followers, were worried.

Carballo, as far as he was concerned, would have been much more worried had he not been going through an uncertainty of his own just then. One Friday in December, around three in the afternoon, he was closing the shop to go down to the Municipal Theater when he realized that someone was waiting for him. It was Amalita Ricaurte, the daughter of Don Hernán: a respected and much-loved mechanic who had an honorable scar on his right arm from a Conservative machete attack, and in whose workshop, a garage behind the old Panóptico, four committee meetings had been held. Amalita said hello to Carballo without approaching, like a frightened animal, and began to walk beside him without even asking him where he was going. She accompanied him silently for three blocks, and only as they arrived at Carrera Séptima and Twenty-sixth Street did she tell him, in a barely audible voice and looking at the ground, that she was pregnant.

It was the result of a chance encounter, but from that moment on it was a permanent reality. Amalita was a small, slight woman, with very large eyes and very black hair, who was three years older than Carballo and had begun to feel she'd missed the boat. She usually went to the Cultural Friday speeches, less out of enthusiasm than to obey her father's orders, and that's how she must have gotten close to Carballo, bit by bit, during the ins and outs of political activism that her father shared with this young man with the strong voice who had already taken on his shoulders the well-being of his whole family.

Years later, recounting the episode to her only son, Amalita would talk about love at first sight without embarrassment, disguising that fleeting and clandestine encounter with grand words like *inevitable* or *destiny*, in such a way that it is not possible to really know how things happened: it's only possible to know how the only woman who can speak of them wanted to remember them. However it was, at the beginning of 1947 Amalita was already living in César Carballo's room, throwing up in the mornings in the Carballos' bathroom, and finding herself in the kitchen of César's mother, who made her a bland milky soup while glancing at her with a stern, forbidding look on her face, and who had already started accusing her of stealing her son, invading her family, and wanting to take over her dead husband's business. There was a hasty but happy wedding in a downtown church and a celebration with *aguardiente* and empanadas. That night, with an empty glass in his hand, Don Hernán Ricaurte hugged his new son-in-law and told him:

"This child is going to be born into a better country. You and me are going to put our shoulders to the grindstone and my grandson is going to be born in a better country."

And Amalita, seeing her slightly drunk husband nod, noticed that she believed that too.

The months of her pregnancy were marked by La Perseverancia committee meetings, which turned into the most loyal of the zone, and by the organization of demonstrations and speeches in Bogotá and the surrounding area. The dedication of her father and husband was no less than that of the rest of the members. When Gaitán began to talk of a great torch-lit march, a spectacle that would stop the hearts of the most skeptical, nobody was surprised when La Perseverancia committee got the job or the challenge of organizing it. Amalita was six or seven months along then. And thus, suffering without anyone's help the rigors of carrying a child in her tired belly, she watched her husband put himself at the head of fund-raising, go house to house asking for coins and passing the hat at committee meetings, and then go around the neighborhood to make sure people would commit to helping to make the torches. César visited local factories to find cheap burlap, visited laundry yards and came back from each one with a broom or mop handle. Carpenters donated legs from broken chairs, and mechanics, recently purchased fuel. Carballo got oil from the railways and donated tacks from his own workshop, and urchins brought him bottle caps from the garbage that he could use to stick the burlap to the wood. In theory, each committee was to supply a certain number of torches, which they'd later sell for two pesos apiece to help fund the movement. César Carballo's committee not only contributed the most torches, but also made enough so that no Gaitanista would have to fight with another for a bit of fire. Don Hernán Ricaurte gave them a great satisfaction when he embraced his son-in-law in public and declared a banality that was also a medal: "Our boy's turned out good." Meanwhile, neither Amalita nor her father nor her husband really wondered why the Gaitanistas were marching. The chief had asked for it, and that was enough.

Nothing like it had ever been seen in Bogotá. That July night, the whole neighborhood went down the hill as far as San Agustín, where they met with the other torch bearers from other neighborhoods: from San Victorino and Las Cruces, from La Concordia and San Diego. At three o'clock in the afternoon, not another soul could have fit in the plaza. The sky was cloudy but it wasn't raining, and someone said that God must undoubtedly be a Gaitanista. The march began to move at a slow pace, as much due to the terrifying solemnity as to the quantity of men and women who could not have walked any faster without stepping on each other. People lit their torches here and there as darkness began to fall, and César Carballo would later speak of the heat they suddenly began to feel inside that beast. They were heading down Carrera Séptima in the direction of the Palace when the sky had turned purple and the eastern hills had been swallowed by darkness. When night fell, it was as if the lights of the whole city had been turned off out of timidity. It was, just as Gaitán had requested, a river of fire. Carballo, among his people, marching shoulder to shoulder beside other Gaitanistas, was sweating from the heat and his eyes stung from the smoke of the torches, but nothing would have made him abandon that privileged place. His comrades' faces were yellow and luminous, and away from the march Bogotá was dark and the horizon blended into the sky, and silhouettes peered out of windows caught between admiration and fright, without even turning on the lights of their sitting rooms or studies, as if they were a little bit embarrassed to exist and not be there, to exist and not be marching with the march, to exist and not be part of the people able to produce this miracle. César heard Gaitán's speech at the end of the march, but he didn't understand much of it, because the emotion of the last few hours had made understanding expendable or perhaps superfluous. He arrived home with his clothes smelling of smoke and his face smudged, but happy, happier than Amalita had ever seen him or would ever see him again.

The country awoke changed. The upper-class Liberals joined the Communists in labeling the chief's march a fascist exercise; they never knew that he, in private meetings, would have agreed with them. He had seen Mussolini enter Rome and had been inspired, and the inspiration had brought him results: now they feared him, they were all afraid, they had all seen what he could awaken in his followers, and they were all wondering what might that man be capable of if they opened the doors of power to him. Later the rumor reached Carballo that Gaitán, in his office, had congratulated his deputies: "Very good, my little fascists. Who do I have to thank for this?" And somebody had mentioned Carballo's name. The rumor was no more than that: somebody had mentioned him. For Carballo, nothing so important had ever happened in his short life. He said to Amalita: "We did this. This was done by us." And he pressed his face against his wife's tummy and told the same thing to the baby on the other side of the protruding belly button: "It was us, we did it for the *jefe* and the chief knows it." That memory, of her young husband talking to her belly with his face illuminated as if he had a lit torch in front of him, stayed with her all her life, and twenty-five days later, when the baby was born, it was not hard to name him Carlos Eliécer: Carlos for Amalita's paternal grand-father, who died in the Battle of Peralonso fighting under the orders of General Herrera, and Eliécer for the man who had given his father a mission on the face of the earth.

They were days of horror. What before were the excesses of an out-of-hand Conservative police force had now turned into a frightful daily spectacle: throats slit open with machetes, women raped, pits dug in the middle of the countryside to bury nameless corpses. On the radio, the bishop of Santa Rosa de Osos exhorted agricultural laborers to be God's soldiers and fight against Liberal atheism, and the rest of the bishops ordered them to get rid of the Red apostates. And the violence was already in the city, timid, sly, peering around the corners, coming out every once in a while to show its dangerous face. After the proclamation of Gaitán as the sole leader of the Liberal Party, Liberals, instead of celebrating, began to be afraid. An old bootblack, a man who had worked the same doorway of the same café since he was a boy, had his red tie cut with a pair of sewing scissors and then the scissors held to his throat, waiting for him to complain. A girl in a red dress was harried for blocks, first insulted and then groped, until a policeman saw what was going on, and managed to get her pursuers to disperse only by pulling out his pistol and firing three times in the air. Along the Carretera del Norte bodies began to appear with coups de grâce: they were Liberals who'd been trying to escape from neighboring Boyacá and hadn't made it. The inventory of deaths kept mounting. The engineer of the Bogotá–Tunja line went out one Sunday at twelve noon and was stabbed to death for not being at Mass, and in the villages of Santander they heard of priests dressing as civilians, pointing out God's enemies, whose (sometimes headless) bodies would show up in the following days under the trees of the plaza. There was terror in the letters that Liberals were writing to Gaitán, but not in the newspapers: for

President Ospina's government, those were the invisible dead. Gaita-nistas were waiting for a sign from their leader to know what to do; at the beginning of 1948, Gaitán gave it. He did what he knew best: organized a multitude and spoke in front of it. But this time was not like the others.

Later they would talk about that February 7 in legendary tones. You have to imagine the scene: the Plaza de Bolívar, under the city's gray sky, had filled with more than a hundred thousand people, but you could hear the footsteps of those still arriving, an old man's cough, the crying of a tired baby on the other side of the plaza. One hundred thousand people: a fifth of the entire city's population was there, an-swering their leader's call. But the crowd didn't shout their support or Long live anybody or Death to anybody, they didn't light torches or raise closed fists, because the chief had asked for one thing: silence. His people were being slaughtered like beasts all over the country, he'd said, but they would not respond to violence with violence. They would give a lesson, yes: they would march in silence and their peace-ful silence would be stronger and more eloquent than the fury of the people rising up. His friends had told him it was impossible, that he could not silence the indignant thousands desiring to scream their rage, that crowds could not be controlled like that. Gaitán, however, gave the order; and when the moment arrived, that uncontrollable mob, made up of poor and angry and nervous people, obeyed as if they were a single spellbound body. That's what César Carballo heard, from his seat with his La Perseverancia comrades on the stone steps of the cathedral. From there, one or two heads above the rest of the crowd, he could see the platform from which the chief was getting ready to deliver the speech of his life. An old woman in *alpargatas*, tak-ing a rest from carrying a bundle of firewood, put it in words that others would have signed: "The doctor has a pact with the devil."

Then Gaitán climbed up onto the platform. In the middle of that supernatural silence, in which Carballo could hear the fabric of his clothes brushing against those standing next to him, Gaitán addressed the president of the Republic to ask that the violence cease, but he did not do so with the sensationalism of other days, instead he did so quietly, with solemnity but also simplicity, as if he were speaking at a friend's funeral. The people accompanying him today, he said, came from all over Colombia with the single intention of defending their rights, and their presence here was testimony to their discipline. "Two hours ago they began flowing into this plaza and there has not been a single shout," he said, "but as with violent tempests, the subterranean power is much stronger." He also said: "Here there is no applause, just thousands of black banners waving." He also said: "This demonstration is happening because of grave events, not for trivial reasons." And then, in the same calm tone in which he'd been speaking until then, he said something that César Carballo took a second or two to understand, but his blood then froze.

"Here are the great majority obeying an order," said Gaitán. "But these masses holding themselves back here would also obey the commanding voice if it told them to exercise legitimate defense."

César Carballo looked around, but nobody seemed surprised: not his comrades from the neighborhood, not a group of men in buttoned-up shirts even though they weren't wearing ties, not the group on their other side, where Carballo recognized a photographer with a thin mustache he'd seen at other demonstrations or maybe at the Friday *tertulias*. *Legitimate defense*: Had he understood right? Was Gaitán issuing a threat? Was this whole thing a show of force, directed at half the country so they would know what this man was capable of? *"Señor presidente,"* Gaitán continued, "this multitude in mourning, these black banners, this crowded silence, this mute cry of hearts is asking you for a very simple thing: that you treat us, our mothers, our wives, our children, and our belongings as you would like to be treated yourselves, as you would like your mother, your wife, your children, and your belongings to be treated." And the people who waved their black banners or looked down at the cobblestones seemed to hear what Gaitán was saying just as Carballo was hearing it, but nobody was furrowing their brow, nobody looked at anyone else to see if it were true what they were hearing, because nobody else seemed to understand what Carballo understood: that Gaitán had just turned, by virtue of a few dormant volcano phrases, into the most dangerous man in Colombia. Only one person echoed his secret worry, one who put into words what he was thinking after the speech ended. The people remained silent, because that was Gaitán's order, and in silence they abandoned the Plaza de Bolívar by all four corners; but as they passed in front of the Casa del Florero, when they were no longer under the balcony, it was as if a taboo was lifted, and an individual taller than Carballo, with a dense black beard, expressed an observation that seemed casual in an accent that was not Colombian:

"This man just signed his own death sentence."

The idea obsessed Carballo from that moment on. The neighborhood committees had stopped meeting, but he managed to get his father-in-law, Don Hernán Ricaurte, to persuade some of their La Perseverancia comrades, and after a few days several militants went along with him on the absurd undertaking of asking Gaitán to be careful. But they didn't do it in person: getting an appointment with the chief, in March of that year, was an impossible task. The ninth Pan-American Conference was approaching, which would bring all the continent's leaders together in Bogotá, and Gaitán was far too busy to deal with his faithful followers' delusions: he had his hands full with the affront of the president, who had left him out of the Colombian delegation. Him, the sole leader of the Liberal Party! Gaitanistas were indignant. The government's implausible argument was that Gaitán, being a brilliant penologist, was not an expert in international law; but the whole country knew the very different truth was that the president had folded to the demands of Laureano Gómez, leader of the Conservative Party, who had threatened to pull out of the conference if the Indian Gaitán were included. Laureano Gómez was the man who, during the long years when the Liberals had been in power, had suggested to the Conservatives *intrepid action and the personal attack* as ways of recuperating their lost country. He was a Franco sympathizer who had publicly and expressly desired the defeat of the Allies. He was the enemy, and the enemy—this was clear to Carballo and to the Empolvados of La Perseverancia—had won the battle.

Gaitán, however, was not afraid. When they managed to get him their proposal of forming a group of bodyguards for him, Gaitán replied with the implacable logic that nobody could kill him, because his murderer would have to know that he would be immediately murdered. "That's my life insurance," said Gaitán. And what if the assassin didn't mind dying? What if the murderer, as in the case of Gandhi's, had accepted his own death? The chief paid no attention. "Things like that don't happen to me," he said. Carballo never got to hear those words. His father-in-law passed them on, and the word of his father-in-law was enough for him.

In spite of the recommendations, Gaitán carried on living his life as normal. He went jogging in the Parque Nacional in the mornings, before going to the office, and he did so alone: he took off his jacket and loosened his tie, and did a loop or two around the park without anyone ever explaining why he didn't sweat like normal people. At night he went out alone and without warning, to visit a friend or take a ride in his Buick and think about things he never revealed to anybody, and returned home late. Carballo knew it—he knew Gaitán went jogging alone in the Parque Nacional and that he went out on nocturnal excursions—because he often accompanied him without Gaitán's knowledge, following him from afar, watching him as an assassin might have watched him. That was how it was: the Empolvados had decided to be their chief's clandestine bodyguards. One morning, Carballo followed him to the Parque Nacional, and there he saw him leave the Buick in front of the clock and start jogging along the lower path; on the upper path, quite a ways behind, Carballo jogged at the same pace as Gaitán. But it was difficult to keep an eye on the slender figure ahead of him and the fist-sized rocks at the same time as the potentially ankle-breaking holes. Coming down the hill, almost at the end of his circuit, Gaitán accelerated. Carballo had to switch directions quickly not to lose sight of him, and as he did so he kicked a stone that fell a few steps in front of Gaitán. Carballo, from behind a eucalyptus, saw him stop and look all around, and discovered for the first time something like fear on his face. He knew in that fleeting instant, Gaitán was considering the possibility that he was being stoned and the next thing would be an ambush or an attack: an *intrepid action*, a *personal attack*. Carballo had no choice but to come out from his hiding place. On Gaitán's face, the relief gave way to irritation.

"And what the hell's this?" he shouted. "What are you doing back there?"

"Here I am, *Jefecito*, following your example, Chief," said Carballo.

"Don't be silly, Carballo," said Gaitán furiously. "What example. Go and get us some votes instead of wasting your time."

He got in his Buick and drove off south. Carballo was happy because the chief knew or remembered his name, but at the same time a revelation appeared in his mind: *He thinks they want to kill him too. The chief has begun to suspect that someone's lying in wait for him.*

He had no proof, of course. But when he talked about his concerns with his comrades in La Perseverancia, he discovered that many of them had begun to think frequently of the possibility that their chief might suffer an attack, and one of them had even received a badly written note meant to say: *Tell Gaitán he should take care.* They were not alone in their apprehensions: Bogotá had begun to breathe an air of paranoia. It was true that the Pan-American Conference had them all nervous: the police had swept through all the neighborhoods arresting and locking up prostitutes and beggars, cleaning up the city so the international delegates would find it tidy and decent, with the only result being that the inhabitants of those neighborhoods found them spectral and tense: a place on the border of a curfew. Everything was changing. The Panóptico, the prison that had first been a convent, had been converted into a museum, as if to try to say that in this city there were no wrongdoers, only artists and philosophers. But outside the peaceful city, the war was still alive.

Its news arrived by irregular channels. People commented that the Boyacá police were planting bombs in the doorways of Liberal houses, and that a Liberal from Duitama had been taken to a nearby cliff and thrown off. Fantasists said that Peronistas had arrived in Bogotá from Argentina to help overthrow the government; other voices said that it was Yankees who had arrived, and were swarming over the city disguised as businessmen or journalists, who in reality were intelligence agents trained to combat the threat of communism. All these things were discussed in the cafés. César Carballo and Hernán Ricaurte were at all the debates and meetings, more like father and son than in-laws. It's safe to assume that each found in the other what he lacked, for they became inseparable in those days: they were together at the Café Asturias when a group of left-wing students, from the Free University, denounced the Pan-American Conference as a veiled way to impose a

Marshall Plan on Colombia; they were together in the Café San Moritz when another group of students, from La Salle University, denounced the presence in Bogotá of agents provocateurs in the service of international socialism. It's not surprising that they should also have been together on the night of April 8, when Jorge Eliécer Gaitán defended Lieutenant Cortés, the man who had murdered for the honor of the army. At around one in the morning, when Gaitán got the verdict of innocence and emerged on the shoulders of a very mixed crowd blending military officers with revolutionaries, Cesár Carballo and Don Hernán Ricaurte shouted their *viva*s and applauded until their hands hurt, and then walked back to La Perseverancia. They said good night without solemnities. It was a victorious night, yes, but it was also just another night. They had no way of knowing the next day would change their lives.

As Don Hernán Ricaurte, the only witness to the events of that day or to their sequence, would later recount, that morning he had been working on a rosewood-colored Studebaker, and shortly before midday he walked down to Carrera Séptima to find someone to have lunch with. He walked south along the joyful or jubilant avenue, which had its lampposts adorned with the flags of the conference and the cleanest sidewalks in the world. The sky was starting to cloud over: it would rain in the afternoon. When he reached the Hotel Granada, Hernán Ricaurte decided to cross Parque Santander to Avenida Jiménez: he would read the news on *El Espectador*'s chalkboard, be angered by what they didn't say as much as by what they did, and then he'd look for a table of Gaitanistas, have an unhurried lunch (it was Friday), and go back to the garage. But he didn't even have to find his comrades: his comrades found him. They were coming out of a hardware shop on Avenida Jiménez, laughing their heads off like a gang of teenagers; they said hello without stopping, and the habit of other days

directed their feet toward the Café El Inca, whose balcony had a privileged view over Carrera Séptima.

Don Hernán Ricaurte did not know that a poet had forever chris-
tened that place as the best street corner in the world, but he would
have agreed. He liked the view: he liked to see the San Francisco
church, its dark stone corner, and the Government Palace recently
cleaned for the foreigners coming for the Pan-American Conference;
he liked, most of all, seeing the Agustín Nieto building, where the
chief had his law office. On the occasional night, when Gaitán stayed
late at the office, the comrades from La Perseverancia would station
themselves there to keep an eye on him, to follow him to the place on
Parque Santander where he usually left his car. Don Hernán Ricaurte,
who knew Gaitán's routines as if they were his own, thought the chief
must be just about to go out for lunch, in who knows what company.
Later he would remember having looked at the clock just then: it was
five to one in the afternoon. He would also remember the exact location of his lunch companions: at the four-sided table, Gonzalo Castro
and Jorge Antonio Higuera were sitting with their backs to the window; he and César Carballo sat across from them—the father-in-law
and son-in-law who seemed more like father and son—so close to the
balcony that the trams seemed to be running under their feet. He
would not remember, however, what conversations filled the distracted
minutes until Carballo, looking toward the street, said calmly: "Look,
there's the *jefe* . . ." But he didn't finish the sentence. Ricaurte saw him
open his eyes wide and stand up, and in the memory he'd keep forever,
in the scene that appeared in his dreams for the rest of his life, Carballo
stretched out a hand, as if to grab something, at the moment the first
shot rang out.

Ricaurte heard two more shots and saw the man with the pistol fire
the fourth. He thought the shots sounded like percussion caps, like the

caps the street urchins put on the tram rails to make them explode; but they weren't percussion caps, because the chief had fallen to the ground and people were shouting. "They killed Gaitán!" somebody shrieked below them. A waitress from El Gato Negro had gone outside and was wailing and holding her head in her hands and then she dried them on her apron: "They killed Gaitancito! They killed him!"

The four of them had lurched down the stairs, making their way through the terrorized crowd with the force of desperation, and once down on the Séptima, Ricaurte saw a policeman capture the man who had fired the shots, and who was trying to escape toward Jiménez, clumsily walking backward. From afar they scrutinized him—badly dressed, badly shaven, a mixture of fury and fear on his face—and they also noticed that the irate mob was already beginning to surround him. The chief, on the other hand, was surrounded by his friends: Ricaurte recognized Dr. Cruz and Dr. Mendoza, who asked that the wounded man be allowed some air, while the waitress from El Gato Negro crouched down and tried to get him to drink a glass of water. People, pushed by an uncontrollable impulse, approached Gaitán to touch him, and among them was Carballo: Ricaurte saw him crouch down beside the body and put a hand on Gaitán's shoulder. It was a fleeting movement, full of intimacy but also timidity, to which Gaitán responded with a little chirp. He's alive, thought Ricaurte; he thought, as well, that the chief would survive. He went around the huddle and arrived beside his son-in-law, whose gaze was contorted with hatred but at the same time was in command of a terrifying reason. He opened his hand and showed Ricaurte what he'd found when he crouched down beside Gaitán: it was a bullet. "Put it somewhere safe," he said to Ricaurte. "Put it in your pocket and don't lose it." And then he heard him say the first of the many strange sentences he'd hear him say that day: "We have to find the other one."

"The other what?" asked Ricaurte. "Were there two?"

"The other didn't fire," said Carballo without looking him in the eye, looking for something farther away. "He was taller, in an elegant suit with a raincoat over his arm. He was the one who signaled, Don Hernán, I saw him from up there. We have to find him."

But the moment had filled with a fatal inertia. People had spilled out onto Carrera Séptima from El Gato Negro and the Colombia and El Inca and the Asturias, and the trams had stopped on their tracks, and onlookers, drawn by the shouting, began arriving from the side streets, and at some point there were so many that nobody knew how the two taxis had made their way through. They lifted Gaitán into one of them, black and shiny: in the middle of the confusion, the orders and counterorders and footsteps coming and going and small or huge hysterics, Ricaurte saw that his recent lunch companion Jorge Antonio Higuera was one of those who helped to lift the body, but then he didn't see him again. "To the Central Clinic," someone shouted. Others shouted: "Call Dr. Trías." The taxis drove south; in the trance of the moment, several people bent down to dip their handkerchiefs in Gaitán's blood. Ricaurte imitated them unthinkingly; he went to the place where the chief had fallen and was surprised at the size of the puddle, black on the pavement, the blood black and shiny even though it was not sunny. A student dipped a page of *El Tiempo* and the waitress dipped a corner of her spotless apron. "They killed the chief," she said, and a friend who had begun to cry said no, they hadn't killed him, the chief was strong.

"Don't worry, *comadre*," she sobbed. "You'll see how the doctor fixes him up."

Meanwhile, a commotion was going on in front of the Granada Drugstore. The shooter had been taken in there for safekeeping, and now the furious crowd was trying to enter the drugstore to drag him out. There were dozens of men who were forcing the metal shutters open any way they could: the bootblacks were banging their wooden crates against them loudly, while the deliverymen raised their iron handcarts furiously and used them as battering rams. The rest clung to the shutters as if to tear them off. "Bring out the miserable wretch!" someone roared. "He's got to pay, make him pay for what he did!" The mob was incited: Ricaurte thought that the man who had shot Gaitán could count the minutes he had left if he fell into the hands of the irate throng. And then, just when the mob began to succeed, he saw that César Carballo was one of them, but he had an absorbed expression, as if something else was catching his attention. "He's coming out," someone shouted from behind, and someone else shouted: "Kill him!" Then with a screech of metal and broken glass, among shouts of dread, Gaitán's attacker came out of the door of the Granada Drugstore, dragged by several hands, torn from his refuge. "Don't kill me!" he begged, and Ricaurte thought he'd started to cry. From up close he looked less of a man than before: he was twenty-three, twenty-four years old? He inspired hatred and pity at once (the brown suit stained with oil or something that looked like oil, the messy, greasy hair), but he had tried to kill the chief, Ricaurte thought, and deserved the people's revenge. A monster of violence welled up in his breast; he took a few steps toward the wretched little man, but at that moment he saw his son-in-law, who was trying to make himself heard in the midst of the rage: "Don't kill him! We need him alive!" he said. But it was too late: an iron cart had smashed down on the shooter's head, and the bootblacks were hitting him with their crates and the sound of breaking bones filled the air, and someone took out a fountain pen and stabbed him several times in the neck and the face. The shooter had stopped protesting: or maybe he was already dead, or he had lost consciousness from the blows or the fear. Someone suggested throwing him under a tram, and for an instant it looked like they would. Someone else said: "To the Palacio!" And the order inflamed the maddened mob, and they began to drag the body of the shooter south. Ricaurte thought of Gaitán, who by then must have been fighting for his life on a stretcher, and he went over to Carballo.

"Come on, son, don't get mixed up in that," he said, taking him by the arm. "We need to be with the *jefe*."

But Carballo resisted. His attention was elsewhere, as if he were drunk. "Didn't you see him, Don Hernán?" he said. "He was right there, didn't you see him?"

"Who, son?"

"The one in the fine suit," said Carballo. "The elegant guy."

Those who were taking the lynched body of the shooter now had an unexpected slipstream behind them, and the Séptima was filling with a furious wave dragging along all those it encountered in its way. Ricaurte could have slipped down Pasaje Santafé and turned onto Carrera Sexta to get to the Central Clinic, but a new sort of conviction had appeared in his son-in-law's gaze that made it impossible not to walk with him: to the Presidential Palace, to take the attacker's body to the Palace, to leave the body for the president so he can know how the Liberals reacted. From afar they could hear the first shots: But who was firing them? Against whom? "They killed the chief," Carballo was saying, and it was the first time Ricaurte heard him say the words. "No, they didn't kill him, the chief is strong," Ricaurte answered, though he didn't even believe it himself: he'd seen the injuries up close, the blood coming out of Gaitán's mouth and the blank, lost look in his eyes, and he knew that nobody came back from those depths. But then Carballo said:

"He was in an elegant suit."

And then right after that: "All this already happened."

Ricaurte didn't understand what he was talking about, but César didn't say anything more, so he didn't insist or question or ask his son-in-law to repeat what he'd said. They were advancing in the direction of the Plaza de Bolívar, in the middle of a growing horde and thirty meters or so from the body of the shooter; they saw the frightened faces of the people on the sidewalks, and from that distance they also saw some of them stepping down from the sidewalk onto the pavement to kick the lifeless body, to spit on it, to shout an obscenity. As they arrived at Eleventh Street, a noisy and furious wave was coming down the eastern sidewalk. It was led by a man in a straw hat brandishing a machete and announcing, between hysterical sobs and promises of revenge, that Gaitán, the chief, had just died.

"To the Palacio!" shouted those who followed him, joining the group dragging the shooter's corpse. Don Hernán Ricaurte felt like he'd boarded a runaway train. Now the train of horror was pulling into the Plaza de Bolívar, heading for the Capitol where, at this tragic hour, the Pan-American leaders were all meeting at the conference. But the crowd immediately doubled back and returned to the Carrera Séptima, as if it had suddenly remembered that its true objective was not to take the dead body of an assassin—because by this time the shooter was a killer—to the steps, but to enter the Palace: enter the Presidential Palace and take revenge, enter the Palace and do to President Ospina what the assassin had done to Jorge Eliécer Gaitán. Ricaurte noticed that in the turn around the Plaza de Bolívar the assassin's body had lost its jacket and shirt like a serpent shedding its skin. Those who had lynched him collected his clothes: one man had made a bundle of the shirt and jacket, and then, as they arrived at Ninth Street, another had taken his trousers off, so the body that arrived at Eighth Street was wearing only a pair of undershorts torn by being dragged over the cobblestones. From the distance, Ricaurte and

Carballo watched the scene with horror: those at the front were trying to lift up the assassin and use his own clothing to tie him to the railings of the Palace gates, as if crucified. But they didn't have time to feel pity, because at that moment a burst of gunfire came from the Palace door, and the angry mob had to flee again, to whip around and take refuge and regroup back in the Plaza de Bolívar. A timid drizzle began to fall. The square kept filling with armed men; minute by minute Bogotá was turning into a city at war.

Toward the south, shop fronts began to burst into flames, and someone even said the Palacio de San Carlos was on fire, and on the radio they were announcing that the offices of *El Siglo* had burned down. Men ready for battle joined the throng from every corner: they had looted hardware stores and barracks, it was later learned, and they arrived with machetes and pipes but also with Mauser rifles and tear gas launchers to join the revolution. Then the rumor began to circulate that the battalion stationed at the Palace had come out to retake the Séptima, and in minutes the people were erecting a barricade between Ninth and Tenth Streets, where there are plaques commemorating the death of General Uribe Uribe. They took chairs and desks and small cupboards from the Capitol, the occupants of which had escaped in official cars by the back door, and behind the barricade they stationed a first line of men armed with weapons that a few minutes earlier had belonged to the police. It was a little after two in the afternoon when, seeing the Presidential Guard approaching, those entrenched behind the barricade began firing.

The Guard shot back. Ricaurte saw a line of soldiers take positions, one knee on the ground, and open fire. From behind, protected by living bodies, he saw three and then four men fall dead on the pavement, but he didn't recognize them: they weren't Gaitanistas from their neighborhood. "Resist! Resist!" cried a voice from one side of the barricade. But the army's aim was more precise, or the inexperience of the rebels too obvious, because men kept falling and those behind them kept pressing forward, stubborn and brave, as if death did not exist. Then Ricaurte looked at Carballo and saw him raise his face: something had caught his attention.

"There are people in the tower," he said.

It was true. In the tower of San Bartolomé College, the Jesuit headquarters, several silhouettes were firing at the crowd. But then, looking around, Carballo and Ricaurte realized there were snipers on every roof, so that in a matter of seconds it became impossible to know where the shots were coming from; it also became impossible to protect themselves. They were penned in: the Guard was advancing from the south and to the north was the San Bartolomé tower, and from the rooftops of Ninth Street more snipers were fearlessly opening fire. The strange thing, Ricaurte would later say, is that nobody seemed to even consider the possibility of fleeing: the whole mob, blinded by the desire for revenge, stayed where it was. Ricaurte realized they had no way out of the cordon. In that precise second, a shot out of nowhere ripped into the chest of the man standing next to him, who hit the ground with a thud and lay there with one leg bent behind the other.

"Get down, son!" Ricaurte shouted.

But Carballo did not obey. Later, telling the story of that day to his daughter and much later to his grandson, Don Hernán Ricaurte would talk about what happened on his son-in-law's face, and he'd try to describe it in detail, with his humble tradesman's vocabulary, the arduous light he saw in Carballo's eyes and on his forehead when he heard him say the last of his incomprehensible phrases.

"Shit," said his son-in-law. "It's like it's happening all over again."

Then a burst of gunfire came from the north, a burst of sniper fire, and Ricaurte dove to the ground. He landed facedown on top of a dead man he didn't recognize; his face found a space that allowed him to hide and breathe at the same time. He felt Carballo drop down beside him: Ricaurte felt his presence (a pressure against his legs) but could not tell what position his body was in. He closed his eyes. There, in that singular space smelling of sweat and damp clothing, the world was quieter and less terrifying than out of it, where bullets whistled through the air. He just had to endure, and that's what Ricaurte did: he endured. He didn't count the minutes, but not too much time passed before the miracle. It had started to rain.

It was a downpour worthy of the month, with fat drops that Ricaurte felt on the nape of his neck and on his back like the fingers of someone trying to get his attention in the street. He thought that God, the God he barely believed in, was at his side, because such a rain was the only thing that could have dispersed the two sides of that battle. Incredibly, he was right: the shots began to taper off as the rain intensified, as if intimidated by the rattle of the water against the tiles, the windows of the bell tower, the stone of the steps. Ricaurte lifted his head very slowly and felt dizzy when he stood up, but he knew that this was his opportunity. He called Carballo, whose weight he still felt on his legs: Carballo didn't answer. Ricaurte found himself alone on top of a pile of three bodies. None of them belonged to his son-in-law. He looked around and then he saw him: he was three or four steps farther south, as if he'd started to walk toward the barricade, and he wasn't facedown, but looking at the sky with his eyes wide open, with his face bathed in rain and a rosette of blood covering the center of his chest. The blood wasn't black, like Gaitán's, because the rain had watered it down: it was pink, a deep pink, and it seemed to be spreading across his white shirt.

"YOU DON'T KNOW how many times he told me all that," said Carlos Carballo, César's son, grandson of Don Hernán Ricaurte. "I don't remember when he told me for the first time, but that's the best proof that he must've started telling me when I was really small. I don't remember having had to ask where my *papá* was, or anything like that: I think Mamá started explaining things to me long before I ever asked her. That's what I think now, of course, because I don't remember a time in my life when I didn't already live with what happened on April 9. With those images I now know as well as if I'd lived through them. With those ghosts, Vásquez, those ghosts who accompany me and stalk me and talk to me. I don't know if you talk to the dead, but I do. With time I've become used to it. Before I just talked to Papá, and sometimes, I won't deny it, to Gaitán. I'd say: Papá knew they were going to kill you, *Jefecito*, why didn't you listen? In those conversations I always called Gaitán 'little chief.' I, who was a few months old when they killed him, talked to him the way I'm sure Papá talked to him. Well, there are worse madnesses, don't you think? There are more dangerous madmen."

I think that was the moment when I began to understand certain important things (or things that would later take on new importance), but my understanding was still too vague to put into words. I think I also had at that moment some intuition: I thought, for example, that Carballo expected a book like a *Who Are They?* of the Gaitán assassination from me. We had spent hours talking; time had melted or stretched, and it didn't help that the curtains in Carballo's apartment, closed as if ours were a secret or clandestine meeting—a meeting of conspirators—made it impossible to know with certainty if it was night or day. Had the sun already set? Had night fallen and dawn broken again? How many hours had we spent there, shut up inside that small, dark, narrow apartment, in the company of ghosts of the past?

"And where is your father buried?" I asked Carballo.

"Yes, there's that," said Carballo. "Well, that's part of the story, of course. You've seen those images, I imagine: what happened on April 9 from about four in the afternoon onward. The fires, the looting, this city looked like the ruins of a bombing raid. Death, Vásquez, death washed over the city. I've always thought that the origin of it all was that group of people taking the dead body, no, the lynched body of the assassin to the Palace. I grew up knowing Papá was there. That one of those dozens of people, dozens who were later hundreds, was Papá. And what can I do: that changes a person's way of seeing everything. I didn't grow up hearing about April 9 like other people might have. I grew up hearing about the day Papá was killed. In other words: the reasons I grew up half orphaned. And then I began to find out, very gradually, that the day was what it was. It's strange to spend your childhood thinking that the important thing about April 9 was the death of your father, not that other man who meant nothing to me, the gentleman who was a politician and who got killed like so many others have been killed. For me the essential thing about April 9 was Papá's death, Papá getting shot and dying there, on top of other dead men, dying like one more corpse among so many, the myriad who had died by then in Bogotá. A child understands these things very slowly. I gradually understood that Papá was not the only man who died: on that day and the three days that followed some three thousand people died in Bogotá and Papá was only one of them."

"One of the first, all the same."

"Yes, but only one. And later, in my teens, I began to understand better how it had all happened. I began to understand that Papá would not have died if that man called Gaitán had not died before him. I began to understand that Papá had fallen into the cracks of an earth-quake, and the epicenter of that earthquake was in front of the Agustín Nieto building, on Carrera Séptima almost at Avenida Jiménez, Bo-gotá, Colombia. Sometimes I think it would have been better not to have understood anything, not known anything: to have grown up with a lie, for example, that Papá had just left one fine day, or that he'd gone to fight in the Korean War, I don't know. Yes, that would have been good, wouldn't it? To think my *papá* was a war hero over in Ko-rea, that he had gone with the Colombian Battalion and died in the Battle of Old Baldy, for example. That's what it's called, right?"

"Yes," I told him. "That's the name of that battle."

"Well, that's not what happened. They told me everything, my grandfather and Mamá. All about that day, all about Papá's life, all that I just told you. All that led up to his death on April 9. And also all that came after."

"After April 9?"

"No, the same day. Grandpa couldn't tell it without his eyes water-ing. Never, not even when I was twenty, when it seemed like the old man didn't remember things, did I ever see him talk about that without getting sad. Imagine him there, standing in front of all those dead bod-ies in front of the Plaza de Bolívar, in a magic moment when the shots had stopped and it no longer seemed as though the world was going to end. But it had ended in a way, because there was his son-in-law dead. Grandpa loved him, loved him a lot. Gaitán was a family thing, too, you know? Families united around Gaitán, and the promises Gaitán made. And there was my grandfather, having to decide at that very instant what to do with the body of his beloved son-in-law. Bogotá was already a city at war, that was obvious. Grandpa always told me he thought for a fraction of a second of calling a policeman, as if normal life would have still been going on, and then he thought no: that normal life had been suspended until further notice. He picked up my father's body, balanced him across his back like a sack of potatoes, and started walking north, thinking of getting back to the neighborhood. My grandfather wasn't strong, Vásquez, he wasn't big, but he managed to lift up Papá and stick close to the cathedral wall so he wouldn't be seen. He walked like that, scared to death, for a couple of blocks. He could hear gunfire in the distance, sometimes it sounded closer. But what made the biggest impression were the display windows: the destroyed windows all the way along the Séptima, the jewelry shops and department stores full of people taking things: refrigerators, radios, armfuls of clothes. He saw a guy with a machete stop another who had a radio in his hands. He took the radio and smashed it on the ground. He shouted: "We're not here to rob! We're here to avenge the *jefe*!" But the majority of people did not agree, and Grandpa felt sorry: what should have been an opportunity for a revolution had turned into a party for delinquents. They stole because they could steal, they killed because they could kill, and they were killed in turn for no rhyme or reason. Once, Grandpa summed it up for me like this: 'They killed people just to watch them fall down dead.'

"Meanwhile, Grandpa kept hoping they wouldn't notice his presence, hoping he could pass by undetected. Two, three blocks with Papá's weight on his back. Then four. Then five. He was sidestepping corpses as he walked, and sometimes there were so many he had to make a detour, because with the weight of Papá he couldn't climb over them: his body weighed so much that he couldn't lift his feet high enough to step over some of the dead bodies. They were mostly men but women too, and he saw some children too, of course. Sometimes he had to stop to rest, put Papá's body down beside a wall and try not to look at him. He always told me that: he tried not to look at him, because he thought if he looked at him he wouldn't have been able to go on. Meanwhile, the rebellious police kept firing, those policemen who were secret, or not-so-secret, Gaitanistas. The furious people kept setting things on fire and looting stores with Jewish names, all those jewelry shops on the Séptima. If there was a hardware store, people grabbed pipes, hacksaws, hammers, axes, whatever might help avenge the chief. If there was a liquor store, the people smashed the windows and took bottles or drank them right there. Those who ran into the Ley on Eleventh Street to shelter from the bullets bumped into those running out with their arms full of clothes. Grandpa walked past the café where he had been sitting when Gaitán was shot, and the tables and chairs were smashed up, and people came out armed with table legs and chair legs and bits of wood. But they didn't even see him. It was as if he were invisible. Around then, he crossed paths with some military tanks driving south down the Séptima. People made way for them, and began to walk behind them, believing they were rebelling soldiers heading for the Palace to overthrow the president. Later he learned that the tanks stopped at Tenth Street, turned around, and opened fire. Grandpa didn't see it, but would hear of it later, and he told me as if he'd seen it. In the end, he no longer knew what he'd seen and what he'd been told. I suppose that happens to all of us.

"When he arrived at Avenida Jiménez, he couldn't go on. He'd carried Papá's body four or five blocks and he had no strength left. He put Papá down and rested for a few minutes, and then, with all the strength he had left, he lifted him again and tried to cross the street. But then a woman running from the regional government building caught his attention, and at that very instant he heard a burst of gunfire and the woman fell dead in the middle of the street. My grandfather saw it all: he saw the woman running, then falling as if her legs had been cut off, and then two more bodies falling, and the screams, and the calls for help.

"If the dead hadn't been those others, it would have been him: because the shots came from soldiers who were positioned at the entrance to the Pasaje Santafé and were firing indiscriminately against anyone who tried to cross the street. Grandpa waited for a long time crouching at the corner, but the soldiers didn't stop firing. There were snipers on the rooftops there too. Grandpa thought that if he could get as far as the Hotel Granada, maybe they'd let him shelter there, maybe they'd help him find an ambulance to take Papá's body home. He dug up strength from who knows where to pick him up one last time and went the other way, walking as fast as he could, and that's when he felt the burning in one ankle and then the pain, and he fell with the body and all, and knew it was all fucked.

"Later, when I was a kid, let's say around sixteen, Grandpa started doing something he'd never done before: ask my forgiveness. To say he was sorry for not having been able to bring Papá's body home, sorry for having left him there on Jiménez. Imagine: he was sorry for not having been able to lift Papá with a shattered ankle in the midst of a hail of bullets, and then for not having gone to find him the next day. But nobody could leave their houses the next day, you know. Anyone who broke the curfew would show up dead. My grandfather told me how they stayed shut up at home listening to the radio, and how he felt ashamed of what his own people were saying, the Liberals, on the stations they'd taken over. Calling for people to kill Conservatives, announcing happily that they'd burned down the houses of oligarchs, telling people to draw their machetes and let the blue blood flow as the red blood had been flowing before. I don't know if you know those transmissions, but they are hair-raising."

"I do know them," I said, and it was true: I think anyone who's ever suffered an obsession with April 9 knows them. The agitators took over the radio waves right after the crime and launched their harangues, their calls for terror, to a disoriented and vulnerable people who were too ready to cling to the consolation of revenge: "War is humanity's menstruation," says one of those harangues. "We Colombians have had fifty years of peace. Let's not give the impression of being the only cowards on earth." Those incendiary speeches called for the assassination of the president and his reduction to ashes, gave instructions on how to fabricate the "clear Molotov cocktail," and exhorted taking government positions "by blood and fire." I thought Carballo was referring to those. But maybe he had other examples in mind, because there were many shameful instances on that day that brought out the worst in everybody.

"Later he went back to look for him," Carballo continued. "He told me, on the eleventh, with his broken ankle and everything, he took a couple of guys from La Perseverancia and went back into the hell of downtown to look for Papá. But he didn't find him. The corpses had started accumulating in the arcades, one next to the other along both walls, and they were like death-scented tunnels, and the smell spilled out and filled the streets. People were walking down the middle of those arcades, trying not to step on other people's dead and looking for their own. Grandpa went through them all, every one, looking for Papá's body. But he didn't find him. He never found him in any of the rest of the inventories of corpses they made over the following days. And he always blamed himself for Papá not having a tomb that we could go visit."

"He ended up in a mass grave," I said.

"It's possible, but nobody ever told me about the mass graves. Or about the trucks full of dead bodies driving out of the city center to the pits, or the possibility that Papá was there, in one of them. I say it's possible, but what other possibility is there? No, I got used to the idea a long time ago: Papá in a mass grave. It's strange, the need for a tomb. It's strange how much tranquility a known grave can bring. I've never had that tranquility of knowing where that body is. And not knowing where our dead are is a silent torment, an entrenched pain, and it screws up your life. Actually what really screws us up is when we don't get to decide exactly what happens to our dead. It's as if death were the moment when you feel you've lost control over something, because of course, if you could prevent a loved one's death, you always would. Death takes away our control. And then we want to control everything up to the last detail of what happens after death. The burial, the cremation, even the fucking flowers, right? Mamá didn't have that possibility, and that always tormented her. That's why I understand so well what happened with Gaitán's body. You know, I suppose, what happened with Gaitán's body."

"They wouldn't allow him to be buried in a cemetery," I said. "They took him home."

At around four in the morning of the tenth, after gangs of drunks had made two attempts to force their way into the Central Clinic to take Gaitán's body, Doña Amparo, the brave woman who had just become his widow, sent for a coffin to take him home. There are several versions, as there are of everything that happened that day: some say it was just to protect the body that had already, a few hours after the crime, turned into a relic; according to others, Gaitán's widow didn't want to give his enemies in government a chance to wash their hands of guilt with a state funeral. Whatever the case, Gaitán's house filled with people in the early hours of the tenth: there, among Gaitanistas from all over the city, were the Empolvados from La Perseverancia, taking six-hour turns to watch over the chief.

"Grandpa was one of them," said Carballo. "He did his shift and then went back out to keep looking for Papá. Later he heard that they'd buried Gaitán right there, in the garden. Every year, on the anniversary of the crime, the comrades from La Perseverancia put on their best clothes and went down to visit the place where the chief was buried. I don't remember how old I was when they took me for the first time, but I was still a child: I might have been nine or ten, but no older than that. No, I think I was nine, yes, nine years old. Of course, visiting Gaitán's grave was what we did instead of visiting Papá's. We went to Gaitán's house and said prayers in the garden and left flowers because we couldn't pray or leave flowers on Papá's grave. But you can see how long it took for me to understand this, and especially how naturally we did so. It doesn't seem odd to me to visit another dead person and pray for my own at the same time. Yes, I knew that the man buried there wasn't Papá, but we said prayers first for Papá and then for him. A child does what he's told and gets used to whatever he's taught, right? Well, we went as a family, we went down the hill from home to Gaitán's house. It was a long walk but we did it as a ritual, it was part of the ritual. Grandpa, Mamá, and I walked, and in the early days other Gaitanistas went, too, but in time they stopped going and it would just be us: the family.

"On those walks, they both told me things. Sometimes, if there was money, they'd buy me an ice cream cone and I'd eat it walking along the street listening to the stories. We always ended up talking about April 9. At one point or another, usually on the way home, but sometimes on the way there, I would say: 'Tell me about the day when Papá went to heaven.' And they would tell me. They told me, I imagine, what they thought suitable for a child my age. Later I grew up, of course, and they gradually added details, and April 9 was no longer *the day when Papá went to heaven* but *the day Papá was killed*.

"And on one of those April ninths, Grandpa told me for the first time about his theory. That's how I put it now, his theory, but that's not how we referred to it in my family. It was simply *what Grandpa thinks.* That was how it went, those were the phrases we used. 'You know what Grandpa thinks . . .' 'Well, speaking about what Grandpa thinks . . .' 'What Grandpa thinks has to do with this . . .' And you didn't have to say anything else, because what we were talking about was clear.

"It was 1964. I was going to turn seventeen and was about to finish school. I was at the top of my class, Vásquez, and I'd already received the news my whole family was expecting: a grant to study at the National University. I was going to study law, which was, according to my family, what Papá would have wanted. More important, it was what Papá would have wanted to do *because Gaitán had done it.* I had begun to read newspapers as if I were going to die the next day. Grandpa would look at me and say: 'Just like his *papá.*' I had also become truly interested in politics. My grandfather noticed, I suppose, because if not there wouldn't have been much reason to tell me what he thought at that moment. That day, April 9, 1964, we were walking back home, and somewhere around Avenida Caracas he suddenly came out with: 'Well, what I think, son, is that your *papá* knew.' I asked: 'Knew what?' And he looked at me as if I were an idiot, with one of those withering looks older people sometimes employ. 'What do you think?' he said. 'He knew who killed our *jefe.*'

"And he began to tell me about what he had seen on my father's face that day, about all the strange phrases he heard him say in a matter of minutes, about his reaction after the shots were fired, which seemed somewhere between suicidal and deranged. He began to tell me that Papá had seen someone else, an accomplice or companion of the assassin who carried a raincoat and wasn't like him: he was dressed elegantly. He said that from there, from the moment he saw him, Papá had begun to behave strangely: he was strange on the Séptima, while they walked behind the body of Gaitán's killer, Roa Sierra, and he was strange later, when they'd set up the barricade. He repeated several times the phrase he'd heard Papá say: 'It's like it's happening all over again.' At that moment, my grandfather didn't understand a thing. That was the last thing Papá said before the sniper's bullet killed him, but Grandpa didn't understand, he couldn't have understood at that moment. That's what he told me: 'At that moment, I didn't understand. But I've come to understand, though it hasn't been easy. And now I want you, son, to understand as well.'

"And by the time we got home I knew this was serious because Grandpa made me go with him to his room, and his room was a place that was off-limits to me. I sat on his bed—he'd never let me sit on his bed before—and then he knelt on the floor. He lifted the bedspread and pulled a wooden drawer out from under the bed, a drawer from some lost piece of furniture, with its lock useless because it didn't have the rest of the cabinet around it. The drawer was full of things, shoes, papers, but mostly books. 'Look, son, look,' he said. 'Your father's books.' He showed me a pamphlet: it was a speech Gaitán had given at the tomb of Rafael Uribe Uribe. He was sixteen years old and the speech was commissioned by the National Youth Center. 'So you can see, my dear boy, what the chief was capable of at your age,' my grandfather said to me. Then he showed me Gaitán's degree thesis, *Socialist Ideas in Colombia*, but he said: 'Not yet.' And then he put a book on my lap. It was *Who Are They?* by Marco Tulio Anzola. On the first page Papá had written his name, *C. Carballo*, and on the last page the date when he finished reading it: *30.X.1945*. 'This one, son. Take it and read it as soon as you can, and then tell me if you understand the same thing I understand.'

"That's what my grandfather said. And it goes without saying, I imagine, that I did: I understood that same thing he understood. Maybe not the first time I read it, maybe not during the first conversation, but I came to understand it in time. That evening in 1964, the April 9 when my grandfather gave me the book that had been my *papá*'s, I began to read it with a single mission: to find there, in those three hundred pages, all that Papá could have remembered in the moment when they killed Gaitán. Of course, I was sixteen years old, and there's very little I could have understood at that moment. But I understood more as the months and years went by: I understood that in Anzola's book, in an ugly and boring book published in 1917, were the keys to what Papá had thought in the last hours of his life, on April 9, 1948. Such an idea is not easy to accept, but I worked hard at it. I read the book twice, three times, then five, then ten, and with every reading some scenes, some isolated sentences surfaced. I read that book, that damned book, and I knew it: I knew the same thing Papá knew a few minutes before he died. It was like being in his head, like seeing the world through his eyes, like being him a few minutes before he was shot. And that is a knowledge I wouldn't wish on anyone. It is a fortune and a privilege, of course it is, but it's a burden, a hard burden to bear. It is what has fallen to me, and it's what I've devoted my life to: to bearing what Papá understood in the last minutes of his life, what my grandfather thought he understood later, that understanding I've inherited from them."

Then I said the only words I could have said at that moment in that place. They were in the form of a question, a question I would perhaps regret, but keeping quiet would have been a form of cowardice and maybe blindness.

"And what understanding was that, Carlos? What was it that your father understood and that you now understand?"

"That the elegant man in front of the Granada Drugstore was no different from the elegant man on Ninth Street. That the tall man in the irreproachable gray suit, as García Márquez describes him, is no different from the man in striped trousers and patent leather ankle boots, as the witness Mercedes Grau described him, and no different from the man the disappeared witness Alfredo García saw in Galarza's carpentry shop, and is no different from the man in the top hat Anzola didn't want to name at the trial. That the elegant man, who incited the inflamed crowd until they lynched Juan Roa Sierra, is no different from the one who asked Uribe's assassins: 'How'd it go? Did you kill him?' Papá understood that the priest who hoped Uribe was in hell in 1914 is no different from another very famous priest who before the Gaitán crime called for the annihilation of Reds. Papá understood that the rumors and anonymous notes that circulated in Bogotá before April 9 were no different from the rumors and anonymous notes that circulated in Bogotá before October 15. He understood that all those people convinced that Gaitán was going to be killed were no different from those who heard, forty days in advance, that Uribe was going to be killed. He understood that, Vásquez, he understood that terrible truth: that they were killed by the same people. Of course I'm not talking about the same individuals with the same hands, no. I'm talking about a monster, an immortal monster, the monster of many faces and many names who has so often killed and will kill again, because nothing has changed here in centuries of existence and nothing ever will change, because this sad country of ours is like a mouse running on a wheel."

THERE ARE TWO WAYS to view or contemplate what we call history: one is the accidental vision, for which history is the fateful product of an infinite chain of irrational acts, unpredictable contingencies, and random events (life as unremitting chaos that we human beings try desperately to organize); and the other is the conspiratorial vision, a scenario of shadows and invisible hands and eyes that spy and voices that whisper in corners, a theater in which everything happens for a reason, where accidents don't exist and much less coincidences, and where the causes of events are silenced for reasons nobody knows. "In politics, nothing happens by accident," Franklin Delano Roosevelt once said. "If it happens, you can bet it was planned that way." The phrase, which I haven't been able to find quoted in any reliable source, is loved by conspiracy theorists, maybe because it comes from a man who decided so much over the course of so long (that is, who left so little space to chance or fate). But what there is in it, if one peers carefully into its foul-smelling pit, is enough to overcome the bravest among us, for the phrase shatters one of the minimal certainties on which we base our lives: that misfortunes, horror, pain, and suffering are unpredictable and inevitable, but if someone can predict or foresee them, they will do anything possible to prevent them. The idea is so terrifying that others know right now that something bad is going to happen and don't do anything to prevent the damage, it is so horrifying even for those of us who have already lost all our innocence and left behind all illusion with respect to human morality, who tend to take this vision of events as a game, a pastime for idle or credulous people, an inveterate strategy to better fight against the chaos of history and the revelation, proven by now a thousand times, that we are their peons or their marionettes. We respond to the conspiratorial vision with our well-trained skepticism and a touch of irony, repeating that there is no proof of the conspiracies, and believers will tell us that the principal objective of every conspiracy is to hide its own existence, and that the fact of not seeing it is the best proof it is there.

That Friday, February 28, 2014, almost a hundred years after one

of the crimes and almost sixty-six since the other one, I was living in a
world like that, ironic, skeptical, a world ruled by chance, chaos, accidents, and coincidences. And what Carlos Carballo was asking me
was to come out for a moment and live in another world, and then
return to mine to tell what I'd seen. He was asking me so that the vision of his father would not be lost. I remembered his words about
truths that don't happen in visible places, truths that don't happen in
the world of what a journalist or historian can recount, those small or
fragile truths that sink into oblivion because those in charge of recounting history never manage to see them or to find out about their
modest existence. And I thought that Carballo's desire was not just to
save from oblivion a truth that had never been born in the world of
historical things, but also to give his father an existence he hadn't ever
had until now. He might not have a tomb, perhaps, and his bones
might never have a stone with his name, but he would have a place to
exist with his name and his memory. That is, with his life: his acts and
his loves and work and enthusiasms, his affiliations and descendants,
his ideas and emotions, his projects and illusions and plans for the future. No, Carballo didn't want me to write a *Who Are They?* of the
Gaitán crime; he wanted me to make a mausoleum of words where his
father could dwell, and he also wanted the last two hours his father
lived to be documented just as he understood them, because that way
his father would not just have a place in the world, but would have
played a part in history.

I understood this and I had an idea. I told him:

"I'm going to write it, Carlos."

He looked up, straightened barely perceptibly, and I noticed there
was a slight trace of tears in his eyes. Or maybe he was just tired, just
as I was after twenty-four hours (or maybe it was more: impossible
to know at this stage) of continuous conversation and arduous

memories. It must not have been February 28 anymore when I said this: we'd spent so much time shut up in there by then that we must have been well into the first day of March.

"You're going to write it?" he said.

"Yes. But in order to do it, I'm going to need to trust you. I need to know you're telling me the truth. I'm going to ask you one question, and I'm only going to ask you once: Do you have the vertebra? Did you take Gaitán's vertebra out of Francisco Benavides's drawer?"

He didn't answer me.

"Let me put this another way, Carlos," I insisted. "I need to take Gaitán's vertebra and Uribe Uribe's skull fragment. I need to return them to Francisco, who is the legitimate heir to those bones. If I take them, I'll write the book. If I don't take them, I won't. It's that simple."

"But he's not the legitimate heir," said Carballo. "The *maestro* gave the cranium to me."

"And the vertebra? Did he give you that too?"

"Francisco wants to give them up," he said.

"He doesn't want to give them up. He wants them to be in a museum, so people can see them. Look, Carlos, those bones don't belong to him or to you: those bones belong to everyone, because the past they contain is all of ours. I want to be able to go to see them when I want. I want my daughters to be able to go see them when they want. More than that: I want to take my daughters to a public place and show them those bones behind glass and explain to them all that those bones can tell."

"But they are evidence," said Carballo. "They're the proof of something we don't see but that might be there. On the skull fragment there might be the sign of a knuckle-duster. In the vertebra there might—"

"That's bullshit," I interrupted him. "Don't talk shit to me. What is in the vertebra? A bullet from a second shooter? You already know that's not the case, and if you don't remember, I'll tell you again what your *maestro* discovered in his 1960 autopsy: There was no second shooter. So in that vertebra there is nothing. And as for the famous knuckle-duster, no trace of that is visible on that piece of bone. The knuckle-duster lives in Anzola's theory, but not in this bone. These bones have not been forensic evidence for a long time. They are not proof, not anymore. They are simply human remains, ruins, yes, the ruins of noble men."

When I went out into the Bogotá morning—that Saturday morning, that March morning—I was carrying Francisco Benavides's possessions in my black knapsack. I put it beside me in the car, on the passenger seat, and I realized, as I drove toward home and my present life with a certain sensation of unreality, that once in a while it occurred to me to take a look at them while I was driving, as if to confirm that all that had happened over the preceding hours was not a product of my morbid imagination. The ruins of noble men: the line from *Julius Caesar* had assailed me (or perhaps I should say: had come to my rescue) as had happened to me so many times before with old Will, whose words helped me give shape and order to the chaos of experience. In that scene, Julius Caesar has just died in the Capitol, stabbed twenty-three times by the conspirators' swords, bled at the foot of Pompey's statue, and Anthony, his friend and protégé, is left alone beside his dead body. "O, pardon me, thou bleeding piece of earth," Anthony says to him, "That I am meek and gentle with these butchers! Thou art the ruins of the noblest man that ever lived in the tide of times."

I don't know if Uribe Uribe and Gaitán were the noblest men of their times, but their ruins, accompanying me on my trip home, had that nobility. Those human ruins were memoranda of our past errors, and at some point they were also prophecies. I remembered, for example, the statement of one of the lawyers of the private prosecution in the Uribe trial. After discounting the participation of anyone other than the two assassins and describing the political nature of the crime as anarchist, he concluded by saying: "Fortunately, the case of General Uribe Uribe has been and must be, God willing, unique in Colombia." He was mistaken, and at my side was the material testimony of that error, but the important thing for me was not that memory of the bones, but what contact with them had caused in the lives of these men: Carlos Carballo, Francisco Benavides, and his now-dead father. And in mine, of course. In mine as well.

Since it was Saturday, I thought it might be all right to show up unannounced at Dr. Benavides's house. He answered the door with his reading glasses still on and a book in his hand; from inside, as if from the back of the house, a sad cello welled up. I didn't have to explain the reason for my visit. He had me go straight upstairs, to his treasure room where all this had started nine years earlier, and received his relics. We talked: I told him about the last hours, omitting a lot, grossly summarizing what I had discovered, for telling the whole thing seemed like a disloyalty to me at that moment, like violating a secret, or maybe because Carballo had made his revelations to me or because they had a single objective, which was to live on in my future book. I told Benavides about the agreement I'd made with Carballo. It was a last-minute deal, when, already saying good-bye, both of us standing on the threshold of his door, he said: "And how do I know you are going to keep your side of the bargain? You're taking these things now and Francisco is going to return them, as you two put it, to donate them to some museum or whatever. How do I know that you're still going to write it afterward?" I then proposed to persuade Benavides to put them out into the world only once my book, Carballo's book, had been published: when it was already living out in the real world, filling it with the stories he had told me and one of them in particular. There, in Benavides's house, I told him, and he agreed; but I noted in his manners that his relationship with Carlos Carballo, his lifelong friend, his father's disciple, had broken forever. And I felt as sorry as if it had been me who had lost an old friend.

Several days later I flew to Belgium to spend a few weeks there, a visit that had been scheduled a long while before to work on a novel. The idea of shutting myself up in an apartment in downtown Brussels to cohabit day and night with my fictional characters and their invented destinies, with no obligation to talk to anyone or answer the phone, had seemed impossible to refuse even if I didn't have dear friends in Belgium who I like to visit whenever I can, for some of them are now of sufficient age that I wonder, after each new visit, if I'll see them alive again next time. But now that the trip was looming, my circumstances had changed: it would no longer be the fictional characters of that novel who would occupy my solitude, but a true story that showed me at every step how little I had understood until this moment my country's past, which laughed in my face, as if making me feel the pettiness of my narrative resources before the disorder of what had happened so many years ago. It would no longer be the conflicts of characters who depended on my will, but my attempts to understand, truly and forever, what Carlos Carballo had revealed over the course of several encounters that were now blending in my memory.

And that's what I did for thirty days and nights. The apartment on the Place du Vieux Marché aux Grains had a studio that overlooked a cobblestone street; beside the wall, between two high windows that let in the cold northern light, there was a desk (with a black leather top and drawers full of worn-down pencils and envelopes from previous users), but I never wrote there, for when I walked in the first day I found myself in a living room the perimeter of which was lined with white cupboards about a meter high, and the next morning that almost continuous surface had been covered with all the papers I'd brought on the trip—copies of old newspapers, photos, books, and notebooks—and the checkered dining table had turned into my workplace. On top of all the surfaces, and on the marble mantelpiece of the unlit fireplace, the documents changed places: little by little, in the early spring days, a possible version of Carballo's story began to come to light: and during my nights of insomnia I read and reread the furious notes I'd taken, until the events that could be seen there, combined with my solitude and exhaustion, provoked something similar to paranoia.

When I went outside for a walk I found a city whose museums, bookshops, and ad-covered walls were all flooded with the memory of the Grande Guerre, and I saw those images I'd seen a thousand times, the barbed wire, the helmeted soldiers in trenches, those faces covered in mud, those big open holes in the ground where shells had exploded. And it occurred to me that two hours away by train Jean Jaurès had been killed (and why not take that train) and that the soldier Hernando de Bengoechea had died a three-hour drive from there (and why not rent a car), but I never managed to make those trips: I hastened back to my cobbled street and my study because I realized I couldn't stop thinking about my Colombian crimes, and I also realized that nothing in that memorious city, or in the possible trips to the past the region could offer, interested me as much as continuing to remember in writing my conversations with the man who believed in conspiracy theories. Other things happened to me in those days, I thought of and discovered other things. For example, I met a man who had been the lover of the writer Senka Marniković. But those anecdotes cannot form part of this book.

I should mention, however, what happened on my return trip. I traveled by way of New York, since it was cheaper than other routes and for other, less practical reasons that aren't relevant, and ended up spending two days in the city instead of the anticipated few hours. I could have spent the time in secondhand-book stores or movie theaters, but the obsession with the events and characters of my still-embryonic book wouldn't allow me an instant of freedom, and I ended up spending a morning feeding it: looking for the places Rafael Uribe Uribe had been when he arrived in the city at the beginning of 1901, in the middle of the War of a Thousand Days. I had no luck: my searches led nowhere. But then I remembered Carballo's theory, stemming from a book called *Secrets of Roulette and Its Technical Tricks*, that Marco Tulio Anzola had escaped to the United States after the trial, and had probably done so with the help of Carlos Adolfo Urueta, Uribe's son-in-law, who was then a diplomat in Washington.

If Anzola had come to New York in those years, I thought, there would be a record of him in the Ellis Island archives, which were open to the public. Idleness is creative: one sunny morning, before going back to the airport to return to Bogotá, I boarded the ferry that takes tourists and other people with time on their hands to the island where the country's immigrants used to arrive, and began to investigate. I didn't have to spend more than an hour searching: there, on the computer screen, was the record of Anzola's entry. His ship, the *Brighton*, had set sail from the Colombian port of Santa Marta. The date of his arrival in New York was January 3, 1919; among his companions was Carlos Adolfo Urueta. The register also records his twenty-eight years of age, the color of his eyes—dark brown—his distinguishing marks— a mole on his left cheek—and his civil status: married. What did Anzola do in New York? How long did he stay in the United States? Who was his wife? Why was he able to write a book on gambling? Months after that book was published, Gaitán was shot dead in

	3	**2**	**4**	**5**	**6**	**7**	**8**	**9**	**10**
	NAME IN FULL.		**Age.**			**Calling or occupation**	**Able to—**	**Nationality. (Country of which citizen or subject.)**	**†Race or people.**	***Last perm**
	Family name.	Given name.	Yrs. Mos.	Sex.	Married or single		Read. / Read what language [or, if exemption claimed, on what ground]. / Write.			Country.
✓	Gonzalez	Luis Carlos	24	M	S	Merchant	Yes Spanish Yes	Colombia	Spanish Am.	Col.
✓	Ramires-Ricaurte	Jorge	28	M	S	Travel...	Spanish and English "	"	"	U.S.
✓	Anzola-Samper	Marco T.	28	M	M	Clerk	" Spanish "	"	"	Colombia
✓	Herrera	Julio E.	25	M	S	Merchant (reporter)	" " "	"	"	

S. S. "BRIGHTON" 3. Passengers sailing from SANTA MARTA.

John R Montgomery
W. S. ...
Jan 3 1919.

Bogotá. Would Anzola have heard about the crime? What conspiracy theory would he have designed or considered then? I took a couple of careless photos and felt like I'd just seen a ghost. I also felt that Anzola had not completely left my life yet. True obsessions don't go so easily.

I returned to Bogotá at the beginning of April. And that was when, one of my first nights back, I caught that late-night news item and saw the image of Carballo at the moment of his arrest, climbing into the police van with the look on his face of a startled prankster. His hands were cuffed behind his back, but he looked relaxed; his head was down between his shoulders, but not to hide, just to avoid bumping it on the edge of the van's doorframe. On the news they accused him of trying to steal Jorge Eliécer Gaitán's serge suit, but I knew that wasn't the case. When the journalist described what had happened, when he said Carballo had used a knuckle-duster to break the glass case within which the suit was exhibited, when he explained in detail that the museum guard had detained Carballo at the moment he laid a hand on the shoulder of the suit jacket, only I knew his intention was not to steal it, but to feel with the palm of his hand the same cloth his father's hand had touched on that fatal day. Relics are that, too, I thought in front of the television, a way of communicating with our dead, and at that moment I noticed that my wife had fallen asleep at my side and I could not discuss the whole business with her. And then I got up out of bed and went to my daughters' room, where they were also asleep, and closed the door and sat down in their green chair decorated with birds and I stayed there, in the darkness of the peaceful room, watching with envy the serenity of their bodies, letting myself be surprised by how much they'd changed since their difficult birth, trying to hear their soft breathing amid the noises of the city: that city that began on the other side of the window and that can be so cruel in this country sick with hatred, that city and that country my daughters would inherit as I had: with its sense and its excesses, its rights and its wrongs, its innocence and its crimes.

AUTHOR'S NOTE

The Shape of the Ruins is a work of fiction. Characters, incidents, documents, and episodes from past or present reality are used here in a novelized form and with the liberties characteristic of the literary imagination. Readers who wish to find coincidences with real life in this book do so at their own risk.

ACKNOWLEDGMENTS

During the three years I spent writing this novel, many relatives, friends, and acquaintances lent me their time, their spaces, their knowledge, their advice or provided a punctual piece of help to solve a problem, and I'd like to put my gratitude on record here. They are: Alfredo Vásquez, the Passa Porta Foundation of Brussels, the Casanovas & Lynch Agency (Mercedes Casanovas, Nuria Muñoz, Sandra Pareja, Ilse Font, and Nathalie Eden), Inés García and Carlos Rovira, Rafael Dezcallar and Karmele Miranda, Javier Cercas, Tatiana de Germán Ribón, Catalina Gómez, Enrique de Hériz, Camilo Hoyos and the Instituto Caro y Cuervo, Gabriel Iriarte, Álvaro Jaramillo and Clarita Pérez de Jaramillo, Alberto Manguel, Patricia Martínez, Jorge Orlando Melo, Hernán Montoya and Socorro de Montoya, Elkin Rivera, Ana Roda, Mónica Sarmiento and Alejandro Moreno Sarmiento, Andrés Enrique Sarmiento, and Fanny Velandia. But my biggest debt is to Mariana, the first recipient of these pages, whose visible or invisible presence gives this book (and the life of its author) something mysteriously resembling harmony.

J.G.V.

Bogotá, September 2015

Juan Gabriel Vásquez is the vanguard of a new generation of Latin American authors who eschew magical realism and are building a powerful modern vocabulary to articulate the complexities of their world. Vásquez is a gripping storyteller of these profound personal and political struggles. As Edmund White wrote on the cover of *The New York Times Book Review* in his review of *The Sound of Things Falling*, Vásquez has written "a page-turner, but it's also a deep meditation on fate and death."

Vásquez has said that "you write because there's a dark corner, and you believe that fiction is a way to shed some light." To read Juan Gabriel Vásquez is to discover and savor a voice destined to become a classic, destined to shed light on those dark corners and on our own experiences.

A gripping and moving story about how we can never truly escape the past

When Gabriel Santoro's book is scathingly reviewed by his own father, a famous Bogotá rhetorician, Gabriel is devastated. Cataloging the life of a longtime family friend, Sara Guterman, a Jewish German immigrant who escaped to Colombia in the 1930s, Gabriel's book seemed an innocent attempt to preserve a piece of his country's rapidly vanishing history. But as Gabriel goes over his research looking for clues to his father's anger, a sinister secret lies locked in the pages. After his father's death, and with the help of Sara Guterman and his father's girlfriend, Angelina, Gabriel peels back layer after shocking layer of history—from the streets of 1940s Bogotá to a stranger's doorstep in 1990s Medellín—to reveal a long-silenced portrait of his family's past: dark, complex, and inescapable.

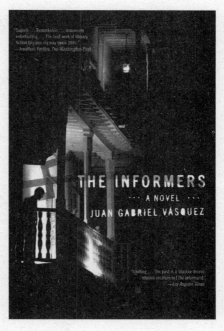

"Juan Gabriel Vásquez's *The Informers* is a thrilling new discovery."

—Colm Tóibín

"[A] remarkable novel. It deals with big universal themes. . . . It is the best work of literary fiction to come my way since 2005 . . . and into the bargain it is immensely entertaining, with twists and turns of plot that yield great satisfaction."

—Jonathan Yardley, *The Washington Post*

A novel about the complexities of literary and cultural thievery, featuring Joseph Conrad, a writer to whom Juan Gabriel Vásquez is often compared

Many years before Joseph Conrad's death in 1924, Colombian-born José Altamirano confessed to Conrad his life's every detail—from his country's heroic revolutions to his darkest solitary moments. Those intimate recollections became *Nostromo*, a novel that solidified Conrad's fame and turned Altamirano's reality into a work of fiction. Now Conrad is dead, but the slate is by no means clear—*Nostromo* will live on and Altamirano must write himself back into existence.

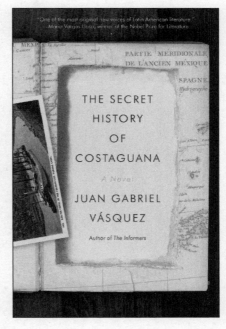

Vásquez takes us from a flourishing twentieth-century London to the lawless fury of a blooming Panama and back, in a labyrinthine quest to reclaim the past—of both a country and a man.

"A potent mixture of history, fiction, and literary gamesmanship . . . [Vásquez's] particular triumph with this novel is to remind us, as Balzac put it, that novels can be 'the private histories of nations.'"
—*Los Angeles Times*

"[An] exceptional new novel . . . When Mr. Vásquez, like Conrad, focuses on the individuals trapped in these national tragicomedies, he displays a keen emotional and moral awareness."
—*The Wall Street Journal*

A brilliant intimate portrayal of the drug wars in Colombia from a master storyteller

This is a story that opens with the visceral image of a hippo, escaped from a derelict zoo once owned by legendary Colombian drug kingpin Pablo Escobar, wandering the countryside outside Bogotá. From there, the mysteries, beauty, and horror of lives amid a world of endemic violence bring us on a sensual and thrilling journey. This is Juan Gabriel Vásquez's most personal, most contemporary novel to date, and a tour de force of style and storytelling.

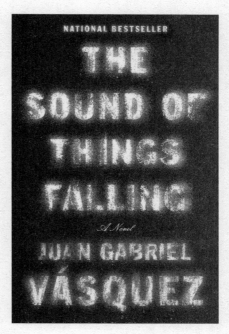

National Bestseller

A *New York Times* Notable Book

International Dublin Literary Award Winner

"[A] brilliant new novel . . . gripping . . . absorbing right to the end. *The Sound of Things Falling* may be a page-turner, but it's also a deep meditation on fate and death."
—**Edmund White**, *The New York Times Book Review*

"Deeply affecting and closely observed."
—**Héctor Tobar**, *Los Angeles Times*

A haunting collection of stories set in Europe

Lovers on All Saints' Day haunts, moves, and seduces. In these seven powerful stories, the genius novelist Juan Gabriel Vásquez brings his keen eye and rich prose to themes of love and memory. There are love affairs, revenge, troubled histories, and tender moments that reveal a person's whole history in a few sentences. These stories share a singular evocative mood and showcase Vásquez's hypnotic writing. He is a humane, deeply insightful writer, and the collection leaves one feeling transformed from the experience of reading, with a greater vision of humanity and society, a greater understanding of relationships and of love.

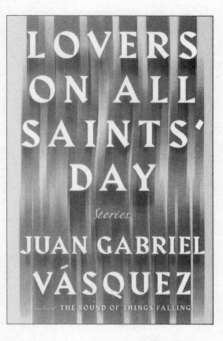

A powerful novel about a legendary political cartoonist

Javier Mallarino is a living legend. He is his country's most influential political cartoonist, the conscience of a nation. A man capable of overturning judges' decisions, and destroying politicians' careers with his art. His weapons are pen and ink.

After four decades of a brilliant career, he's at the height of his powers. But this all changes when he's paid an unexpected visit by a young woman who upends his personal history and forces him to reconsider his life and work, questioning his position in the world.

In this intimate novel, Vásquez brilliantly plumbs universal experiences to create a masterly story, one that reverberates long after you turn the final page.

"Spare but powerful . . . A brisk and sophisticated study of a conscience in crisis." —*Kirkus Reviews* (starred review)

"A reverberant new work about a life suddenly challenged." —*Library Journal*